FRONTISPIECE.

MY WAYWARD PARDNER;

OR,

MY TRIALS

WITH

JOSIAH, AMERICA, THE WIDOW BUMP,

AND ETCETERY.

BY

JOSIAH ALLEN'S WIFE,

(MARIETTA HOLLEY,)

AUTHOR OF "MY OPINIONS AND BETSEY BOBBET'S," "SAMANTHA AT THE
CENTENNIAL," &C.

"Wimmen is my theme, and also Josiah."

Illustrations by True W. Williams.

PUBLISHED BY SUBSCRIPTION ONLY.

HARTFORD, CONN.:
AMERICAN PUBLISHING COMPANY.
1890.

TO JOSIAH AND AMERICA.

WITH THE HOPE THAT HE AND SHE BOTH WILL PUT THEIR
BEST FOOT FORWARD AND WALK OFF NOBLY IN
THE PATH OF RIGHT THIS BOOK
IS DEDICATED BY
THEIR AFFECTIONATE FRIEND AND WELL WISHER,

JOSIAH ALLEN'S WIFE.

PREFACE.

I told Josiah that I guessed I would write a book about several things—and wimmen. Says I, "My mind has been dretful agitated lately about that certain lot of female wimmen that are sufferin' more than tongue can tell. Why," says I, "when I think of their agony and wrongs, it fairly makes the blood bile in my veins. I love the female sect," says I firmly, "I am one of 'em myself."

Says he (not wantin' me to say a word about it), "Let 'em write about it themselves."

Says I, "Josiah Allen, do you remember when you fell down through the barn and broke your limb, and most broke your other leg?"

"Yes," says he, "but what of it?"

Says I, "What if I had stood still in the buttery winder, and hollered at you to help yourself, and if you was in pain to get out of it?"

"Well," says he, "let 'em get some of their own folks to do the writin' then. They haint none of your folks, nobody won't expect nothin' of you." (He had reasons for not wantin' me to tell all I knew about certain things.)

But I says in solemn tones, " Do you remember that time you fell, Josiah Allen, and I, bein' bound down by rheumatizm, couldn't do nothin' but blow the dinner-horn for help, and Sam Snyder come on the run, and fetched you in, and went after the doctor?"

" Throw that leg in my face, if you want to, but what of it?"

Says I, " Them sufferin' female wimmen are bound down fur more painfully and gauling than you wuz. I haint the strength to lift 'em up myself, but I am a goin' to toot the horn for help. I am a goin' to blow through it powerful breaths of principle and warnin'; and mebby another Samuel, an uncle of mine, that I honor and admire, may hear it, and start off on the run, and lift the hull of them poor female wimmen up, out of their pain and humiliatin' situation. He can do it if he is a mind to," says I, " as easy as Sam Snyder lifted you, and easier, for he sweat powerful, and most dropped you once or twice. And," says I firmly, " my mind is made up, Josiah Allen, I shall holler for Samuel."

" Wall, wall, holler away, for all I care." He had strong reasons for not wantin' me to speak a word about certain things, and his tone was very snappish, snappisher than it had been for over seven weeks. But such trials do great spirits no harm; no, it only lifts 'em up above their own earthly peace and happiness, and sets 'em more firmly and stiddily on their loftier spears.

I sithed, but I didn't contend another word with him, only jest that sithe, and then I commenced to write my book.

WHAT THE BOOK IS ABOUT.

JOSIAH ALLEN GOES ASTRAY.

A curious World and a curious Coincidence—Realms of Mystery—Josiah Acts queer and Sits on a Volcano—"Wait till Evenin'"—Widow Bump and Her Nutcakes are Discussed—How She Ruined the Tailors—A tedious Evening and a Night of Woe—Fearful Words from the sleeping Josiah—"The real Josiah, Where was He?"—A mysterious Sign—Firm Resolves—"Pardners Must Be Watched"—Duty Tackled—Josiah Stays at Home—Samantha's powerful Weapons victorious, and the Widow Bump Forgotten...19—51

KITTY SMITH AND CALEB COBB.

A Visit from One of the Smiths Who is Poor and Proud—Kitty's Secret, which Must Be Kept—Her Would-be Lover, and how She Encouraged Him—Sketch of Kellup the Hearse-driver and His Experiences with Hair dyes—Why He Didn't Marry—Blamed by the Census-taker—How Nine Girls Lost Him—How He Killed Jane Sofier—The Death-Blow—His Warning to Women—Old Cobb and His Arguments—A Sermon by Samantha—The old, old Story Rehearsed—Kitty's Kiss—Fun for Kitty.................52—91

JOSIAH GOES INTO BUSINESS.

Josiah, Hankering for Speculation and Neighbors, Repairs the old House and Rents It to "a beautiful Family" from Zoar—Rumors that They were Smoked out—Josiah Feels neat, and Loves to Neighbor—So Do the Spinkses, Their Cow, and Their Hens—They Borrow Feather Beds, Pantaloons, and Pork—Their Twin "Takes to Him"—He Nurses the Twin, Sleeps with the Boys, Chases the Cow, and Takes "solid Comfort"; but "Gets mad" at last, and Meditates Murder—Summary Process—Adieu to the Spinkses...92—120

MORALIZIN' AND EPISODIN'.

Josiah Longs for more Speculation and Comes Home "as
cross as a Bear"—An Epoch of History—The new Head-
dress and how It Was Bought—Caleb Cobb's Opinions
thereof, and of extravagant Members of the Meetin'-house
—Samantha Rejoins, Holding up Nature Wreathed in
Beauty as a Pattern, and Advocating Charity toward both
the Rich and the Poor—Two Sides to Everything—Naming
the Baby—Caleb Changes the Subject, and Starts off to
Borrow the Stun-bolt,...............................121—153

JOSIAH UNDERTAKES MORE BUSINESS.

How old Ben Mandagool Made Money—Josiah Wants to do
likewise, but Knowing Samantha will Object, Feels cross,
Looks mauger, and at last Says He Wants to take Summer
Boarders—Affection *vs.* Principle—Samantha Yields—
Josiah Engages Boarders, and Figures out the Profits—
A Competency at last!—"Get a Girl"—The Tip-toe of
Expectation—Arrival of the Dankses—Tremendous
Appetites—Victuals and Profits Disappear—The Secret
out—More Trouble—A heavy Bill, and how he Flatted
the Colt and Squshed the Grin'-stun—How They Made
Ghosts and Were hard on the Tom Turkey—Night-walk-
ing and Historicks—Arrival of old Danks—The Crisis—
Josiah's Wrath—How He Scared Danks, and how Danks
Scared him—Samantha Speaks of Matrimony and its
Responsibilities, and Consoles all Matrimourners—A Law-
suit and its Result...................................154-188

A VISIT FROM MISS RICKERSON.

A windy Day—The Simons of the Desert—Good Advice to
Women—Preparing for an Emergency—"Likely Creeters"—Now and then—Vain Experiments—The miscar-
ried Letter—"She is Coming to-day!"—Arrival of Miss
Rickerson, she that Was an Allen—Her flattering Tongue
—How She Scared Caleb Cobb, Extolled the Spring Corset,
and made Josiah Think he was handsome—Our four old
Fathers and their chilly Blue Laws—"Praise your Friends
while they Are Living"—Samantha Holds firm, but Cooks
good Victuals, and Does well by Alzina Ann........189-204

CASSANDRA'S TEA PARTY.

History of Cassandra and her Misfortune—History of her bashful Husband, Nathan Spooner—Some of his Adventures and Experiences—How he Went hungry to Please Himself, and Feasted to Please Others—How he Courted Cassandria—Scenes at the Wedding—The Tea-party, and how Alzina Entertained Nathan—"The Image of his Pa"—At the Tea-table, and how Nathan Said Grace—Untimely Remarks—Samantha to the Rescue—After Supper—Alzina Walks with Cassandra in the Garden—She Slanders Josiah and Calls him a "humbly Creeter"—Samantha Appears on the Scene—A Tableau—Sarcastic Remarks about People who Take Liberties with their Friends—Alzina's Confession—The Walk homeward........205—229

THE LORDS OF CREATION.

Josiah Is proud and tickled because he Is a Man—His Opinion of "Wimmen"—What old Error Would do if They Made the Laws, and where York State Would Be—Samantha Points out a Monument of Man's Economy and Wisdom with Her new Tow-mop—A Reminiscence—Under the Meetin'-house Shed—Guilt Arrayed in festal Robes to Lure the Unwary....................................230—240

A EXERTION FOR PLEASURE.

Josiah's new "Idee," which Samantha Discourages—The Folly of Chasing Pleasure—Exertion to the Lake Resolved on—Caleb Sacrifices his own Pleasure for the Welfare of the Fair Sect—He Is not Their Natural Enemy, but Can't Marry Them all—Preparations—Early to Bed—Visitors, and a Conference Meetin'—"Galluses and Night Caps"—A Wild Night—Dreams—Josiah Wears T. Jefferson's Uniform—The Start—Arrival at the Lake—How Twenty Old Fools "Sot Sail"—Overboard—Sea-sick and weak as Cats—On the Sand-Beach—Demoralized Vittles—Wasps and Muskeeters—Histing an Umbrell—Josiah Meets with Two Accidents, and Retires to Meditate—A Search for Josiah—Josiah Wears a Shawl and Looks meachin'—The Return to the Main-land, and Ride Homeward in the Rain—The Rheumatiz Takes Hold—"Is this Pleasure, Josiah Allen?"..241—269

1*

A VISIT TO THE CHILDREN.

"The Croup Is around"—A Slave to Conscience—Caleb
Enquires about Kitty's Health, and Decides that He May
Marry Her—Why He Did not Write to Her, and why He
Wore old Clothes—A Funeral at Log London—A Load of
Company—The Start for Jonesville—Thomas J. and Mag-
gie—Providence and the Weather—Arrival at Whitfield's
—A pretty Sight—Portraits of little Samantha Joe and
Her Pa and Ma—The Sun and Sunflower—The Kiss of
Welcome—A Talk with Tirzah Ann, Who Says They Are
Going off for Rest and Pleasure—"Miss Skidmore Is Go-
ing, and all genteel People Go"—Samantha's Advice,
"Better Let Well Enough Alone," is Rejected—Who
need a Change of Scene and who do not—The Stiff-necked
Miss Skidmore—Who Leads the Jonesville Aristocracy?—
How Samantha Prescribed for her, and Was Winked out
—"Burdock Won't Help Her"—Proud Keturah Allen—
Samantha's Ideas of People who Put on Airs and Feel
above Her..270—302

TIRZAH ANN TO A WATERIN' PLACE.

How Tirzah Ann, Whitfield, and Samantha Joe, Went off for
Rest, and how they Came back as poor as 3 Snails—Tirzah's
Story of her Experiences and Wrongs at Miss Skidmore's
Tavern—How She Resolved at Starting to outdo the Skid-
mores—How they Rested and Recreated—Midnight in the
fourth Story of a Waterin' Place—The young Man who
Was Crossed in Love, and the young Maiden Who
Owned a Melodeon—Wails of Woe—How the Baby Was
Skairt into the Historicks—Bathin', deep Water, Cramps
and Drowndin'—Pulled out by the Hair—Too much
Mineral Water—How Whitfield Played Polo (a Game
Josiah Wants to Play) and Was Hit by a base Ball—How
He Danced too much, and Got Disabled—Evenin' Parties,
Dancin' and Flirtin'—The Worst of All; Tirzah's dread-
ful Confession, Which must be Kept a Secret; "She
Flirted with a Man!"—About Her Trouble with Whit-
field in consequence, how He Was jealous, and how a
Separation Was imminent—"Such Doins!"—Piles of
Money Spent, and Morals Totterin'—Bought Wit is the
best..303—329

MISS BOBBET LETS THE CAT OUT.

An old Acquaintance—Sorrows of Her domestic Life, and her great Consolation—The Dignity of Marriage—Simon's horrible Horrors—A Present for Betsey—A Summer Evening's Scene—Josiah and the high-tide Level of Love —The Stranger in the Kitchen—How He Looked, and What He Said—Why He didn't Set down—He Calls for some Cider, and Persisting in his Demands, is Driven from the House at the Point of Samantha's Umberel— Tobacco, and why People Use it—A Visit from Betsey, who Says the Intruder is Elder Judas Wart, Who is Sealed to Widder Bump, who has been Forwarded to Utah by Express—Betsey Tells about his disabled Wives, and about the Mormon Meetin's in Jonesville—Shocking Disclosures—"Bobbet Went to 'em and so did Josiah Allen!"—Fearful Words—Samantha Groans aloud, and Feels Wicked—The Mormon Wimmen's Appeal to Emily (She that was a Webb) and Samantha—A Woman to be proud of—Direlection in Duty—Samantha's firm Resolve to be up and Doin'—She Hankers to Tackle Elder Wart and America, and Gets madder and madder.........330—354

A SERENADIN' EPISODE, ETC.

Betsey Bobbet's new Poem, Entitled "A Wife's Story," and Published in the *Gimlet*—She Laments her Wedded Life and (although proud to Think she Married Simon) "to be a Widder is her Theme"—"Husbands are Tryin'," and Simon's Loss would be Betsey's Gain—The pathetic Story of E. Wellington Gansey who Came from the Ohio to Visit his Childhood's Home—He is Welcomed by His early Playmates, Has a good Time, and Resolves to Move back to Jonesville—Josiah and Others Are so elated that They Go to Serenade Him—Samantha, Left alone in the House, Has exciting Experiences—She Hears Noises, Gets Skairt, and Expects to be Burgled and Rapined— She is finally Appeared to and Talks with the Ghost— Poor Tamer Mooney and Her horrible Words—"Bloody Indians, Yells, and Tomyhawks!"—Rousting the Neighbors—Reappearance of Josiah—What Hit Him—What Hit Old Bobbet—What Hit the Editor of the *Augur*— What Hit Old Gansey, etc.—Eliab leaves His Childhood's Home, and Starts for the Ohio by the first Train....355—396

JUDAS WART AND SUFFERIN' WOMEN.

Josiah has a Stitch, Comes in on a Broom-handle, and is Made
comfortable—The Elder Wart also Comes in, Seems
dreadful Tickled, and Makes some complimentary Remarks—Josiah Overhears them, and Forgets his "Stitch"
—Samantha Rescues the Elder, who, in retaliation,
Twits Josiah about "a certain Widder" to whom He
Had Been partial—Josiah Denies the Imputation and
Gets luny—His strange Hallucination, and Memories of
his Childhood—Samantha, being again "Approached"
by the Elder, Gets mad and Threatens him with the Tea-
kettle—He Wants to "Argue," and Samantha Tackles
Him—What Mormons Worship—Who they Rob and
Murder—What they Covet, and Get, too—The Wretched-
ness of Mormon Wimmen, and especially of Wife No. 1
—Ruined Morals—Beelzebub's own Timber—A Voice
from Old Babylon and the Turkey—No Acquaintance
with Thalos and Mr. Plato—The Elder Gets "Sassy,"
and Samantha Declares She Will Appeal to her Uncle
Samuel, who, though a little distracted and run down by
his domestic Troubles, Can and Will Stop Mormonism
—The Elder's parting Shot, which Josiah Resents by an
Attack in the Rear—"A skairter Man never Lived"..397—469

A CRISIS WITH KELLUP.

Kitty Departs, and Kellup Calls to See her 5 Minutes after-
ward—He is greatly Depressed—"Wimmen is what's the
Matter"—He is sorry for Kitty, and says he will Write to
her—On Reflection he Authorizes Samantha to tell her he
Will Marry her whether or no, even if She is poor—
Remembering Sofier's Fate, he "Dassent" do an Errand
at Marier's House—A Visit from Cassandra and her
young Babe—How Nathan Treated his Heir—A mysterious Decree—Thrillin' News—Kitty Smith Disappears from
the Scene—So Does Miss Smith the Elder—So Does Wart
(the Elder)—So Does Kellup and the Hearse—A pastoral
Scene—Samantha, Reclining by the Brook-side, Listens
to a Bird as he Sings and Swings; Watches the Sky and
Golden-rod Reflected in the Stream; Meditates on the Old
and the New, the Steadfast and the Changing; and
Thinks how swift the Water is a Runnin' toward the
Sea..470—490

THE PICTURES

MR. WILLIAMS HAS MADE.

		PAGE
1. Frontispiece ....(FULL PAGE)............		
2. "The Tedious Evening Waned Away" ....(FULL PAGE)............		18
3. Portrait of the Widder Bump............................		24
4. An Ideal Family ....(FULL PAGE)..........		28
5. Measured by the Widder...		32
6. Josiah Dreaming...		36
7. Those "Awful Words" ....(FULL PAGE)............		40
8. A Solemn Warning...		42
9. Josiah's Disappointment...................		47
10. Kitty Smith ....(FULL PAGE)............		54
11. Kellup...		59
12. The Woman Question...................		63
13. The Deserted...		65
14. Paying Her Way...		67
15. How Jane was Roped in......................(FULL PAGE)............		69
16. The Death-blow		71
17. A Judgment Seat...		74
18. Swingin' Out..		83
19. A Cob(B) Without Corn......................(FULL PAGE)............		85
20. Kitty's Kiss		87
21. Josiah Feels Neat		93
22. Arrival of the Spinkses...		97
23. Yoked but not Mated.......................(FULL PAGE)............		100
24. Josiah Neighbors..		102
25. Borrowin' Josiah..		106
26. Spinks'es Cow—A Night Scene ....(FULL PAGE)......... .		108
27. Our Hen-dairy..		110
28. Josiah's Vow		117
29. Danger Ahead		118
30. The new Head-dress..		121
31. Apple Blossoms...		123
32. How it might have been...		124
33. Hard at it...		126

34. Nature's Ocean Boudoir ....(Full Page)............ 129
35. Nature's Work.. 131
36. Baby Piller Case.. 135
37. Feeling Christian... 137
38. "Blessings on Them all" .... (Full Page)..... 141
39. A Heavenly Messenger.. 143
40. The wreathed Spear.. 145
41. A Guiding Hand 150
42. "What's the Matter, Josiah?"................................. 154
43. A Poetical Simely ....(Full Page)............ 158
44. Josiah's Idee... 161
45. Early Birds... 162
46. Our Boarders,......................(Full Page)............. 165
47. A Surprised Colt.. 170
48. Exercising the Gobbler...................................... 172
49. A Heavy Bill ....(Full Page)......... 176
50. "Shut that Door".. 192
51. Arrival of Miss Rickerson.................................. 196
52. Kellup's Conundrum.. 202
53. Nathan Spooner.. 206
54. Nathan Snickers... 207
55. Pudding and Milk.......   209
56. The Family Night-cap..................(Full Page)......... 211
57. "Nathan Sot Down".. 214
58. Cassandra's Misfortune.............. ......(Full Page)..... 217
59. Bad for Nathan.. 222
60. Face to Face.. 226
61. A Monument of Men's Economy................................. 233
62. On the Ragged Edge....   236
63. Under the Meeting-house Shed............(Full Page)........ 238
64. Routed out.. 246
65. "Murder Will out".. 247
66. Samantha's Dream.......................(Full Page)......... 249
67. Facing Trouble.........................(Full Page)... 253
68. Bound for the Island........................ 255
69. On the Beach... 257
70. Discouraged Excursionist..................(Full Page)..... 260
71. A desperate Situation...................................... 264
72. Homeward Bound........................(Full Page)......... 267
73. The End of the Exertion.................................... 269
74. Moving Josiah.. 271
75. Dressed for the Occasion....   274

76. A Roadside Visit...............................(Full Page)............ 279
77. A Happy Home.. 282
78. Little Samantha Joe... 283
79. Josiah Still 286
80. The Annual Turnout.........................(Full Page)............ 289
81. Mrs. Skidmore 292
82. Keturah Allen.. 295
83. View of Jonesville......................(Full Page)............ 300
84. "A Pitiful Sight"...........................(Full Page)............ 306
85. Keepin' Up Her End.. 309
86. Midnight at a Watering-place.............(Full Page)............ 312
87. Wail of Woe... 314
88. Quavers and Shakes... 316
89. Doin' Their Level Best... 318
90. How Josiah Would Play Polo.............(Full Page)............ 320
91. The Rescue... 323
92. "It Tasted awfully".. 324
93. A Sad Scene.. 325
94. Tirzah Ann Flirts With a Man.............(Full Page)............ 327
95. A Present for Betsey.. 331
96. Friendly Feelin's.. 332
97. Meeting the Elder.. 335
98. A Threatnin' Attitude.. 341
99. Miss Bobbet Tells About Josiah..........(Full Page)............ 344
100. "A Rarity to 'em".. 348
101. Bobbet and Josiah Talkin'... 352
102. Old Toil's Bride...........................(Full Page)............ 357
103. The Wild-Eyed Woman... 363
104. No Answer.. 367
105. E. Wellington Gansey.. 370
106. Burglers... 379
107. The Ghost.. 380
108. Tamer Mooney... 383
109. The Serenading Party... 384
110. The Bruised Josiah... 387
111. The Serenade...........................(Full Page)............ 390
112. "Mandana! Mandana!".. 395
113. A Stitch in the Back......................(Full Page)............ 398
114. Elder Judas Wart... 400
115. Rescuing the Elder... 401
116. Hot Water... 407
117. "Less Argue".............................(Full Page)............ 409

118. Mountain Meadows.. 417
119. An Angel of Peace.. 430
120. Mr. and Mrs. Plato.. 436
121. The Hindoo Mother.. 441
122. A Fallen Angel 443
123. The Old Man.. 450
124. Our Distracted Uncle.......... 453
125. The Call to Duty.... ....(Full Page)............ 455
126. Helps for the Heathen.. 457
127. Josiah Ends the Argument...............(Full Page)............ 464
128. Departure of the Elder... 467
129. Takin' a Reef.. 475
130. Marier Burpey... 480
131. "Do You Want a Pair of Boots?"............................... 484
132. Thrilling News......................(Full Page)............ 486

"THE TEDIOUS EVENING WANED AWAY."

JOSIAH ALLEN GETS ASTRAY.

I HAVE said, and said it calmly, that this is the
curiousest world I ever see in my life. And I
shan't take it back. I hain't one to whiffle round and
dispute myself. I made the statement cool and firm,
and shall stand by it. And truly if I never had said
or thought anything of the kind, what I see with my
own eyes last Friday night, and heard with my own
ear before mornin' dawned, would have convinced me
that I was in the right on't.

It's happenin' on a Friday, too, was strange as
anything could be strange. It was on Friday that
Mr. Columbus discovered the New World, and it was
on a Friday (though some time after) that I discovered new regions in my pardner's mind. Realms of
mystery, full of strange inhabitents That Christo-
pher and me should both make such startlen and
momentious discoveries on the same day of the week
is a coincidence curious enough to scare anybody most
to death.

Yes, this world is a curious place, very, and holler, holler as a drum. Lots of times the ground seems to lay smooth and serene under your rockin' chair, when all the time a earthquake may be on the very p'int of busten' it open and swollerin' you up—chair and all. And your Josiah may be a-settin' right on top of a volcano, unbeknown to you. But I am wanderin' off into fields of poesy, and to resoom and proceed.

It was along the latter part of winter, pretty nigh spring, when my companion Josiah seemed to kinder get into the habit of going to Jonesville evenin's. When I would beset him to go and get necessaries, groceries, and etcetery, he would say :

"Wall, I guess I'll wait till evenin', and then I'll hitch up and go."

He'd done it a number of times before I noticed it in particular, bein' took up alterin' over my brown alpacka, and bein' short on't for pieces and strained in my mind whether I would get out new backs without piecin' 'em acrost the shoulder-blades. I don't get much time to sew, bein' held back by housework and rheumatiz, and the job had hung on, and wore on me powerfully, body and mind. Wall, every day or two he would make that curious remark, without my noticin' of it (as it were):

"Wait till evenin', and I ll hitch up and go."

And I wouldn't say nothin', and he'd go, and wouldn't get back till nine o'clock or after. Wall, as time went on, and my mind grew easier about my

dress (I concluded to take the overskirt and make
new backs and sleeves, and I got it cut foamin', could
have cut it profuse and lavish, if it had been my way),
and my mind bein' onstrained, and noticin' things
more, I thought it looked sort o' peculier that Josiah
should be so uncommon willin' to go to the store evenin's for necessaries and things, when he had always
been such a case to stay to home nights ; couldn't get
him out for the Doctor hardly. Collery morbeus
couldn't hardly start him, nor billerous colic.

It was on that Friday night after Josiah had started,
that I, havin' finished my dress, sot there a knittin',
and my mind bein' sot free, it got to thinkin' over
things. Thinkin' how I told him that mornin' that
the tea was a-runnin' out, and I should have to have
some that day, and he says :

" Wall, after supper I'll hitch up and go."

And I says to him sort o' mechanically (for my
mind was almost completely full of alpacka and waist
patterns—I had concluded late the night before to
take the overskirt) :

" What has come over you, Josiah Allen ? I
couldn't never use to get you out nights at all."

He didn't explain, nor nothin', but says agin, in
that same sort of a curious way, but firm :

" You make the tea last through the day, Samantha,
and to-night I'll hitch up and go."

And then he beset me to have a chicken pie for
dinner, and I, bein' in such a hurry with my sewin',

didn't feel like makin' the effort, and he told me I *must* make it, for he had had a revelation that I should.

Says I, " a revelation from who ?"

And he says, " From the Lord."

And I says, " I guess not."

But he stuck to it that he had. And I finally told him, " that if it was from the Lord he would probable get it, and if it wuzn't, if it wuz as I thought, a revelation from his stomach and appetite, he most probable wouldn't get it." And I kep' on with my sewin'. I laid out to get a good, wholesome dinner, and did. But I couldn't fuss to make that pie, in my hurry. His revelation didn't amount to much. But it was curious his talkin' so—awful curious.

I got to thinkin' it all over agin as I sot there a-knittin', and I felt strange. But little, little did I think what was goin' on under my rockin'-chair, unbeknown to me.

About half past 7 Josiah Allen got home. I asked him what made him come so soon, and he said sunthin', as he took off his overcoat, about there not bein' no meetin' that night, and sunthin' about the Elder bein' most sick. And I s'posed he meant conference meetin', and I s'posed he meant Elder Bamber. But oh! if I had only known who that Elder was, and what them meetin's was, if I had only known the slippery height and hollerness of the volcano Josiah Allen was a-sittin' upon, unbeknown to me! But I didn't know nothin' about it, and so I sot there, calm and serene in my frame, for my mind bein' onharnessed, as I may say, speakin' in a poeticule way, from the cares it had been a-carryin', I felt first rate. And so I sot there a-knittin', and Josiah sot by the stove seemin'ly a-meditatin'. I thought likely as not, he was a-thinkin' on religious subjects, and I wouldn't have interupted him for the world. But pretty soon he spoke out sort 'o dreamily, and says he :

"How old should you take the Widder Bump to be, Samantha ? "

"Oh, about my age, or a little older, probable," says I. "What makes you ask ?"

"Oh, nothin'," says he, and he sort o' went to whistlin', and I went on with my knittin'. But anon, or mebby a little before anon, he spoke out agin, and says he :

"The Widder Bump is good lookin' for a widder, hain't she ? And a crackin' good cook. Sometimes," says he in a pensive way, "sometimes I have almost thought she went ahead of you on nutcakes."

Her nutcakes was pretty fair ones, and midelin' good shaped, and I wuzn't goin' to deny it, and so I says :

"What of it, Josiah ? What if she duz ?"

There hain't a envious hair in my head (nor many gray ones for a woman of my age, though I say it that shouldn't). I hain't the woman to run down another woman's nutcakes. My principles are like brass, as has been often remarked. If a woman can make lighter nutcakes than I can (which, give me good flour and plenty of sour cream, and eggs, and other ingregiencies, I shall never believe they can)—why, if they can, runnin' down their nutcakes don't make mine any higher up. There is where folks make a mistake—they think that runnin' other folks down lifts them higher up; but it don't, not a inch.

THE WIDDER BUMP.

So I kep' on knittin', cool as the heel of the sock I was knittin' on. Pretty soon Josiah broke out agin:

"The Widder Bump hain't got no relations, has she, Samantha, that would be a kinder hangin' on, and livin' on her, if she should take it into her head to marry agin?"

"I guess not," says I. "But what makes you ask, Josiah?"

"Oh, nothin', nothin' in the world. I hadn't no reason in askin' it, not a single reason. I said it,

Samantha," says he, speakin' in a sort of a excited, foolish way, " I said it jest to make talk."

And agin he went to whistlin', strange and curious whistles as I ever heard, and haulin' a shingle out of the wood-box, he went to whittlin' of it into as strange shapes as I ever see in my life. I looked at him pretty keen over my specks, for I thought things was goin' on kinder curious. But I only says in a sort of a dry tone :

" I am glad you can think of sunthin' to say, Josiah, if it hain't nothin' but widder. Howsumever," says I, speakin' in a encouragin' tone, seein' how dretful meachin' he looked, and thinkin mebby I had been too hard on him, " Widder is better than no subject at all, Josiah, though I don't call it a soarin' one. But I can't see," says I, lookin' at him uncommon keen over my specks, " I can't see why you foller it up so awful close to-night. I can't see why the Widder Bump is a-running' through your mind to-night, Josiah Allen."

"Oh! she hain't! she hain't!" says he, speakin' up quick, but with that dretful meachin' and sheepish look to him.

" I am a talkin' about her, Samantha, jest to pass away time, jest to make myself agreeable to you."

" Wall," says I, in a dryer tone than I had hitherto used, " don't exert yourself too hard, Josiah, to make yourself agreeable. You may strain your mind beyond its strength. I can stand it if you don't say nothin' more about the Widder Bump. And time," says I, "I guess time will pass away quick enough without your takin' such pains to hurry it along."

And then I launched out nobly on that solemn theme. About time, the greatest of gifts; how it come to us God-given; how we ort to use it; how we held our arms out blindly, and could feel the priceless treasure laid in 'em, close to our hearts, unbeknown to us; and how all beyond 'em was like reachin' em out into the darkness, into a awful lonesomeness and emptiness; how the hour of what we called time was the only thing on God's earth that we could grip holt of; how it was every mite of a standin place we could lift the ladder on for our hopes and our yearnin's, our immortal dreams to mount heavenward; how this place, the Present, was all the spot we could stand on, to reach out our arms toward God, and eternal safety, and no knowin' how soon that would sink under us, drop down under our feet, and let us down into the realm of Shadows, the Mysterious, the Beyond. "And still," says I, "how recklessly this priceless treasure is held by some; how folks talk about its bein' too long, and try to get ways to make it go quicker, and some," says I, dreamily, "some try to make it pass off quicker by talkin' about widders."

I don't think I had been more eloquent in over five weeks, than I was in talkin' upon that theme. I was very eloquent and lengthy, probable from $\frac{1}{4}$ to $\frac{1}{2}$ an hour. I talked beautiful on it. A minister would have said so if he had heard me, and he would have

AN IDEAL FAMILY.

been likely to thought highly of it, and my gestures, for the waves that I waved outwards with my right hand was impressive, and very graceful. I held the sock in my right hand, as I waved it out; it was a good color, and it floated out some like a banner. I felt well, and acted well, and I knew it. And I thought at the time that Josiah knew it, and was proud of me, and felt more affectionate to me than his common run of feelin's towards me wuz, for most the minute I got through episodin', he broke out, and says he:

"Don't you think you are a workin' too hard, Samantha? Don't you think it would be easier for you if you had some woman here a livin' to help you? And," says he, dreamily, "she might be a fryin' the nutcakes while you was a brilin' the beef-steak, and cookin' other provisions."

I was exceedingly affected by his tender feelin's towards me, (as I supposed,) and says I, in affectionate axents:

"No, I can get along, Josiah."

But oh! if I had known! If I had known what thoughts was a runnin' through his mind, how different my axent would have been. My axent would have been so cold it would have froze him stiffer'n a mush-rat, jest one axent would, it would have had that deadly icyness to it. Blind bein' that I was, a speakin' tender and soft to him, and knittin' on his heel, (a double stitch, too, to make it firmer,) and he a settin' of his own accord up on top of that volcano that was

2

ready to bust right out, and burn up all my happiness, and swaller down and engulf my Josiah. What feelin's I felt as I thought it all over afterwards.

Wall, I sot there a knittin' on his heel, and occasionally makin' eloquent and flowery speeches, and he, from time to time, a speakin out sudden and sort o' promiscous, a praisin' up the Widder Bump, and sort o' mixin' her up with religion, and seals, and revelations, and things, and anon, when I would take him to do about it, a whistlin', and whittlin' shingles into curious and foolish shapes, curiouser than I ever remembered to see him whittle, and whistlin' more sort o' vacant and excentrick whistles than I ever remembered hearin' him whistle—dretful loud whistles, some of 'em, and then dwindlin' down sudden and unexpected into low and dwindlin' ones. And I a wonderin' at it, and thinkin' things was a goin' on strange and curious. And then anon, or about that time, or anyway, as soon as I would have time to meditate on men's curious and foolish demeanors at times—why I would give up that it was one of their ways, and he would get over it, knowin' that they mostly did get over 'em.

And so the long, tejus evenin' waned away. And Josiah locked the doors, and wound up the clock, and greased his boots, and went to bed. But oh! little did I know all the while he was a windin' and a greasin', and I a knittin', and the carpet seemed to lay smooth and straight under us, all the time a earthquake was a rumblin', and, to use a poetical and figurative expression, a snortin' down under us, unbeknown to me.

Wall, that night my pardner, Josiah Allen, at two different times, once about midnight, and once about the time the roosters crowed—at two separate times, which I am ready to testify and make oath to, he spoke right out in his sleep, and says:

"Widder Bump!"

And that is the livin' truth, and I have always been called truthful, and don't expect to take up lyin' now, at my age. How many more times he said it, while I was a sleepin' peacefully by his side, I can't say. But them two times I heard and counted, and my feelin's as I lay there and heard them awful words can't never be told nor sung; no, a tune can't be made curious enough to sing 'em in.

Then I gin up, fully gin up, that sunthin' was wrong. That a great mystery was hangin' over my Josiah and the widder, or to one of 'em, or to somebody, or to sunthin'.

Oh the feelin's that I felt, as I lay there and heard them words. I wuzn't jealous that I will contend for; but what words them was for a affectionate, lovin' pardner to hear from the lips of a sleepin' Josiah.

"Widder Bump!"

I was not jealous. I would scorn to be. There wuzn't a jealous hair in my foretop, and I knew it, or my back hair. And I knew I was better lookin' than the widder, though she was wholesome lookin'.

She was the widder of Sampson Bump; he died with collery morbeus, and she moved to Jonesville and set up a tailoress shop, and had been called likely. Though the wimmen of Jonesville had gi'n in that their husbands never had so many clothes made in the same length of time, and a good many of the men had got scolded considerable by their wives for runnin' through with their property, and goin' so deep into their store-clothes. But the men had all gi'n in that ready-made clothes ripped

MEASURED BY THE WIDDER.

so it was a perfect moth to buy 'em, and it was fur cheaper to hire 'em made by hand. And Josiah had started up about the middle of winter, and wanted to have her measure him for a vest, and get a new overcoat made. Josiah Allen didn't need no vest, and I put my foot right down on it. But I had her come to the house and make the overcoat, and while she was there I run a splinter under my finger-nail, and was disabled, and I kep' her a week to do housework.

As I say, she had always been called likely, though she seemed to be sort o' shaky and tottlin' in her religion. She had been most everything sense she come to Jonesville, not quite 2 years. She jined the Methodists first, then the 'Piscopals, then the Universalers, and then the Camelites. And I s'posed at this present time she was a Camel. I had hearn' talk that she was a leanin' towards the Mormons, but I had always made a practice of disputin' of it, knowin' how hard it was for good lookin' wimmen to get along without bein' slandered by other wimmen. I always dispised such littleness, and so I had come out openly and stood up for her, and called her a Camel. But I learnt a lesson in this very affair. I learnt to be more mejum than I had been, and I thought I knew every crook and turn in mejumness, I had always been such a master hand for it. But in dispisin' littleness and jealousy in other wimmen, and tryin' to rise above it, I had riz too fur. *She wuzn't a Camel!* And while the other wimmen had been spiteful and envious, I had been a lyin'— though entirely unbeknown to me, and I don't s'pose I shall ever be hurt for it.

As I have said, and proved, I wuzn't jealous, but oh, what groans I groaned, as I heard for the second time them fearful words from the lips of my pardner— " Widder Bump!"

It was awful dark in the room, perfectly dark, but darker fur in the inside of my mind, and gloomier. How I did groan, and turn over agin and groan. And then I'd try to look on the bright side of things, right there in the dark. Thinkses I, I know I am better lookin' than she is, and would be called so by good judges. To be sure, her heft was in her favor; her heft was a little less than mine, mebby 100 pounds or so, and she could most probable get around spryer, and act more frisky. But thinkses I, when a man loves a woman devotedly, when he carrys her in his heart, what is a few pounds more or less? Thinkses I, a hundred pounds hain't more than a ounce to him under the circumstances; he don't sense it at all. So I'd try my best to look on the bright side, (right there in the dark,) and I'd say to myself, my Josiah's affections are sound, they are wrapped completely round me. And then I'd look on the dark side, and think how I had hearn that men's affections was loose and stretchy, some like the injy rubber ribbins you get to put round papers. How it will set tight round one, and hold it seemin'ly so close that there don't seem to be room for another single one, and then how easy it will stretch out and hold tight round another one— and another one—and et cetery—and et cetery. Seemin' to set jest as easy round the last ones, and hold 'em jest as tight and comfortable as the first one. And then I'd groan, and turn over agin and groan. And once my groan (it was a louder one than

my common run of groans, and deeper,) it waked
Josiah Allen right up out of a sound sleep, and he was
skairt, and riz right up in the end of the bed, and says
he, in tones tremblin' with emotion and excitement:

"What is the matter, Samantha?"

And I never let on what ailed me, but told him in
tones that I tried to make calm and even, (and as
lofty as I could when I knew I was talkin in a parable
way) that it was a pain that was a goarin' of me. I
didn't lie. I wuz in pain, but I didn't feel obleeged to
explain the parable to him, and tell him where the
pain wuz. I didn't tell him it was in my heart. And
he thought it was in my shoulder-blades; he thought
it was the rheumatiz. And he wanted to know, in
affectionate tones, "if he shouldn't rub my back, or if
he shouldn't get me the spirits of turpentine, or the
camfire?"

But I told him no. I knew that turpentine was a
master hand to strike in, but it couldn't never go
down deep enough to strike at the feelin's I felt—and
camfire never was made strong enough to case off a
wounded spirit, or bathe it down.

But I held firm, and didn't say nothin'. And
Josiah lay down agin, and in ½ a minute's time was
fast asleep, and a dreamin'. What was his dream?
Into what land was his mind a journeyin'? And who
was his companion? *Was it Widder Bump?* At that
fearful thought it seemed as if I should expier. I
dassent groan for fear of roustin' up my pardner, and

so I had to stand it with sithin'. Sithes wouldn't wake him up. And oh! what fearful and tremenjous sithes I sithed for the next several moments. I hain't afraid to bet that the best judge of sithes that ever lived would have said that he never heard any that

JOSIAH DREAMING.

went ahead of these, nor see deeper ones, or more melancholy. Why my feelin's was dreadful, and can't be described upon. There it was, dark as pitch. It was jest before daylight, when it is the darkest time in the hull night. And there my companion wuz. Where wuz he? I couldn't tell, nor nobody. His body lay there by my side. But the real Josiah, where wuz he? And who was with him where he wuz? Oh! what feelin's I felt! what sithes I sithed!

What blind creeters we are, anyway. Our affections reach out like a wild grape-vine, layin' hold of sunthin', or somebody, a twistin' and a clingin', till death on-clinches of 'em, jest as foolish, jest as blindly. Human love is strong, but blinder than a mole.

How is that grape-vine to know what it is a clingin' to? Blind instinct moves it to lay holt of sunthin', and hang on till it is tore away, or sot fire to, or wrenched off by some power outside of itself, and killed, and destroyed. But how can it tell whether it is clingin' round a live oak or a bean-pole? Round sunthin' that is sound to the core, or holler as a pipes-tail? Round sunthin' that will draw it along the ground, draggin' it through mud and mire into a perfect swamp hole and bog, soilin' its bright leaves, dwarfin' its free growth, poisenin' it with dark and evil shadows? Or whether it will draw it up towards the clear heavens and the sunlight, and hold it up there by its strength—a happy vine, growin' fresh and bright, sendin' out blessed tendrils touchin' nothin' less pure than God's own sweet atmosphire.

Now I worshipped that man, Josiah Allen. And I thought he loved the very ground I walked on as devotedly as I did hisen. I thought I knew every crook and turn in that man's mind. And now, after livin' together over 20 years, that man had done what
2*

he had done; talked the hull evenin' long about a
certain widder, and even in his sleep had uttered them
fearful and agonizin' words—" Widder Bump!"

And there I was, a strong woman in every way—
strong in intellect and principles, strong in my love
for him, strong in my heft. And here I was, powerless as a rag-babe. No more strength nor knowledge
in the matter than the rag-babe would have. No more
power in my hand to lift up the veil of mystery that
was hangin' round my Josiah than there would be in
the babe's, not a mite. Josiah's mind wasn't the
strongest mind in the world—I had always known
that, and had made a practice of remindin' him of it
frequent, when I see it would be for his good. But
now, now there wuzn't a intellect powerful enough on
the face of the earth to foller it up and overthrow it.
Out of the reach of friend or foe; beyond perswasion,
ridicule, reasonin', or entreaty; out of the reach of
me, his Samantha. He had gone off a travelin' without no change of clothin', or railroad tickets. Settin'
off on a journey, unshackled by pardners, bundles, and
umberells. A soarin' free and calm through that wonderful land. The ring on my finger held him before
earthly courts and constables, but there he was a wanderin', a free Josiah. Was I a wanderin' with him?
Did his soul reach out to me from that realm—hold to
me so close as to draw my spirit to his adown them
shadowy streets, into them mysterious homes, over
whose silent threshold no curious foot may pass?

THOSE "AWFUL WORDS."

Was his lawful pardner with him there, where she should be? Was his thought loyal to me, where there was no law, no influence, or constraint to make him constant—or was he a cuttin' up and a actin', flirtin' in spirit with the phantom thought of a Widder Bump? Here I would sithe powerful, and turn over agin, and sithe.

And so the tejus night passed away. But one great determination I made there in them fearful moments of darkness and mystery, one powerful resolve I made, and determined to keep: I would hold firm. And never let my pardner know I was a mistrustin' anything. But every minute of the time, day and night, I would keep the eye of my spectacles open, and try to find out what was a goin' on. But little, little did I think what it was that was a goin' on. Little did I realize the size and heft of the earthquake that was a rumblin' and a roarin' under that feather-bed unbeknown to me. But more of this hereafter and anon.

The next mornin' sunthin' happened to me that, comin' as it did jest at this curious and tryin' time, was enough to scare anybody most to death. I had a sign; a mysterious warnin'. I happened to take up the last *World* while my dish-water was a heatin', and the very first words the eye of my spectacles fell on—right there in broad daylight—entirely unexpected to me, I read these awful words:

A meetin'-house steeple had fell flat down the day before—fell right down into a man's door-yard, sudden

and unexpected, broke a
hen-coop and five lengths
of fence, and skairt 'em
most to death. They
thought, them folks did,
that that steeple stood
firm and sound. They
never mistrusted it was
a tottlin'. And it had
stood straight and firm
for year after year, probable for over 20 years.
But there come along a
gust of wind too strong
for it, and over it went
right into their door-
yard; its lofty head was
bowed into the dust, the
hen-coop and fence was
squshed down forever,
and they was skairt.

I don't believe too
much in signs and won-
derments, yet I don't
s'pose a man or a woman
lives who hain't got a
little streak of supersti-
tion and curiousness in
'em. I s'pose livin' as

we do with another world that we don't know nothin'
about pressin' so close about us on every side, livin'
in such curious circumstances makes us feel sort o'
curious.

Some as Miss Arden felt, the one that Mr. Tennyson
wrote about, she that was Ann Lee. When her husband Enock got lost she wouldn't gin up that he was
dead, and marry to another man, till she opened the
Bible and looked for a sign. I have heard Thomas J.
read it so much that Ann seems near to me, almost
like one of the Smiths. But though Ann did find a
sign, and was mistaken in it, or didn't give it the right
meanin', I was determined to read mine right. I felt
a feelin' in my bones that them words was meant to
me for a warnin; was gin to me as a sign to meditate
on. If a meetin' house steeple could tottle, my Josiah's
morals was liable to tottle; if that steeple fell right
down flat into a man's door-yard, breakin' down and
squshin' what it had broke down and squshed, my
Josiah was liable to fall flat down in a moral way, and
sqush down all my earthly comfort and happiness; and
I felt a feelin' that if I would save him I must be up
and a doin'.

Now if them folks had mistrusted that that steeple
was gettin' shaky, they could have tied it up, mebby,
and kep' it straight. And I was determined that if
tyin' up, or anything of that sort, would keep my
Josiah up, he should be tied. I am speakin' poetically,

and would wish to be so understood. Ropes was not in my mind, neither tow strings.

And then as I come to think things over, and look at the subject on every side, as my way is, I felt a feelin' that I hadn't done as I ort. My mind had been on a perfect strain for 2 weeks on that alpacka dress, and I hadn't kep' watch of my pardner as pardners ort to be watched over. Men are considerable likely critters, but they are sort o' frisky in their minds, onstiddy, waverin' kinder. They need a stiddy bit, and a firm martingill, to drive 'em along straight in the married life, and keep their minds and affections stabled and firm sot onto their lawful pardners. I have said that there wasn't a jealous hair in my head, not a hair. But filosify and deep reasonin' has learnt me severe and deep lessons. Even after the fearful night I had passed, the awful words I had listened to from the lips of a sleepin' Josiah, still filosify whispered to me that my pardner was as good as the common run of men, and I, in strainin' my mind on store-clothes, had neglected things of far more importance; I had neglected lookin' after my companion as men ort to be looked after. The cat, to use a poetical and figurative expression, had been away, and the mouse had gone to playin'. Or, to bring poesy down to prose, and to common comprehension, the cat had been fixin' over a brown alpacka dress, and the mouse had got to follerin' up a Widder Bump in his mind.

I believe when the man goes to cuttin' up and actin',

if the female pardner, upheld by principle, would take
a microscope and look over her past, she would more'n
as likely as not come bunt up against some fault of
her own, some neglect, some carelessness, some things
she had done that she ortn't to done, or some things
she hadn't done that she ort. She could trace back
their cuttin's up and actin's to some little unguarded
moments, when through hurry, or carelessness, or
neglect, she had let the lines and martingills of tenderness and watchfulness drop out of her hand, and
had let her pardner go a caperin' off with nothin' but
a halter on, a prancin' up and down society like a 3-
year old colt that hadn't had a bittin' rig on. Pardners have got to be humored. They have got to be
made comfortable and happy in their own homes;
their companions has got to make themselves attractive to 'em, or they won't be attracted. Viniger won't
draw flies worth a cent. And pardners *have got* to be
watched; for this is the law and the profit.

They have got to be reined up to the post of duty,
and hitched there. They are naturally balky, and
love to shy off side-ways, and there haint no use
denyin' of it.

I tell you, I had deep thoughts that day as I went
round the house a doin' up my work; awful deep ones,
and a sight of 'em, probable as many as 2 dozen a minute right along through the day; some solemn and
affectin' ones, about as solemn as they make, and some

more hopeful like, and chirk. I tell you, my mind got
fairly tuckered out by the middle of the afternoon.

But with Samantha, regret, repentance, and reform-
ation foller right straight on after each other, jest like
3 horses hitched in front of each other drawin' a heavy
load. I see there was a duty in front of me to tackle;
I see that I must not let Josiah Allen go off to Jonesville another night without his pardner. I must leave
cares and store-clothes in the back-ground, and come
out nobly, and make my home and myself agreeable to
my pardner, and keep a keen and vigilant eye onto his
proceedin's and goin's on.

So that evenin' along towards night, when he spoke
out in that same sort o' strange and curious way about
Jonesville, and that "after supper he guessed he'd
hitch up and go."

Then it was that I spoke up mild and firm as my
soap-stun, and said, "I guessed I'd go, too." He
looked brow-beat and stunted by my remark, and says
he: "I am most afraid to have you go out in such
muggy weather, Samantha. I don't believe you realize
how muggy it is."

Says I, in a brave, noble tone: "It hain't no mug-
gier for me than it is for you, Josiah Allen, and if you
go, I go, too."

"Wall," says he, with that same dumb-foundered
and stunted mean, "the old mare hadn't ort to go out
agin to-night; she lost a shoe off last week. I don't
believe we had better try to go."

Says I coolly: " Do jest as you are a mind to, but if you must go, it is my duty to stand by you and go, too; if my pardner has got a hard job in front of him to tackle, it is my duty to tackle it, too."

JOSIAH'S DISAPPOINTMENT.

"Wall," says he, " I guess I'll go out to the barn and onharness. The old mare hadn't ort to go out with her off shoe in such a condition."

But as he drawed on his overhauls, I heard him mutter sunthin' to himself about "its bein' the last night the Elder would be there till fall." But I over-heard him, and says I:

"You know, Josiah Allen, that Elder Bamber has

gin up goin' home; his mother's fits is broke up, and he hain't a goin'. And there'l be meetin's right along every night jest as there has been."

They've been holdin' protracted meetin's to Jonesville for quite a spell, and I s'posed them was the meetin's that Josiah meant. Ah! little, little did I know what Elder he meant, or what meetin's. But he knew me too well to tell me. He knew well the soundness and heft of my principles. He hadn't lived with 'em above 20 years without findin' 'em out. But more of this hereafter and anon.

When Josiah come into the house agin, and sot down, he had that same sort o' cross, brow-beat look to him. And he spoke out sort o' surly like: "Hain't it about supper-time, Samantha? And if you've got over bein' in such a dreadful hurry with that dress, mebby you'll have time to get a little sunthin' better to eat. I declare for't," says he in a pitiful tone, "you have most starved me out for a week or two. And you hain't seemed to have had time to say a word to me, nor nothin'. Your mind hain't seemed to be on me a mite. And," says he, with a still more depressted and melancholy look, "a cream-biscuit is sunthin' I hain't seen for weeks. Nothin' but bread! bread!"

Oh! how my conscience smited me as I heard them words—it smited and smarted like a burn. Yet at the same time his words kind o' chirked me up, they made me think what a powerful arrow I had in my hands to shoot down my sorrow with. They made me

feel that it wuzn't too late to save my pardner, and
that was a sweet thought to me.

Yes, with a thankful and grateful heart, I grasped
holt of that weepon that had defended me so many
times before on hard battlefields of principle. I held
that weepon firm and upright as a spear, and says I :

" Josiah, you shall have as good a supper as hands
can get." Says I, " Besides the common run of vittles
we jenerally have for supper, cake and tarts and such
stuff, what do you say, Josiah Allen, to havin' a
briled chicken, and toast, and mashed-up potatoes, and
cream biscuit, and peaches ?"

His mean changed in a minute. I never see a mean
in my hull life look more radient than hisen did as I
spoke them words. And my breast heaved with such
happy and grateful emotion that it most bust off 2
buttens in front (them buttens wuzn't what they was
recommended to be ; there was sunthin' wrong about
'em in the shanks). Though the mournful and mysterious episode and Widder Bump was remembered,
yet I felt a feelin' that I should win my pardner back
—I should save his sole alive.

But yet I had solemn feelin's, I can tell you, all the
while I was a mixin' up them cream biscuit, and
brilein' that chicken, and makin' that toast, and
mashin' up them potatoes, and puttin' plenty of cream
and butter into 'em.

I well knew I was a handlin' my most powerful
weepons. I knew if them failed, I was ondone.

I had meditated so many times and so deep onto this subject, that I knew every crook and turn in it. How a man's conscience, his moral faculties, and his affections was connected by mighty and resistless cords to his appetite. I knew well that when his morals was tottlin', when he was wild, balky, fractious, and oneasy, good vittles was the panaky that soothes. And when the mighty waves of temptation was tostin' him to and fro—when scoldin's seemed futile, and curtain lectures seemed vain, extra good vittles was the anchor that wimmin could drop down into them seethin' waters, knowin' that if that didn't holt, she could, in the words of the Sammist, "give up the ship."

Yes, as Josiah Allen see me a gettin' that supper he grew calm, peaceful, his demeaner towards me grew sweet and lovin', his affections seemed to be stabled and firm sot onto me. I see, and I can tell you I was a proud and happy woman as I see it, that the anchor I had throwed cverboard was a grapplin' the rock. Agin, as in days past and gone, in different crysises of my life, philosophy, principle, and Samantha conquered.

The supper was a success. The spring chicken was plump and tender, but not more tender than Josiah's demeanor to me as he partook of that refreshment. The cream biscuit was light and warm; so was my heart as I see my happy pardner eat the 7th one. The peaches was delicious and sweet; so was my

Josiah's smile onto me, as I dipped out the 4th sass plate full and handed it to him. And after supper he sot there by my side calm and peaceful, and the Widder Bump and all other earthly cares and agonys seemed to be forgot.

But it wuzn't till long afterwards, it wuzn't till the 4th day of the next September, though I mistrusted, I mistrusted strong before, but it wuzn't till then, that I knew for certain what a glorious and momentious victory I had won that day. What great and awful responsibilities was a devolvin' onto them cream biscuit, and hangin' round that chicken and toast and potatoes. I felt solemn feelin's a gettin' that supper, and curious ones a eatin' of it. But oh, what feelin's should I have felt if I had known what a earthquake was a rumblin' and a roarin' under that table unbeknown to me.

Oh, what blind creeters the fur seein'est of us are, how powerless are the most magnifyest spectacles to see the brinks that pardners are a hangin' over unbeknown to us. But of this, more hereafter and anon.

KITTY SMITH AND CALEB COBB.

WE have got a dretful pretty girl a-stayin' with us now, one of the relation on my side, one of the Smiths. When we heard she was a comin', Josiah kinder hung back from the idee at first. But as I see him a hangin' back, I calmly, and with dignity, took the Widder Doodle, one of the relations on his side, and mildly yet firmly threw her in his face. It hit him jest right, the idee did, and I hain't heard a word sense of murmurin's or complainin's about the Smiths.

I enjoy her bein' here the best that ever was. We have took lots of comfort sense she come. Not that happiness and security has caused me to shut that open eye of my spectacle. No! that is still on the watch, vigilent and keen, and if there is anything a goin' on, I feel that it cannot long he hid from that eye. But everything has seemed calm and peaceful, Josiah is affectionate and almost tender in his mean to me. And I learn from the neighbors that the Wid-

(52)

KITTY SMITH.

der Bump has gone off on a visit to her folkses. But still that eye of my speck is sleepless. Not once has it closed itself in slumber, and still I *hold firm*.

Kitty Smith is a pretty girl, as pretty a one as I ever see. The Smiths, as I have said to Josiah a number of times, was always pretty fair lookin'. He thinks so too, only when he is fractious. She looks a good deal as I did when I was her age; Josiah owned up to me the other night that she did. We had had a splendid good supper, and he felt well, and he said so of his own accord. And then she favors her mother considerable, a good-lookin' woman as I ever see, and smart.

Kitty is very fair complected, smooth, as delicate as a sea shell, with curly hair almost gold-colored, only bearin' a little on the brown, kinder fruzzly and fluffy on top, blowin' all over her forward when she goes out in the wind, or anything. And her forward bein' white as snow, when the little gold rings and curls are a blowin' all over it, they look well. She has got sort 'o pinky cheeks, and her eyes are big and dark, and kinder grey like, and all runnin' over with fun and mischief. She is the biggest witch out. And her lips are red as two roses, and always a laughin', them and her eyes; I don't know which laughs the most. Her name is Kitty, and she is just as affectionate as a little kitten, and as playful.

I think a sight on her. And I love to look at her. I always did love to look at a handsome woman.

There are some wimmen that it gauls to see a female handsomer than they be, but it never did me. I always loved to see handsome pictures, and a beautiful woman's face is a picture with a soul in it.

I set a great deal of store by her, and so does Josiah and the childern; they are all a quarrelin' now which will have her the most. But we shan't none of us have her long, I s'pose. For she has told me in strict confidence, and if I tell, it must not go no further, for it *must be kep'!* She don't want Josiah and the childern to get holt of it, knowin' they would plague her most to death. She is engaged to be married to a awful smart-lookin' feller. She showed me his picture—a keen-eyed, noble-lookin' chap, I can tell you, and well off. His father owns the big manufactory where her father was overseer when he died, and where her mother keeps boarders now. His father stood out, at first, about his marryin' a poor girl. And Kitty come off out here for a long visit; her mother wanted her to; they are both proud, and won't force themselves into no company. But Mark—that is the young feller's name—Mark stands firm, and the old man is a comin' round gradual. Kitty, though she jest worships Mark, won't go there till she is welcome, and I bear her out in it. That is why she is here on such a long tower. But she knows it is all a comin' out right; her mother says it is; and Mark writes to her every day or two, and she is happy as a bird.

But she is a little too full of fun sometimes, and thoughtless. She don't realize things as she ort, and as she will when she is older. Now there is a young feller here in Jonesville that has got after her, Caleb Cobb, or Kellup, as everybody calls him. And just out of pure fun she lets him foller her up. I feel bad about it, and so I have told Josiah. But he said "she didn't mean no more hurt than a kitten did, a-playin' with a mouse."

Says I, "Josiah Allen, hain't it bad for the mouse?"

"Wall," says Josiah, "it no need to have been a mouse then."

Says I, "That is a dretful deep argument, Josiah." Says I, "I should be afraid to be so smart, if I was in your place. I should be afraid they'd want me to Congress."

My tone was witherin' and dry as a fish. But Josiah didn't feel withered up. The fact is, he hates Kellup, and loves to see him fooled, that is the truth on't. Kellup's father is the cabinet-maker to Jonesville, and Kellup drives the hearse, and he comes to see Kitty in it. His father does sights and sights of business out in the country all round Jonesville, and every time Kellup is called out with it, on his way home he will go milds and milds out of his way for the privilege of stoppin' and seein' her. And he'll hitch that hearse to the front gate, and come in and try to court her. Why, anybody would think a pestilence had broke out in our three housen, our'n, and

3

Tirzah Ann's, and Thomas Jefferson's, to see that hearse hitched in front of 'em every day or two. It works me up and gives me awful feelin's. But Kitty jest giggles and laughs over it, and Josiah and the children encourages her in it. They hate Kellup like pisen.

And he is one of the stingiest, disagreeablest, conceitedest, self-righteousest creeters that I ever see in my life. And pretends to be religious. Why, I spose tight is no name for his tightness. Somebody made the remark that he was a wolf in sheep's clothing. And Thomas J. said it wasn't nothin' but the sheep's hide, then, for if it had been the hull pelt he'd sell the wool offen it quicker'n a wink.

And he thinks he is so beautiful, and dangerous to wimmen. But I never could bear his looks. He has got great big black eyes, dretful shaller, no depth to 'em, some like huckleberries, only bigger, but jest about as much soul and expression into 'em as a huckleberry has. And a saller skin and low forward, with sights of hair and whiskers. The curiousest hair, and the singularest whiskers that I ever did see.

They are very heavy and bushy, and he bein' pretty well along in years, they would be as grey as two rats. But bein' a bachelder, and wantin' to pass off as a young man, he colors 'em. Which would be all perfectly proper and right, and no more than lots of folks do; but the peculiarity is, he is so uncommon tight that he wont buy hair dye, but makes experiments with himself, steeps up things, roots and herbs, and stuffs he can buy cheap, minerals and things, cateku, and so 4th, and pusly. And so you hardly ever see him twice with his hair and whiskers and eyebrows the same color. And I'll be hanged if he haint some of the time the curiousest lookin' creeter that was ever seen out side of a menagery.

KELLUP.

If he would only settle down on one color and keep it up, it wouldn't be so bad for him. London brown hair and whiskers wouldn't look so awful bad after you get used to 'em, or cateku color, or madder red. But he thinks, I spose, that he will hit on sunthin' cheaper than he has hit on; so he will keep on tamperin' with 'em, and makin' experiments, and you won't no sooner get used to seein' 'em cinneman color, than the very next thing they will be a bright pusly color, or sorrel. It jest spiles his looks, and so I have told Josiah.

And he said " It was hard spilin' anything that was born spilt." And I told him " That no human bein' was ever born with pusly-colored hair and whiskers."

And he said "He was born a dumb fool!"

And I didn't deny it, and didn't try to, only I scolded him powerful and severe on the "dumb."

His hair and whiskers, as I say, are always some new and curius shade, very changeable and oncertain, as to color, but they are always greasy. He uses sights and sights of hair oil; he makes it himself out of lard, scented up high with peppermint. He uses peppermint essence on his handkerchy, too (he gathers his own peppermint and makes it, and uses it lavish). He says that is the only vain, worldly luxury he indulges in. He says he feels guilty about usin' up his property in it, but it is such a comfort to him that he don't feel as if he can give it up.

His clothes are always very cheap and poor lookin', when he is dressed up the most, but he dresses very poor the most of the time, for principle, he says, to try to wean the wimmen from him as much as he can.

And take him with them clothes of hisen, and that curius lookin' hair and whiskers all round his chin, and up the sides of his face, he is as sepulchral and singular a lookin' a chap as I ever laid eyes on.

He is a bachelder, Kellup is, not from necessity, he says, but because he has found it so hard to select one from the surroundin' wimmen that want him. He has told me that the two main reasons why he didn't marry, one was, he found it so awful hard to select one out of so many, and the other, it was so tryin' to him to hurt the feelins' of them he would have to slight if he made a choice.

Why, he talked with me about it over two years ago. He was in to our house one day, and Josiah had been a attin' him about his not gettin' married, and after Josiah went out, he talked to me confidential. I s'pose it is that sort of a noble, lofty look, to my face, that makes folks confide in me so much. Says he,

"I am tender-hearted, Josiah Allen's wife. I am too tender-hearted for my own good. There is so many wimmen that want me, and it would cut me, it would cut me like a knife to have to disapinte so many."

He stopped here for me to say sunthin', and I remarked, in a sort of a dry tone, that I wouldn't worry about 'em, if I was in his place."

"Wall," says he, "I shouldn't worry, if I was like some men. I should slash right in and marry, without payin' any attention to other wimmens feelin's. But if I should kill half a dozen wimmen or so, Josiah Allen's wife, I feel that I never should forgive myself."

Here he stopped agin, and I see that he wanted me to say sunthin' ; and not knowin' exactly what to say, I said sort o' mechanically, without really thinkin' what I was a sayin', that it would be a good stroke of business for his father.

"Yes," says he, "but the profits we should make wouldn't much more than half pay me for the feelin's I should have a thinkin' I was the means of their dyin' off.

"Why," says he, takin' out his pocket handkerchief and wipin' his forward, till the room smelt as strong as a peppermint sling,—"there haint a woman in Jonesville but what would jump at the chance of marryin' of me. But they mustn't calculate too strong on it. I wouldn't be the one to tell 'em right out plain that there wasn't no hopes of gettin' me. That would be a little too heartless and cold-blooded in me. But they mustn't build up too high castles in the air about it, for I may not marry at all.'

"Like as not you wont," says I, speakin' not quite so mekanikle, but with considerable more meanin'. "I shouldn't wonder a mite if you didn't."

"No," says he, foldin' his arms and lookin' haughtily at a picture of a woman over the wood-box.

"No; the thing of it is I am so tender-hearted, and hate so to cause sufferin'.

"I can't," says he, knittin' up his eyebrows (they was a kind of a olive green that day), "I *can't* marry all the wimmen that want me. That is a settled thing. Anybody with half a mind can see that. I *can't* do it. And so what would the result be if I should make a choice, and marry one. One woman made happy, and cruelty, wanton, bloody cruelty, to all other wimmen fur and near. Would that one woman's happiness," says he, knittin' up his eye-brows as hard as I ever see any knit, and I have seen some considerable hard knittin' in my day, "would that one woman's happiness go anywhere near makin' up for the agony that

would rack the breasts of other wimmen, and tear
their heart-strings all to flitters? That is the question," says he, lookin' gloomily into the wood-box,

THE WOMAN QUESTION.

"that is wearin' on me night and day, and what shall
I do to do right?"

"Wall," says I, "I can't advise you. I wouldn't
marry, if I thought it was a goin' to kill ten or a
dozen; and I wouldn't marry anyway, unless I got a
chance."

"Chance!" says he haughtily. "Why, there haint
a woman in the country but what would jump to have

me; that is," says he in a reasonable tone, "if they wasn't too old to jump, or wasn't disabled in some way, rheumatiz, or sunthin, or sprains. They all want me."

"Why," says I, tryin' to chirk him up, and make him feel better, "I thought it was right the other way. I thought you had got the mitten more'n a dozen times. There was Polly Bamber"—

"Oh, well. Polly Bamber loved me to distraction. She tried to conceal it from me. She refused me, thinkin' it would make me fiercer to marry her. But she got fooled. I only asked her three times. She was waitin' for the fourth, and I spose she was as disapinted as a girl ever was. I was sorry for her; my heart fairly ached for her; but I had a man's dignity to keep up, and I left her."

"Wall, there was Betsey Gowdey."

"Betsey would have had me in a minute, if it hadn't been for influences that was brought to bear on her. She just as good as told me so. I s'pose she felt awfully to lose me; but she bore up under it better than I thought she would. I thought like as not she would break completely down under it."

"Wall," says I, tryin' my best to chirk him up, "there was Mahala Grimshaw, and Martha Ann Snyder, and Jane Boden, and Serena Rumsey, and Serepta Mandagool."

"Them girls was sorry enough, when it was too late. They lost me, every one of them girls did, by puttin' on airs and pretendin' not to want me. Pretendin' to make fun of me, jest for an outside show. I see right through it. But I took 'em at their word, and when they said they wouldn't have me, I jest left 'em, and paid no attention to what they suffered after I left. Sometimes I have thought that mebby I was too harsh with 'em, to punish 'em so; but I did it, and I'd do it agin if it was to do over. They no need to have been so deceitful. They might expect to suffer for it, and I am glad they did."

"There was Nabby Ellis," says I dreamily.

"Oh, Nabby was all right. It was envy and jealousy that broke that up. Sam Larkins jest

3*

filled her ears about me, I know he did; if he hadn't, and hadn't married her himself, Nabby would have gin her ears to have had me. I think she thinks more of me to day than she does of Sam; but I keep out of her way all I can; I don't want to harrow up her feelin's. I am a young man of principle, if there ever was one.

"Now I know of several married wimmen that I am obleeged to treat cool and distant, for their own good. What good would it do me?" says he, knittin' up his eyebrows agin.

"What good could it do me for a lot of married wimmen to get over head and ears in love with me? They know they can't get me. And though they may feel hurt at my coldness at the time, when they come to think it over they must know I am actin' for their good in the long run, by bein' cold and distant to 'em, and tryin' my best to wean 'em from me.

"Some young men don't seem to have no idee or care about the sufferin' they cause on every side of 'em. They will trample right round over female hearts, as if there wusn't no more feelin' in 'em than in tan bark, and as if it didn't hurt 'em and bruise 'em to tread on 'em. But it haint my way. I don't think a young man can be too careful about such things. Why, I am so careful and conscientious that if I thought it was necessary for females' peace of mind, and the good of surroundin' wimmen, I would be willin' to wear a veil over my face the hull time."

I looked him full and keen in the face, over the top of my specks, and told him calmly that I didn't think it was necessary.

"Wall," says he, "I am jest that tender-hearted, that I would do it. I am too tender-hearted for my own good. I know that very well. Now I want to get married, I want to badly; but there them two reasons stand, right in front of me, headin' me off. It haint the expense of keepin' a wife that holds me back, for I could more than make her pay her way, doin' the housework for father and me and five workmen.

PAYIN' HER WAY.

No, it is clear principle that is headin' me off. I may get reckless after a while."

Says he, with a sort of a bitter mean onto him: "I may get so carried away with some girl's looks, and so

hankerin' after matrimony, that I shall forget my conscience and principle, and slash right in and marry
her, and let the other wimmen go to wrack and ruin.
But then agin when I think what the consequences
would probable be, why then I tremble."

And he kinder shook some as if he had a chill.

Says he: "When I think of Jane Sofier Burpy.
When I think what my feelin's was as I drove her
hearse to the buryin'-ground. When I think how I
felt durin' that ride—why, I think I will never meddle
again with any women, in any way, shape, nor manner. When I think how she wilted right down like a
untimely flower cut down by the destroyer."

"Why," says I, "she died with a bile; that was
what ailed her,—a carbuncle on her back."

"Yes," says he, with a unbelievin' look on his face,
"so the doctors said; so the cold world said. But I
think it was sunthin' deeper."

"Why," says I, "a bile couldn't go no deeper than
her'n went. It was dreadful. It was the death of
her."

Says he: "I have always had my own idee of what
ailed her. I know what that idee is, and I know what
a guilty conscience is. I wuzn't careful enough. I
didn't mean no harm to her, Heaven knows I didn't.
But I wuzn't careful enough. I boarded two weeks
with her mother the spring before she died. And I
can see now where I missed it, where I did wrong. I
wuzn't offish enough to her. I treated her too friendly.

HOW JANE WAS ROPED IN.

I was off my guard, and didn't notice how my attractions was bein' too much for her.

"I paid her little attentions to the table, such as passin' her the mashed-up potatoes and the beans. I talked with her, more or less. Once I helped her hang out the clothes-line. I brought her letters from the post-office. Twice I helped her into a wagon. I was onguarded. I think then was the time I give her her death-blow."

And oh! what a harrowin' and remorseful look he did cast into that wood-box, as he said this.

THE DEATH BLOW.

"She died in the fall. And my feelin's durin' that fall I shall never forget. If that thing should happen agin, and my feelin's prey on me as they preyed then, I couldn't stand it through more than seven or eight more such cases. I know I couldn't. I have been careful since then. When I'm obliged to board now

I don't board in any house where there is a woman under seventy-five years of age. And sometimes I am most afraid it is resky then.

And agin he looked as gloomy at that wood-box as I ever see a box looked at. And he waited a minute or two. Mebby he waited for me to say sunthin' but I didn't say it, and he kep' on:

"Several times sense that I have started up, and thought that I would marry anyway, and leave the result. But it has seemed to be broke up every time providential, and I'd make up my mind in the end not to have 'em. But after awhile agin I will start up, and almost make my mind up, that marry I will, no matter what the result may be. But there it is agin; I am too tender-hearted. That is where the stick is with me. I know jest how skurce men are, and how wimmen feel towards 'em. I know jest how they get their minds sot on 'em, and how they feel to loose 'em. I have got principle, Josiah Allen's wife. I am principle clear to the back-bone."

"Wall," says I, "I don't know but you be. I can't dispute you, not knowin' how it is."

"It may end," says he, with a bitter look at the woman over the wood-box, "it may end by my not marryin' at all. But if I don't marry, where will the blame lie?"

Says he, speakin' up louder and more excited than he had spoke up:

"I have been blamed; blamed in public places;

right in the grocery, and on the post-office steps;
blamed by the trustees of the public school; blamed
by the old man that keeps the children's toy-store;
blamed by the census man for shiftlessness, and slack-
ness, in not increasin' the population.

"But where does the blame rest? Is it with me, or
with the wimmen that act so like furyation that it is
impossible for me to make a choice amongst 'em?

"If I should tell them men that the reason I had
lived along, year after year, without marryin' was that
I was so tender-hearted, they would laugh at me."

"I hain't a doubt of it," says I heartily and decid-
edly.

"Yes, they would hoot at me, so little can they
enter into such a heart as mine. But I can't always
live along in this way. Some day there may be a
change. I give wimmen warnin' that there may be."

And so he went on for two hours, if it was a minute. Repeatin' it over and over agin, till I was as sick
as a dog of hearin' of it. But knowin' he was talkin' to
me in confidence, I didn't want to come right out plain,
and tell him what I thought of him. But I was glad
enough when he got through and started off of his
own accord.

But since Kitty come he has been to our house more
than ever. He has acted crazy as a loon about her.
Though true to his principle, he asked Josiah the other
day, "if consumption run in her family, and if he

thought it would go too hard with her if he didn't make up his mind to marry her."

Old Cobb is well off, but he and Kellup works hard, and fares hard. They stent themselves on clothes, and I

A JUDGMENT SEAT.

don't s'pose they allow themselves hardly enough to eat and drink. And all the literary feasts and recreations they allow themselves is to set round in stores and groceries, on dry-goods boxes and buttertubs, a-findin' fault with the government, spittin' tobacco-juice at the stove, and fixin' the doom of sinners. Kellup is harder on 'em than the old man is. Old Cobb thinks there won't be more'n half the world saved; Kellup thinks there won't be more than a quarter, if there is that.

They argue powerful. Have come to hands and blows frequent. And once Kellup knocked the old man down, he was so mad and out of patience to think the old man couldn't see as he see about the Judgment. You know there is sights and sights said on that subject now and wrote on it; and Kellup and the old man will borrow books and papers that are wrote on it, some on one side and some on the other, and then they'll quarrel agin over them. And they've tried to draw me into their arguments time and agin. But I have told 'em that I was a master hand to work where I was needed most, and I didn't seem to be needed so much a judgin' the world, and settlin' on jest how many was a goin' to be saved or lost, as I did a mindin' my own business, and tryin' to read my own title clear to mansions in the skies. Says I: "I find it a tuckerin' job to take care of one sinner as she ort to be took care of, and it would make me ravin' crazy if I had to take care of the hull universe."

It fairly makes me out of patience, when there is so much work our Master sot for us to do for His sake, it fairly makes me mad to see folks refuse to do a mite of that work, but tackle jobs they hain't sot to tackle.

Why, the Lord don't, like a good many human bein's, ask impossibilities of us. He only wants us to do the best we can with what we have got to do with, and He will help us. He never refused help to a earnest, strugglin' soul yet. But He don't calculate nor expect us to judge the world, I know He don't. Why, our Saviour said, in that hour when it seemed as if the God and the man was both speakin' from a heart full of a human longin' for love and a divine pity and tenderness for sorrowful humanity,—He said, "If you love me, feed my sheep." He said it twice over, earnest and impressive. He meant to have it heard and understood. And once He said, seemin'ly so afraid the childern wouldn't be took care of, "Feed my lambs." That is a good plain business, tryin' to feed them every way, doin' our best to satisfy all their hunger, soul and body. That is the work He wants us to do, but He never gave a hint that He wanted us to judge the world. But He said out plain and square more'n once, "*Judge not.*" Then what makes folks try to do it? What makes 'em pass right by flocks and flocks of sheeps needy and perishin' every way, pass right by these little lambs of Christ, hungry and naked, stumblin' right over 'em without pickin' of 'em up? Why, they might fall right over quantities of dead sheeps and dyin' lambs, and not know it, they are so rampent and determined on tacklin' jobs they hain't sot to tackle, crazy and sot on judgin' the world.

Why, everybody says they never did see such a time as it is now for arguin' and fightin' back and forth on that subject. Why, the papers are full of it. " Is there a Hell?" And "How deep is it?" And "How many are a goin' there?" And "How long are they a goin' to stay?" Books are wrote on it, and lectures are lectured, and sermons are preached on both sides of the Atlantic; and Kellup and his father are by no means the only ones who get mad as hornets if anybody disputes 'em in their views of the Judgment.

But I am glad enough that I don't feel that way, for it would make me crazy as a loon if I thought I was sot to judge one soul, let alone the universe.

Why, how under the sun would I go to work to judge that one soul, and do it right? I could see some of the outward acts, ketch glimpses of the outside self. But how could I unlock that secret door that shuts in the real person,—how could I get inside that door that the nearest and the dearest never peeked through, that God only holds the key to—the secret recesses of the immortal soul—and behold the unspeakable, the soarin' desires, and yearnin's, and divine aspirations—the good and true intentions—the dreams and visions of immortal beauty, and purity, and goodness—and the secret thoughts that are sin—the unfolded scarlet buds of wrong, and the white folded buds of purity and holynesses, each waiting for the breath of circumstance, of change, and what we call chance, to unfold and blossom into beauty or hejusness? How could my eyes see if I should put on 'em the very strongest spectacles earthly wisdom could make—how could they behold all the passion and the glory, the despair and the rapture, the wingéd hopes and faiths, the groveling, petty fears and cares, the human and the divine, the eternal wonder and mystery of a soul?

And if I could once ketch a glimpse of this—that I never shall see, nor nobody else—if I could once get inside the mystery of a mind, how could I judge it right? How could I go to work at it? How could I tackle it? Good land, it makes me sweat jest to think on't. How could I test the strength of that mighty network of resistless influences that draws that soul by a million links up toward Goodness and down toward Evil—binds it to the outside world, and the spiritual and divine? How could I get a glimpse of that unseen yet terrible chain of circumstances, the inevitable, that wraps that soul almost completely round? How could I ever weigh, or get the right heft if I could weigh 'em, of all the individual tendencies, inherited traits, sins, and goodnesses that press down upon that soul? How could I tell how the affections, powerful critters as I ever see, was a drawin' it one way, and where? and how fur? And ambitions and worldly desires, how they was a hawlin' it another way, and where to? and when? How true, noble aims and holy desires was pushin' it one way, and ignoble impulses, petty aims and littleness, self-seekin', and vainglory was givin' it a shove the other way? Good land! if I could see all these, and see 'em plain—which no one ever can or will—but if I could, how could I ever sort 'em out, and mark 'em with their right name and heft, and calculate how far they was a drawin' and a influencin' that soul, and how fur it had power to resist? How could the eyes of my spectacles ever see jest how fur down into the depths of that soul shone the Divine Ideal, the holy, stainless image of what we pray to be,—and jest how fur the mists that rise up from our earthly soil darken and blind that light? Good land! I couldn't do it, nor Josiah, nor nobody.

We are blind creeters, the fur-seein'est of us : weak creeters, when we think we are the strong-mindedest. Now, when we hear of a crime, it is easy to say that the one who committed that wrong stepped flat off from goodness into sin, and should be hung. It is so awful easy and sort o' satisfactory to condemn other folks'es faults that we don't stop to think that it may be that evil was fell into through the weakness and blindness of a mistake. Jest as folks fall down suller lots of times a gropin' round in the dark tryin' to find the outside door, and can't. Doin' their best to get out where it is lighter, out into the free air of Heaven, and first they know, entirely unbeknown to them, they open the wrong door, and there they are down suller, dark as pitch, and mebby with a sore and broken head.

And if a wrong is done wilfully, with a purpose, it is easy to think of nothin' but the wrong, and not give a thought to what influences stood behind that soul, a pushin' it off into sin. Early influences, sinful teachin's drunk down eagerly before the mind could seperate the evil from the good. Criminal inheritances of depraved tastes, and wayward and distorted intellect, wretched, depressing surroundings, lack of all comfort, hope, faith in God or man, ignorance, blind despair, all a standin' behind that soul pushin' it forward into a crime. And then when we read of some noble, splendid act of generosity, our souls burn within us, and it is easy to say, the one who did that glorious deed should be throned and crowned with honor—not thinkin' how, mebby unbeknown to us, that act was the costly and glitterin' varnish coverin' up a whited sepulchre. That deed was restin' on self-seekin', ambitious littleness.

Yes, we are blind creeters. And there is but One who holds the key to the terror, the glory, and the mystery of a soul. He, only, can see and judge. He whose age is ageless, and who can therefore alone judge of the mighty flood of influences that pour down upon the soul from that ageless past, swayin' it with mysterious power. He whose life fills that boundless future—Eternity—He alone knows the strength of those mighty forces drawin' us thither. He who sees the unseen—whose eyes can alone pierce the clouds that close so dark about us, and behold the host of shadowy forms that surround us on every side, angels and demons, things present, things to come, life, and death, and every other creature—He only knows their power over us. He who alone knows the meaning of life, the mystery of our creation. And all that keeps me from bein' ravin' distracted in even meditatin' on this is to calm myself down on this thought, that there is One who knows all. And He alone can judge of what He alone can see. He, the just and loving One, will do right with the souls He made.

Why, if I didn't lean up against that thought, and lean heavy, I should tottle and wobble round to that extent that I should fall to pieces—be a perfect wrack and ruin in no time. And another thought that gives me sights of comfort is, He don't need none of my help in judgin' the world. And if I was ever glad of anything in my life, I am glad of that. Why, in my opinion, it is irreverent, the very height of audacity, to dare to affirm what shall be the doom of a single soul.

Then to think of the countless millions on earth, and who sleep in its bosom—and the countless, countless worlds that fill endless and boundless space, the unnumbered hosts of the ageless past, and·the endless future—the Eternity—and jest to speak that word almost takes away my breath—and then to think of us, poor, blind little aunts, on a aunt-hill, deciding on this mighty mystery, writin' books, preachin' sermons, givin' lectures, one way and another, judgin' the fate of these souls, and where they are goin' to, and quarrelin' over it. In my opinion it would be

better for us to spend some of the breath we waste in
this way in prayer to Him who is Mighty, for help in
right living. Or, if we can't do any better with it, let
us spend a very little of it, mebby ½ of it, in coolin'
porridge for the starvin' ones right round us; that
would be better than to spend it as we do do, in
beatin' the air, quarrelin' on who is goin' to be saved,
and how many. Them's my idees, but, howsomever,
everybody to their own mind. But good land! I am
a eppisodin', and a eppisodin', beyond the patience of
anybody. And to resoom and proceed:

As I was a sayin' of Kellup and his father, I s'pose
there's lots of things said about 'em that there hain't
no truth in. Now I don't believe that they chaw
spruce-gum for dinner, and eat snow and icicles in the
time of 'em—not to make a stiddy practice of it.
Why, they couldn't stand it, not for any length of time.
But you know when anybody gets their name up for
any particular thing, it is dretful easy—don't take
hardly a mite of strength—to histe it up a little higher.
But I see this myself, with my own eye.

Last Thanksgivin' I was in the meat-shop to Jonesville, a buyin' a turkey, and some lamb, and oysters,
and things. I was goin' to have the childern home to
dinner. And Kellup come in, and said his father
thought it was such hard times they wouldn't try to
keep Thanksgivin' this year. But he told his father it
showed a ungrateful heart for all the mercies and ben-
efits that had been bestowed on 'em durin' the year,

and it was settin' a bad example to sinners round 'em
to not celebrate it; so he had carried the day, and they
was goin' to swing right out, and buy half a pound of
fresh beef, and celebrate.

And he bought it, and beat the butcher half a cent
on that. I think myself that he is as tight as the bark

SWINGIN' OUT.

to a tree, but I don't believe he is any tighter. But
they say he is as tight agin.

Like myself and Josiah, Kellup is a member of the
Methodist meetin'-house. And he is a dretful case to
exhort other folks. And jest like them that don't do
nothin' themselves, that never did a noble, generous

4

act in their lives, he is a great case to talk about other folks'es duty. And jest like them that are too stingy to draw a long breath for fear of wearin' out their lungs, he is a great case to talk about other folks'es givin'.

If anybody has decent clothes and vittles, he is always talkin' about their extravagance, and how much they could do for the sufferin' poor round 'em with the money. And a man could starve to death right on the road in front of him, and all he would do would be to stop that hearse, and exhort him from the top of it. Not a cent would he give if the man died right there in under the hearse. I despise such Christians, and I always shall; and there are lots of 'em all round us, who are always talkin' about workin' for Christ, and all the work they do is with their tongues. I say such religion is vain; empty as tinglin' brass, and soundin' thimbles.

From the time he wore roundabouts, Kellup's father promised him that jest as quick as he got big enough he should drive that hearse, and it has lifted him up, that hearse has, and always made him feel above the other boys. He has always seemed to think that was the highest station in life he could get up onto. We all think that the reason he comes to see Kitty on it, is he thinks he looks more stately and imposin' on it than he would walkin' afoot. And when the childern, the little Jonesvillians, hoot at him, and make all manner of fun of him, he thinks they envy him, and it

A COB(B) WITHOUT CORN.

makes him act haughtier than ever, and more proud-spirited, and stiff-necked.

As I say, I feel bad, and I take Kitty to do about it every time I see her a'most. And she'll say:

"Oh, Auntie! it is too rich!"

And she'll laugh, and kiss me, and coax me not to be cross about it, till she makes most as big a fool of me as she does of Kellup, and I tell her so.

But I stand firm, and try to make her feel a realizin' sense

KITTY'S KISS.

how it looks to have a hearse standin' round pro-miscous every few days, hitched to our front gate. It is a solemn thing to me. And would be to anybody who looked at things serious and solemn. Most every subject has several sides to it, and some has more'n 20. And folks ort to tutor themselves to hold a subject right up in their hands, and look **on** every side of it. But Kitty don't try to. The humorous side of things is the side she meditates on. And she thinks that Kellup's travelin' round after her on that hearse has a funny side to it. But I can't see it. It is a solemn thing to me to see it drive up to our gate any time o' day, and be hitched there, while he comes in and tries to court her. Why, it looks fairly wicked to me, and I tell her so. And then she'll giggle and laugh, and make a perfect fool of Kellup. Or, that is, improve on the job; for truly Nater helped her powerful at his birth. Nater did a good job in that line— in the fool line. Though you couldn't make him think he was most a fool, or leanin' heavy that way, not if you should drive the fact into his head with a hammer. It is one of the hardest things in the world to make folks believe. They'll own up to bein' a fool twice as quick.

But as I say, it worries me most to death. And there is only jest one thing that keeps me from comin' right out and puttin' a stop to it, and tellin' Kellup she is a foolin' of him. I have meditated on it powerful. And sometimes I have thought that he needs such a affliction. Sometimes I have thought that, bein' so overbearin', and haughty, and big-feelin', that such a takin' down is what he needs to lift him up (morally).

But though that principle holds up my spirit, it is a hard trial to my spirit, and to the eye of my spectacles. And I'll say to Josiah, every time I see him drive up, and groan loud as I say it: "I should think he'd know better than to go a courtin' with a hearse."

But he says: "Keep still; it don't hurt you any, does it?"

That man enjoys it. He has wicked streaks, and I tell him so. And says I:

"Josiah Allen, you don't seem to know what solemnity is, or what wickedness is."

And he says: "I know what a dumb fool is."

And that is all the help I can get. And I s'pose I shall have to let it go on. But I feel like death about it. When he comes here, and Kitty don't happen to be here, he will always begin to exhort me on religion. He is the disagreeablest, self-righteousest creeter I ever see, and that I won't deny.

" Oh," says he to me yesterday—there had been a funeral up by here, and when he came back he hitched the hearse, and come in. And he began to exhort me, and says he: "I have been a thinkin' of it all day, —how glad I am that salvation is free."

I felt wore out with him, and says I: "Well you may be glad. For if it wasn't free, you wouldn't have any—not a mite. You wouldn't either if you had to pay a cent for it."

Before he could say anything, Kitty come in. She had been out to the barn with Josiah to feed the sheep. She looked like a blush-rose; her eyes a dancin' and a sparklin'. And Kellup acted spoonier than any spoon I have got on my buttery shelves.

JOSIAH GOES INTO BUSINESS.

JOSIAH Allen has got a sort of a natural hankerin' after makin' money easy. A sort of a speculatin' turn to his mind, which most men have. But not havin' the other ingregiences that go with it to make it a success, his speculations turn out awful, 2 episodes of which I will relate and set down. One pleasant evenin' Josiah had jest got back from carryin' Kitty Smith to Tirzah Ann's. Tirzah Ann had sent for her to stay a spell with her. And Josiah had got back and put the horses out, and sot by the fire a meditatin' to all outward appearance. When all of a sudden he broke out and says:

"Samantha, I love to make money easy."

"Do you?" says I, in a mechanicle way, for I was bindin' off the heel of a sock of hisen, and my mind was sort o' drawed out by that heel, and strained.

"Yes," says he, crossin' his legs, and lookin' dretful wise at me, "Yes, I love to, like a dog. I love to kinder speculate."

I had bound off the last stitch, and my mind bein' free it soared up noble agin, and I says firmly and impressively:

"Good, honest hard work is the best speculation I ever went into, Josiah Allen."

"Yes," says he, with that same dretful wise look, "wimmen naterally feel different about these things. Wimmen haint got such heads onto 'em as we men have got. We men love to make money by a speck. We love to get rich by head work."

I jest give one look onto his bald head, a strange, searchin' look, that seemed to go right through his brains and come out the other side. I didn't say anything, only jest that look, but that spoke (as it were) loud.

He looked kinder meachin', and hastened to explain.

"I am goin' to fix up that old house of our'n, Samantha, and rent it," says he. "I am goin' to make piles and piles of money out of it, besides the comfort we can take a neighborin'." "And," says he, "I love to—to neighbor, Samantha—I love to deerly."

Says I in calm tones, but firm: "There are worse neighbors, Josiah Allen, than them that are livin' in the old house now."

"Livin' there now?" says he. And his eyes stood out from $\frac{1}{4}$ to a $\frac{1}{2}$ a inch in surprise and horrer.

"Yes," says I, "you'll find, Josiah Allen, that take it right along from day to day, and from year to year, that there are worse creeters to neighbor with than Peace, and Quiet, and Repose."

"Dummit! scare a man to death, will you?"

Says I: "Stop swearin' to once, Josiah Allen, and instantly!"

My mean was lofty and scareful, and he stopped. But he went on in a firm and obstinate axent: "I am determined to fix up that house and rent it. Wimmen can't see into business. They haint got the brains for it. You haint to blame for it, Samantha, but you haint got the head to see how profitable I am goin' to make it. And then our nearest neighbors live now well onto a quarter of a mile away. How neat it will be to have neighbors right here by us, all the time, day and night." And agin he says dreamily: "If I ever loved anything in this world, Samantha, I love to neighbor."

But I held firm, and told him he'd better let well enough alone. But he was sot as sot could be, and went on and fixed up the house. It was a old house right acrost the road from our'n. One that was on the place when we bought it. All shackly and run down; nobody had lived in it for years. And I knew it wouldn't pay to spend money on it. But good land! he wouldn't hear a word to me. He went on a fixin' it, and it cost him nearer a hundred dollars than it did anything else—besides lamin' himself, and blisterin' his hands to work on it himself, and fillin' his eyes

with plaster, and gettin' creeks in his back, a liftin' round and repairin'.

But he felt neat through it all. It seemed as if the more money he laid out, and the worse he got hurt, the more his mind soared up, a lottin' on how much money he was goin' to make a rentin' it, and what a beautiful time he was a goin' to enjoy a neighborin'. He would talk about neighborin' most the hull time days, and would roust me up nights if he happened to think of any new and happifyin' idea on the subject. Till if ever I got sick of any word in the hull dictionary, I got sick of that.

Well, jest as quick as the house was done, and he pushed the work on rapid and powerful, fairly drove it, he was in such

4*

a hurry, nothin' to do but he must set off huntin' up a renter, for he couldn't seem to wait a minute. I told him to keep cool. Says I "You'll make money by it if you do."

But no! he couldn't wait till somebody come to him. He wouldn't hear a word to me. He'd throw wimmen's heads in my face, and say they was week, and wuzn't like men's. He was so proud and haughty about the speck he had gone into, and the piles and piles of money he was goin' to make, that once or twice he told me that I hadn't no head at all. And then he'd hitch up the old mare, and go off a huntin' round and enquirin'. And finally one day he come home from Jonesville tickled to death seeminly. He'd found a family and engaged 'em—Jonathan Spinks'es folks. They was to Jonesville a stayin' with Miss Spinks'es sister, Sam Thrasher's wife, and they had heerd of Josiah's huntin' round; so they hailed him as he was a goin' by, and engaged it, made the bargain right there on the spot. And as I said, he was tickled to death almost, and says to me in a highlarius axent:

"They are splendid folks, Samantha."

Says I in very cold tones: "Are they the Spinkses that used to live to Zoar?"

"Yes," says he. "And they are a beautiful family, and I have made a splendid bargain. 50 dollars a year for the house and garden. What do you think now? I never should have known they was a lookin' for a house if I hadn't been a enquirin' round. What do you think now about my keepin' cool?"

Says I mildly, but firmly: "My mind haint changed from what it wuz more formally."

"Wall, what do you think now about my lettin' the old house run down, when I can make 50 dollars a year, clear gain, besides more'n three times that in solid comfort a-neighberin'?"

Says I, firm as a rock, "My mind hain't changed, Josiah Allen, so much as the width of a horsehair."

"Wall," says he, "I always said wimmen hadn't no heads, I always knew it. But it is agravatin', it is dumb agravatin', when anybody has done the head-work I have done, and made such a bargain as I have made, to not have anybody's wife appreciate it. And I should think it was about time to have supper, if you are goin' to have any to-night."

I calmly rose and put on the teakettle, and never disputed a word with him whether I had a head or not. Good land! I knew I had one, and what was the use of arguin' about it? And I didn't say nothin' more about his bargain, for I see it wouldn't do no good. 'Twas all settled, and the writin's drawed. But I kep' up a severe thinkin'. I had heard of Spinks'es folks before. It had come right straight to me. Miss Ebenezer Gowdey, she that was Nabby Widrick, her nephew's wive's step-mother, old Miss Tooler, had lived neighber to 'em. And Miss Tooler told Nabby, and Nabby told me, that they was shiftless creeters. But when bargains are all made, it is of no use tryin' to convince Josiahs. And I knew if I should tell Josiah what I had heard he'd only go to arguin'

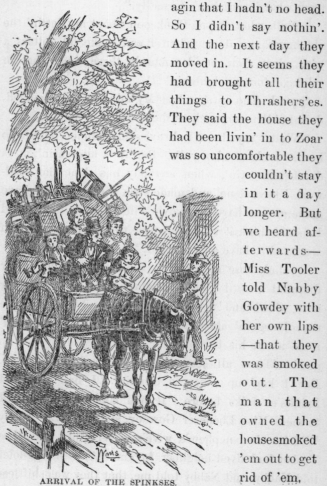

ARRIVAL OF THE SPINKSES.

agin that I hadn't no head. So I didn't say nothin'. And the next day they moved in. It seems they had brought all their things to Thrashers'es. They said the house they had been livin' in to Zoar was so uncomfortable they couldn't stay in it a day longer. But we heard afterwards— Miss Tooler told Nabby Gowdey with her own lips —that they was smoked out. The man that owned the house smoked 'em out to get rid of 'em,

Wall, as I said, they come. Mr. Spink, his wife, and his wife's sister (she was Irish), and the childern. And oh! how neat Josiah Allen did feel. He was over there before they had hardly got sot down, and offered to do anything under the sun for 'em, and offered 'em everything we had in the house. I, myself, kep' cool and collected together. Though I treated 'em in a liberal way, and in the course of two or three days I made 'em a friendly call, and acted well towards 'em.

But instead of runnin' over there the next day, and two or three times a day, I made a practice of stayin' to home considerable; and Josiah took me to do for it. But I told him I treated them exactly as I wanted them to treat me. Says I, "A mejum course is the best course to pursue in nearly every enterprise in life, neighberin' especially. I begin as I can hold out. I lay out to be kind and friendly to 'em, but I don't intend to make it my home with them, nor do I want them to make it their home with me. Once in two or three days is enough, and enough, Josiah Allen, is as good as a feast."

"Wall," says he, "if I ever enjoyed anything in this world I enjoy neighberin' with them folks. And they think the world of me. It beats all how they worship me. The childern take to me so, they don't want me out of their sight hardly a minute. Spink and his wife says they think it is in my looks. You know I *am* pretty lookin', Samantha. They say the baby will cry after me so quick. It beats all what friends we have got to be, I and the Spinkses, and it is agravatin', Samantha, to think you don't seem to feel towards 'em that strong friendship that I feel."

Says I, "Friendship, Josiah Allen, is a great word. True friendship is the most beautiful thing on earth; it is love without passion, tenderness without alloy. And," says I, soarin' up into the realm of allegory, where, on the feathery wings of pure eloquence, I fly frequent, "Intimacy hain't friendship. Two men may sleep together, year after year, on the same feather-bed, and wake up in the mornin', and shake hands with each other, perfect strangers, made so unbeknown to them. And feather-beds, nor pillers, nor nothin' can't bring 'em no nigher to each other. And they can keep it up from year to year, and lock arms and prominade together through the day, and not get a mite closer to each other. They can keep their bodies side by side, but their souls, who can tackle 'em together, unless nature tackled 'em, unbeknown to them? Nobody. And then, agin, two persons may meet, comin' from each side of the world; and they will look right through each other's eyes down into their souls, and see each other's image there; born so, born friends, entirely unbeknown to them. Thousands of milds apart, and all the insperations of heaven and earth; all the influences of life, education, joy, and sorrow, has been fitting them for

YOKED BUT NOT MATED.

each other (unbeknown to them): twin souls, and they not knowin' of it."

"Speakin' of twin—" says Josiah.

But I was soarin' too high to light down that minute. So I kep' on, though his interruption was a-lowerin' me down gradual.

"There is a great filisofical fact right here, Josiah Allen," says I, tryin' to bring down and fit the idee to my pardner's comprehension, for it is ever my way to try to convince, as well as to soar in oritory. "You may yoke up the old mare and the brindle cow together and drive 'em year after year in a buggy. But you can't make that horse into a cow, or make that old cow whinner. It can't be done. And two wimmen may each of 'em have half a shear, and think they will screw 'em together and save property, and cut some with 'em. But if one of them halves is 2 or 3 inches shorter than the other, and narrower, how be they goin' to cut with 'em? All the screws and wrenches in creation can't do no more than hold 'em together. It hain't no use if they wuzn't made to fit each other in the first place, unbeknown to them." Says I, "Some folks are j'ined together for life in jest that way, drawn together by some sort of influence, worldly considerations, blind fancy, thoughtlessness, and the minister's words fasten 'em, jest as these shears was. But good land! after the vapory, dreamy time of the honeymoon is passed through, and the heavy, solid warp and woof of life lays before 'em for

them to cut a path through it, they'll find out whether
they fit each other or not. And if they don't, it is
tejus business for 'em, ex-
tremely tejus, and they'll find
it out so."—"Speakin' of
twin—" says Josiah.

His persistent and stiddy

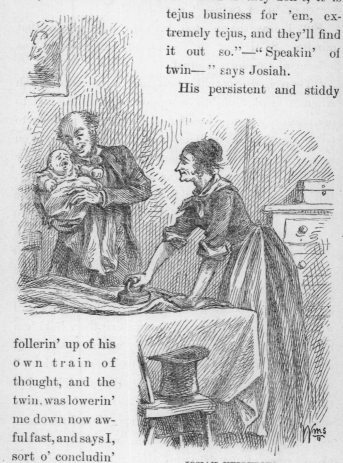

follerin' up of his
own train of
thought, and the
twin, was lowerin'
me down now aw-
ful fast, and says I,
sort o' concludin'
up, " Be good and

JOSIAH NEIGHBORS.

kind to everybody, and Mr. Spinks'es folks, as you
have opportunity ; but before you make bosom friends

of 'em, wait and see if your soul speaks." Says I, firmly, " Mine don't, in this case."

"Speakin' of twin," says Josiah agin, " Did you ever see so beautiful a twin as Mr. Spinks'es twin is ? What a pity they lost the mate to it! Their ma says it is perfectly wonderful the way that babe takes to me. I held it all the while she was ironin', this forenoon. And the two boys foller me round all day, tight to my heels, instead of their father. Spink says they think I am the prettiest man they ever see, almost perfectly beautiful."

I give Josiah Allen a look full in his face, a curious look, very searchin' and peculiar. But before I had time to say anything, only jest that look, the door opened, and Spinks'es wive's sister come in unexpected, and said that Miss Spink wanted to borrow the loan of ten pounds of side pork, a fine comb, some flour, the dish-kettle, and my tooth-brush "

I let her have 'em all but the tooth brush, for I was determined to use 'em well. And Josiah didn't like it at all because I didn't let that go. And he said in a fault-findin', complainin' axent "that I didn't seem to want to be sociable."

And I told him that "I thought borrowin' a toothbrush was a little *too* sociable."

And he most snapped my head off, and muttered about my not bein' neighborly, and that I didn't feel a mite about neighborin' as he did. And I made a vow, then and there (inside of my mind), that I wouldn't say a word to Josiah Allen on the subject, not if they borrowed us out of house and home. Thinkses I, I can stand it as long as he can; if they spile our things, he has got to pay for new ones; if they waste our property, he has got to lose it; if they spile our comfort, he's got to stand it as well as I have; and, knowin' the doggy obstinacy of his sect, I considered this great truth, and acted on it, that the stiller I kep', and the less I said about 'em, the quicker he'd get sick of 'em; so I held firm. And never let on to Josiah but what it was solid comfort to me to have 'em there all the time a most; and not have a minute I could call my own; and have 'em borrow everything under the sun that ever was borrowed: garden-sass of all kinds, and the lookin'-glass, groceries, the old cat, vittles, cookin' utensils, stove-pipe, a feather-bed, bolsters, bed-clothes, and the New Testament.

They even borrowed Josiah's clothes. Why, Spink wore Josiah's best pantaloons more than Josiah did. He got so he didn't act as if he could stir out without Josiah's best pantaloons. He'd keep a tellin' that he was goin' to get a new pair, but he didn't get 'em, and would hang onto Josiah's. And Josiah had to stay to home a number of times jest on that account. And then he'd borrow Josiah's galluses. Josiah had got kinder run out of galluses, and hadn't got but one pair of sound ones. And Josiah would have to pin his pantaloons onto his vest, and the pins would lose out, and it was all Josiah could do to keep his clothes on.

It made it awful bad for him. I know one day, when I had a lot of company, I had to wink him out of the room a number of times, to fix himself so he would be decent. But all through it I kep' still, and never said a word. I see we was loosin' property fast, and had lost every mite of comfort we had enjoyed, for there was some of 'em there every minute of the time, a most, and some of the time two or three of 'em. Why, Miss Spink used to come over and eat breakfast with us lots of times. She'd say she felt so mauger that she couldn't eat nothin' to home, and she thought mebby my vittles would go to the place. And besides losin' our property and comfort, I'll be hanged if I didn't think sometimes that I should lose my pardner by 'em, they worked him so. But I held firm. Thinkses I to myself, it must be that Josiah will get sick of neighborin', after a while, and start 'em off. For the sufferin's that man endured couldn't never be told nor sung.

Why, before they had been there a month, as I told sister Bamber,—she was to our house a visitin', and Josiah was in the buttery a churnin', and I knew he wouldn't hear,—says I: "They have borrowed everything I have got, unless it is Josiah."

And if you'll believe it, before I had got the words out of my mouth, Miss Spinks'es sister opened the door, and walked in, and asked me "if I could spare Mr. Allen to help stretch a carpet."

And I whispered to sister Bamber, and says I: "If

they haint borrowed the last thing now; if they haint borrowed Josiah."

But I told the girl "to take him an' welcome." (I was very polite to 'em, and meant to be, but cool.)

BORROWIN' JOSIAH.

So I took holt and done the churnin' myself, and let him go. And he come home perfectly tuckered out. Wasn't good for nothin' hardly for several days. He got strained somehow a pullin' on that carpet. But after that they would send for him real often to help do some job. They both took as much agin liberty with Josiah as they did with me; they worked him down almost to skin and bones. Besides all the

SPINKS'ES COW—A NIGHT SCENE.

rest he suffered. Why, his cow-sufferin' alone was perfectly awful. They had a cow, a high-headed creeter; as haughty a actin' cow as I ever see in my life. She would hold her head right up, and walk over our fence, and tramp through the garden. I didn't know how Josiah felt about it, but I used to think myself that I could have stood it as well agin if it hadn't been so high headed. It would look so sort o' independent and overbearin' at me, when it was a walkin' through the fence, and tramplin' through the garden. Josiah always laid out his beds in the garden with a chalk-line, as square and beautiful as the pyramids, and that cow jest leveled 'em to the ground. They tied her up nights, but she would get loose, and start right for our premises; seemed to take right to us, jest as the rest of 'em did. But I held firm, for I see that gettin' up night after night, and goin' out in the night air, chasin' after that cow, was coolin' off my companion's affection for the Spinkses.

And then they kept the awfulest sight of hens. I know Josiah was dretful tickled with the idee at first, and said, "mebby we could swap with 'em, get into their kind of hens."

And I told him in a cautious way "that I shouldn't wonder a mite if we did."

Wall, them hens seemed to feel jest as the rest of the family did; didn't seem to want to stay to home a minute, but flocked right over onto us; stayed right by us day and night; would hang round our doors and door-steps, and come into the house every chance they could get, daytimes; and nights, would roost right along on the door-yard fence, and the front porch, and the lilack bushes, and the pump. Why, the story got out that we was keepin' a

OUR HEN-DAIRY.

hen-dairy, and strangers who thought of goin' into the business would stop and holler to Josiah, and ask him if he found it profitable to keep so many hens. And I'd see that man shakin' his fist at 'em, after they would go on, he would be that mad at 'em. Somehow the idee of keepin' a hen-dairy was always dretful obnoxious to Josiah, though it is perfectly honorable, as far as I can see.

Finally, he had made so much of 'em, the two boys got to thinkin' so much of Josiah that they wanted to sleep with him, and he, thinkin' it wouldn't be neighborly to refuse, let 'em come every little while. And they kicked awfully. They kicked Josiah Allen till he was black and blue. It come tough on Josiah, but I didn't say a word, only I merely told him "that of course he couldn't expect me to sleep with the hull neighborhood," so I went off, and slept in the settin'-room bedroom. It made me a sight of work, but I held firm.

At last Spink and his wife, and his wife's sister, got into the habit of goin' off nights to parties, and leavin' the twin with Josiah. And though it almost broke my heart to see his sufferin's, still, held up by principle, and the aim I had in view, I would go off and sleep in the settin'-room bedroom, and let Josiah tussle with it. Sometimes it would have the colic most all night, and the infantum, and the snuffles. But, though I could have wept when I heerd my pardner a groanin' and a sithein' in the dead of night, and a callin' on heaven to witness that no other man ever had the sufferin's he was a sufferin', still, held up by my aim, I would lay still, and let it go on.

It wore on Josiah Allen. His health seemed to be a runnin' down; his morals seemed to be loose and totterin'; he would snap me up every little while as if he would take my head off; and unbeknown to him I would hear him a jawin' to himself, and a shakin' his fist at nothin' when he was alone, and actin'. But I kep' cool, for though he didn't come out and say a word to me about the Spinkses, still I felt a feelin' that there would be a change. But I little thought the change was so near.

But one mornin' to the breakfast-table, as I handed Josiah his fourth cup of coffee, he says to me, says he:

"Samantha, sposen we go to Brother Bamberses to-day, and spend the day. I feel," says he, with a deep sithe, "I feel as if I needed a change."

Says I, lookin' pityingly on his pale and haggard face, "you do, Josiah," and says I, "if I was in your place I would speak to Brother Bamber about the state of your morals." Says I, in a tender yet firm tone, "I don't want to scare you, Josiah, nor twit you, but your morals seem to be a totterin'; I am afraid you are a back-slidin', Josiah Allen."

He jumped right up out of his chair, and shook his fist over towards the Spinks'es house, and hollered out in a loud, awful tone:

"My morals would be all right if it wuzn't for them dumb Spinkses, dumb 'em."

You could have knocked me down with a pin-feather (as it were), I was that shocked and agitated; it had all come onto me so sudden, and his tone was so loud and shameful. But before I could say a word he went on, a shakin' his fist vehementer and wilder than I ever see a fist shook:

"I guess you be neighbored with as I have been, and slept with by two wild-cats, and be kicked till you are black and blue, and mebby you'd back-slide!"

"Says 1: "Josiah Allen, if you don't go to see Brother Bamber to-day, Brother Bamber shall come and see you. Did I ever expect to live," says I, with a gloomy face, "to see my pardner rampagin' round worse than any pirate that ever swum the seas, and shakin' his fist, and actin'. I told you in the first on't, Josiah Allen, to begin as you could hold out."

" What if you did?" he yelled out. " Who thought we'd be borrowed out of house and home, and visited to death, and trampled over by cows, and roosted on; who s'posed they'd run me over with twin, and work me down to skin and bone, and foller me 'round tight to my heels all day, and sleep with me nights, and make dumb lunaticks of themselves? Dumb em!'"

Says I in firm accents, " Josiah Allen, if you swear another swear to-day, I'll part with you before Squire Baker." Says I, " It betters it, don't it, for you to start up and go to swearin'."

Before Josiah could answer me a word, the door opened and in come Miss Spink'ses sister. They never none of 'em knocked, but dropped right down on us unexpected, like sun-strokes.

Says she, with a sort of a haughty, independent

5

mean onto her (some like their cow's mean), and directin' her conversation to Josiah :

"Mr. Spink is goin' to have his likeness took, to-day, and he would be glad to borrow the loan of your pantaloons and galluses. And he said if you didn't want your pantaloons to go without your boots went with 'em, he guessed he'd wear your boots, as his had been heel-tapped and might show. And the two boys bein' so took up with you, Mr. Allen, their Ma thought she'd let 'em come over here and sleep with you while they was gone ; they didn't know but they might stay several days to her folks'es, as they had heard of a number of parties that was goin' to be held in that neighborhood. And knowin' you hadn't no little childern of your own, she thought it might be agreeable to you to keep the twin, while they was gone —and—and—"

She hadn't got through with her speech, and I don't know what she would have tackled us for next. But the door opened without no warnin', and in come Miss Spink herself, and she said that "Spink had been urgin' her to be took, too, and they kinder wanted to be took holt of hands, and they thought if Josiah and me had some kid gloves by us, they would borrow the loan of 'em ; they thought it would give 'em a more genteel, aristocratic look. And as for the childern," says she, "we shall go off feelin' jest as safe and happy about 'em as if they was with us, they love dear Mr. Allen so." And says she with a sweet smile, "I have lived on more places than I can think of hardly—we never have lived but a little while in a place, somehow the climates didn't agree with us long at a time. But never, in all the places we have lived in, have we ever had such neighbors, never, never did we take such solid comfort a-neighborin', as we do here."

Josiah jumped right upon his feet, and shook his fist at her, and says he, in a more skareful tone than he had used as yet:

" You have got to stop it. If you don't stop neigh-berin' with me, I'll know the reason why."

Miss Spink looked skairt, and agitated awful, but I laid hands on him, and says I, "Be calm, Josiah Allen, and compose yourself down."

" I won't be calm!" says he; "I won't be composed down."

Says I, firmly, still a-keepin' between him and her, and still a-layin' holt of him, " You must, Josiah!"

" I tell you I *won't*, Samantha! I'll let you know," says he, a-shakin' his fist at her powerful, " I'll let you know that you have run me over with twin for the last time; I'll let you know that I have been trampled over, and eat up by cows, and roosted on, and slept with for the last time," says he, shakin' both fists at at her. " You have neighbored your last neighbor with me, and I'll let you know you have."

Says I, " Josiah Allen, I tell you to compose your-self down."

"And I tell you again, Samantha, that I *won't!*"

But I could see that his voice was sort 'o lowerin' down, and I knew the worst was over. I spoke sort 'o soothin'ly to him, and told him, in tender axents, that he shouldn't be neighbored with another mite; and finally, I got him quieted down. But he looked bad in the face, and his sithes was fearful.

My feelin's for that man give me strength to give Miss Spink a piece of my mind. My talk was calm, but to the purpose, and very smart. It was a very little on the allegory way. I told her jest how I felt about mejum courses; how sweet and happyfyin' it was to pursue 'em.

Says I, " Fire is first-rate, dretful comfortin' for warmin' and cookin' purposes; too much fire is bad, and leads to conflagrations, martyrs, and etcetery. Water is good; too much leads to drowndin', dropsy, and-so-forth. Neighborin' is good, first-rate, if follered mejumly. Too much neighborin' leads to weariness, anarky, kicks, black and blue pardners, and almost delerious Josiahs."

As quick as I mentioned the word kick, I see a change in Josiah's face; he begun to shake his fist, and act; I see he was a-growin' wild agin; Miss Spink see it too, and she and her sister fled.

That very afternoon Josiah went to Jonesville and served some papers onto 'em. They hadn't made no bargain, for any certain time, so by losin' all his rent, he got rid of 'em before the next afternoon. And says he to me that night, as he sot by the fire rubbin' some linement onto his legs where he had been kicked, says he to me :

"Samantha, if any human bein' ever comes to rent that house of me, I'll shoot 'em down, jest as I would a mushrat."

I knew he had lost over two hundred dollars by 'em,

JOSIAH'S VOW.

and been kicked so lame that he couldn't stand on his feet hardly. I knew that man had been neighbored almost into his grave, but I couldn't set by calmly and hear him talk no such wickedness, and so says I :

"Josiah Allen, can't you ever learn to take a mejum course ? You needn't go round huntin' up renters, or murder 'em if they come nigh you." Says I, "You must learn to be more moderate and mejum."

But he kep' right on, a-pourin' out the linement on his hand, and rubbin' it onto his legs, and stuck to it to the last. Says he, "I'd shoot him down, jest as I would a mushrat; and there hain't a law in the land but what would bear me out in it."

MORALIZIN' AND EPISODIN'.

ANYBODY would have thought that this episode (Spink episode) would have sickened Josiah Allen of launchin' out into any more headwork, and tryin' to made money on a speck. But if you'll believe it, Jonathan Spink'ses folks hadn't been gone three weeks—for Kitty come back the day after Spink'ses folks left, and she only stayed with us two weeks that time, havin' promised to stay a spell to Thomas Jefferson's, and it was only a few days after she went— and then I knew by Josiah's legs—the black-and-blue spots hadn't begun to wear off; they had just begun to turn yaller—and then I knew by my head-dress, too—when that man come home from Jonesville one night, cross as a bear.

I said I knew by my new head-dress. I well remember I had wore it that afternoon for the first time, some expectin' very genteel company, and wantin' to look well. But the company didn't come, and Kellup Cobb did. He come to bring home a cent he had

(119)

borrowed the night before at the missionary meetin'
to send for his annual gift to the heathens. And he
noticed my new cap in a minute. He looked witherin'
and overbearin' at it, and in a sort of a back-handed,
underground way, that I can't bear, nor never could,
he begun to throw hints at me about it. About
married women and members of meetin'-housen
spendin' their money in such extravagance, when
they might spend it in spreadin' the Gospel in be-
nighted lands—and about how awful wicked it was to
be so dressy—and et cetery, et cetery.

My cap *wuz* middlin'-foamin' lookin'. I couldn't
deny it, and didn't try to. It wuzn't what you might
call over and above dressy, but it was handsome, and
very nice. The ribbin on it cost me 18 pence per yard,
and the cap contained two yards and a half; it was
very nice. But none too good for me, my Josiah said.

He is what you may call a close man at a bargain.
(Tight, would perhaps be a better word to express his
situation.) But he loves dearly to see me look beautiful.
And he is very gay in his tastes; red is his favorite
color, and the more fiery shades of yellow; he would
be glad to see me dressed in these tints all the time.
But I don't encourage him in the idee. Not that I
think one color is wickeder than another, but they
don't seem to be becomin' to my style and age.

Now this new head dress, I had picked it out and
selected it with my pardner by my side, and he whispered to me loud, as I was a-selectin' of it: "If you

have *got* to have a new cap, Samantha, for mercy's sake get a red one."

But I whispered to him that I should look like a fool with a red cap on, and to keep still.

And then he whispered agin, in a more anxious tone: "Wall then, for pity's sake do get yeller, or

THE NEW HEAD-DRESS.

sunthin' that has got a little color to it. Black! black! the whole of the time; you look jest like a mourner."

I had a black one on my hand at that time, admirin'

5*

of it, and most settled on it. But Josiah's mean was such as I was a-settlin', that I, as a devoted pardner, and a woman of principle, compromised the matter with Josiah and Duty, by purchasin' one trimmed with a sort of a pinky, lilock color. It was very becomin' to me. But I won't deny, as a woman who is bred to tellin' the truth, and not gin to deceit and coverin' up,—I won't deny that the first time I tried that head-dress on after I got home, I had my curious feelin's. I thought mebby it was wrong for me to buy such costly ribbin, and so much of it. And then I worried about the color, too. Thinkses I, mebby it is too young for me; too young for a woman who owns a bald-headed pardner and a grandchild, and who has but few teeth left in her head.

My conscience is a perfect old tyrent, and jest drives me round more'n half the time. I am willin' to be drove by her as fur as I ort to be. But sometimes, I declare for't, I get so tuckered out with her drivin's, that I get fairly puzzled, and wonderin' whether she knows herself all the time jest what she is about; whether she is certain that she is always a drivin' me in the right road; and how fur I ort to be drove by her, and when, and where to; and whether I ort to let my intellect and common sense lay holt and help her drive. As I say, she run me considerable of a run on this head-dress. I had a awful time of it, and won't deny it, and I was on the very pint several times of carryin' it back. But when Kellup come right out, and gin such powerful hints about it; about extravagance, and wickedness, and vanity; and about married wimmen settin' sinful patterns to them outside of meetin'-housen, and that it didn't look likely, and et cetery, et cetery, and so forth.

Why, as he went on a hintin' so powerful strong, and givin' such burnin' glances onto that head-dress, why, I sort o' sprunted up, and begun to see things on the other side plainer than I had seen 'em.

APPLE BLOSSOMS.

Then says I, as the eyes of my specks rested upon the apple-boughs that filled the north kitchen winder with a glow of rosiness and sweetness:
"The Lord don't seem to think as you do, Kellup. Jest see how He has dressed up that old apple-tree,"

Says I : " No fashionable belle in New York or Paris village can ever hope to wear garments so daintily fine and sweet. No queen nor empress ever wore or ever will wear for their coronation robes such splendid and gorgeous raiment as the common spring suit of that old apple-tree."

HOW IT MIGHT HAVE BEEN.

Says Kellup, holdin' his head well up in the air, and drawin' his lips down with a very self-righteous drawin', that I knew meant head-dress, though he didn't come right out and say it :

" I despise and detest the foolishness of display. There is more important and serious business on earth than dressin' up to look nice."

"That is so," says I, "that is jest as true as you live. Now that old apple tree's stiddy business and theme is to make sweet, juicy apples; but at the same time that don't hender her from dressin' up, and lookin' well. The Lord might have made the apples grow in rows right round the trunk from top to bottom, with no 'foolishness of display' of the rosy coloring and perfume—but He didn't. He chose in His wisdom, which it is not for you or me to doubt, to make it a glory and a delight to every beholder. So beautiful that the birds sail and sing with very joy in and out of the sweet branches, and the happy bees hum delightedly about the honey-laden cells, and she whose name was once Smith, has been made happy as a queen all day long, by jest lookin' out of that window down into the fragrant, rosy depths of sweetness and light."

"Wall," says Kellup, lookin' keen at my head-dress, "I don't consider it likely, anyway, to spend so much time a dressin' up—it is a shiftless waste of time, anyway."

"Why," says I; for the more he scolded me, the plainer I see the other side of things. So curious are human bein's constituted and sot.

"Nater has always been considered likely—I never heard a word against her character, and she is stiddy minded, too, and hard workin'. She works hard, Nater does. She works almost beyond her strength sometimes. She has sights of work on her hands all the hull time, and she has a remarkable knack of turnin' off tremendous day's works. And I never in my hull life heard her called shiftless or slack. But what a case she is to orniment herself off; to rag out and show herself in so many different colors. And if she feels better to be dressed up and fixed off kinder pretty while she's to work, I don't know whose business it is. I never was no case myself to dress up in white book muslin, or pink silk, or bobonet lace, or anything of that kind, when I was a doin' hard jobs, such as makin' soap, and runnin' candles, and cleanin' house, and etcetery. And when I have got to be out in the rain when it is all drabbly and muddy, why I jest wrap up and look like fury. But she don't. No! I have known her time and agin to tie the most gorgeous and shinin' rainbow round her old waist and jest lay herself out to look foamin' and dressy, right there in the rain.

HARD AT IT.

"It beats all how she does fix herself up. But it don't hurt my feelin's at all. I never was a mite jealous of other females lookin' better than I did. The better they look, the better I enjoy lookin' at 'em. And if Nater can dress up better and look better while she is a doin' her spring work and all her other hard jobs than I can, good land! how simple it would be in me to blame her. There is where I use such cast-iron reason. You don't ketch me a blamin' other folks for their little personal ways and habits that don't do nobody no hurt. She is well off, Nater is, and able to do as she is a mind to; she has got plenty to do with; she don't have to scrimp herself to buy flowers, and tossels, and rainbows. If she did, I shouldn't approve of it in her, not at all. I despise folks goin' beyond their means to look pretty. I think it is wicked, and the height of dretfulness. But if them that are abundantly able and willin' want to look nice, I say, let 'em look."

And I cast a conscious and sort of a modest glance up into the lookin'-glass that hung over the table. I could jest ketch a glimpse of my head-dress, and I see that its strings floated out noble, and I see at the same glance that he was still lookin' witherin' at it. But I didn't care a mite for it. I was jest filled with my subject (that side of it, for every subject has got more'n a dozen sides to it), and the more he cast them witherin' looks onto me the more I wuzn't withered—but soared up in mind, and grew eloquent.

And I went on fearfully eloquent about Nater, and the way she fixed herself up perfectly beautiful—right when she was a workin' the hardest.

"Why," says I, "when she goes way down into the depths of the under world to make iron, and coal, and salt, and things that has got to be made, and she has got to make 'em—why, she can't be contented way down there in the dark, all alone by herself, without deckin' herself off with diamonds, and all sorts of precious gems, and holdin' up wreaths of shinin' crystal, enameled fern fronds, and hangin' clusters snowy white, and those shinin' with every dazzlin' hue.

" And way down on the ocean floor, fifteen miles or so down below, where she would naturally expect nobody would come a visatin'—why, way down there, where she must know that there hain't no company liable to drop in on her onexpected, yet every minute of the time she is all ornimented off with pearls, and opal-tinted shells, daintest green and crimson sea-grass, gem-like purple astreas, wonderful pink and white coral wreaths—all strange and lovely blossoms of the sea.

" What tongue can tell the wonders of the beauty she arrays herself with way down there in the dark alone. How every little bud of beauty is wreathed around with other marvels of loveliness—how all about one tiny little bit of a blossom will be twined other wonderful little flowerin' vines, starred with crystal bells.

" No tongue can ever describe it—not mine, certainly, for I say but little myself, and that little is far too small to express these wonders of beauty.

" And then right round here, when she is to work right here in our fields, doin' her common run of hard work—such as makin' wheat, and oats, and other grain. No matter how hot the weather is, or muggy; no matter whether she is behindhand with her work, and in a awful hurry—she always finds time to scatter along in the orderly ranks of the grain, wild red poppies and blue-eyed asters. And I never in my life, and Josiah never did, see her ever make a solid ear of corn without she hung on top of it a long silk tossel.

NATURE'S OCEAN BOUDOIR.

And I don't believe she ever made a ton of hay in the world, if she had her own way about it, but what she made it perfectly gay with white daisies and butter-cups.

"And all the gardens of the world she glorifies, and all the roads, and hedges, and lanes, and by-ways. No matter how long and crooked they are, or how tejus, she scatters blossoms of brightness and beauty over them all.

"And clear up on the highest mountains, under the shadow of the everlastin' snows, she will stop to lay a cluster of sweet mountain anemones and Alpine roses on the old bosom—for she is a gettin' considerable along in years, Nater is. Not that I say it in a runnin' way at all, or spiteful, or mean. But I s'pose she is older than we have any idee

NATURE'S WORK.

of—as old agin as folks call her.   But she acts young, and looks so.   She holds her age remarkable, as has been often remarked about a person whose name was once Smith.

"Why, she acts fairly frisky and girlish sometimes. Way down in the lowest valleys, down by the most hidden brook-side, she will sit down to weave together the most lovely and coquetish bunches of fern and grasses, and scarlet and golden wild flowers, and deck herself up in 'em like a bride of 16.   You never ketched her runnin' in debt for a lot of stuff though —her principles are too firm.   But she goes on makin' beauty and gladness wherever she goes, and lookin' handsome, and if it had been wicked the Lord wouldn't have let her go on in it.   He could have stopped her in a minute if He had wanted to.   She does jest as He tells her to, and always did.

"And," says I, with considerable of a stern look onto Kellup, "if Nater—if she who understands the unwritten language of God, that we can't speak yet— if she, whose ways seem to us to be a revelation of that will of the Most High—if she can go on wreathing herself in beauty, I don't think we should be afraid of gettin' holt of all we can of it—of all lovely things.   And I don't think," says I, givin' a sort of a careless glance up into the lookin'-glass, "that there should be such a fuss made by the world at large about my head-dress."

"But," says Kellup, a groanin' loud and violent,

" it is the wickedness of it I look at. To follow the vile example of the rich. And oh! how wicked rich folks be. How hard-hearted, how unprincipled, and vile." And agin he groaned, deep.

Says I, " Don't groan so, Kellup," for it was truly skairful to hear him.

Says he, " I will groan!" Says he, " The carryin's on and extravagance of the rich is enough to make a dog groan."

I see I couldn't stop his groanin', but I went on a talkin' reasonable, in hopes I could quell him down.

Says I, " There is two sides to most everything, Kellup, and some have lots of sides. That is what makes the world such a confusin' place to live in. If things and idees didn't have but one side to 'em, we could grab holt of that side, hold it close, and be at rest.

" But they do. And you must look on both sides of things before you make a move. You mustn't confine yourself to lookin' on jest one side of a subject, for it hain't reasonable."

" I won't try to look on both sides," says he with a bitter look. " That is what makes folks onsettled and onstabled in their views, and liberal. But I won't. I am firm and decided. I am satisfied to look on one side of a subject—on the good old orthodox side. You won't ketch me a whifflin' round and lookin' on every side of a idee."

" Wall," says I, calmly, for to convince, and not

to anger, is ever my theme and purpose. And knowin' that to the multitude truth is most often palatable if presented in a parabolical form, and has been for centuries often imbibed by them in that way, entirely unbeknown to them. And knowin' that the little scenes of daily life are as good to wrap round morals and cause 'em to be swallowed down unbeknowin', as peach preserves are to roll round pills, I went on and says :

" If you won't look on only one side of a subject, Kellup, you may find yourself in as curious a place as Melvin Case was last fall. His wife told it herself to Miss Gansey, and Miss Gansey told the editor of the Augurs'es wife, and the editor of the Augurs'es wife told Miss Mooney, and she told the woman's first husband's mother-in-law that told me. It come straight.

" It was a very curious situation, and the way on't was : Melvin Case, as you know, married Clarinda Piller of Piller P'int, down on the Lake Shore road. Wall, they had been married 23 years and never had no childern, and last fall they had a nice little boy. He was a welcome child, and weighed over 9 pounds.

" Wall, Malvin thought the world of his wife, and bein' very tickled about the boy, and feelin' very affectionate towards his wife at the time, he proposed at once that they should call him after her maiden name —Piller. Of course she give ner willin' consent, and they was both highly tickled. But you see, bein' blinded by affection and happiness, they didn't look on

only one side of the idee, and they never studied on
how the two names was a goin' to look when they was
put together, till after he had wrote it down in the
Bible ; and then he paused, with his pen in his hand,
and looked up perfectly horrified at his wife, who was

BABY PILLER CASE.

holdin' the baby in her arms and lookin' over his
shoulder, and she looked perfectly dumbfoundered at
him, for they see it looked awful—Piller Case.

"Now you are lookin' at one side of the subject, but
there is another side to it, Kellup,—there is as sure
as you live and breathe.

"God knows too much cannot be said or sung about the duty the rich owe to the poor. They cannot study too correctly, and follow too closely the pattern that He, the loving Elder Brother, set them. He who was so tender in His compassion; so helpful and thoughtful to the claims of the poor and humble. But charity is a big word, and it has more than one side to it. It means charity to the poor, under whose lowly roofs He once entered, a child of the poor, and so consecrated them honorable for all time. Those who were His closest friends through His toilsome earthly life ; those whom He loved first, and loved last ; cared for even in that supreme moment of His most triumphant and glorious ignominy. Shall not His followers forever love and bless those He hallowed by His tender care in such a moment ? Yes, charity to the poor first. But we mustn't stop there, Kellup. We may want to set right down in front of that side of the word, and stay there. But we mustn't. If we want to view this heavenly word on every side we must walk round on the other side of it, and see that it means, too, charity to the rich. A higher, subtler quality of charity it calls for in us than the other.

"For I can tell you, Kellup, some folks say it is a tough job for one to keep a sweet, charitable, loving spirit towards them that are richer, more successful, and happier than they be. Hard for 'em to rejoice over the good fortune of the great. Hard for 'em to keep from judgin' them severely—from feelin' envious over the good fortune they cannot share.

"We are exhorted to feel sorry for the man who falls down and breaks his leg. We are exhorted to feel christian toward

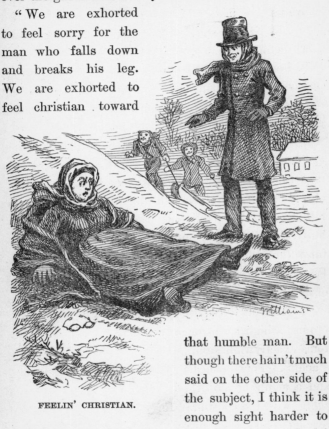

FEELIN' CHRISTIAN.

that humble man. But though there hain't much said on the other side of the subject, I think it is enough sight harder to feel christian towards that man when we are a layin' flat on the ice, or slippery sidewalk, and he is a standin' up straight.

"It is easy to deceive ourselves; easy to give very big, noble names to very small emotions. And if we

feel uncomfortable to see some one else who has always
stood on the same level with ourselves suddenly lifted
above us,—no matter how worthily he may have earned
that more exalted station,—we may call that uncomfortable feelin' any name we please. We may call it a
holy horror of worldly-mindedness—a hauntin' fear
lest he be jeopardizin' his immortal soul, by settin' up
on that loftier spear. And mebby it is. I hain't a
goin' to come right out and say that it hain't. But I
will say this, for there hain't no harm in it, and it
can't make no trouble. I will say that if we feel this
uncomfortable feelin' we ort to keep a close watch of
our symptoms. For though that gripin' pain in the
left side may be a religious pain, yet there is a possi-
bility that it may be envy. And if it is, it requires
fur different treatment. And it may be a self-righteous,
Pharasaical feelin' that our Lord seemed to hate worst
of any feelin' we could feel.

"I tell you it requires the very closest dognosing
(to use a high learnt medical phrase) to get the symptoms exactly right, and see exactly what aches we are
a achin'. For the heart that we imagine is a gripin'
and a achin' at sinful worldly-mindedness, may be a
achin' with the consumin' fever of spite, and envy and
revenge,—the heart-burnin' desire and determination to
bring the loftier and the nobler down in some way on
a level with ourselves, if not by fair means, with the
foul ones of malice and slander and lies.

"I don't say it is so; but I say, let us be **careful,**

and let us be charitable to all,—the rich and the poor,
—for charity, Kellup, like the new linen ulsters, covers
a multitude of sinners.

"Now," says I, metaforin' a little, as I might have
known I should before I got through, "now if I was a
woman, and should say that to wear diamonds was
wicked, or to live in a beautiful home full of books and
pictures, and all the means of ease and culture was an
abomination to me, and wicked, when I was hankerin'
in the very depths of my soul to be wicked in jest that
way, if I only had the wherewith to be wicked with,
why, that holy horror I professed would be vain in
me; empty as soundin' brass and tinglin' symbols.
Let us be honest and true first, and then put on more
ornamental christianity afterwards; there hain't no
danger of our gettin' any too much of it, that is, of the
right kind.   Envy and hypocracy and cant look worse
to me than diamonds ; and I would wear the diamonds
as quick agin—if I got the chance."

Kellup didn't look a mite convinced. But I kep'
right on, for though I am a woman that says but little,
yet when I begin to convince anybody I always want
to finish up the job in a handsome, thorough way, and
then I felt real eloquent ; and I tell you it is hard,
even for a close-mouthed woman, it is hard for 'em
when they feel as eloquent as I did then to keep from
swingin' right out and talkin', and I didn't try to stop
myself ; I kep' right on, and says I :

"It is a mistake in you and in me if we think that
6

every rich person is necessarily a hard-hearted one; if we think a tender heart cannot beat jest as warmly and truly aginst a ermine robe, as a shabby overcoat; aginst a rich boddist waist, as a calico bask. There are little, stingy, narrow, contracted souls in every station-house of life, high ones and low ones; and there are loving, generous ones, visey versey, and the same. And God bless those tender hearts where-ever they are; those who in lofty places organize the great charities whose benefactions bless the nations in famine, in war, and in the calamity of national sick-ness and distress. And Heaven bless the lowly toilers of life, whose humble gifts out of their scanty means are in God's sight equally as great.

"The little blue potato-blossom laid upon the pillow of the sick by the child of poverty—we think the per-fume of that little odorless flower will rise to Heaven as sweet as the most royal blossom given by the child-ren of kings. The blossoms of true charity are all sweet in Heaven's sight."

And says I, lookin' up to the ceilin' in a almost rapped eloquence of mean, and a lofty fervency and earnestness of axent:

"Heaven bless all the generous, loving hearts that beat under any and every colored robe; under the shabby garb of poverty; the somber hue of some con-secrated sisterhood of compassion; under the quaint Quaker garb, or the bright silks of the Widder Albert's generous daughters; those who conscientiously wear

"BLESSINGS ON THEM ALL!"

sober clothing, and those who jest as innocently wear
brighter apparel. Heaven bless them all; the gray-
robed sisterhood of Mercy, God's dove-colored angels,
who lean over the beds of the sick and the sorrowing,

A HEAVENLY MESSENGER.

and whose shadows falling by the beds of pain the
sad-eyed soldiers kiss; Catholic or Protestant, whatever their creed, they have the divinest gift of the
three—the divine gift of Charity. God made them
all—the rose and the gray; the blue sky, the rainbow,
and the soft shadow of the twilight clouds. He made
the earth for His beloved; nothing is too good for

them, or too beautiful. And why should one color boast over another, as being purer-minded, and less wicked ? "

I had been very eloquent, and felt considerable eloquent still, but happenin' to let the eye of my speck fall for a minute on Kellup, I see by the awful unbelievin' look on his face that I had got to simplify it down to his comprehension. I see that he did not understand my soarin' ideas as I would wish 'em to be understood.

Not that I blamed him for it. Good land! a tow string hain't to blame for not bein' made a iron spike. But at the same time it is bad and wearisome business for the one who attempts to use that tow string for a spike—tries to drive it into the solid wall of argument and clinch a fact with it. I had said a good deal about beauty, but it semede as if I wanted to say sunthin' more, and I went on and said it:

"Some folks seem to be afraid of beauty; as 'fraid of it as if it was a bear. They seem to be more afraid of lettin' a little beauty into their lives than they be of lettin' the same amount of wickedness in. You would think a man was awful simple who would spend his hull strength in puttin' up coverin's to his windows to keep out the sunshine and fresh air, and not pay any attention to the obnoxious creeters, wild-cats, burglars, and etcetery that was comin' right into the open front-door. And it hain't a mite more simple than it is for them, for they take so much pains a puttin' up iron bars (as it were) across the windows of their souls to keep beauty and brightness and innocent recreation out of it, that they have no time to see how uncharitableness and envy and malice and hatred and a hull

regiment of just ers are troopin' front-door unbe-

"They seem to despisin' beauty, merit in them to and feel hauty ous toward the liest thing God don't feel so, think it is wicked of all the beauty that I can, con- duty to humanity

"There are must be done must hold the upright. We principles stiddy

such ugly creet- right into the known to them. take a pride in as if it was a look down upon, and contemptu- divinest and love- ever made. I Kellup. I don't for me to lay holt and happiness sistently with my and Josiah. some things that first of all. We spear firm and must carry our and firm. But

we have a perfect right and privilege to wreath that spear and them principles with all the blossoms of brightness and innocent happiness we can possibly lay holt of. Them is my opinions. Howsomever, everybody to their own mind."

"Beauty the divinest thing God ever made!" says

Kellup in a hauty, ironical tone. "How dare you be so wicked, Josiah Allen's wife? I call it awful wicked to talk so."

Says I, "I don't believe anything is wicked that lifts us right up nearer to Heaven. I don't mean to be wicked."

"Wall, you be," says he, speakin' up sharp. "Worshipin' beauty, worshipin' the creature instead of the creator."

Says I, "Can you tell me, Kellup, what that spirit of beauty is, that you are so sot aginst?" Says I, feelin' more and more eloquent as I dove further and further into the depths of the subject than I had doven—and the more I went on about it the more carried away I wuz and lost, till before I had gone on 2 minutes I was entirely by the side of myself, and carried completely out of Kellup Cobb's presence, out of Josiah Allen's kitchen, out into the mighty waste of mystery that floats all round Jonesville and the world:

"What is this spirit of beauty—there is something, some hidden spirit, some soul of inspiration, in all beautiful things, pictures, poetry, melody—a spirit that forever eludes us, flies before us, and yet smiles down into our souls forever with haunting, glorious eyes. What is this wonderful spirit, this insperation that thrills us so in all sweetest and saddest melodies, in lovely landscapes, in the soft song of the summer wind, and the mournful refrain of ocean waves, in sunset, and the weird stillness of a starry midnight?

That thrills us so in all glorified legends of heroism— and in that divinest poem of a noble life.—That haunts us, and so fills our souls with longing that sometimes we imagine we can catch a glimpse of it in the clear look of some inspired eye ; but almost e'er we behold it, it is gone. Some fleetin' echo of whose voice we fancy we have caught in the lofty refrain of some heavenly melody—but, e'er our soul could hardly listen, the sweet strain was drowned in the discord of human voices. Ah! sometimes the veil has seemed but thin between us, as we stood for brief, blissful moments on the mountain tops of our best and noblest emotions, so transparent, and glowing with inner brightness, that we could almost behold the face of an angel behind the shining barriers. But the mists swept coldly up, and the sweet face was lost in the cloudy, earthly vapors.

"If we could reach it, if we could once reach out our longing arms, and touch that wonderful, illusive soul of beauty, if we could hold it with our weak, mortal grasp, and look upon it face to face—can you tell me, Kellup, what it would be? Can you tell me how pure, and holy, and divine a shape it would be? The Ideal of Beauty that forever rises before us—this longing for perfection implanted in our souls? We cannot believe by bad spirits, but by the Ever Good. This ideal that every poet and artist soul has longed for, prayed for, but never reached—this ideal of purity which we strive to mould in clay; poor, crumblin', imperfect clay, that will not, however earnestly we toil, take the clear shape of our dreams. Can you tell me, Kellup, that it is not the longing of the mortal for the immortal, the deathless cry of the human for the divine?

"To me, it is the surest proof of immortality. For we know that our God is not cruel, and we cannot think He would hold out to us a lovely gift only to mock us with glimpses of its glory, and then withdraw it from us forever.

"And this ideal of perfection that we have so striven and prayed to realize—perhaps these longings and strivings are perfecting that image in our lives, unbeknown to us; and when the clay that wraps it round drops off, shall we behold it in glad wonder in the land of the King? Shall we see that the dull stroke of care and the keen blow of suffering helped most to mould it into beauty? Surely, surely, He will one day give the desire of our souls. Surely there is a land of immortal purity, immortal beauty, where to the souls of all who truly aspire the dim shadow light of our hope will be lost in the bright glory of fulfillment."

Says Kellup, castin' the witherin'est look onto my head-dress that he had cast onto it, and clingin' close to his old idee, as close as a idee ever was clung to, says he, comin' out plain:

"That head-dress is a shame, and a disgrace. You wouldn't ketch me in no such extravagance. The money had better have been took and distributed round amongst the poorer classes in the country."

I don't s'pose I ort to, and I don't know exactly how it happened that I did, but I won't deny it, that comin' down so awful sudden off of the height of eloquence I had been a soarin' on, bein' brought down so awful short and sort o' onexpected, it did, and I won't deny it, it did, for as much as a minute and a half, make me mad. It sort o' jarred me all over, and I spoke up sharp, and says I:

"There are exceptions to every ruler, as scholars have always said. But as a general thing, the people who deny themselves all the beauty and brightness of life, are the very ones who deny it to others. Those who talk the most about others' extravagance, and what great things they would do if they was in other folks'es places, are the very ones who, if they wuz there, wouldn't do nothin'. It is the tight ones of earth who talk the most about looseness: how awful loose they would be under certain circumstances. But I believe, and Josiah duz, that they wouldn't under the very loosest circumstances ever be loose, but would always be tight. And them who says the least often does the most. Them who scold the least about other folks'es duty, often do their own duty the best. Curious. But so it is.

"And those who love to put beauty into their own lives, are often the ones who love to bless other lives —are the ones whose hearts ache at the pleading of a sorrowful eye—whose hearts thrill clear to their center at the voice of a hungry child.

6*

"And if the heart is thrilled in the right way, that thrill always trembles right down into the portmoney, and trembles it open, and jars the money right out of it. The money that will make that hungry cry change into a thankful one, and that wistful look change into a rejoicin' one.

"Why," says I in a earnest, lofty tone, wantin' to convince him, "look at that female I have been a talkin' about; look at Nater. See what she duz. You have had to give up that no other female ever loved the beautiful as she duz. And you have got to give up that no other female was ever so great-hearted, so compassionate and generous."

And havin' by this time got all over my little temporary madness, I went on agin about her, beautiful. Somehow I always do talk eloquent about Nater. I guess it is because I think so much of her.

Says I: "No tenderer care does she give to the monarch on his throne than she gives to the little bare-foot peasant child, or the little foolish sparrer. She takes no greater thought to guide the great ship freighted with noble lives, and help her plow her way through the billows, than she takes to guide the way of the sea-bird over the wild waters, or the flight of the frightened northern birds fleeing southward through the trackless sky before the snows.

"Good to all, generous, helpful to all, patient to all And at the last she just opens her loving arms and gives rest to all, simple and gentle, serf and monarch; to the prosperous and happy, and to all the heavy-hearted, all the broken-hearted, all the worn, the defeated, the despairin' souls; the saint and the sinner alike, without rebuking or questioning; she jest reaches out her arms to them all, and gives them rest."

Says Kellup: "I guess I'll go out and look at Josiah's new stun-bolt. I don't know but what I shall want to borry it bimeby to draw some stuns."

And he started off—and I was glad he did.

JOSIAH UNDERTAKES MORE BUSINESS.

WALL that was the very night, as I said, that Josiah Allen come home so awful cross. And what under the sun ailed him I could not imagine. He had been clever when he left home,—very; he had had a extra good breakfast, and he was the picture of happiness; and his morals seemed stiddy and firm. And comin' off so sudden onto such fearful fractiousness, it worried me.

But little did I think he was plannin' more headwork. If I had I should have worried fur more. But he wuz. Old Ben Mandagool, a friend of Josiah's, was takin' in boarders, and makin' money by 'em. And that very day (unbeknown to me) he had throwed them boarders, six of 'em, into Josiah's face, and the pile of money he had made by 'em, and twitted him that if it wasn't for his wife he could make jest as much. Old Mandagool knew well how I felt about takin' in boarders; he knew I was principled against it, and sot. Mandagool misuses his wife shamefully;

makes a perfect underlin' of her; works her down to skin and bone; they don't live happy together at all. And he seems to be envious of anybody that does live agreeable with their pardner, and loves to break it up. And so it went on for a number of days; he a twittin' Josiah how if it wuzn't for his wife he could have his way, and make money, (and Josiah loves to have his own way dearly,) and throwin' them half a dozen boarders into his face, and it hain't no wonder that Josiah felt hurt. And it hain't no wonder, constituted as men be, that he was exceedingly cross to me. But knowin' how cast-iron my mind was when it was made up, he never let on what ailed him. And I was skairt most to death to see him look so mauger, and act so restless and oneasy, and crosser'n any bear out of a circus.

How strange and mysterious things be in this world. Lots and lots of things we can see the effects of,— powerful effects,—but can't ketch a glimpse of the causes. I could see the crossness, and bear it; but what the cause of it was, was concealed from me by a impenetrable vail. And I, jest as poor, blind mortal bein's will do, when they stand in front of mysteries, and don't want to own they are puzzled by 'em, would make up reasons in my own mind, and call 'em facts. Thinkses I to myself: he is a enjoyin' poor health, or else he is a gettin' back-slid. And one day I says to him, says I:

"Josiah Allen, what is the matter with you? You

don't act like the same man you did several days ago. I am goin' to steep up some catnip and thoroughwort tea, and see if it won't make you feel better,—and some boneset."

"I don't want none of your boneset and catnip."

Says I: "You know, Josiah Allen, that you are enjoyin' very poor health. You enjoy as bad agin health as you did along in the winter."

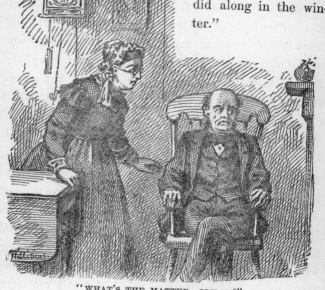

"WHAT'S THE MATTER, JOSIAH?"

"My health is well enough," says he sort o' surly like.

"Wall then," says I in still more anxious tones, "if it hain't your health that is a sufferin', is it your mor-

als ? Do they feel totterin', Josiah ? Tell your pardner how they feel."

" Dummit, my morals feel all right."

Says I sternly : " Stop that swearin' instantly and to
once." And I went on in reasonable tones : " If you
hain't enjoyin' poor health, Josiah, and your morals
are firm, why is there such a change in your mean ?"
Says I : " Your mean don't look no more like your old
one than if it belonged to another man."

But instead of answerin' my affectionate and anxious
inquiries, he jumped up and started for the barn. And
so it went on for over 4 days ; I a knowin' sunthin'
ailed him, and couldn't get him to tell ; he a growin'
crosser and crosser, and lookin' maugerer and maugerer, and I a growin' alarmed about him to that extent that I knew not what to do. And finally one
mornin' to the breakfast table, I says to him in tones
that would be answered :

" Josiah Allen, you are carryin' sunthin' on your
mind." And says I firmly : " Your mind hain't strong
enough to carry it alone ; your pardner *must* and *will*
help you carry it." He see determination in my eye-
brow, and he finally up and told me. How he was a
hankerin' to take in summer boarders ; how he wanted
to get back the money he had lost in some way, and
he knew there was piles and piles of money to be made
by it ; and it was such pretty business, too,—nothin'
but fun to take 'em in ; anybody could take such perfect comfort with 'em, besides bein' so awful profitable ;

and knowin' my principles rose up like cast-iron against the idee, it was a wearin' on him.

I didn't say nothin'. Some wimmen would have throwed Jonathan Spink and his wife in her pardner's face, and some wimmen would have throwed the twin and the hull of the family. But I didn't. I knew my pardner was a sufferin' fearfully, and my affection for him is like a ox'es, as has been often remarked. No, I only said in a cold, cautious tone : " Will you pass me the buckwheat-cakes, Josiah, and the syrup ? "

But them words, them buckwheat-cakes, was only a vail (as it were) that I threw over my feelin's, tryin' to hide 'em from my pardner. For oh ! what a wild commotion was goin' on inside of me between my principles and my affection. And of all the wars that ever devastated the world, that is the most fearful ; though it may be like many others, a silent warfare. Yes, when love—such a love as my love for Josiah—and principles strong and hefty as my principles are, get to fightin' with each other, and kickin' back and forth, and ragin', and as I may say, in a practical and figurative way, snortin' and prancin',—then ensues and follers on a time long to be remembered.

I was principled against takin' in summer boarders. I had seen 'em took in, time and agin, and seen the effects of it, and I had said, and said calmly, that for people like us boarders was a moth. I had said, and felt, that when a woman does her own housework it was all she ort to do to take care of her own men folks,

A POETICAL SIMELY.

and her house, and housen stuff, and common run of visitors,—and hired girls I was immovably sot against from my birth.

Home seemed to me to be a peaceful haven, jest large enough for two barks,—Josiah's bark and my bark,—and when foreign schooners (to foller up my poetical simely), when foreign schooners and periogers sailed in, they generally proved to be ships of war, pirate fleets stealin' happiness and ease, and runnin' up the skeliton of our dead joys at their mast-heads. But I am a episodin', and wanderin' off into fields of poesy, and to resoom and go on:

It would be in vain and only harrow up the reader's feelin's to tell how the long struggle went on inside of my mind. But when I say that my pardner daily grew before my eyes crosser and more fearfully cross, and mauger and more awfully mauger, any female woman who has got a beloved companion and a heart inside of her breast bones, knows how the conflict ended. I yielded and gin in, and the very day I gin my consent Josiah went and engaged 'em. He'd heard of 'em from old Mandagool. He had boarded 'em the summer before, and he said they wanted to get board again in Jonesville, though for some reason Mandagool didn't seem to want to board 'em himself. I thought to myself that looked squally. I never liked old Mandagool,—not for a minute,—but I didn't say a word. Neither did I say anything when he told me there was 4 childern in the family that was a comin'.

No; I held firm. The job was undertook by me for the savin' of my pardner. I had undertook it in a martyr way, and I wuzn't goin' to spile the job by murmerin's and complainin's.

But oh! how animated Josiah Allen was the day he come back from engagin' of 'em. His appetite come back powerfully; he eat a immense dinner. His crossness had disappeared, his affectionate demeanor all returned; he would have acted as spoony as my big iron spoon if he had had so much as a crumb of encouragement from me. But I didn't encourage him. There was a loftiness and majesty in my mean (caused by my principles) that almost awed him. I looked first-rate, and acted so. But oh, how highlarious Josiah Allen was! He was goin' to make so much money by 'em. Says he, with a happy look:

" If a man loses money by one speck, he must launch out into another speck and get it back again." Says he: " I have tried to make money easy, time and agin, and now I have hit the nail on the head; now I can make up my loss, and get independently rich. Why, besides the pure happiness we shall enjoy with 'em, the solid comfort, jest think of four dollars a week for the man and his wife, and two dollars a piece for the childern. Less see," says he dreamily:

" Twice 4 is 8, and no orts to carry; 4 times 2 is 8, and 8 and 8 is 16. Sixteen dollars a week. Why, Samantha," says he, " that will support us; there hain't no need of our liftin' our fingers agin, if we could only keep 'em right here with us always."

"Who is goin' to cook and wait on 'em?" says I almost coldly. Not real cold, but sort o' coolish like. For I hain't one when I tackle a cross to go carryin' it along groanin' and cryin' out loud all the way. No! if I can't carry it cheerfully, I'll drop it. So, as I say, my tone wasn't frigid, but sort o' cool like. "Who'll wait on 'em?"

"Get a girl! get two girls! Think of sixteen dollars a week. You can keep a variety of hired girls if you want to. Yes," says he, with a blissful expression and joyous axent, "besides the

JOSIAH'S IDEE.

sweet rest and comfort we are a goin' to take with 'em, we can have everything else we want. Thank Heaven we have now got a compeatency."

"Wall," says I in the same tones, or about the same, —coolish, but not frigid,—"time will tell."

Wall, they come on a Monday mornin', on the six
o'clock train.   Josiah had to meet 'em to the depot,

and he was so afraid he
should miss 'em, and
somebody else would
undermine him, and get
'em as boárders, that he
was up about three o'clock,
and went out and milked
by candle-light, so's to be

EARLY BIRDS.

sure and be there in season. And I had to get up
and get his breakfast before daylight, feelin' like a

a fool, too, for he kep' me awake all night a'most, walkin' round the house, and fallin' over chairs and things,—sort o' gropin' round,—lightin' matches to look at the clock to see what time it was. And if he said to me once, he said 30 times durin' that night: "It would be jest my luck to have somebody get in ahead of me to the cars, and undermind me at the last minute, and get 'em away from me."

Says I, in dry tones (not so dry as I had used, but dryish): "I guess there won't be no danger, Josiah."

But the very last thing I heard him say, in fearful and fractious tones, as he got into that democrat, was: "It would be jest like old Mandagool to undermind me."

Wall, about a quarter to 7 he driv up with 'em. A tall, spindlin', waspish-lookin' woman, and 4 childern. The man, they said, wasn't comin' till Saturday night. I thought the woman had a singular look to her when I first see her, and so did the oldest boy, who was about 13 years old. I thought he looked dretful white in the face, and sort o' strange like. He looked like his ma, only he was fleshy,—dretful sort o' fleshy,— flabby like. And as they walked up from the gate, side by side, I thought I never in my hull life see a waspisher and spindlener woman, or a curiouser lookin' couple. The other 3 childern that come behind seemed to be pretty much of a age, and looked healthy, and full of the old Harry, as we found out afterwards they indeed was.

Wall, I had a hard tussle of it through the day to cook and do for 'em. Their appetites was tremenjous, specially the woman and the oldest boy. They wasn't healthy appetites. I could see that in a minute. Their eyes would look holler and hungry, and they would look voraciously at the empty deep dishes and tureens, after they had eat 'em all empty,—eat enough for 4 men. Why, it did beat all. Josiah looked at me in silent wonder and dismay, as he see the vittles disappear before that woman and boy. The other three childern eat about as common healthy childern do, —each of 'em about twice what Josiah and me did. But there wasn't nothin' mysterious about them. But the woman and boy made me feel curious, curiouser than I had ever felt, for truly I thought to myself if their legs and arms hain't holler, how do they hold it. It was to me a new and interesting spectacle, to be studied over and filosofied upon. But to Josiah it was a canker, as I see the very first meal. I could see by the looks of his mean that them two appetites was sunthin' he hadn't reckoned and calculated upon. And I could see plain, havin' watched the changes of my pardner's mean as close as astronomers watch the moon, I could see that them two appetites was a wearin' on him.

Wall, I thought mebby they was kinder starved out, comin' right from a city boardin'-house, and a few of my good meals would quell 'em down.

But no, instead of growin' lighter them two appe-

OUR BOARDERS.

tites of their'n seemed, if possible, to grow consuminer and consuminer, though I cooked lavish and profuse, as I always did. They devoured everything before 'em, and looked hungry and wistful at the plates and table-cloth. Josiah looked on in perfect agony I knew, though he didn't say nothin' (he is very close). And it seemed so awfully mysterious to me. I would get so lost reasonin' and felosifyin' on it; whether their legs was holler or not holler; and if they was holler, how they could walk round on 'em; and if they wasn't holler, where the vittles went to. Why, studyin' so deep into it, bringin' all the deep scientific facts I could think on to bear onto it, I don't know but I should have gone ravin' distracted if she hadn't herself up and told me what the matter was.

They had got tape-worms—she and the oldest boy; immense ones, so the doctor said, and they had to eat to satisfy 'em. That explained it, and I felt relieved. And I told Josiah, for I love that man, and love to happify him when I possibly can. But if you'll believe it, that man was mad; and he vowed he would charge extra for 'em. It was after we went to bed I told him, and I had to talk low, for their room was right over our'n. Says I, in a low but firm whisper:

"Don't you do no such thing, Josiah Allen. Do you realize how it would look; what a sound it would have to community?"

"Wall," he hollered out, "do you s'pose I am goin' to board all the tape-worms in the world free of ex-

pense? Do you s'pose I am goin' to have 'em all con
gregate here, and be boarded on me for nothin'? I
took men and wimmen and childern to board. I didn't
agree to board anything else, and I won't, nuther. It
w,uzn't in the bill."

"Do you keep still, Josiah Allen. She'll hear you,"
I whispered.

"I say it wuzn't in the bill," he hollered out agin.
I s'pose he meant it wasn't in the bargain, but he was
nearly delirious (he is very close—nearly tight).
But jest that minute,—before I could say a word,—
we heard a awful noise right over our heads; it sounded
as if the hull top of the house had fell in.

Says Josiah: "The old chimbly has fell in."

Says I: "I think it is the ruff."

And we both started for up-stairs on the run. I
sent him back from the head of the stairs, for in the
awful fright he hadn't realized his condition, and wasn't
dressed. I waited for him at the top of the stairs, for
to tell the truth, I dassent go on. He hurried on his
clothes, and went in ahead,—and there she lay; there
Miss Danks was on the floor in a historical fit. Josiah,
thinkin' she was dead, run in and ketched her up, and
went to puttin' her on the bed; and she, jest as they
will in historicks, clawed right into his hair, and tore
out above half he had on that side. She then struck
him a fearful blow in the eye—made it black and blue
for over two weeks. She didn't know what she was

about; she wuzn't to blame—though the hair was a great loss to him, and I won't deny it.

Wall, we stood over her most all night to keep the breath of life in her; and the oldest boy, bein' skairt, it brought on some fits that he was in the habit of havin',—a sort of fallin' fits; he would fall anywheres; he fell onto Josiah twice that night, and almost knocked him down. He was awful large for his age; dretful big and fat. It seemed as if there was sunthin' wrong about his heft, it was so oncommon hefty for a boy of his age. He looked bloated. His eyes, which was a pale blue, seemed to be kinder sot back in his head, and his cheeks stood out below, some like baloons; and his mouth was kinder open a good deal of the time, as if it was hard work for him to breathe; he breathed thick and wheezy,—dretful oncomfortable. His com plexion was bad, too; sallow and sort o' tallery lookin'. He acted dretful logy and heavy at the best of times, and in them fits he was as heavy and helpless as lead.

Wall, that was the third night after they got there, and from that night, as long as they stayed there, she had the historicks frequent and violent, and Bill had his fallin' fits. And you wouldn't believe if you hadn't seen 'em, how many things he broke a fallin' on 'em in them fits. It beat all how unfortunate he was. They always come onto him unexpected, and it seemed as if they would always come onto him while he was in front of sunthin' to smash all to bits. And I says to Josiah, says I: " Did you ever see, Josiah Allen, any-

7

body so unfortunate as that boy in his fits? It seems
as if he'll break everything in the house if it goes on."

Says he, "'Tis a pity his cussed neck don't break!"

A SURPRISED COLT.

I don't know as I ever gin Josiah Allen a firmer,
eloquenter lecture against swearin' than I did then.
But in my heart I pitied him, for it was only the day
before that he fell as he was a lookin' at the colt. It
was only a week old, but Josiah sot his eyes by it, and
the boy was admirin' of it—there wasn't nothin' ugly
about him—but a fit come on, and he fell onto the colt,
and the colt not expectin' of it, and bein' unprepared,
fell flat down, and the boy on it; and the colt jest lived,

that is all. Josiah says it never will be worth anything; he thinks it broke sunthin' inside. As I said,
there wasn't a ugly thing about Bill. He'd be awful
sorry when he broke things, and squshed 'em, and
flatted 'em all out a fallin' on 'em.

All I blamed him for was his prowlin' round so
much. I thought then, and I think still, seein' he
knew his own heft, and knew he had 'em, and was
liable to have 'em, he'd done better to have kep' still,
and not tried to got round so much. But his mother
said he felt restless and oneasy. I couldn't help likin'
the boy; and when he fell right into my bread that I
had a risin' and spilte the hull batch, and when he fell
acrost the table in the parlor and broke everything
that was on it, and when he fell onto a chicken-coop
and broke it down and killed a hull brood of chickens,
and when he fell onto some tomato plants of a extra
kind which Josiah had bought at a great expense and
sot out, and broke 'em off short, I didn't feel like
scoldin' him. I s'pose it was my hefty principles that
boyed me up; them and the sweet thought that would
come to me—mebby Josiah Allen will hear to me
another time, mebby he'll get sick of summer boarders
and to takin' of 'em in.

I s'pose it was these lofty feelin's that kep' me up;
truly if it hadn't been I don't know how I could have
lived, cookin' as much as I had to, and goin' through
with what I did, historics, and fallin' fits, and etcetery,
etcetery.

And the 3 smaller children was ugly; there haint no other name made that will describe their demenors and acts, only jest that word, ugly.

They made me more work than all my housework put together. A handlin' everything, and a breakin' everything, and a ridin' the turkeys, and actin', and performin'.

I spose they was told more'n a hundred times by me and Josiah to *not* ride that turkey gobbler. And I don't spose there was ever any other children on earth, only jest them 3, that would have dast to

EXERCISING THE GOBBLER.

gone near it. Why, I have seen right-minded and moral children time and agin weep and cry when they seen it comin' nigh 'em, it was so powerful lookin', and high-headed. But good land! first thing I'd know I'd see one on 'em right on that gobbler, pretendin' to ride it; they almost killed that Tom Turkey.

And then all of a sudden we'd hear the fannin' mill a goin' full blast, and Josiah would run to the barn, and there they would be a runnin' dirt through it, slates, stuns, or anything. And then I'd hear the wheel a goin' up stairs, buzzin' as if it would break its old band, and up I'd go, and there they'd be a spinnin' of my best rolls. And five different times I took the youngest one out of the flour barrel, where they was a makin' a ghost out of him, to appear to the oldest one —they loved to scare that boy into fits, they loved it dearly.

And they'd lay to and eat between meals all the preserves and jell and honey they could get holt of, unbeknown to me; they wasted twice over every day what their board come to. But I kep' still, and held firm. Thinkses I the medicine is bitter, but it is goin' to do good; the patient is feelin' the effects of it. For Josiah looked awful as the days went by. He see he had made a terrible mistake; he see that he'd done better to have listened to his faithful pardner. He see where he had missed it. But pride kep' him silent, only in the little unguarded speeches that he would make in sudden moments of anger and agony, unbeknown to him. Such as sayin' in loud, quick axents:

"Dummit, I can't stand it so much longer." Or in low, plaintive tones, "Did Heaven ever witness such tribulation?"

I'd ketch him a sayin' that as he would be a bringin' Bill in, for Josiah would have to lift him and lug him in when he would fall out doors. That in itself I could see was a underminin' my pardner's strength and his back bones. And I shall always believe that was the reason why Danks stayed out of the way. It was underhanded in him; he knew that boy was heavy as lead, and he knew he would fall when he had 'em, and would have to be fetched in, and so he jest stayed away and let Josiah do all the luggin' and liftin'.

It was three weeks before that man come, and Josiah didn't look like the same man. What with chasin' after them three littlest boys, and carryin' round Bill in his fallin' fits, and havin' the care of providin' more provisions than was ever devoured on earth before by the same number of people, and bein' kep' awake night after night by Miss Danks'es historicks, and the oldest boy's walkin' in his sleep (I don't know as I have mentioned it, but Bill was liable to appear to us any time, and have to be headed up stairs agin) —take it all together, Josiah looked like a shadder. And thinkses I to myself, almost wildly, my principles was hefty, and they are hefty; I have said I would stand firm, and I have stood firm. But oh, must I, must I see my pardner crumple down and die before my face and eyes?

It was Josiah's pride that stood in the way of his startin' of 'em off. He couldn't bear to give in to me that he was in the wrong on it, and I was in the right on it. He couldn't bear to come right out openly and own up to his pardner how deceived, and fooled, and

A HEAVY BILL.

took in he had been. Men's pride is high, it towers up like a meetin'-house steeple, and when it tottles and falls down, great is the fall thereof. I knew this, divin' into the mysterious ingregiencies of men's naters so deep as I had doven, I knew this great filisofical fact as well as I knew the dimensions of the nose on my pardner's face. And so I shuddered to myself as I thought it over, and pondered on what the end would be. But I held firm on the outside, and never let on how agonized and burdened in soul I was. My mind is like a ox'es for strength, and very deep.

This was on a Friday mornin' that I had this melancholy revery, as I looked out of the buttery window, as I stood there a washin' dishes to the sink, and see Josiah come from the barn a luggin' Bill in. He had had a fit, and fell acrost the grin'-stun where Josiah was a grindin', and Josiah had to drop everything and come a luggin' of him in. He broke some of the runnin'-gear of the grin'-stun that time. Josiah had it fixed so he could put a pail of water on top of it, and it would water itself while he was a grindin', but Bill had fell right acrost it and flatted it all down. It cost Josiah upwards of seven shillin's to make that loss good.

Wall, that night old Danks come. It was most bedtime when he come, and I didn't see him much that night. She had the historicks the first part of the night, Miss Danks did, but we knew he was with her, so we sort o' gin up the care to him. Bill got up in his sleep, and went to prowlin' round as usual in the kitchen. But Josiah headed him off up-stairs, and locked the chamber door onto him, and let his father tussle with him. He had a fallin' fit, we both think, —Josiah and me do, that he had,—and fell onto his father, and knocked him down. We don't know it for certain, but we think so. For we heard the awfulest katouse you ever did hear. It sounded as if the house was a comin' down, and then we heard groanin' and sithin' and low, very low swearin'.

Of course we couldn't sleep none while such a rumpus was a goin' on, and historicks and everything, and he a tryin' to quell 'em down, but we lay and rested, which was a good deal for us. Wall, in the mornin', if you'll believe it, Danks told us (Miss Danks and the childern had gone down into the orchard to eat some strawberries), and Danks up and told Josiah and me that he was goin' off agin that day, on the afternoon train. He did look bad, I'll say that for him; his sufferin's was great. But he hadn't ort to shirk 'em off onto somebody else; he hadn't ort to throw a historicky wife onto perfect strangers, and bring a lot of childern, perfect young hyenas, into the world, and then caper off, and let other folks tussle with 'em.

But I held firm. I knew a crysis was approachin' and drawin' nigh, but I wasn't goin' to say nothin'; I held firm; only I says in a mecanical and sort of wonderin' way:

"Goin' away to-day?"

"Yes," said Danks, "it is a case of life and death; I must go."

And then all of a sudden Josiah Allen bust right out, and oh! what a scene of wild excitement rained down for the next several moments. Josiah riz right up, and hollered out to Danks louder than I most ever hearn him holler,—loud enough to be hearn for half a mile, though Danks was within half a foot of him. Says he, in that loud, scareful, wild tone:

"If you leave this house for half a minute, without takin' your family with you, I'll prosecute you, and throw you into jail, and take the law to you."

It skairt Danks dretfully; it come so unexpected onto him, he fairly jumped. And it started me for a minute, though my principles are so solid and hefty that they hold down my composure and keep it stiddy better'n a iron wedge, makin' my presence of mind like a ox'es for strength.

Says Josiah, in that awful and almost deafenin' tone of hisen, and with a mean as wild and delerious as a mean ever looked on earth:

"I hain't a wet-nurse, and I'll let you know I hain't, and Samantha hain't a horsepittle. Here I have," says he, in a still more agonizin' tone, "here I have for week after week kep' stiddy company with fallin' fits and historicks. I have been broke to pieces a luggin' boys! and rode to death by childern! and eat up by tape-worms! And there has got to be a stop put to it, or somebody is goin' to get hurt."

7*

He was perfectly delerious, and I says to him sooth-in'ly:

"Be calm, Josiah!"

"I won't be calm, Samantha!"

But Danks had got over bein' skairt, and begun to look cross,—crosser'n a bear. And he spoke out, in a pert, hateful tone, old Danks did, and says he:

"'Tain't nothin' to me; I don't have the fallin' fits nor the historicks." He looked dretful mad, and spoke up as pert and impudent to my pardner as if it was Josiah's business to tussle with them fits and things, instead of hisen.

I had thought I wouldn't put in my note at all, but I hain't one to stand by and see my pardner imposed upon. And then, too, I felt in the name of principle I ort to speak. I felt a feelin' that mebby here was a chance for me to do good. And when he spoke out agin, more impudenter and hatefuler than before, "that it wasn't nothin' to him," says I:

"It is sunthin' to you." And then I went on powerful and eloquent. I can tell you I talked deep and solemn to that man about what he took onto him-self when he sot out in matrimony; about the respon-sibility of marriage, and bringin' childern into the world; the responsibility to God and man of usherin' eternal souls into this world for everlasting joy or mis-ery; the terrible responsibility to these souls and to God, the righteous Judge; and the terrible responsi-bility to the world of lettin' loose in it such mighty powers for good or evil,—a set of likely creeters, bless-ings and benefactors forever, or shacks and sources of uncounted misery, made so greatly by early care and culture; influences that will go on and on for all time, growing and widening out all the time, till no mind but the Eternal can reckon up or even imagine the awful consequences for good or evil of one human soul. "How dare anyone," says I, "lightly and irreverantly even think on the subject,—much less tackle it."

I talked beautiful on the subject, and deep, deeper than I had for some time. I felt fearfully eloquent, and acted so, and very noble. But Danks acted mad, mad as a hen. And he snapped out agin:

"Who made any calculations on fallin' fits and such things? I didn't."

Why, that man almost took my head off, he snapped me up so. But I didn't care; I knew I was a talkin' on principle, and that reflection is a high rock to lean and rest the moral back against. That thought is a thick umberell to keep off the little hailstuns of imper-tinence and impudence that might otherwise hurt one's self-respect and mortify it. I felt well and noble in my mind, and acted well, very. I kep' right on cool and collected together.

And says I, "That is one great reason why any one ort to consider well on't. They ort to know that this is one of them jobs that you can't calculate on exactly how it is a comin' out. You must take the chances. There is lots of undertakin's jest so—jest as hard to

tell how it is a comin' out as some things in Nater.
Now the greatest of minds can't figger out exactly to
a minute what time the butter will come—or how a
marriage is a goin' to turn out—or jest when it will
stop rainin', or begin—or when the old hen will lay.

"The world is a curious place, and in lots of undertakin's you have to step out blindfold and ketch holt
of the consequences, good or bad. The blinders will
be took offen our eyes sometime, probable, but the time
is not yet. And marriage, I take it, is one of the very
reskiest undertakin's you can undertake. It may lead
you into a happiness as pure and lofty as a certain
couple I could mention have enjoyed for the neighberhood of 20 years. It may, and then again it
mayn't. But there is one great comfort in this that
there hain't in some things, such as rain, and thunder
storms, and etcetery. You needn't enlist in this warfare if you hain't a mind to—that is a sweet and con-
solin' thought—if you feel scareful over it. But if
you do enlist you must take the chances of war, you
must take the resks. And if it wasn't a resky piece
of business to embark in, why did them old fathers
put these words in the marriage service, ' for richer,
or for poorer.' They knew what they was about, them
old fathers did. They knew they couldn't tell whether
it would turn out rich as rich could be with blessings
and bliss, or poor as poverty. Them old fathers knew
that, and bein' likely men and sound-moraled, they fixed

that halter so that folks couldn't squirm their necks out of it every time they got oneasy and worrysome.

"Historical fits, and etcetery," says I, in reasonable tones, "might come under the head of 'worse.' But you can't slip your head out; that vow holds you, for better or worse. You no need to have tackled that vow, but you did, and now you ort to stand up under it; that is law, and that is gospel too, which don't always go together."

"Well, what of it," says Danks; "what if it duz? What are you goin' to do about it?"

Oh, how surly and mad that man did look. His mean would have skairt some wimmen, but it didn't me; mebby it would if I hadn't been talkin' on such high principle, but that boyed me up.

"Why," says I, "as I have said more'n 40 times, folks ort to get it into their heads that it is a great and serious subject that ort to be considered and prayed over and meditated upon. They ort to realize that gettin' married is a solemn thing; solemner, if anything, than it is not to, and that has always been considered a very solemn thing, very. But instead of lookin' on it in this serious and becomin' way, folks will caper and prance off into matrimony in jest as light and highlarious and triflin' a way as if they was headin' a row of fantasticks on the 4th of July. They don't consider and filosifize on it that the fantasticks can take off their uniforms at night, and be themselves agin, but the matrimourners can't. They can't do it nohow; there they be, matrimourners. No matter how bad they feel, and how disappointed they be by the looks of the state they have got into, they can't get out of it. They are matrimourners, and can't help themselves.

"The state of wedlock has got a high, slippery wall round it, as high up as eternity, and as low down as the same. It is a wall that can't be stepped acrost and climbed over. It is a wall that a man or a woman can't sneak out and creep up on without fallin' back— it is too slippery. It is a wall that can't be broke down, and jumped over only on Bible grounds. And then when you do take that jump on Bible grounds, oh how fatiguein' that leap is. How much happiness and ease of mind the matrimourner has to drop in the jump, drop forever. And how much trouble he has to carry with him, and disquietude of mind, and condemnation, and upbraidin's, and gossip, and evil speaking, and hateful memories, and hauntin' ones, and travel of soul and body. Oh, what a time that matrimourner duz have."

"I thought," says he, with that surly, mad look of hisen, "I thought you was one that preached up liberty, freedom, and etcetery."

"So I be," says I. "Hain't I jest been a doin' of it? Hain't I jest said that no man or woman ort to be drove into the state of matrimony by anybody only jest their own selves? But after they lay holt, and drive themselves in, they ortn't to complain. But, as I have said frequent, they'll find after they have drove themselves in that it is the curiousest state that ever was made. None of our States of America will compare with it for curiosity,—and some of our'n are exceedingly curious, take 'em laws and all, to wit: Havin' a man in congress to make laws that imprison a man for havin' two wives, while he himself, proud and hauty, a settin' up a makin' that law, has four on 'em. Exceedingly curious that is, and to wit: Fixin' penalties against crime and vice, and then sellin' licenses to encourage and make it respectable. Oh! how curious, how curious some of our states be! But the state of matrimony is far curiouser. It is curiouser in the beginning—some like a conundrum. States have to be admitted into the Union; a union admits you into that state. And then, it is bounded on every side by divinest possibilities of happiness, or the most despairin' ones, and no knowin' which will break over the frontier, and capture you. Sweetest and most rapturous joys may cover its soil as thick as blossoms on a summer prairie, or angry passions and disappointments and cares may crunch 'em down under foot, and set fire to 'em. Peace and trust and tenderness may rain over that state, or anarky and sizm."

"Yes, and fallin' fits," says Danks, with a bitter tone, "and historicks."

"Yes," says I calmly, "matrimourners ort to take all the blessings and enjoyments and comforts with a thankful heart, and they ort to have the courage and the nobility and the common sense to take all the evils, fallin' fits, historicks, and etcetery, and etcetery, with a willin' mind. You ort," says I firmly, " you ort to have figured it all out. You ort to have figured out the hull sum, orts and all, and seen what was to carry, and got the right answer to it, before you drove yourself into that state."

" How could I see to carry historicks ? how could I figured 'em out ? " says he bitterly.

But I kep' right on : " You ort to have studied it out, whether you was strong enough to stand the climate, with its torrid weather and its frigid zones, its sweet summery winds and its blasts, its squalls and hurrycains. But as I have said 40 times, if I have once, after you have drove yourself into that state, you ort to hist up your moral umberell, and make the best on't."

Danks didn't look convinced at all. He muttered sunthin' agin about fits and other things, and how he hadn't made no calculations on 'em ; and I felt fairly out of patience, and went to allegorin', as I might have known I should before I got through. (It is next to impossible for me to be so eloquent as I was then without allegorin' some).

" Why," says I, " when a man buys a farm, he must be a natural fool, or else a luny, if he expects and calculates the sun to shine on it every day the year round. He must make calculations for rain and snow, sun

shine and thunder.   He can't expect it all to be ripe
wheat and apple-sass.   He buys it with his eyes open;
buys it with all its possibilities of good or evil; and
don't expect, if he hain't a fool, to shirk out of carryin' of 'em.''

"Who has shirked out of carryin' of 'em?" says
Danks.   "I hain't."

"You have!" says Josiah, a jumpin' up and hollerin' at him agin; and his face was red as a fire-bran'.

"I hain't!" says Danks.

"You have!" says Josiah.   "And don't you dispute
me agin if you know what is good for yourself.   You
have shirked out of carryin' that dumb boy of your'n,
in his dumb fits.   And I let you know that I have
broke my back for the last time a luggin' him round,
or somebody or sunthin' is goin' to get hurt, and I can
tell you so—dummit!"

I felt as if I should sink.   My Josiah was almost
doin' what Miss Job advised Mr. Job to do when he
was smote with agony and biles.   He was almost a
swearin'.   But here was where I and the late Miss
Job differ.   I knew my pardner's sufferin's was intense,
and them sufferin's was terrible to me.   But still I
says in a reprovin', but tender and pityin' tone:

"Be calm, Josiah!"

"I won't be calm!" says he.

Says I: "Josiah, you must; you are almost delerious."   Says I: "You are a swearin', Josiah! be
calm!"

"Wall, I tell you agin that I won't be calm; and I tell you agin, *dummit!* there now! *dummit!*"

Oh! how my pardner did look, how his axent did sound, as he uttered them fearful and profane words. And then before I could put in a soothin' word to soothe him, Danks spoke right out, and says he:

"You promised to take 'em for all summer, and if you don't I won't pay you a cent for their board, and you can't make me."

Here Josiah turned as white as a white milk-pail, and groaned to that extent that I thought he was a goin' to faint away.

And as it turned out, the law was on Danks'es side. Josiah made 'em all go that very day, but he couldn't get a cent from 'em. He hired a lawyer to prosicute Danks, but Danks, bein' sharp-witted and ugly (and sometimes I think that such trials as he underwent, if anybody don't take 'em as a means of grace, makes anybody ugly. I can't help feelin' sorry for Danks, after all). But as I was a sayin', Danks worked it in such a way that Josiah lost the case, and had to pay the costs on both sides. They was heavy bills,—most as heavy as Bill Danks,—and take it with what we lost boardin' of 'em, and what the childern tore to pieces, and Bill smashed and squshed down, a fallin' on 'em,—take it all together, it is a loss that makes Josiah Allen groan now every time he thinks on it. We don't either of us think his back will ever feel as it did before. He strained it beyond its strength.

A VISIT FROM MISS RICKERSON.

IT was about a week after the Danks'es departure and exodus. It was a cool day for the time of the year, and very windy. And I was settin' calm and peaceful, hullin' some strawberries for dinner. For my companion, Josiah Allen, had gone to Jonesville, and I wanted to have dinner ready by the time of his arrival. But I had only jest got my potatoes pared and over the stove, when I heard the old mare and him drive into the barn-yard. He had come sooner than I looked for. But it didn't excite me; I was prepared. For not knowin' exactly the time of his arrival, I had made ready for any emergency. I had drawed the table out, and put the table-cloth on; and I felt at rest, and peaceful.

Let wimmen whose pardners are wont to rampage round and act, when they come in and find dinner only jest begun—let 'em not tell any wrong stories or exagerations or parables, let 'em not bandy words or argue, but let 'em, jest before he comes in, draw out

(189)

the table and throw the table-cloth on, and everything will move on peaceful; their pardners will think dinner is most ready, and as they glance at that snowy table-cloth their wrath will leave 'em, and they will demean themselves like lambs.

I only tell what I have learnt from experience. And any little crumbs of wisdom and knowledge that I have gained by hard experience, and through tribulation, I am willin' to share freely, without money and without price, with the female sect; I think so much of 'em, and wish 'em so well. Now jest this one little receipt, —this table-cloth performance,—would have been worth dollars and dollars to me if I had known it when I was first a pardner. But I never found it out till I had been married over thirteen years, and had been jawed accordingly, when I was belated and dinner wasn't ready. Why no woman would have any idee of its value till they try it. Men are as likely creeters as the earth affords, if you only know how to get along with 'em. And wimmen has to try various ways and measures. I learnt this jest by tryin' it as a experiment. I have tried a good many experiments— little harmless ones like this. Some of 'em work, and some don't.

Wall, I sot there hullin' my berries, and listenin' to the wind, which was a roarin' round the house. Seems as if I never heard it blow no harder. It blowed for all the world as if it had been kep' in through sickness in its family, or sunthin', and was out now for the first time, on a regular spree.

And though it didn't come right out and sing 'em in plain words, yet it seemed to be a roarin' it down the chimbley, and blowin' it through the orchard and round the corners of the house, and whistlin' it through the open buttery window—the song that other elevated and gay spirits indulge in, about bein' fairly determined and sot to not go home till mornin'.

It blowed fearfully. But I was calm and peaceful, knowin' the table-cloth was on, and Josiah would act first-rate. And then, when a tempest is a howlin' and a actin' out-doors, it seems as if I enjoy more than ever the safety and sweet repose and happiness of my own hearth-stun (which last is a poetical simely, our hearth not bein' stun at all, but iron, with a nickel platin' round it).

Wall, there I sot, feelin' well and lookin' well. I had combed my hair slick, and put on a clean gingham dress,—when Josiah Allen opened the door and walked in. He glanced at the table-cloth, and a calm, contented look settled upon his eye-brow, but he left the door open behind him as composed as if he had been born in a saw-mill; and says I:

"Josiah Allen, if there was a heavy fine to pay for shettin' up doors, you wouldn't never loose a cent of your property in that way." And says I, clutchin' my pan of strawberries with a firmer grip, for truly it was a movin' and onstiddy, and my apron was a flutterin' like a banner in the cold breeze: "If you don't want me to blow away, Josiah Allen, shet up that door."

"Oh shaw! Samantha. You won't blow away; you are too hefty. It would take a hurrycane and a simon, too, to tackle you, and lift you."

'SHUT THAT DOOR'

"Simon who?" says I, in cold axents, caused partly by my frigid emotions and the cool blast, and partly by his darin' to say any man could take me up and carry me away.

"Oh! the simons they have on the desert. We

hearn Thomas J. read about 'em. They'll blow camels away, and everything."

Says I dreamily: "Who'd have thought twenty years ago, to have heard that man a courtin' me, and callin' me a zephire and a pink posy and a angel, that he'd ever live to see the day he'd call me a camel."

" I hain't called you a camel. I only meant you was hefty, and camels was hefty, and it would take a simon or two to lift you round, either on you."

"Wall," says I, in frigid tones, "what I want to know is, are you a goin' to shet that door ?"

" Yes, I be, jest as quick as I change my clothes. I don't want to fodder in these new briches."

I rose with dignity,—or as much dignity as I could lay holt of, half bent, tryin' to keep five or six quarts of strawberries from spillin' all over the floor,—and went and shet the door myself, which I might have known enough to done in the first place, and saved time and breath. For shettin' up doors is a accomplishment that Josiah Allen never will master. I have tutored him up on lots of things since we was married, but in this branch of education he has been too much for me. Experiments have been vain; I have about gin up.

In the course of ten or fifteen minutes, Josiah come out of the bedroom lookin' as pleasant and peaceful as you please, with his hands in his pantaloons pockets, seemin'ly searchin' their remotest depths, and says he in a off-hand, careless way:

" I'll be hanged if there hain't a letter for you, Samantha."

" How many weeks have you carried it 'round, Josiah Allen?" says I. " It would scare me if you should give me a letter before you had carried it round in your pockets a month or so."

" Oh! I guess I only got this two or three days ago. I meant to handed it to you the first thing when I got home. But I hain't had on these old breeches sence that day I went to mill."

" Three weeks ago to-day," says I, in almost frosty axents, as I opened my letter.

" Wall," says Josiah cheerfully, as he hunted round in the bedroom for his old hat, " I knew it wuzn't long, anyway."

I glanced my gray eye down the letter, and says I in agitated tones :

" Come out here, Josiah Allen, and let me look at you, and wither you! She that was Alzina Ann Allen is comin' here a visatin'. She wrote me three weeks ahead, so's to have me prepared. And here she is liable to come in on us any minute, now, and find us all unprepared." Says I, " I wouldn't have had it happen for a ten-cent bill to had one of the relation on your side come and ketch me in such a condition. There the curtains are all down in the spare room. Bill Danks fell and dragged 'em down onto the floor under him, and mussed 'em all up, and I washed 'em yesterday, and they hain't ironed. And the carpet in the settin'-room up to mend, where he fell onto it with a lighted candle in his hand and sot it afire. And not a mite of fruit-cake in the house, and she a comin' here to-day. I am mortified most to death, Josiah Allen. And if you had give me that letter, I should have hired help and got everything done. I should think your conscience would smart like a burn, if you have got a conscience, Josiah Allen."

"Wall, less have a little sunthin' to eat, Samantha, and I'll help round."

"Help! What'll you do, Josiah Allen?"

"Oh! I'll do the barn chores, and help all I can. I guess you'd better cook a little of that canned sammen I got to Jonesville."

Says I coldly, "I believe, Josiah Allen, if you was on your way to the gallus, you'd make 'em stop and get vittles for you—meat vittles, if you could."

I didn't say nothin' more, for, as the greatest poets have sung, "the least said, the soonest mended." But I rose, and with outward calmness opened the can of salmon, and jest as I put that over the stove, with some sweet cream and butter, if you'll believe it, that very minute she that was Alzina Ann Allen drove right up to the door, and come in. You could have knocked me down with a hen's feather (as it were), my feelin's was such; but I concealed 'em as well as I could, and advanced to the door, and says I:

"How do you do, Miss Rickerson?" She is married to Bildad Rickerson, old Dan Rickerson's oldest boy.

8

She is a tall, bony woman, light-complected, sandy-haired, and with big, light-blue eyes. I hadn't seen

ARRIVAL OF MISS RICKERSON.

her for nineteen years, but she seemed dretful tickled to see me, and says she:

"You look younger, Samantha, than you did the first time I ever seen you."

"Oh, no!" says I, "that can't be, Alzina Ann, for that is in the neighberhood of thirty years ago."

Says she, "It is true as I live and breathe, you look younger and handsomer than I ever see you look."

I didn't believe it, but I thought it wouldn't look well to dispute her any more ; so I let it go ; and mebby she thought she had convinced me that I did look younger than I did when I was eighteen or twenty. But I only said " That I didn't feel so young any way. I had spells of feelin' mauger."

She took off her things, or "wrappers," as Tirzah Ann says it is more genteel to call 'em. She was dressed up awful slick, and Josiah helped the driver bring in her trunk. And I told her jest how mortified I wuz about Josiah's forgettin' her letter, and her ketchin' me unprepared. But good land! she told me that " she never in her hull life see a house in such beautiful order as mine was, and she had seen thousands and thousands of different houses."

Says I, " I feel worked up and almost mortified about my settin'-room carpet bein' up."

But she held up both hands—they was white as snow, and all covered with rings—and says she, "If there is one thing that I love to see more than another it is to see a settin'-room carpet up, it gives such a sort of a free, noble look to a room."

Says I, " The curtains are down in the spare bed-room, and I am almost entirely out of cookin'."

Says she, " If I had my way, I never would have a curtain up to a window. The sky always looks so pure and innocent somehow. It is so beautiful to set and look up into the calm heavens, with no worldly obstructions between, such as curtains. It is so sweet to sit in your chair, and knit tattin', and commune with holy nature. And cookin'," says she, with a look of complete disgust on her face, " why I fairly despise cookin'. What's the use of it?" says she, with a sweet smile.

" Why," says I, reasonably, " if it wasn't for cookin' vittles and eatin' em, I guess we shouldn't stand it a great while, none of us."

I didn't really like the way she went on. Never, never, through my hull life, was I praised up by any-body as I was by her durin' the three days that she stayed with us. She praised everything fur beyond what they would bear.

I believe in praisin' things that will stand praisin'. Nothin' does any one more good than appreciation. Honest admiration, sympathy, and good-will put into words are more inspirin' and stimulatin' than tongue can tell. They are truly refreshin'. I think as a rule we New Englanders are too cold in our means. Mebby it is settin' on Plymouth Rock so much, or leanin' up against Bunker Hill Monument ; or mebby we took it from our old Puriten four-fathers, and mebby them four old men ketched cold in their demeaniers from settin' under the chilly blue light of their old laws, or took the trait from the savages. Any way, we are too undemonstrative and reticent (them are very hefty words, and it is seldom indeed that I harness up a span of such a size to carry my idees.

As a general thing I don't have idees so hefty but

what I can draw 'em along with considerable small words. And I prefer 'em always, as bein' easier reined in, and held up, and governed. Why, I have seen such awful big words harnessed in front of such weak little idees that they run away with 'em, kicked in the harness, got all tangled up, and made a perfect wrack and ruin of the little idee. Hence, I am cautious, and if I owned droves of 'em, I should be on the safe side, and handle 'em careful and not drive 'em hardly any. But these two I have heard Thomas J. use in jest this place, and hain't a doubt but they are safe and stiddy as any ever was of their size.)

Thomas J. said, and I believe, that we are too bashful, or shy, or sunthin', too afraid of expressin' our hearty appreciation, the honest, friendly admiration and regard we entertain for our friends. But if my friends like me, or my work, I want 'em to tell me of it, to give me the help, and encouragement, and insperation this knowledge will bring. A few sympathetic, cheerin' words and a warm smile and hand-clasp will do more good than to wait and cut the praise on marble, when the heart they would have cheered and lightened is beyond the touch of joy or pain. I think it is not only silly, but unchristian, to be so afraid of tellin' our friends frankly how pleasant and admirable we think them, *if we do think so*. But let us not lie. Let us not praise what won't stand praisin'. Now when Alzina Ann Rickerson told me that I was as pretty as any wax doll she ever see in her life—and if my intel-

lect and Shakespeare's intellect was laid side by side,
Shakespeare's would look weak and shiftless compared
with mine—and when she said that my old winter
bunnet that I had wore on and off for thirteen years
was the most genteel and fashionable, and the loveliest
piece of millionary she ever sot her eyes on, she was
goin' too fur. Why, that old bunnet wouldn't hardly
hold together to stand her praisin'. And she praised
up everything. She flattered Kellup Cobb so, when
he happened to come in there one mornin', that it
skairt him most to death.

He had been up by on his father's business, and as
he come along back he stopped the hearse and come
in to see when Kitty was a comin' back, and to see if
he could borrow Josiah's stun-bolt that afternoon to
draw some stuns. He was goin' to wait till Josiah
come back from the factory to see about it, but Alzina
Ann praised him up so, and looked so admiringly at
him, that he dassent. As a general thing I think
Kellup is afraider than he need to be of doin' hurt and
gettin' wimmen in love with him, but now I'll be
hanged if I blame him for thinkin' he was doin' dam-
age. Why, she praised him up to the very skies.

She pretended to think that his hair and whiskers
and eyebrows was the natural color. They was a sort
of a greenish color that mornin'—he had been a tamperin' with 'em agin, and tryin' experiments. He had
been a usin' smartweed and sage, as I found out afterwards, and they bein' yellow before, the two colors

together made 'em a sort of a dark bottle-green—made him look as curious as a dog, and curiouser than any dog I ever laid eyes on.

But oh, how Alzina Ann did praise 'em up. You'd have thought, to heard her go on, that she had all her hull life been longin' to ketch a glimpse of jest such colored hair and whiskers. She said they looked so strikin', and she never had seen anything like 'em in her life before, which last I don't doubt at all. And then she would glance out at the hearse, and tell him he looked so noble and impressive on it, it give him such a lofty, majestic look, so becomin' to his style. And then she would branch off again and praise up his looks.

Why, I don't wonder a mite that Kellup thought he was ensnarin' her affections and doin' harm.

He follered me out onto the back stoop, where I was feedin' a chicken that the old hen had forsook, and I was bringin' up as a corset. He follered me out there, and whispered, with a anxious look, that he was goin' to start for home that minute, that he dassent wait another minute to see Josiah about the stun-bolt; and, says he, with a awful anxious look:

"I am afraid I have done hurt as it is, but Heaven knows I didn't mean to."

I threw the corset another handful of dough, and told him, in a encouragin' tone, that "I guessed he hadn't done much harm."

"Why," says he, "don't you s'pose I could see for

myself what I was a doin'? She was a gettin' head
over heels in love with me. And," says he, frownin'
and knittin' up his eyebrows:

"What good will it do to have another married
woman a droopin' round after me?"

KELLUP'S CONUNDRUM.

Says I, mechanically, as I put some fresh water on
the corset's dish:

"I thought you wanted to see Josiah about the stun-
bolt, you said you needed it."

"Yes, I need the stun-bolt, but I need a easy conscience more. I had ruther lug the stuns in my arms,
and crack my back, and bruise my stomach, than crack

the commandments and strain my principles. I see
from her actions that I have got to leave at once, or no
knowin' what the consequences will be to her. I am
afraid she will suffer now, suffer intensely. But what
can a man do?" says he, frownin' heavily. "They
have got to go around some, and do errants. And if
wimmen lay traps for 'em on every side, and make fools
of themselves, what is a man to do? But I don't want
to do harm, Heaven knows I don't."

And he started for the gate almost on the run. And
I was jest a goin' in when Alzina Ann come out to 'the
back door herself, and happenin' to see the corset, she
said "she should rather have it for a pet, and it was
far handsomer and more valuable than any mockin'-
bird, or canary, or parrot she ever laid eyes on." And
so she kep' on in jest that way. And one mornin'
when she had been goin' on dretfully that way, I took
Josiah out one side and told him "I couldn't bear to
hear her go on so, and I believed there was sunthin'
wrong about it."

"Oh, no," says he, "she means every word she says.
She is one of the loveliest creeters on earth. She is
most a angel. Oh!" says he, dreamily, "What a
sound mind she has got. How fur she can see into
things."

Says I, "I heard her a tellin' you this mornin' that
you was one of the handsomest men she ever laid eyes
on, and didn't look a day over twenty-one."

"Wall," says he, with the doggy firmness of his sect,

8*

"she thinks so; she says jest exactly what she thinks."
And says he, in firm axents, "I am a good-lookin' feller, Samantha—a crackin' good-lookin' chap; but I
never could make you own up to it."

I didn't say nothin', but my gray eye wandered up,
and lighted on his bald head. It rested there searchin'ly and very coldly for a moment or two, and then
says I sternly, "Bald heads and beauty don't go
together worth a cent. But you was always vain,
Josiah Allen."

Says he, "What if I wuz?" And says he, "She
thinks different from what you do about my looks.
She has got a keen eye in her head for beauty. She
is very smart, very. And what she says, she means."

"Wall," says I, "I am glad you are so happy in
your mind. But mark my words, you won't always
feel so neat about it, Josiah Allen, as you do now."

Says he in a cross, surly way, "I guess I know what
I do know."

I hain't a jealous hair in the hull of my foretop or
back hair, but I thought to myself, I'd love to see
Josiah Allen's eyes opened; for I knew as well as I
knew my name was Josiah Allen's wife, that that
woman didn't think Josiah was so pretty and beautiful. But I didn't see how I was goin' to convince him,
for he wouldn't believe me when I told him she was
a makin' of it; and I knew she would stick to what
she had said, and so there it was. But I held firm,
and cooked good vittles, and done well by her.

CASSANDRA'S TEA PARTY.

THAT very afternoon we was all invited to take tea with she that was Cassandra Allen, Miss Nathan Spooner, that now is. And we all went, Alzina Ann, Josiah, and me.

Cassandra didn't use to be likely. She had a misfortune when she was a girl. It is six years old now. But all of a sudden she took a turn, and went to behavin'. She learnt the dress-maker's trade, experienced religion, and jined the Methodist Church. And folks begun to make of her. I didn't use to associate with her at all, Josiah didn't want me to, though she is his 2nd cousin on his father's side. But jist as quick as she went to behavin', we went to makin' of her. And the more she behaved, the more we made; till we make as much of her now as we do of any of the relation on my side, or on hisen And last fall she was married to Nathan Spooner. She got acquainted with him about two years ago.

Nathan is a likely feller, all that ails him is he is

bashful, too bashful for any sort of comfort. But
Cassandra is proud-spirited, and holds him up, and I
tell Cassandra "I dare say he'll get over it by the time

NATHAN SPOONER.

he gets to be a old man. I tell her "I shouldn't
wonder at all if by the time he got to be seventy or
eighty, he would talk up quite well." I try to make
her feel well, and encourage her all I can.

But bein' proud-spirited, it works her up awfully to have Nathan get over the fence, rather than meet a strange woman, and walk in the lot till he gets by her. And it mortified her dretfully, I s'pose, when she introduced him to our new minister and his wife, to have him instead of bowin' to 'em, and speakin', turn his back to 'em, and snicker.

NATHAN SNICKERS.

But he couldn't help it, I told her he couldn't. I was present at the time, and I could see, his mouth bein' a little open, that his tongue was dry, and parched, and his eyes wild and sot in his head.

He has the worst of it, as I told Cassandra—it don't hurt nobody else so bad as it does him. But I s'pose it has been almost the means of his death, time and agin—through his not dastin' to call for anything to eat when he is away from home, and not dastin' to eat it when it is on the table. And then again, sometimes, through his not dastin' to stop eatin' when he gets at it.

He went to Bobbets' one day in the fall of the year, —it was a year ago this present fall. Cassandra was a sewin' for Miss Bobbet. They had jest had some new corn ground, and they had a new corn puddin' and milk for dinner.

Nathan had been to dinner jest before he went in there. His mother had had a boiled dinner, and mince pie, and etcetery—he had eat a awful dinner, and was so full he felt fairly uncomfortable. But Miss Bobbet urged him to set down and eat, and wouldn't take no refusal. She thought he was refus-in' because he was bashful, and she urged him out of his way, telling him he *must* eat, and he, not dastin' to refuse any longer, thought he would set down and eat a few mouthfuls, if he could, though it seemed to him as if he couldn't get down another mouthful.

But when he stopped, Cassandra, thinkin' it was bashfulness that made him stop, and thinkin' a good deal of him then—and wantin him to eat all the pud-din' he wanted, she told him she shouldn't think he showed good manners at all, if he didn't eat as much as she did, anyway. So he dassent do anything else then, only jest eat as long as they wanted him to, and

PUDDING AND MILK.

he did. Miss Bobbet would press him to have his bowl filled up again with milk, and Cassandra would urge him to have a little more puddin', and he not dastin' to stop, after she had said what she had, I spose he eat pretty nigh three quarts. It almost killed him. He vomited all the way home, and was laid up bed-sick for more'n two weeks.

And he has destroyed his clothes dretfully. Now hats,—I spose it took pretty nigh all he could earn to

keep himself in hats.   When he would go to any new
place, or evenin' meetings or anything, he would muss
'em so, rub 'em, and everything—why, he couldn't
keep no nap on a hat at all, not for any length of time
—he would rub 'em so, and poke at em, and jab 'em,
and wring 'em when he was feelin' the worst.   Why,
he got holt of Josiah's hat, thinkin' it was hisen, one
night at a church social; they appointed Nathan to
some office, and he wrung that hat till there wasn't no
shape of a hat to it.   When Josiah put it on to go
home, it was a sight to behold.   Anybody would have
thought that it was the fashion in the Allen family to
wear hats for night-caps, and this had been the family
hat to sleep in for years.   Josiah was for makin' him
pay for the wear and tear of it.   But I wouldn't hear
a word to it.   I told him breakin' bruised reeds, or
smokin' flax, would be tender-hearted business compared to makin' anybody pay for such sufferin's as
Nathan Spooner had suffered that night.   Says I, " if
he wrung one mite of comfort out o' that hat, for pity
sake don't begrech it to him."

Why, I have been so sorry for that feller that I
didn't know what to do.   Now when he was a courtin'
Cassandra (and how he ever got up spunk enough to
court a mouse, is a mystery to me), Cassandra used
to sew for me, and he would come there evenin's to
see her, and set the hull evenin' long and not say
nothin', but jest look at her, and twirl his thumbs one
over the other.   And I told Josiah " I felt bad for

THE FAMILY NIGHT-CAP.

him, and it seemed as if his thumbs must give out after a while, and it looked fairly solemn to me, to see 'em a goin' so, for evenin' after evenin', and week after week, without any change."

And Josiah said there was a change. He said about the middle of the evenin' he changed thumbs, and twirled 'em the other way.

I don't know whether it was so or not. I couldn't see no change; and I told Josiah I couldn't.

How under the sun he ever got up courage to ask her to marry him, is another deep and mysterious mystery, and always has been. But there are strange things in this world that there hain't no use tryin' to pry into and explain. But in his feeble way, he courted her a good deal, and thought everything of her, anybody could see that. And he popped the question to her, or she to him, or it popped itself, —anyway it was popped, and they was married.

They said he suffered dretfully the day he was married, and acted strange and bad. They said he seemed to act sort o' paralyzed and blind. And she had to take the lead, and take holt of his hand, and lead him up to the minister, instead of his leadin' her.

Some made fun of it, but I didn't. I told 'em I presumed he was fairly blind for the time bein', and sort o' numb, and didn't sense what was passin' round him.

It made it as bad agin for him, to think he fell jest

after they was married. You see he sort 'o backed off to set down, for he needed rest. And feelin' so weak and wobblin' and sort o' tottlin', he didn't back quite fur enough, and sot

NATHAN SOT DOWN.

right down on the floor. It hurt him awfully, I s'pose, from their tell. He was tall, and they say he struck hard. But he was too bashful to have a doctor, or make any fuss, only jest set there where he wuz. Some think he would have sot there all night, and not tried to make a move towards gettin' up at all. But Cassandra was proud-spirited, and helped nim up onto his feet. But they said he acted jest exactly like a fool.

And I told 'em in reasonable axents "that I presumed he wuz a fool for the time bein'." Says I, "When anybody's senses are gone, they are a fool." Says I, "It is jest as bad to be skairt out of 'em, as be born without 'em, as long as it lasts."

But says I, "He knows enough when he hain't skairt to death." And he does. He is industrious, and so is she, and I shouldn't wonder if they got along first-rate, and done well.

Wall, when we got there, Nathan was settin' by the stove in the settin'-room. He was afraid of Alzina Ann, and was too bashful to set down, or stand up, or speak, or anything. And when she asked him "how his health was," he didn't say nothin', but looked down on the floor, and under his chair, and into his hat, as if he was tryin' to find his health, and drive it out, and make it tell how it was.

But she asked him over agin—she was perfectly heartless, or else she didn't notice his sufferin's. And the second time she asked him, he sort o' looked under his chair agin, and into his coat pocket, and seemed to give up findin' his health and makin' it speak for him, so he said, sort o' dry and husky, sunthin' about bein' "comfortable."

Which was one of the biggest stories Nathan Spooner had told sence he j'ined the meetin'-house, for he wuzn't comfortable; far from it. His face was

red as blood, and he was more than half blind, I could
see that by the looks of his mean. But after awhile
he seemed to revive up a little. He wuzn't afraid of
me and Josiah, not very. And after Alzina Ann and
Cassandra got engaged in talkin, he said quite a
number of words to us, as rational and straight as
anybody. But Alzina Ann had to bring back his
sufferin's agin, and worse than he had suffered.

I hadn't said a word to Alzina Ann about Cassandra's misfortune; I hadn't mentioned the child to her.
He is a dretful humbly child, about the humbliest boy
I ever see in my life. He looks fairly pitiful he is so
humbly, and he hain't more than half-witted, I think.
But Alzina Ann couldn't keep still; she had to flatter
somebody, or sunthin', so she had to begin agin:

"How much! how much! that beautiful little boy
looks like his pa! Don't you think so?" says she to
Cassandra.

And then she would look at Nathan, and then at
the boy, in that rapt, enthusiastic way of her'n. And
says she to Cassandra:

"Hain't it a comfort to you to think he looks so
much like his pa?"

And Cassandra's face would get red as blood, and
I could see by her looks that she hadn't the least
idee what to say, or do, she was so awful wretched,
and feerfully uncomfortable. And truly if Nathan
Spooner could have sunk right down through the floor
into the suller, right into the potato-ben, or pork-

CASSANDRA'S MISFORTUNE.

barrell, it would have been one of the most blessed reliefs to him that he ever enjoyed.

If she had said what she had to say, and then left off ; but Alzina Ann never'll do that ; she has to enlarge on her idees. And so she would keep a-askin' Cassandra in that rapturous, admirin' way of her'n, if she didn't think her boy had the same noble, handsome look and manners that his father had. And Cassandra's face and Nathan's would be as red as two red woolen shirts. And then Alzina Ann would look at the child's pug nose, and then at Nathan's, which is a sort of a Roman one, and the best feature on his face, as Josiah says. She would look from one nose to the other as if she admired both of 'em so she couldn't hardly stop lookin' at 'em, and would ask Nathan "if folks hadn't told him before how much his little boy resembled his pa ?"

And Nathan didn't say nothin' but jest set there red as blood, his eyes fixed and glarin' on the opposite wall, a watchin' it as close and wishful as if he expected to see a relief party set out from it to befriend him, and shoot him down where he sot, or drag him off into captivity. Anything that would relieve him of his present sufferin's he would have hailed gladly. I could see that by his mean.

But at supper-time worse was in store for him. Her supper was good—good enough for anybody. She haint got a great deal to do with, but bein' a little afraid of Alzina Ann, and bein' proud-spirited and wantin to make a good appearance, Cassandra had sent over and borrowed her mother-in-laws's white-handled knives, and entirely unbeknown to Alzina Ann I had carried her over some tea-spoons and other things for her comfort, for if Cassandra means to do better, and try to get along and be respectable, I want to encourage her all I can, so I carried her the spoons.

But all the time Cassandra was a settin' the table, Nathan looked worse and worse; he looked so bad it didn't seem as if we *could* keep him out of the suller. He realized what was in front of him.

You see Cassandra, bein' so determined to do better, and start right in the married life, made a practice of makin' Nathan ask a blessin'. But he bein' so uncommon bashful, it made it awful hard for him when they had company. He wuzn't a professor, nor nothin', and it come tough on him. He looked more and more as if he would sink all the while she was a gettin' the supper onto the table. And when she was a settin' the chairs round the table he looked so bad that I didn't know but what he would have to have help to get to the table. And he would give the most pitiful and beseechin' looks onto Cassandra that ever was, but she would shake her head at him, and look decided, and then he would look as if he would wilt right down agin.

So, when we got set down to the table, Cassandra give him a real firm look, and he give a kind of a low groan, and shet up his eyes, and Cassandra, and me, and Josiah put on a becomin' look for the occasion, and shet up our'n, when, all of a sudden, Alzina Ann— she never asked a blessin' in her own house, and forgot that other folks did—she spoke out in a real loud, admirin' tone, and says she:

"There! I will say it, I never see such beautiful knives as them be, in my hull life. White-handled knives, with a gilt of sun-flowers on 'em, is something I always wanted to own, and always thought I would own. But never, never did I see any that was so perfectly beautiful as these are."

And she held her knife out at arm's length, and looked at it admirin'ly, and almost rapturusly.

Nathan looked bad, dretful bad, for he see by Cassandra's looks that she wuzn't goin' to set him free from the blessin'. And he sort o' nestled round, and looked under the table, a wishful and melancholy look, as if he had hopes of findin' a blessin' there: as if he thought mebby there might be one a layin' round loose on the floor that he could get holt of, and so be sot free himself. But we didn't none on us reply to Alzina Ann, and she seemed to kind o' quiet down, and Cassandra give Nathan another look, and he bent his head, and shet up his eyes agin, and she, and me, and Josiah shet up our'n. And Nathan was jest beginnin' agin, when Alzina Ann broke out afresh, and says:

"What wouldn't I give if I owned some knives like

them? What a proud and happy woman it would make me."

That rousted us all up agin, and never did I see—unless it was on a funeral occasion—a face look as

BAD FOR NATHAN.

Nathan's face looked. Nobody could have blamed him a mite if he had gin up then, and not made another effort. But Cassandra bein' so awful determined to do jest right, and start right in the married life, she winked to Nathan agin, as firm and decided a wink as I ever see wunk, and shet up her eyes, and Josiah and I done as she done, and shet up our'n.

And Nathan (feelin' as if he *must* sink), got all ready to begin agin. He had jest got his mouth opened, when says Alzina Ann, in that rapturus way of her'n:

"Do tell me, Cassandra, how much did you give for these knives, and where did you get 'em?"

Then it was Cassandra's turn to feel as if she must sink, for, bein' so proud-spirited, it was like pullin' out a sound tooth to tell Alzina Ann they was borrowed. But bein' so sot in tryin' to do right she would have up and told her. But I, feelin' sorry for her, branched right off, and asked Nathan "if he layed out to vote republican or democrat."

Cassandra sithed, and went to pourin' out the tea. And Nathan, feelin' so relieved, brightened up, and spoke up like a man, the first words he spoke out loud and plain, like a human bein', that day—says he:

"If things turn out with me as I hope they will, I calc'late to vote for old Peter Cooper."

I could see by the looks of Josiah's mean that he was a gettin' kinder sick of Alzina Ann, and (though I haint got a jealous hair in the hull of my back-hair and foretop) I didn't care a mite if he wuz. But truly worse wuz to come.

After supper Josiah and me was a settin' in the spare room close to the window, a lookin' through Cassandra's album, when we heard Alzina Ann and Cassandra out under the window a-lookin' at the posy beds, when Alzina Ann says:

9

"You must excuse my lookin' at you so much, Cassandra, but you are so lovely and fair-lookin' that I can't keep my eyes offen you. And what a noble-appearin' husband you have got—perfectly splendid! And how pleasant it is here to your house—perfectly beautiful! Seein' we are such friends to her, I feel free to tell you what a awful state I find Josiah Allen's wife's house in. Not a mite of a carpet on her settin'-room floor, and nothin' gives a room such a awful look as that. She said it was up to mend, but, between you and me, I don't believe a word of it. I believe it was up for some other purpose, somethin' she didn't want to tell.

"And the curtains was down in my room, and I had to sleep all the first night in that condition. I might jest as well set up, for I could not sleep, it looked so. And when she got 'em up the next mornin', they wuzn't nothin' but plain, white muslin. I should think she could afford something a little more decent than that for her spare room. And she hadn't a mite of fruit cake in the house, only two kinds of common-lookin' cake. She said Josiah forgot to give her my letter, and she didn't get word I was comin' till about ten minutes before I got there; but, between you and me, I never believed that for a minute. I believe they got up that story between 'em to excuse it off, things lookin' so. If I wuzn't such a friend of hern, and didn't think such a sight of her, I wouldn't mention it for the world. But I think everything of her, and everybody knows I do, so I feel free to talk about her.

"How humbly she has growed! Don't you think so? And her mind seems to be kind o' runnin' down. For how under the sun she can think so much of that simple old husband of hern is a mystery to me, unless she is growin' foolish. If it was your husband, Cassandra, nobody would wonder at it, such a splendid, noble-appearin' gentleman as he is. But Josiah Allen was always a poor, insignificant-lookin' creeter; and now he is the humbliest, and foolishest, and meachin'est-lookin' creeter I ever see in human shape. And he looks as old as Grandfather Rickerson, every mite as old, and he is most ninety. And he is vain as a pea-hen."

I jest glanced round at Josiah, and then instinctively I looked away agin. His countenance was perfectly awful. Truly, the higher we are up the worse it hurts us to fall down. Bein' lifted up on such a height of vanity and vain-glory, and fallin' down from it so sudden, it most broke his neck (speakin' in a poetical and figurative way). I, myself, havin' had doubts of her all the time, didn't feel nigh so worked up and curious, it more sort o' madded me, it kind o' operated in that way on me. And so, when she begun agin to run Josiah and me down to the lowest notch, called us all to naught, made out we wuzn't hardly fit to live, and was most fools, and then says agin:

"I wouldn't say a word aginst 'em for the world if I wuzn't such a friend to 'em—"

Then I riz right up, and stood in the open window;

FACE TO FACE.

and it come up in front of me some like a pulpit, and I s'pose my mean looked considerable like a preacher's when they get carried away with the subject, and almost by the side of themselves.

Alzina Ann quailed the minute she sot her eyes on

me, as much or more than any minister ever made a congregation quail, and, says she, in tremblin' tones:

"You know anybody will take liberties with a friend that they wouldn't with anybody else."

Says I, in deep, awful tones, "I never believed in knockin' folks down to show off that we are intimate with 'em."

"Wall," says she, "you know I do think everything in the world of you. You know I shouldn't have said a word aginst you if I wuzn't such a warm friend of yourn"

"Friend!" says I, in awful axents, "friend! Alzina Ann Rickerson, you don't know no more about that word than if you never see a dictionary. You don't know the true meanin' of that word no more than a African babe knows about slidin' down hill."

Says I, "The Bible gives a pretty good idee of what it means: it speaks of a man layin' down his life for his friend. Dearer to him than his own life. Do you s'pose such a friendship as that would be a mistrustin' round, a tryin' to rake up every little fault they could lay holt of, and talk 'em over with everybody? Do you s'pose it would creep round under windows and backbite and slander a Josiah?"

I entirely forgot for the moment that she had been a talkin' about me, for truly abuse heaped upon my pardner seems ten times as hard to bear up under as if it was heaped upon me.

Josiah whispered to me: "That is right, Samantha!

give it to her!" and, upheld by duty and that dear
man, I went on, and says I:

"My friends, those I love and who love me, are
sacred to me. Their well-being and their interest is
as dear to me as my own. I love to have others praise
them, prize them as I do; and I should jest as soon
think of goin' round tryin' to rake and scrape sunthin'
to say aginst myself as aginst them."

Agin I paused for breath, and agin Josiah whispered:

"That is right, Samantha! give it to her!"

Worshipin' that man as I do, his words was far
more inspirin' and stimulatin' to me than root beer.
Agin I went on, and says I:

"Maybe it hain't exactly accordin' to Scripture, but
there is somethin' respectable in open enmity—in beginnin' your remarks about anybody honestly, in this
way: 'Now I detest and despise that man, and I am
goin' to try to relieve my mind by talkin' about him
jest as bad as I can;' and then proceed and tear him to
pieces in a straightforward, manly way. I don't s'pose
such a course would be upheld by the 'postles. But
there is a element of boldness and courage in it
amountin' almost to grandeur, when compared to
this kind of talk: 'I think everything in the world of
that man. I think he is jest as good as he can be, and
he hain't got a better friend in the world than I am;'
and then go on, and say all you can to injure him.

"Why, a pirate runs up his skeleton and cross-bars

when he is goin' to rob and pillage.   I think, Alzina Ann, if I was in your place I would make a great effort, and try and be as noble and magnanimous as a pirate."

Alzina Ann looked like a white hollyhawk that had been withered by a untimely frost.   But Cassandra looked tickled (she hadn't forgot her sufferin's, and the sufferin's of Nathan Spooner).   And my Josiah looked proud and triumphant in mean.   And he told me in confidence, a goin' home (and I wouldn't wish it spoke of agin, for folks might think it was foolish in me to tell such little admirin' speeches that a companion will make in moments of harmony and confidence).   But he said that he hadn't seen me look so good to him as I did when I stood there in the winder, not for much as thirteen years.   Says he:

"Samantha, you looked almost perfectly beautiful."

That man worships the ground I walk on, and I do hisen.

THE LORDS OF CREATION.

JOSIAH Allen is awful tickled to think he is a man. He has said so to me, time and agin. And I don't wonder a mite at it. Men are first-rate creeters, and considerable good-lookin'. I have always said so. And they have such glorious chances to be noble and grand, and to *work* for the true and the right, that I don't wonder a mite that Josiah feels just as he duz feel.

And when Josiah tells me how highly tickled he is he is a man—when he says it in a sort of a pensive and dreamy way, kinder miselanious like—I don't resent it in him but on the contrary approve of it in him, highly. But once in a while he will get to feelin' kind o' cross and uppish, and say it to me in a sort of a twittin' way, and boastin'.

Mebby he will begin by readin' out loud to me sunthin' against wimmen's rights, in the *World* or almanac, or some other high-toned periodical; sometimes it will be awful cuttin' arguments aginst wimmen. And after he gets through readin' it he will

(230)

speak out in such a sort of a humiliatin' way about
how awful tickled he is, he is a man, so he can vote,
and help keep the glorious old state of New York on
its firm basis of nobility, morality, and wise economy.

Why, says he to me the other afternoon (feelin'
fractious was the cause of his sayin' it at the time),
says he: "Wimmen are dretful simple creeters; gos-
sipin', weak, weak-minded, frivolous bein's; extravagant, given to foolish display. They don't mind the
cost of things if they can only make a big show. So
different from men, they be. Why," says he proudly and
boastfully, "you never in your life ketched a man gos-
sipin' over their neighbors' affairs. You never see 'em
meddlin' the least mite with scandal and evil talkin'.
Men are economical, sound-minded. They spend only
jest what they need, what is useful—nothin' more, not
a cent more. Why," says he, "take it with wimmen's foolish extravagance and love of display, what
would the glorious old state of New York come to if
it was sot under her rain? And they are so weak,
too,—wimmen be. Why, old Error would take 'em by
the nose" (Josiah, I think, is a practicin' allegory. He
uses flowery rhetoricks and simelys as much agin as he
used to use 'em.) And he repeated agin, with a haughty
look: "Old Error would take 'em by the nose, as it
were, and lead 'em into all sorts of indiscretions, and
weakness, and wickedness, before they knew it.

"Why, if we men of New York state had a woman's
incapability of grapplin' with wrong, and overthrowin'
9*

of it. if we had her love of scandal and gossip; if we
had her extravagance and love of display, where
would the glorious old state of New York be to-day?
Where would her morals be? Where would her finan-
kle and money affairs be?"

And Josiah leaned back in his chair, and crossed
his legs over each other, as satisfied and contented a
crossin' as I ever see, and says agin:

"If I was ever proud and tickled about anything in
my life, Samantha Allen, I am tickled to think I am a
man."

He had been readin' a witherin' piece out of the
almanac to me—an awful deep, skareful piece aginst
wimmen's suffrage. And feelin' cross and fractious,
he did look so awful overbearin' and humiliatin' onto
me, on account of my bein' a woman, that I sprunted
right up and freed my mind to him. I am very close-
mouthed naturally, and say but very little, but I can't
stand everything.

While he was talkin' I had been a fixin' a new tow
mop that I had been a spinnin' into my patented mop-
stick, and had jest got it done. And I riz right up
and pinted with it at a picture of the new capitol at
Albany that hung over the sink. It was a noble and
commandin' gesture (though hard to the wrist). It
impressed him dretfully, I could see it did. I had that
sort of a lofty way with me as I gestured, and went on
in awful tones to say:

"When you look at that buildin', Josiah Allen, no

wonder you talk about wimmen's extravagance and foolish love of display, and the econimy and firm common sense of the male voters of the state of New York, and their wise expenditure of public money. When you and a passel of other men get together and vote to build a house costin'

A MONUMENT OF MEN'S ECONOMY.

nine or ten millions of dollars to make laws in so small that wimmen might well be excused for thinkin' they was made in a wood-shed or behind a barn-door."

Says I, lowerin' down my mop-stick, for truly my

arm was weary—gesturin' in eloquence with a mop-stick is awful fatiguin'—says I, "As long as that monument of man's wisdom and econimy stands there, no man need to be afraid that a woman will ever dast to speak about wantin' to have any voice in public affairs, any voice in the expenditure of her own property and income tax. No, she won't dast to do it, for man's thrifty, prudent common sense and superior econimy has been shown in that buildin' to a extent that is fairly skareful."

It is a damper onto anybody when they have been a talkin' sarcastical and ironical, to have to come out and explain what you are a doin'. But I see that I had got to, for ever sense I had lowered my mop-stick and axent, Josiah had looked chirker and chirker, and now he sot there, lookin' down at his almanac, as satisfied and important as a gander walkin' along in front of nineteen new goslin's. He thought I was a praisin' men. And says I, comin' out plain, "Look up here, Josiah Allen, and let me wither you with my glance! I am a talkin' sarcastical, and would wish to be so understood!"

But I was so excited that before I had fairly got out of that ironical tone, I fell into it agin deeper than ever (though entirely unbeknown to me), and says I:

"As to woman's love of gossip and scandal, and man's utter aversion to it, let your mind fall back four years, Josiah Allen, if you think it is strong enough to bear the fall."

And I went on in a still more ironicler tone. I
don't know as I ever see a more ironicler axent in my
hull life than mine was as I went on, and says:

" How sweet it must be for men to look back and
reflect on it, that while wimmen gloated over the
details of that scandalous gossip, not a man through-
out the nation ever gave it a thought. And while
female wimmen, crazy and eager-eyed, stood in knots
at their clubs and on street corners holdin' each other
by the bunnet-strings a talkin' it over, and rushed
eagerly to the post-office to try to get the latest details,
how sweet to think that the manly editor all over the
land stood up in man's noble strength and purity, and
with a firm eye on the public morals and the welfare
of the young and innocent, and happily ignorant,
refused to gratify woman's rampent curiosity, and said
nothing of the matter, not a word, in editorial or news
column; but all through those long months filled up
their pages with little moral essays, and cuttin' articles
on their hatred of gossip and scandal. And when,
with unsatisfied, itchin' ears, wives would question
their husbands concernin' the chief actors in the
drama, their pure-minded husbands would rebuke
them and say, ' Cease, woman, to trouble me. We
know them not. We have as yet spake no word upon
the subject, and we will not be led into speakin' of it
by any woman, not even the wife of our youth."

Josiah looked meachener and meachener, till, as I
got through, it seemed as if he had got to the very

bounds of meach. He knew well how many times
that old mare had gone to Jonesville for the last
World, long before its time, so in hopes it would be a
little ahead of its time, so he could get the latest

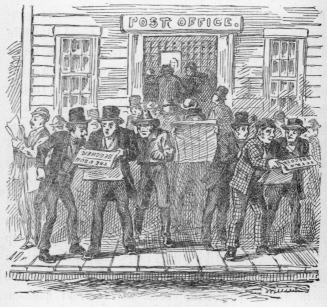

ON THE RAGGED EDGE.

gossip and scandal, and get ahead of old Gowdey, who
took the *Times*, and old Cypher, who took the *Sun*.
He knew jest how that post-office was fairly blocked up
with men, pantin' and sweaty with runnin', every time
the other mails come in.   And he knew well, Josiah
Allen did, how he and seven or eight other old Methodist brethren got to talkin' about it so engaged out

UNDER THE MEETING-HOUSE SHED.

under the meetin'-house shed, one day, that they forgot themselves, and never come into meetin' at all. And we wimmen sisters had to go out there to find 'em, after the meetin' was over. He remembered it, Josiah Allen did, I see that by his mean.

He didn't say a word, but sot there smit and conscience-struck. And then I dropped my ironical tone, and took up my awful one, that I use a talkin' on principle. I took up my very heaviest and awfulest one, as I resumed and continued on.

"I would talk if I was in your place, Josiah Allen, about wimmen's ruinin' old New York State if they voted. I would soar off into simelys if I was in your place, and talk about their bein' led by the nose into wickedness—and grow eloquent over their weakness and inability to grapple with error—when ten hundred thousand male voters of the state stand with their hands in their pockets, or whittlin' shingles, or tradin' jack-knives, or readin' almanacs, and etcetery, and let an evil go right on in their midst that would have disgraced old Sodom.

" Why, it is a wonder to me that the pure waters of old Oneida don't fairly groan as they wash up on the shores that they can't cleanse from this impurity, but would if they could, I know. She don't approve of it, that old lake don't—she don't approve of anything of that kind, no more than I do. She and I and the other wimmen of the state would make short work of such iniquities if we had our say.

" But there them ten hundred thousand male voters stand, calm and happy, all round the Community, in rows and clusters; porin' over almanacs, and whistlin' new and various whistles (Josiah had broke out into a very curious whistle) and contemplate the sin with composure and contentment.

And superintendents of Sabbath-schools and Young Men's Christian Associations will make excursions to admire them and their iniquity, to imbibe bad thoughts and principles unconsciously, but certainly, as one inevitably must when they behold a crime masked in beauty, in garments of peace and order and industry. And railroad managers will carry the young, the easily-impressed, and the innocent at half price, so eager, seemin'ly, that they should behold sin wreathin' itself in flowers, guilt arrayin' itself in festal robes to lure the unwary footsteps."

" Wall," says Josiah, " I guess I'll go out and milk."

And I told him he had better.

AN EXERTION AFTER PLEASURE.

WALL, the very next mornin' Josiah got up with a new idee in his head. And he broached it to me to the breakfast table. They have been havin' sights of pleasure exertions here to Jonesville lately. Every week a'most they would go off on a exertion after pleasure, and Josiah was all up on end to go too.

That man is a well-principled man as I ever see, but if he had his head he would be worse than any young man I ever see to foller up picnics and 4th of Julys and camp-meetin's and all pleasure exertions. But I don't encourage him in it. I have said to him time and again: "There is a time for everything, Josiah Allen, and after anybody has lost all their teeth and every mite of hair on the top of their head, it is time for 'em to stop goin' to pleasure exertions."

But good land! I might jest as well talk to the wind! If that man should get to be as old as Mr. Methusler, and be goin' on a thousand years old, he would prick up his ears if he should hear of a exertion. All summer long that man has beset me to go to 'em, for he wouldn't go without me. Old Bunker Hill himself hain't any sounder in principle than Josiah Allen, and I have had to work head-work to make excuses and quell him down. But last week they was goin' to have one out on the lake, on a island, and that man sot his foot down that go he would.

We was to the breakfast-table a talkin' it over, and says I:

"I shan't go, for I am afraid of big water, anyway."

Says Josiah: "You are jest as liable to be killed in one place as another."

Says I, with a almost frigid air, as I passed him his coffee: "Mebby I shall be drounded on dry land, Josiah Allen, but I don't believe it."

Says he, in a complainin' tone: "I can't get you started onto a exertion for pleasure any way."

Says I, in a almost eloquent way: "I don't believe in makin' such exertions after pleasure. As I have told you time and agin, I don't believe in chasin' of her up. Let her come of her own free will. You can't ketch her by chasin' after her no more than you can fetch up a shower in a drowth by goin' out doors and runnin' after a cloud up in the heavens above you. Sit down and be patient, and when it gets ready the refreshin' rain-drops will begin to fall without none of your help. And it is jest so with pleasure, Josiah Allen; you may chase her up over all the oceans and big mountains of the earth, and she will keep ahead of you all the time; but set down and not fatigue your-yourself a thinkin' about her, and like as not she will come right into your house unbeknown to you."

"Wall," says he, "I guess I'll have another griddle-cake, Samantha."

And as he took it, and poured the maple-syrup over it, he added gently, but firmly:

"I shall go, Samantha, to this exertion, and I should be glad to have you present at it, because it seems jest to me as if I should fall overboard durin' the day."

Men are deep. Now that man knew that no amount of religious preachin' could stir me up like that one speech. For though I hain't no hand to coo, and don't encourage him in bein' spoony at all, he knows that I am wrapped almost completely up in him. I went.

Wall, the day before the exertion Kellup Cobb come into our house of a errant, and I asked him if he was goin' to the exertion; and he said he would like to go, but he dassent.

"Dassent!" says I. "Why dassent you?"

"Why," says he, "how would the rest of the wim-men round Jonesville feel if I should pick out one woman and wait on her?" Says he bitterly: "I hain't perfect, but I hain't such a cold-blooded rascal as not to have any regard for wimmen's feelin's. I hain't no heart to spile all the comfort of the day for ten or a dozen wimmen."

"Why," says I, in a dry tone, "one woman would be happy accordin' to your tell."

" Yes, one woman happy, and ten or fifteen gauled —bruised in the tenderest place."

" On their heads ? " says I enquirin'ly.

" No," says he, " their hearts. All the girls have probable had more or less hopes that I would invite 'em—make a choice of 'em. But when the blow was struck, when I had passed 'em by and invited some other, some happier woman, how would them slighted ones feel ? How do you s'pose they would enjoy the day, seein' me with another woman, and they droopin' round without me ? That is the reason, Josiah Allen's wife, that I dassen't go. It hain't the keepin' of my horse through the day that stops me. For I could carry a quart of oats and a little jag of hay in the bottom of the buggy. If I had concluded to pick out a girl and go, I had got it all fixed out in my mind how I would manage. I had thought it over, while I was ondecided, and duty was a strugglin' with me. But I was made to see where the right way for me lay, and I am goin' to foller it. Joe Purday is goin' to have my horse, and give me seven shillin's for the use of it and its keepin'. He come to hire it just before I made up my mind that I hadn't ort to go.

" Of course it is a cross to me. But I am willin' to bear crosses for the fair sect. Why," says he, a comin' out in a open, generous way, " I would be willin', if necessary for the general good of the fair sect—I would be willin' to sacrifice ten cents for 'em, or pretty nigh that, I wish so well to 'em. I *hain't* that

enemy to 'em that they think I am. I can't marry
'em all, Heaven knows I can't, but I wish 'em well."

"Wall," says I, "I guess my dish-water is hot; it
must be pretty near bilin' by this time."

And he took the hint and started off. I see it
wouldn't do no good to argue with him, that wimmen
didn't worship him. For when a feller once gets it
into his head that female wimmen are all after him,
you might jest as well dispute the wind as argue with
him. You can't convince him nor the wind—neither
of 'em—so what's the use of wastin' breath on 'em.
And I didn't want to spend a extra breath that day,
anyway, knowin' I had such a hard day's work in front
of me, a finishin' cookin' up provisions for the exertion, and gettin' things done up in the house so I could
leave 'em for all day.

We had got to start about the middle of the night,
for the lake was 15 miles from Jonesville, and the old
mare bein' so slow, we had got to start an hour or two
ahead of the rest. I told Josiah in the first on't, that
I had jest as lives set up all night, as to be routed out
at two o'clock. But he was so animated and happy at
the idee of goin' that he looked on the bright side of
everything, and he said that we would go to bed before
dark, and get as much sleep as we commonly did.
So we went to bed the sun an hour high. And I was
truly tired enough to lay down, for I had worked dretful hard that day, almost beyond my strength. But
we hadn't more'n got settled down into the bed, when

we heard a buggy and a single wagon stop at the gate, and I got up and peeked through the window, and I see it was visitors come to spend the evenin'. Elder Bamber and his family, and Deacon Dobbins'es folks.

ROUTED OUT.

Josiah vowed that he wouldn't stir one step out of that bed that night. But I argued with him pretty sharp, while I was throwin' on my clothes, and I finally got him started up. I hain't deceitful, but I thought if I got my clothes all on, before they came in, I wouldn't tell 'em that I had been to bed that time of day. And I did get all dressed up, even to my handkerchief pin. And I guess they had been there as much as ten minutes before I thought that I hadn't took my night-cap off. They looked dretful curious at me, and I felt awful meachin'. But I jest ketched it off, and never said nothin'. But when Josiah come out of the bedroom with what little hair

"MURDER WILL OUT."

he has got standin' out in every direction, no two hairs a layin' the same way, and one of his galluses a hangin' most to the floor under his best coat, I up and told 'em. I thought mebby they wouldn't stay long. But Deacon Dobbins'es folks seemed to be all waked up on the subject of religion, and they proposed we should turn it into a kind of a conference meetin'; so they never went home till after ten o'clock.

It was most eleven when Josiah and me got to bed agin. And then jest as I was gettin' into a drowse, I heerd the cat in the buttery, and I got up to let her out. And that rousted Josiah up, and he thought he heerd the cattle in the garden, and he got up and went out. And there we was a marchin round most all night.

And if we would get into a nap, Josiah would think it was mornin', and he would start up and go out to look at the clock. He seemed so afraid we would be belated, and not get to that exertion in time. And there we was on our feet most all night. I lost myself once, for I dreampt that Josiah was a drowndin', and Deacon Dobbins was on the shore a prayin' for him. It started me so, that I jist ketched holt of Josiah and hollered. It skairt him awfully, and says he, "What does ail you, Samantha? I haint been asleep before, to-night, and now you have rousted me up for good. I wonder what time it is."

And then he got out of bed again, and went and looked at the clock. It was half past one, and he said "He didn't believe we had better go to sleep again, for fear we would be too late for the exertion, and he wouldn't miss that for nothin'."

"Exertion!" says I, in a awful cold tone. "I should think we had had exertion enough for one spell."

SAMANTHA'S DREAM.

But as bad and wore out as Josiah felt bodily, he was all animated in his mind about what a good time he was a goin' to have. He acted foolish, and I told him so. I wanted to wear my brown and black gingham and a shaker, but Josiah insisted that I should wear a new lawn dress that he had brought me home as a present, and I had jest got made up. So, jest to please him, I put it on, and my best bonnet.

And that man, all I could do and say, would put on a pair of pantaloons I had been a makin' for Thomas Jefferson. They was gettin' up a milatary company to Jonesville, and these pantaloons was blue, with a red stripe down the sides—a kind of a uniform. Josiah took a awful fancy to 'em, and says he:

"I will wear 'em, Samantha; they look so dressy."

Says I: "They hain't hardly done. I was goin' to stitch that red stripe on the left leg on again. They hain't finished as they ort to be, and I would not wear 'em. It looks vain in you."

Says he: "I will wear 'em, Samantha. I will be dressed up for once."

I didn't contend with him. Thinks I: we are makin' fools of ourselves by goin' at all, and if he wants to make a little bigger fool of himself, by wearin' them blue pantaloons, I won't stand in his light. And then I had got some machine oil onto 'em, so I felt that I had got to wash 'em, anyway, before Thomas J. took 'em to wear. So he put 'em on.

I had good vittles, and a sight of 'em. The basket
10

wouldn't hold 'em all, so Josiah had to put a bottle of red ross-berry jell into the pocket of his dress-coat, and lots of other little things, such as spoons and knives and forks, in his pantaloons and breast-pockets. He looked like Captain Kidd, armed up to the teeth, and I told him so. But good land! he would have carried a knife in his mouth if I had asked him to, he felt so neat about goin', and boasted so on what a splendid exertion it was goin' to be.

We got to the lake about eight o'clock, for the old mare went slow. We was about the first ones there, but they kep' a comin', and before ten o'clock we all got there.

The young folks made up their minds they would stay and eat their dinner in a grove on the mainland. But the majority of the old folks thought it was best to go and set our tables where we laid out to in the first place. Josiah seemed to be the most rampant of any of the company about goin'. He said he shouldn't eat a mouthful if he didn't eat it on that island. He said, what was the use of goin' to a pleasure exertion at all if you didn't try to take all the pleasure you could. So about twenty old fools of us sot sail for the island.

I had made up my mind from the first on't to face trouble, so it didn't put me out so much when Deacon Dobbins, in gettin' into the boat, stepped onto my new lawn dress, and tore a hole in it as big as my two hands, and ripped it half offen the waist. But Josiah

FACING TROUBLE.

havin' felt so animated and tickled about the exertion, it worked him up awfully when, jest after we had got well out onto the lake, the wind took his hat off and blew it away out onto the lake. He had made up his

BOUND FOR THE ISLAND.

mind to look so pretty that day that it worked him up awfully. And then the sun beat down onto him; and if he had had any hair onto his head it would have seemed more shady.

But I did the best I could by him. I stood by him and pinned on his red bandanna handkerchief onto his head. But as I was a fixin' it on, I see there was sunthin' more than mortification ailed him. The lake was rough and the boat rocked, and I see he was beginnin' to be awful sick. He looked deathly. Pretty soon I felt bad, too. Oh! the wretchedness of that time. I have enjoyed poor health considerable in my life, but never did I enjoy so much sickness in so short a time as I did on that pleasure exertion to that island. I s'pose our bein' up all night a'most made it worse. When we reached the island we was both weak as cats.

I sot right down on a stun and held my head for a spell, for it did seem as if it would split open. After a while I staggered up onto my feet, and finally I got so I could walk straight, and sense things a little. Though it was tejus work to walk, anyway, for we had landed on a sand-bar, and the sand was so deep it was all we could do to wade through it, and it was as hot as hot ashes ever was.

Then I began to take the things out of my dinner-basket. The butter had all melted, so we had to dip it out with a spoon. And a lot of water had swashed over the side of the boat, so my pies and tarts and delicate cake and cookies looked awful mixed up. But no worse than the rest of the company's did.

But we did the best we could, and the chicken and cold meat bein' more solid had held together quite well, so there was some pieces of it considerable hull, though it was all very wet and soppy. But we separated 'em out as well as we could, and begun to make preparations to eat. We didn't feel so animated about eatin' as we should if we hadn't been so sick to our stomachs. But we felt as if we must hurry, for the man that owned the boat said he knew it would rain before night. by the way the sun scalded.

There wasn't a man or a woman there but what the presperation and sweat jest poured down their faces. We was a haggard and melancholy-lookin' set. There was a piece of woods a little ways off, but it was up quite a rise of ground, and there wasn't one of us but what had the rheumatiz more or less.

ON THE BEACH.

We made up a fire on the sand, though it seemed as if it was hot enough to steep the tea and coffee as it was.

After we got the fire started, I histed a umberell and sot down under it, and fanned myself hard, for I was afraid of a sunstroke.

Wall, I guess I had set there ten minutes or more, when all of a sudden I thought, where is Josiah? I hadn't seen him since we had got there.   I riz up and asked the company almost wildly if they had seen my companion, Josiah.

They said, "no, they hadn't."

But Celestine Wilkin's little girl, who had come with her grandpa and grandma Gowdy, spoke up, and says she :

"I seen him goin' off towards the woods.   He acted dretful strange, too ; he seemed to be a walkin' off sideways."

"Had the sufferin's he had undergone made him delerious ? " says I to myself ; and then I started off on the run towards the woods, and old Miss Bobbet, and Miss Gowdy, and Sister Bamber, and Deacon Dobbins'es wife all rushed after me.

Oh, the agony of them two or three minutes ! my mind so distracted with fourbodin's, and the presperation and sweat a pourin' down.   But all of a sudden, on the edge of the woods, we found him.   Miss Gowdy weighin' a little less than me, mebby 100 pounds or so, had got a little ahead of me.   He sot backed up against a tree, in a awful cramped position, with his left leg under him.   He looked dretful uncomfortable. But when Miss Gowdy hollered out :

"Oh, here you be.   We have been skairt about you. What is the matter ?"

He smiled a dretful sick smile, and says he :

"Oh, I thought I would come out here and meditate a spell.   It was always a real treat to me to meditate."

A DISCOURAGED EXCURSIONIST.

Just then I come up a pantin' for breath, and as the wimmen all turned to face me, Josiah scowled at me, and shook his fist at them four wimmen, and made the most mysterious motions of his hands towards 'em. But the minute they turned round he smiled in a sickish way, and pretended to go to whistlin'.

Says I, "What is the matter, Josiah Allen? What are you off here for?"

"I am a meditatin', Samantha."

Says I, " Do you come down and jine the company this minute, Josiah Allen. You was in a awful takin' to come with 'em, and what will they think to see you act so?"

The wimmen happened to be a lookin' the other way for a minute, and he looked at me as if he would take my head off, and made the strangest motions towards 'em; but the minute they looked at him he would pretend to smile, that deathly smile.

Says I, "Come, Josiah Allen, we're goin' to get dinner right away, for we are afraid it will rain."

" Oh, wall," says he, "a little rain, more or less, hain't a goin' to hender a man from meditatin'."

I was wore out, and says I, " Do you stop meditatin' this minute, Josiah Allen!"

Says he, " I won't stop, Samantha. I let you have your way a good deal of the time ; but when I take it into my head to meditate, you hain't a goin' to break it up."

Jest at that minute they called to me from the

shore to come that minute to find some of my dishes.
And we had to start off. But oh! the gloom of my
mind that was added to the lameness of my body.
Them strange motions and looks of Josiah wore on
me. Had the sufferin's of the night, added to the
trials of the day, made him crazy? I thought more'n
as likely as not I had got a luny on my hands for the
rest of my days.

And then, oh how the sun did scald down onto me,
and the wind took the smoke so into my face that
there wasn't hardly a dry eye in my head. And then
a perfect swarm of yellow wasps lit down onto our
vittles as quick as we laid 'em down, so you couldn't
touch a thing without runnin' a chance to be stung.
Oh, the agony of that time! the distress of that pleasure exertion! But I kep' to work, and when we had
got dinner most ready, I went back to call Josiah again.
Old Miss Bobbet said she would go with me, for she
thought she see a wild turnip in the woods there, and
her Shakespeare had a awful cold, and she would try
to dig one to give him. So we started up the hill
again. He set in the same position, all huddled up,
with his leg under him, as uncomfortable a lookin'
creeter as I ever see. But when we both stood in
front of him, he pretended to look careless and happy,
and smiled that sick smile.

Says I, " Come, Josiah Allen, dinner is ready."

" Oh! I hain't hungry," says he. " The table will
probable be full. I had jest as lieves wait."

"Table full!" says I. "You know jest as well as I do that we are eatin' on the ground. Do you come and eat your dinner this minute."

"Yes, do come," says Miss Bobbet, "we can't get along without you."

"Oh!" says he, with that ghastly smile, a pretendin' to joke, "I have got plenty to eat here—I can eat muskeeters."

The air was black with 'em, I couldn't deny it.

"The muskeeters will eat you, more likely," says I. "Look at your face and hands; they are all covered with 'em."

"Yes, they have eat considerable of a dinner out of me, but I don't begrech 'em. I hain't small enough, nor mean enough, I hope, to begrech 'em one good meal."

Miss Bobbet started off in search of her wild turnip, and after she had got out of sight Josiah whispered to me with a savage look, and a tone sharp as a sharp axe:

"Can't you bring forty or fifty more wimmen up here? You couldn't come here a minute, could you, without a lot of other wimmen tight to your heels?"

I begun to see daylight, and after Miss Bobbet had got her wild turnip and some spignut, I made some excuse to send her on ahead, and then Josiah told me all about why he had gone off by himself alone, and why he had been a settin' in such a curious a position all the time since we had come in sight of him.

10*

It seems he had sot down on that bottle of rass-berry jell. That red stripe on the side wasn't hardly finished, as I said, and I hadn't fastened my thread properly, so when he got to pullin' at 'em to try to wipe off the jell, the thread started, and bein' sewed on a machine, that seam

A DESPERATE SITUATION.

jest ripped right open from top to bottom. That was what he had walked off sideways towards the woods for. But Josiah Allen's wife hain't one to desert a

companion in distress. I pinned 'em up as well as I
could, and I didn't say a word to hurt his feelin's, only
I jest said this to him, as I was a fixin' em: I fastened
my grey eye firmly and almost sternly onto him, and
says I:

"Josiah Allen, is this pleasure?" Says I, "You
was determined to come."

"Throw that in my face agin, will you? What if
I was? There goes a pin into my leg! I should think
I had suffered enough without your stabbin' of me with
pins."

"Wall then, stand still, and not be a caperin' round
so. How do you s'pose I can do anything with you a
tousin' round so?"

"Wall, don't be so aggravatin' then."

I fixed 'em as well as I could, but they looked pretty
bad, and there they was all covered with jell, too.
What to do I didn't know. But finally I told him I
would put my shawl onto him. So I doubled it up
corner-ways as big as I could, so it almost touched the
ground behind, and he walked back to the table with
me. I told him it was best to tell the company all
about it, but he jest put his foot down that he wouldn't,
and I told him if he wouldn't that he must make his
own excuses to the company about wearin' the shawl.
So he told 'em he always loved to wear summer shawls;
he thought it made a man look so dressy.

But he looked as if he would sink all the time he
was a sayin' it. They all looked dretful curious at

him, and he looked as meachin' as if he had stole sheep—and meachin'er—and he never took a minute's comfort, nor I nuther. He was sick all the way back to the shore, and so was I. And jest as we got into our wagons and started for home, the rain began to pour down. The wind turned our old umberell inside out in no time. My lawn dress was most spilte before, and now I give up my bonnet. And I says to Josiah:

"This bonnet and dress are spilte, Josiah Allen, and I shall have to buy some new ones."

"Wall! wall! who said you wouldn't?" he snapped out.

But it wore on him. Oh! how the rain poured down. Josiah havin' nothin' but a handkerchief on his head felt it more than I did. I had took a apron to put on a gettin' dinner, and I tried to make him let me pin it on his head. But says he, firmly:

"I hain't proud and haughty, Samantha, but I do feel above ridin' out with a pink apron on for a hat."

"Wall then," says I, "get as wet as sop if you had ruther."

I didn't say no more, but there we jest sot and suffered. The rain poured down; the wind howled at us; the old mare went slow; the rheumatiz laid holt of both of us; and the thought of the new bonnet and dress was a wearin' on Josiah, I knew.

There wasn't a house for the first seven miles, and after we got there I thought we wouldn't go in, for we had got to get home to milk, anyway, and we was both

HOMEWARD BOUND.

as wet as we could be. After I had beset him about the apron we didn't say hardly a word for as much as thirteen miles or so; but I did speak once, as he leaned forward, with the rain drippin' offen his bandanna handkerchief onto his blue pantaloons. I says to him in stern tones:

"Is this pleasure, Josiah Allen?"

He give the old mare a awful cut, and says he:

"I'd like to know what you want to be so agrevatin' for."

I didn't multiply any more words with him, only as we drove up to our doorstep, and he helped me out into a mud-puddle, I says to him:

THE END OF THE EXERTION.

"Mebby you'll hear to me another time, Josiah Allen."

And I'll bet he will. I hain't afraid to bet a ten cent bill that that man won't never open his mouth to me again about a pleasure exertion.

A VISIT TO THE CHILDREN.

IT was a fair and lovely forenoon, and I thought we would go and spend the day with the childern. Kitty Smith had gone the day before to visit a aunt on her mother's side to Log London. She was a layin' out to stay 3 or 4 weeks, and I declare, it seemed lonesome as a dog—and lonesomer. And I told Josiah that I guessed we would go to Jonesville and visit the childern, for we hadn't been there to stay all day with 'em for a number of weeks. He sort o' hung back, and said he didn't know how to spend the time. But I only says, decided like and firm, and in a solemn and warnin' way:

"You can do as you are a mind to, Josiah Allen, and as your conscience will let you. But croup is round, that I know, and I worried last night a good deal about little Samantha Joe."

Says he: "I will hitch up the old mare this minute, Samantha, and do you throw your things on as quick as you can." And he started for the barn almost on the run.

My natural nature is very truthful and transparent, —almost like rain-water,—and little figurative expressions like these are painful to me—very. But every woman who has a man to deal with for above twenty

MOVING JOSIAH.

years will know that they *have* to use 'em in order to move men as men ort to be moved.

I won't come right out and lie for nobody—man or beast. Croup *was* round promiscus in Jonesville, and I *had* worried about little Samantha Joe. But my conscience told me, as I tied up my back hair, and hooked up my dress, that I had talked in a sort of a parable way. And it smote me; not so hard as it had smote; but hardish.

And if there ever was a old tyrant on the face of the earth, my conscience is one. It won't let me do nothin' the least mite out of the way without poundin' me almost to death. Sometimes I get fairly tuckered out with it.

Wall, I had jest finished hookin' up my dress, and was a pinnin' on my collar at the lookin'-glass, when, happenin' to throw one of the eyes of my spectacles out of the window, I see Kellup Cobb a drivin' up; and he hitched the hearse to the front gate, and come in.

He looked quite well for him. His hair and whiskers was a good, dark, tan color, bearin' a little on the orange. Quite a becomin' color to him, he bein' so saller.

He inquired where Kitty was. And then he wanted to know most the first thing he said, and his mean looked anxious as he said it, "If her health was a keepin' up?"

"Why, yes," says I, "why shouldn't it?"

"Wall," says he, "I was obleeged to go away on business, and couldn't get here last week, and I didn't know how she would take it. I should have wrote to her," says he, "but not havin' quite made up my mind whether I would marry her or not, I thought it would be cruel to her to pay her such a close attention as a

letter would be. It wuzn't the postage that I minded.
Three cents wouldn't have stood in the way of my
writin' to her, if I had made up my mind full and
complete.

"But," says he, a knittin' up his forward hard,
"them two old reasons that did stand in the way of
my marryin' stands there now—stands there a headin'
of me off. It hain't so much because she is a poor
girl that I hesitate. No, that wouldn't influence me
much, for she is sound and healthy, good to work, and
would pay her way. No, it is them wimmen! What
will be done with the rest of the wimmen that I shall
have to disapinte?

"But," says he, lookin' gloomy into the oven, "I
have jest about made up my mind that I will marry
her, whether or no, and leave the event to Providence.
If I do, they'll have to stand it somehow. They hadn't
ort to expect, and if they used a mite of reason they
wouldn't expect, that a man would sacrifice himself
always, and keep single forever, ruther than hurt their
feelin's."

Says he, lookin' as bitter and gloomy into that oven
as a oven was ever looked into, "Even if ten or a
dozen of 'em die off, the law can't touch me for it, for
if ever a man has been careful, I have been. Look at
my clothes, now," says he, lookin' down on himself
with a sort of a self-righteous, admirin' sort of a
look, "I wore these old clothes to-day jest out of solid
principle and goodness towards wimmen. It wuzn't

to be savin', and because it looked like rain. No, I
knew I had got to be round amongst wimmen a good
deal, to-day, a settlin' up accounts, and so I wore this
old overcoat of father's.
I have got a brand new
one, but I wouldn't wear
it round amongst 'em.

DRESSED FOR THE OCCASION.

"I am on my guard, and they can't come back on
me for damages. They have only got themselves to
blame if they are ondone. They might have realized

that they couldn't all have got me.   And I have jest
about made up my mind that I will run the resk and
marry her.   She is to Log London, you say.   It happens jest right," says he, a brightenin' up.

"There is a funeral down that way, to-morrow, not
more than thirteen or fourteen miles from there, and I
will go round that way on my way back, and call and
see her."

I declare his talk sickened me so that I was fairly
sick to my stomach.   It was worse than thoroughwort
or lobelia, and so I told Josiah afterwards.   But I
didn't say a word back to him, for I knew I might jest
as well try to convince the wind right in a whirlwind
that it hadn't better blow, as to convince him that he
was a fool.

But, as he got up to go, I told him that I had a little
mite of business of my own with him.   You see our
new minister, Elder Bamber, is a likely feller as ever
drawed the breath of life, and hard-workin'—couldn't
get a cent of his pay from the meetin'-house.   They
had got into a kind of a quarrel, the men had, and
wouldn't pay what they had signed.   And I proposed
to the women, the female sisters, that we should try to
get him up a present of 50 dollars to last 'em through
the storm—the meetin'-house storm.   For they was
fairly sufferin' for provisions, and clothes, and stuff.
And as Kellup was a member of the same meetin'-
house, and talked and sung powerful in conference
meetin's, I thought it wouldn't be no more than right

for me to tackle him, and get him to pay a little sunthin' towards it.   So I tackled him.

"Wall, Sister Allen," says he, in that hypocritical,
sneakin' way of hisen (he was always powerful at
repeatin' Scriptural texts), "I can say with Peter,
'Silver and gold have I none, but such as I have I will
give unto thee.'"

"Wall, what is it?" says I.   "What are you goin'
to give?"

Says he, "I will work for the cause.   If religion is
worth anything," says he, a rollin' up the whites of
his eyes, "it is worth workin' for—it is worth makin'
sacrifices for."

"So I think," says I, in a very dry tone.   "And I
want a half a dollar out of you."

"No!" says he, kinder puttin' his hand over his
pocket, as if he was afraid a cent would drop out of it.
"No! I will do better than that.   To-night is our conference meetin', and I will talk powerful on the subject."

Says I, coldly: "Wind is a powerful element, but it
hain't a goin' to blow comfort into the Elder's household,
nor meat and flour into his empty buttery-shelves, nor
fire-wood into his wood-box.   Song and oritery are good
in their place, but they hain't goin' to feed the starvin'
or clothe the naked."   Says I, in more reasonable
tones: "As I said, wind is good in its place—I hain't
a word to say aginst it—but jest at the present time
money is goin' to do the Elder more good than the

same amount of wind can." And says I, in the same firm but mild tone: "I want a half a dollar out of you." Says I: "The Elder is fairly sufferin' for things to eat and drink and wear. And you know," says I, "that if ever there was a good, earnest, Christian man, it is Elder Bamber. He is a Christian from the top of his head to the sole of his boots. He don't wear his religion on the top of his head for a hat, and take it off Sunday nights. It goes clear through him, and works out from the inside."

"Yes," says Kellup, a clutchin' his pocket with a firmer grip, " he is a worthy man, and I should think the thought of his noble and lofty mission would be meat and drink to him. It probable is. It would be to me—and clothin'. Oh!" says he, a rollin' up his eyes still further in his head, "oh! the thought of savin' souls; what a comfort that must be to the Elder; what a rich food for him."

Says I, in colder tones than I had used yet, for I was fairly wore out with him: "The Elder can't eat souls, and if he could he would starve to death on such souls as your'n, if he eat one every five minutes."

He didn't say nothin' more, but onhitched his hearse and started off. I don't know but he was mad, and don't care. But though I didn't get a cent from him or his father, I raised 50 dollars with my own hands and the might of my shoulder-blades, and sent it to him in a letter marked, " From friends of religion and the Elder."

Wall, jest as Josiah driv up with the old mare, a hull load of company driv up from the other way—come to spend the day. I was disappinted, but I didn't murmur. I took 'em as a dispensation, killed a fat duck, and made considerable of a fuss; done well by 'em. They come from a distance, and had to start for home the sun 2 hours high. And I told Josiah it was so pleasant I guessed we would go to Jonesville then, and he (havin' that babe on his mind) consented to at once and immediately. So we sot off. About half a mile this side of Jonesville we met Thomas J. and Maggie jest a settin' off for a ride. We stopped our 2 teams and visited a spell back and forth. I wouldn't let 'em go back home, as they both offered and insisted on, but made an appintment to take dinner with 'em the next day, Providence and the weather permittin'. And then we drove on to Whitfield's. And I don't never want to see a prettier sight than I see as we driv up.

There Tirzah Ann sot out on the portico, all dressed up in a cool mull dress. It was one I had bought her before she was married, but it was washed and done up clean and fresh, and looked as good as new. It was pure white, with little bunches of blue forget-me-nots on it, and she had a bunch of the same posys and some pink rose-buds in her hair, and on the bosom of her frock. There is a hull bed of 'em in the yard. She is a master hand for dressin' up and lookin' pretty, but at the same time is very equinomical, and a first-

A ROADSIDE VISIT.

rate housekeeper. She looked the very picture of health and enjoyment—plump and rosy, and happy as

A HAPPY HOME.

a queen; and she was a queen. Queen of her husband's heart; and settin' up on that pure and lofty throne of constant and deathless love, she looked first-rate, and felt so.

It had been a very warm day, nearly hot, and Whitfield I s'pose had come home kinder tired. So he had stretched himself out at full length on the grass in front of the portico, and there he lay with his hands under his head, a laughin', and a lookin' up into Tirzah Ann's face as radiant and lovin' as if she was the sun and he a sun-flower. But that simely, though very poetical and figurative, don't half express the good looks, and health, and rest, and happiness on both their faces, as they looked at each other, and then at that *babe*.

LITTLE SAMANTHA JOE.

That most beautifulest and intelligentest of childern was a toddlin' round, first up to one of 'em and then the other, with her bright eyes a dancin', and her cheeks red as roses. You see their yard is so large and shady, and the little thing havin' got so it can run round alone, is out in the yard a playin' most all the time, and it is dretful good for her. And she enjoys it the best that ever was, and Tirzah Ann enjoys it, too, for after she gets her work done up, all she has to do is to set in the door and watch the little thing a playin' round, and bein' perfectly happy. The

minute she ketched sight of the old mare and me and
her grandpa, she run down to the gate as fast as her
little feet could carry her. She had a little pink dress
on, and pink stockin's, and white shoes, and a white
ruffled apron, with her pretty, shining hair a hangin'
down in curls over it, and she did, jest as sure as I
live and breathe—she *did* look almost too beautiful
for earth. I guess she got a pretty good kissin' from
Josiah and me, and then Whitfield and Tirzah Ann
come a hurryin' down to the gate, glad enough to see
us, as they always be.

Josiah, of course, had to take that beautiful child
for a little ride, and Whitfield said he guessed he
would go, too. But I got out and went in, and as we
sot there on the stoop, Tirzah Ann up and told me
what she and Whitfield was a goin' to do. They was
goin' off for the summer for a rest and change. And
I thought from the first minute she spoke of it that it
was foolish in her. Now rests are as likely things as
ever was ; so are changes.

But I have said, and I say still, that I had ruther lay
down to home, as the poet says, "on my own delightful feather-bed," with a fan and a newspaper, and take
a rest, than dress up and travel off 2 or 300 milds
through the burnin' sun, with achin' body, wet with
presperation and sweat, to take it. It seems to me
that I would get more rest out of the former than out
of the more latter course and proceedin'. Howsumever, everybody to their own mind.

11

Likewise with changes: I have said, and I say still, that changes are likely and respectable, if you can get holt of 'em; but how can you?

Havin' such powerful and eloquent emotions as I have, havin' such hefty principles a performin' inside of my mind, enjoyin' such idees, and faiths, and aspirations, and longin's, and hopes, and despairs, and everything—I s'pose that is what makes me think that what is goin' on round me, the outside of me, hain't of so much consequence. I seem to live inside of myself (as it were) more than I do on the outside. And so it don't seem of so much consequence what the lay of the land round me may happen to be, whether it is sort o' hilly and mountainous or more level-like; or whether steam-cars may be a goin' by me (on the outside of me), or boats a sailin' round me, or milk-wagons.

You see the real change, the real rest, would have to be on the inside, and not on the outside. Nobody, no matter how much their weight may be by the steel-yards, can carry round such grand, hefty principles as I carry round without gettin' tired; or enjoy the lofty hopes, and desires, and aspirations that I enjoy, and meditate on all the sad, and mysterious, and puzzlin' conundrums of the old world as I meditate on 'em, without gettin' fairly tuckered out.

Great hearts enjoy greatly and suffer greatly. And so sometimes, when heart-tired and brain-weary, if I could quell down them soarin' emotions and make 'em lay still for a spell, and shet up my heart like a buro-draw, and hang up the key, and onscrew my head and lay it onto the manteltry-piece, then I could go off and enjoy a change that would be refreshin' and truly delightful. But as it is, from Jonesville clear to the Antipithies, the puzzlin' perplexities, the woes, and the cares of the old world foller right on after us tight as our shadders. Our pure and soarin' desires, our blind mistakes, and deep despairs; our longin's, strivin's, memories, heartaches; all the joys and burdens of a soul, has to be carried by us up the steepest mountains or down into the lowest vallies. The same emotions that was a performin' inside of our minds down in the Yo Semity, will be a performin' jest the same up on the Pyramids.

The same questionin' eyes, sort o' glad and sort o' sorrowful, that looked out over New York Harbor will look out over the Bay of Naples—and then beyond 'em both, out into a deeper, more mysterious ocean, the boundless sea that lays beyond everything, and before everything, and round everything, that great, misty sea of the Unknown, the Hereafter; tryin' to see what we hain't never seen, and wonderin' when we shall see it, and how? and where? and wherefore? and if things be so? and why?

Tryin' to hear the murmur of them waves that we know are a washin' up round us on every side, that nobody hain't never heard, but we know are there; the mighty Past, the mysterious Future. Tryin' to ketch a glimpse of them shadowy sails that are floatin' in and out forever more, with a freight of immortal souls, bearin' them here, and away. We know we have sailed on 'em once, and have got to again—and can't ketch no glimpse on 'em—can't know nothin' about 'em—sealed baby lips, silent, dead lips, never tellin'

JOSIAH STILL.

nothin' about 'em. Each soul has got to embark and sail out alone, out into the silence and the shadows—sail out into the mysterious Beyond.

We can't get away from ourselves, and get a real change, nohow, unless we knock our heads in and make idiots and lunys of ourselves. Movin' our bodies round here and there is only a shadow of a change, a mockery, as if I should dress up my Josiah in soldier coats or baby clothes. There he is inside of 'em, clear Josiah, no change in him, only a little difference in his outside circumstances.

Standin' as we do on a narrow belt of land, which is the Present, and them endless seas a beatin' round us on every side of us, bottomless, shoreless, ageless—and we a not seein' either on 'em; under them awful, and lofty, and curious circumstances, what difference does it really make to us whether we are a layin' down or a standin' up—whether we are on a hill, or down in a valley—whether a lot on us get together in cities and villages, like aunts on a aunt-hill; or whether we are more alone, like storks or ostridges?

This is a very deep and curious subject. I have talked eloquent on it, I know, and my readers know. But I could go on and filosifize on it jest as powerful and deep for hours and hours. But I have already episoded too far, and to resoom and continue on. I told Tirzah Ann that I thought it was foolish in her.

And she said, "It was very genteel to go away from home for the summer." She said, "Miss Skidmore was goin'." She is the other lawyer's wife to Jonesville, and Tirzah Ann said she was bound to not come in behind her. She said, "Miss Skidmore said that nobody who made any pretensions to bein' genteel stayed to home durin' the heated term."

"What do they go away for, mostly?" says I, in a cool tone, for I didn't over and above like the plan.

"Oh! for health and—"

"But," says I, "hain't you and Whitfield enjoyin' good health?"

"Never could be better health than we both have got," says she; "but folks go for health and pleasure."

"Hain't you a takin' comfort now," says I, "solid comfort?"

"Yes," says she, "nobody can be happier than Whitfield and I are every day of our lives."

"Wall," says I coolly, "then you had better let well enough alone."

"But," says she, "folks go for a rest."

"Rest from what?" says I. "It seems to me that I never in my hull life see nobody look more rested than you and Whitfield do." Says I, askin' her right out plain, "Don't you feel rested, Tirzah Ann?"

"Why yes," she said, "she did."

"Wall," says I, "I knew you did from your looks. Don't you and Whitfield feel fresh and vigorous and rested every mornin', ready to take up the labor of the day with a willin' heart? Do you either of you have any more work to do than is for your health to do? Don't you find plenty of time for rest and recreation every day as you go along?" Says I: "It is with health jest as it is with cleanin' house. I don't believe in lettin' things get all run down, and nasty, and then once a year tear everything to pieces, and do up the hull cleanin' of a year to once, and then let everything go again for another year. No! I believe in keepin' everything slick and comfortable day by day, and year by year. In housens, have a daily mixture of cleanin' and comfort. In health, have a daily mixture of labor, recreation, and rest. I mean for folks like you and Whitfield, who can do so. Of course some have to

THE ANNUAL TURNOUT.

work beyond their strength, and stiddy; let them take their rest and comfort when they can get it; better take it once a year, like a box of pills, than not at all. But as for you and Whitfield, I say again, in the almost immortal words of the poet, 'better let well enough alone.'"

"But," says she, "I want to do as other folks do. I am bound not to let Miss Skidmore get the upper hands of me. I want to be genteel."

"Wall," says I, "if you are determined to foller them paths, Tirzah Ann, you mustn't come to your ma for advice. She knows nothin' about them pathways; she never walked in 'em."

I could see jest where it was. I could see that Miss Skidmore was to the bottom of it all—she and Tirzah Ann's ambition. I could lay the hull on it to them 2. The Skidmores hadn't lived to Jonesville but a little while, and Miss Skidmore was awful big-feelin' and was determined to lead the fashion. She wouldn't associate with hardly anybody; wouldn't speak to only jest a few. And when she wuz to parties, or anywhere, she would set kind o' stunny and motionless —some as if her head was stiff and she couldn't bend it.

Why, I s'posed the first time I see her appear— it was to quite a big party to Elder Bamber'ses—why, I s'posed jest as much as if I had it on myself, that she had a stiff neck; s'posed she had took cold, and it had settled there. I never mistrusted it was tryin' to act genteel that ailed her. I see when I was intro-

duced to her that she acted sort o' curious and stunny,
and I stood by and watched her (sunthin' as I would
a small circus), and I see that she acted in jest that
way to most everybody that was introduced to her.

MISS SKIDMORE.

And I knew, judgin' her by myself, that she would
want to move her head more and act more limber if
she could, so I up and told her in a friendly way, that
if I was in her place I would steep up some camfrey

roots, and take 'em three times a day; and at night I would take some burdock leaves, and wilt 'em, and bind 'em on her neck. Says I:

"Burdock will take that stiffness out of your neck if anything will."

But Sister Bamber winked me out, and told me what ailed her; told me she kep' her head up in that sort of a stiff way, and sot in them stunny, motionless autitudes and postures, in order to be genteel and aristocratic. And I felt like a fool to think I had been a recommendin' burdock for it. For I knew in a minute that when anybody held their neck craned up in that way in order to act genteel and aristocratic—good land! I knew burdock couldn't help 'em any. I knew it was common sense they wanted, and a true dignity, and the sweet courtesy of gentle breeding,—burdock couldn't help 'em. Why, some said she felt above old Skidmore himself, and thought she was kinder stoopin' to associate with him, and talk with him. I don't know how true that was, but I know she tried to be dretful genteel, and put on sights of airs. And Tirzah Ann bein' ambitious, and knowin' she looked a good deal better than she did, and knew as much agin', and knowin' that Whitfield was as good agin a lawyer as her husband was, and 3 times as well off, wasn't goin' to stand none of her airs. She did seem to sort o' look down on Tirzah Ann, and feel above her, and it madded Tirzah Ann awfully, for she never felt as I did on that subject.

11*

Now if anybody wanted to put on airs, and feel above me, I shouldn't do a thing to break it up—not a thing. I should filosofize on it in this way: because they felt as if they was better than I was, that wouldn't make 'em so; if it would, why I should probable get up more interest on the subject. But it wouldn't. It wouldn't make 'em a mite better, nor me a mite worse, so what hurt would it do, anyway? It wouldn't hender me from feelin' as cool and contented and happy as a cluster cowcumber at sunrise, and it would probable make them feel sort o' comfortable and good, so I should be glad they felt.

But not bein' jealous dispositioned by nater, and and havin' so many other things to think of—soarin' and divin' so high and deep into curious and solemn subjects as I have soared and doven, I s'pose folks might feel milds and milds above me, and I not mistrust what they was a doin'; never find it out in the world unless I was told of it.

Now when Tirzah Ann was about 14 or 15, she that was Keturah Allen, a haughty, high-headed sort of a woman, come to our house a visitin'; stayed most all winter. She was a woman who had seen better days; had been quite fore-handed; and she kep' her fore-handed ways when her four hands (as you may say in a figirative way) was gone and used up. She was real poor now, hadn't nothin' to live on hardly, and I told Josiah that we would invite her to stay quite a spell,

thinkin' it would be a help to her. She was a distant
cousin of Josiah; probable as fur off as 7th or 8th.

She had a very disagreeable, high-headed, patron-
izin' way with her; very proud and domineerin' and
haughty in her demeanier. But I never had it pass
my mind that she was a feelin' above Josiah and me.

KETURAH ALLEN.

But I s'pose she wuz. I s'pose, from what I found out
afterwards, that she did feel above us, right there in
our own house, for as much as 11 weeks, and I never
mistrusted what was goin' on. And I don't s'pose I
should have found it out to this day if Tirzah Ann
hadn't see it, and up and told me of it.

I see she was awful disagreeable, dretful hard on the nerves and the temper. But I took her as a dispensation, and done, if anything, better by her than I would if she had been more agreeabler. I felt a feelin' of pity and kindness towards her, a kind of a Biblical feelin' that should be felt towards the froward —my principles was a performing round her in a martyr way, and a performin' first rate.

When Tirzah Ann come here (she had been off on a visit), and before she had been home a day, she found out what she was up to. She always had a sort of a jealous, mistrustin' turn, Tirzah Ann had. And says she that night, as we was a washin' the dishes to the sink, I a washin' and she a wipin':

"Cousin Keturah feels above you, mother."

"Why, how you talk," says I. "I never mistrusted what she was a doin'."

And she had kept watch of little things that I hadn't noticed or thought of, and says she:

"She did that, mother, because she felt above you."

"Why, is that so?" says I. "I thought she done it because she thought so much of me."

And I kep' on, serene and calm, a washin' my tea-plates. And Tirzah Ann looked keen at me, and says she:

"Don't you believe I am tellin' you the truth, mother? Don't you believe she does feel above us?"

"Oh, yes," says I, "I persume you are in the right

on't, though I never should have mistrusted such a thing in the world."

"Wall, what makes you look so serene and happy over it?"

"Why, I am thinkin', Tirzah Ann, whether she gets enough comfort out of it to pay her for her trouble. I hope she does, poor thing, for she hain't got much else to make her happy."

"You do beat all, mother," says Tirzah Ann; "you don't seem to care a mite whether anybody puts on airs and feels above you or not."

And says I, "That is jest how it is, Tirzah Ann; I don't."

"Wall, it makes me mad!" says she, a rubbin' the teapot hard.

Says I, "What earthly hurt does it do to us, Tirzah Ann? Can you tell?"

"Why, no!" She couldn't really tell what particular hurt it done, and she rubbed the teapot a little slower and more reasonable.

"Wall," says I, coolly, "then let her feel. It probable does her some good, or else she wouldn't tackle the job."

And jest as I had argued with Tirzah Ann about she that was Keturah Allen, jest so I had argued, and did argue about Miss Skidmore. But I couldn't convince her—she stuck to it.

"It does look so poor, mother, so fairly sickish, to see anybody that hain't got nothin' under the sun to make 'em feel proud, put on such airs, and try to be so exclusive and haughty."

And says I, " Such folks *have* to, Tirzah Ann." Says I, " You'll find, as a general thing, that they are the very ones who do it. They are the very ones who put on the most airs, and they do it because they *have* to. Why," says I, " divin' so deep into filosify as I have doven, it is jest as plain to me as anything can be, that if anybody has got uncommon goodness, or intellect, or beauty, or wealth, and an assured position, they don't have to put on the haughtiness and airs that them do that hain't got nothin'. They don't *have* to ; they have got sunthin' to hold 'em up, they can stand without airs."

I had talked it all over with Tirzah Ann lots of times, but it hadn't done her a mite of good, as I could see, for I hadn't got through reveryin' on the subject, nor begun to, when she up and says agin:

" Miss Skidmore says that all the high aristocracy of Jonesville, if they are aris*to*krits," says Tirzah Ann—" that is the way she pronounces it, they say she can't read hardly,—if they are aris*to*krits, and not imposters, they will go away during the summer for a change. And I say, if a change is necessary for her and old Skidmore, why Whitfield and I have got to have a change, if we die in the attempt."

" A change!" says I, in low axents, a lookin' round the charmin', lovely prospect ;—the clean, bright cottage, with its open doors and windows, and white ruf-

VIEW OF JONESVILLE.

fled curtains wavin' on the cool breeze; the green velvet grass, the bright flower beds, the climbing, blossoming vines, the birds singin' in the shady branches overhead, and in the orchard; the blue lake lyin' so calm and peaceful in the distance, shining over the green hills and forests; and the wide, cloudless sky bending over all like a benediction.

"A change!" says I, in low, tremblin' tones of emotion. "Eve wanted a change in Paradise, and she got it, too."

"But," says Tirzah Ann, for my tone impressed her fearfully, "don't you believe in a change for the summer? Don't you think they are healthy?"

I thought I wouldn't go into the heights and depths of felosophy in which I had flew and doven—she had heard me time and agin, and eloquence is very tuckerin' especially after you have been doin' a hard day's work—so I merely said:

"When anybody is bakin' up alive in crowded cities; when the hot sun is shinin' back on him from brick walls and stony roads; when all the air that comes to them comes hot and suffocatin', like a simon blowin' over a desert; to such, a change of body is sweet, and is truly healthy. But," says I, lookin' round again on the cool and entrancin' beauty and freshness of the land and other scape, "to you whom Providence has placed in a Eden of beauty and bloom, to you I again repeat for the 3d time that line of eloquent and beautiful poetry,—' Better let well enough alone.'"

I could see by the looks of her face that I hadn't convinced her. But at that very minute Josiah came back, and hollered to me that "he guessed we had better be goin' back, for he was afraid the hens would get out, and get into the turnips."

He had jest set out a new bed, and the hens was bewitched to eat the tops off. He had shut 'em up, but felt it was resky to not watch 'em. So we started off. But not before I had told Whitfield my mind about the plan. He looked more convinced than Tirzah Ann did, a good deal more. But I no need to have builded up any hopes on that, onto his mean, for I might have known that when a man loves a woman devotedly, and they haint been married—wall, anywheres from 1 to 4 or 5 years, her influence over him is powerful, and never can be told. She moulds him to her will as easy as clay is moulded in the hands of Mr. Potter. Sometimes she moulds honer into him, and then again dishoner; sometimes she moulds him comfortable, and then again she moulds him hard, and powerful oncomfortable. These things are curious, but useful and entertainin' to study on, and very deep.

TIRZAH ANN TO A WATERIN' PLACE.

WALL, if you'll believe it, after all my eloquent talk, and reasonin', and everything, the very next week they set off on their journey after a change, on that exertion after rest and pleasure. They come to see us the day before they went, but their plans was all laid, and tickets bought, (they was goin' to the same place and the same hotel and tavern Skidmore's folks was), so I didn't say nothin more—what was the use? Thinkses I, bought wit is the best if you don't pay too much for it; they'll find out for themselves whether I was in the right on't or not.

But bad as I thought it was goin' to be, little did I think it was goin' to be so bad as it wuz. Little did I think that Tirzah Ann would be brought home on a bed. But she was. And Whitfield walked with two canes, and had his right arm in a sling. But as I told Josiah, when anybody chased up pleasure so uncommon tight, it wasn't no wonder they got lamed by it. For pleasure is one of the curiousest things in the world to ketch,—speakin' in a coltish and parable way. Almost impossible to ketch by chasin' her. And if anybody don't believe me, let 'em get up some mornin' before sunrise, and take a halter, and start off a purpose, and see if they can overtake her;—see if they can ketch her, and put a bit and martingill onto her. See if they don't find she is skittish and balky, and shies off when they go to put the bits in her mouth. And see, when they think they have got the upper hands of her, whether she don't throw 'em head over heels, and caper off agin in front of 'em.

I have spoke in a parable way, and would not wish to be understood a thinkin' pleasure is a horse. Far from it. But this is a very deep subject, and would be apt to carry any one beyond their depth if not simplified and brought down to human comprehension.

The first time I went to see 'em after they got back, Tirzah Ann told me all about it. She could set up some then. But if it wasn't a pitiful sight to see them three—Whitfield, Tirzah Ann, and the babe. To see how their means looked now, and then to look back and think how they had looked the last time I had seen 'em in that very place. Why, as I looked at 'em, and see how feeble, and mauger, and used up they all looked, there wasn't hardly a dry eye in my head. Tirzah Ann told me it was a lesson that would last her through her hull life. Why, she said right out plain, that if she should live to be 3 or 400 years

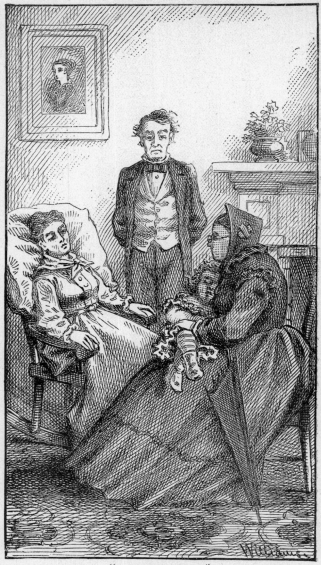

"A PITIFUL SIGHT."

old, she shouldn't never forget it, and I don't believe
myself that she would.

There they was, she and Whitfield, poor as 2 snails.
I never see either of 'em in half so poor order
before. They hadn't no ambition nor strength to
work. Their morals had all got run down. Their
best clothes was all wore out. And that babe! I
could have cried, and wept, to see how that pretty little thing was lookin'. Poor as a feeble young snail, and
pale as a little white cotton piller-case. Her appetite
was all gone, too. She had always been used to sweet,
fresh milk—the milk from her own heifer, white as
snow, with a brindle back, that her grandpa give
her for the name of Samantha. It gives dretful sweet,
rich milk. And the babe almost lived on it. And all
the milk they could get for her there was sale milk,
sour half the time, and at the best full of adultery, so
Whitfield said. And I don't think anything that happened to them on their hull tower made Josiah and
me so mad as that did. To think of that sweet little
babe's sufferin' from adulted and sour milk. It made
us so awful indignant that we can't hardly speak
peacible now, a talkin' about it.

And then they was all cooped up together in a little
mite of a room, and she was used to bein' out-doors
half the time, and had a great, cool, airy room to sleep
in nights; and bein' shet up so much, in such close,
bad air, it all wore on her, and almost used her up.
Oh! how pale she was, and mauger, and cross! Oh!

how fearfully cross! She would almost take our
heads off, Josiah's and mine, (as it were,) every time
we would speak to her. It was dretful affectin' to me
to see her so snappish; it reminded me so of her
grandpa in his most fractious hours, and I told him it
did. Josiah felt bad to see her so; it cut him down
jest as bad as it did me.

And then to see Whitfield's and Tirzah Ann's
demeaniers and means! Why jest as sure as I live
and breathe they didn't seem no more like their old
means and demeaniers than if they belonged to perfect strangers, and I told Tirzah Ann so.

And she bust right out a-cryin', and says she,
"Mother, one week's more rest would have tuckered
me completely out. I could not have stood it, I
should have died off."

I wiped my own eyes, I was so affected, and says I,
in choked-up axents, "You know I told you how it
would be, I told you that you was happy enough to
home, and you hadn't better go off in search of
pleasure."

Says she, bustin' right out agin, "One week more of
pleasure and recreation would have been my death-
blow."

Says I, "I believe it. But," says I, knowin' it was
my duty to be calm, "It is all over now, Tirzah Ann.
You hain't got to go through the pleasure agin. You
hain't got to rest any more. You must try to over-
come your feelin's. Tell your ma all about it," says I,

thinkin' it would mebby do her good, and get her mind offen it quicker.

So she up and told me the hull story. And I see plain that Miss Skidmore was to the bottom of it all.

KEEPIN' UP HER END.

She and Tirzah Ann's determination to not let her get ahead of her, and be more genteel than she was. Tirzah Ann said she was jest about sick when they started, for she found out most the last minute that Miss Skidmore had one dress more than she had, and a polenay, and so she sent at once for materials and ingregients, and sot up day and night and worked till she had got hers made, full as good and a little ahead of Miss Skidmore's.

Wall, they started the same day, and went to the same place, a fashionable summer resort, and put up to the same tavern, a genteel summer tavern, to rest and recreate. And Miss Skidmore bein' a great, healthy, strong, raw-boned woman, could stand as much agin rest and recreation as Tirzah Ann could.

Why, Tirzah Ann said the rest was enough to wear out a leather woman, and how she ever stood it for two weeks was more than she could tell.

You see she wasn't used to hard work. I had always favored her, and gone ahead with the work myself, when she lived to home; and Whitfield had been as careful of her as he could be, and jest as good as a woman to help her, and so the rest come tough on her; it was dretful hard on her. But as hard as the rest was for her, I s'pose the recreation was as bad agin; I s'pose it was twice as tough on her.

You see she had to dress up 3 or 4 times a day, and keep the babe dressed up slick. And she had to prominade down to the waterin' place and drink at jest such a time. And go a-ridin' out on the water in boats and yots; and had to play crokay, and be up till midnight every night to parties. You see she had to do all this, ruther than let Miss Skidmore get on ahead of her, and do more than she did, be more genteel than she was, and rest more.

Their room was a little mite of a room up four

MIDNIGHT AT A WATERING PLACE.

flights of stairs, and Tirzah Ann never could climb stairs worth a cent; and it leaked awful—the rain come down round the chimbley. But they had to take that room or none, the house bein' so full and runnin' over. And Whitfield thinkin' they could rest better in it than they could on the fence or door-step, took it. But if there happened to come up a storm in the night, a thunder-storm or anything, they would have to histe their umberells and lay under 'em. They must have looked as curious as 2 dogs, and I told 'em so.

The room bein' so high up, it wore on Tirzah Ann —she never could climb stairs worth a cent. And then it was so small, the air was close, nearly tight, and hot as a oven. And the babe bein' used to large, cool rooms, full of fresh, pure air, couldn't stand the hotness and the tightness, and it begun to enjoy poor health, and it cried most all the time. And to home it could play round out in the yard all day a'most, and here it hung right onto its ma. And before long she begun to enjoy poor health.

And then the room on one side of 'em was occupied by a young man who was learnin' to play on the flute. He had been disappointed in love, and he would try to make up tunes as he went along, sort o' tragedy style, and dirge-like. The most unearthly, and woe-begone, and soul-harrowin' sounds, they say that they ever heard or read of. They say it was enough to make any one's blood run cold in their vains to hear 'em.

He kept his room most of the time, and played day and night. He had ruther be alone day times, and

WAILS OF WOE.

think of that girl, and lament over her, and play about her, than go into company; and nights he couldn't sleep, owin' to his trouble, so he would set up and play. They was sorry for him, they said they was. They said they knew he must have been in a awful state, and his sufferin's intense. or he couldn't harrow up anybody's feelin's so. But that didn't make it none the easier for them.

Tirzah Ann and Whitfield are both tender-hearted

and sympathetic by nature; if they hadn't been, it wouldn't have been so hard on 'em. But they both say that tongue never can express the sufferin's they underwent from that flute, and from the feelin's they felt for that young man. They expected every day to hear that he had made way with himself, his sufferin's seemed so great. Such agonizin' wails of woe he would blow into that flute! and he would groan and writhe so when he wasn't a playin'.

Twice Whitfield went to bed with his clothes on, he was so certain the young feller couldn't stand it till mornin', and would need help.

The room on the other side of 'em was occupied by a young woman who owned a melodeon. She went into company a good deal, and her spells to play would come on nights, after she got home from parties. She had a good many bo's, and was happy dispositioned naturally, and they said some nights it seemed as if there wouldn't be no end hardly to her playin', quick pieces, waltzes, and pokeys bein' her theme—and love songs, which she would sing very sentimental and impressive, and put in sights of quavers and shakes—they said it did seem as if they never see so many quavers and trills as she trilled and quavered.

Tirzah Ann and Whitfield both said that they knew what it was to be young, they had been young themselves, not much more'n two years ago, and they knew by experience what it was to be lovesick, and they

12

wanted to sympathize with happiness and gayity of
heart, and they didn't want to do nothin' to break up
her highlarity of spirits. But still it come dretful
tough on 'em. I s'pose the sufferin's couldn't never

QUAVERS AND SHAKES.

be told nor sung that they underwent from them 2
musicianers.

And the babe not bein' used to such a racket nights
would get skairt, and almost go into historical fits.
And two or three nights Tirzah Ann had 'em, too—
the historicks. I don't see what kep' Whitfield up;

he says no money would tempt him to go through with it agin. I s'pose Tirzah Ann almost tore him to pieces. But she wasn't to blame; she didn't know what she was a doin'.

It hain't no use to blame Tirzah Ann now, after it is all over with. And she sees it plain enough now; she is sufferin' enough from the effects of it—her tryin' to keep up with Miss Skidmore, and rest as much as she did, and recreate as fur, and do all that she done. And that is where her morals got all run down, and Whitfield's, too.

To think of them two—she that was Tirzah Ann Allen, and Whitfield Minkley—to think of them two, brought up as they had been, havin' such parents and step-parents as they had, settin' under such a preacher as they had always set under—to think of them two a dancin'! and a flirtin'!

Why, if anybody had told me, if it had come through two or three, I would have despised the idee of believin' of it. But it didn't come through anybody; she owned it up to me herself. I couldn't hardly believe my ear when she told me, but I had to.

They had parties there every evenin' in the parlors of the tavern, and Miss Skidmore went to 'em all, and danced, and so they went, and they danced. I didn't say nothin' to hurt her feelin's, her mean looked so dretful, and I see she was a gettin' her pay for her sinfulness, but I groaned loud and frequent while she was a tellin' me of this (entirely unbeknown to me).

Here was where Whitfield got so lame. He never
had danced a step before in his life—nor Tirzah Ann,
neither. But Skidmore and his wife danced every

DOIN' THEIR LEVEL BEST.

night till after midnight, and Tirzah Ann was so
ambitious she was determined that she and Whitfield
should recreate and dance as much as they did, if
they fell dead a doin' of it. And not bein' used
to it, it almost killed 'em. Besides loosenin' their
morals so that it will be weeks and weeks before they
get as strong and firm as they was before. When

HOW JOSIAH WOULD PLAY POLO.

morals get to tottlin' and wobblin' round, it is almost impossible to get 'em as firm as they was before.

But truly they got their pay. Whitfield not bein' used to it, and bein' so tuckered out with the recreation and rest he had been a havin', it lamed him dretfully, rheumatiz sot in, and his sufferin's was intense. And then a base-ball hit him—or anyway he got hurt awfully when he was a playin' some game, base-ball, or billiards, or polo. That is a game, polo is, that I never heard on in my life before, and Josiah was awful interested in it when I told him about it. And he said he should deerly love to learn to play it. That man acts frisky now, a good deal of the time, and is a great case to foller up new idees.

But I told him it would be dretful foolish for him to try to learn it, for the old mare had enough to do now, without that. It is played on horseback, and from the name I s'pose they try to hit each other with poles, or hit the horses, or sunthin'. I don't really understand it well enough to give directions about playin' it straight and correct.

But Josiah was all carried away with the idee, and stuck to it he should love to play it, love to like a dog. Says he: "How I should enjoy to take a game with old Bobbet. Why," says he, "let me get onto the old mare, and give me a good, strong hop-pole, and I believe I could fetch the old man down the first blow."

But I discourage the idee, and don't mean to let him undertake it. Says I, "Josiah Allen, it stands you

in hand at your age to not go to caperin' round, and
actin', and get all the other old men in Jonesville all
rousted up about it, and a actin'. And I should
think," says I, "that one lame one in the family is
enough, without your chasin' after pleasure on the old
mare, and mebby both of you get killed in the job."

I guess I have kinder broke it up; I don't believe
he will try to learn the game. But as I was a sayin',
in that or some other of the games Whitfield got hit
on his elbo, right on his crazy-bone, and I s'pose it
made him most crazy. But the doctor thinks with
the best of care he may get over it, and use his arm
again.

Tirzah Ann's dancin' didn't give her the rheumatiz;
it seemed to hurt her more inwardly, the doctor says,
brought on a kind of weakness. But where she got
her death-blows (as it were), what laid her up, and
made her bed-sick, was goin' in bathin', and drinkin'
so much mineral water. Ridin' out on the water so
much come hard on 'em both, for it made 'em sick as
snipes. Every ride was so severe on 'em it almost
spilte their stomachs. Tirzah Ann never could bear
deep water—was always afraid of it. But she wasn't
goin' to have Miss Skidmore bathe, and she not, not if
she drounded herself in the operation. So she went
in, and got skairt the minute the water was over her
knees; it skairt her so she had sort o' cramps, and
gin up she was a droundin'. And that made it worse
for her, and she did crumple right down in the water,

and would have been drounded if a man hadn't res-
cued her. She was a sinkin' for the 3d time when he
laid holt of her hair, and dragged her out. She hain't

got over the fright yet,
and I am afraid she
never will.

THE RESCUE.

The mineral water,
they say, tasted awfully. And Tirzah Ann bein' very
dainty always about what she eat and drunk, it went
against her stomach so she couldn't hardly get a
tumbler-full of it down. But Miss Skidmore, bein' so
tough, could drink 8 tumblers-full right down, and it
seems it lifted her up dretfully. They said she acted

haughty and overbearin' because Tirzah Ann couldn't
drink so much as she could, into a quart or two.   She
put on airs about it.   And Tirzah Ann couldn't stand

"IT TASTED AWFULLY."

that, so one day, (it was the day before they come
home,) she drinked 5 tumblers-full right down.   And
I s'pose a sicker critter never lived than she was.

I s'pose they was awful skairt about her, and she was skairt about herself. She thought she was a dyin', and made Whitfield promise on a Testament to carry

A SAD SCENE.

her back to Jonesville the next day, dead or alive. And he, bein' a master hand to keep his promise, was as good as his word, and brought her home the next day on a bed.

She got up in a day or two so as to be about the house. But they have been laid up for repairs, as you may say, ever since. They are sick critters now, both on 'em. I have seen awful and deplorable effects

12*

from rest and recreation before, but never, *never* did
I see awfuller or deplorabler than they are both a sufferin' from. They both say that one week's rest more
would have been their death blows, and finished 'em
for this world, and I believe it.

And besides the outward sufferin's that are plain to
be seen, there are inward hurts that are fur, fur
worse. Outside bruises and hurts can be reached with
arneky and wormwood, but who can put a mustard
poultice on a bruised spirit, and a weakened moral?
Nobody can't do it.

Now what I am a goin' to say, what I am a goin' to
tell now, I wouldn't have get round for the world—*it
must be kept!* If I didn't feel it to be my boundin'
duty to write the truth, and the hull truth, and if
it wuzn't for its bein' a solemn warnin' to them who
may have felt a hankerin' to go off on a tower after
rest; if it wuzn't for this I couldn't write the awful
words. But I wouldn't have it told for anything; I
wouldn't have it get round for the world. It *must* be
kept. But sense I am on the subject I will tell it jest
as it is. But it *must not* go no further. Tirzah Ann
didn't tell it right out to me, but I gathered it from
little things I heard her and Whitfield say, and from
what I heard from others that was there. I mistrust,
and pretty much know, that Tirzah Ann flirted.
Flirted with a man!

You see, Miss Skidmore wantin' to appear fashionable and genteel, and do as other genteel wimmen did,

TIRZAH ANN FLIRTS WITH A MAN.

flirted with men. And I know jest as well as I want to know that Tirzah Ann did, not wantin' to be outdone. I know she and Whitfield quarreled dretfully, for the first time in their lives,—that I had right from Tirzah Ann's own mouth. But she didn't tell me what it was about. She looked sort o' meachin', and turned the subject, and I hain't one to pump. But I s'pose, from what they both told me, that they come pretty nigh partin'. And I know, jest as well as if I see her at it, that Tirzah Ann bein' so ambitious, and not wantin' to be outdone by Miss Skidmore, went to flirtin', and I mistrust it was with old Skidmore himself. I know he and Whitfield don't speak. Tirzah Ann never could bear the sight of him, but I s'pose she wanted to gaul Miss Skidmore.

Oh! such doin's, such doin's! It worked up me and Josiah dretfully. As I told him, "where would their morals have been, if they had rested and recreated much longer?"

And he groaned aloud, and said what gauled him the worst was to think of the piles and piles of money they had throwed away. Says he: "It will cramp 'em for months and months,"—and it will.

MISS BOBBET LETS THE CAT OUT.

MY companion Josiah havin' bought a quantity of
fresh fish, I thought I would carry one over to
Miss Betsey Slimpsy,—she that was Betsey Bobbet,—
thinkin' mebby it would taste good to her. Betsey hain't
well. Some think she is in a gallopin' consumption, but
I don't. I think it is her workin' so hard, and farin' so
hard. She has to support the family herself, almost
entirely; she don't have enough to eat a good deal of
the time, so folks say; she hain't got any clothes fit to
wear; and she has to be such a slave, and work so
awful hard, that it don't seem as if she is half as
bright as she used to be. As she says, if it wasn't
for the dignity she got by bein' married, it didn't seem
as if she could keep up. But that, she says, is a great
comfort to her.

But she looks bad. She don't get no sleep at all,
she says, or none to speak of. Simon's horrors are
worse than I ever dremp' horrors could be. They are
truly horrible. Every night he pounds on the head-

board, yells awful, prances round, and kicks. Why, Betsey says, and I believe her, that she is black and blue most the hull time, jest from kicks. I am sorry for Betsey.

Wall, I give her the fish,—she seemed awful glad

A PRESENT FOR BETSEY.

of it,—and visited with her a little while, and then, as supper-time was approachin' and drawin' near, I histed my umberell, and started out on my homeward return.

It was a lovely evenin'. It had been a very hot day,

but the sun had sot down (as it were) behind the trees to cool himself off, and the earth, takin' advantage of his temporary retirement, seemed to foller on and do likewise. So I walked along on the green grass, under

FRIENDLY FEELIN'S

the swayin' branches of the apple-trees that bent down over the highway—great, liberal-hearted trees, stretching their strong brown arms out in blessing and benediction—out over their own rich, cultivated soil and the dusty highway, over foe and lover, tramp, and

Josiah Allen's wife. I liked that in the trees—liked it first-rate in 'em. It made me feel well to walk in their refreshin' shade.

The apples were ripenin' in the clusterin' boughs, birds sang in the branches, the blue sky shone down lovin'ly. The wayside blossoms grew thick at my feet, the grass was like a velvet carpet under' em, and, most beautiful scene of all, my Josiah stood in the barn-door, nailin' on a board.

Oh! how first-rate I did feel and look. I knew I was a lookin' well. I knew it jest as well as I wanted to, before I met my companion's admirin' look, as he asked me, in considerable tender tones, if I knew whether there was any more of them tenpenny nails left.

I told him there wuzn't. And then, oh! how ad mirin' he looked at me agin, as I told him he had better hurry and finish the door, as I was goin' right in to put on the tea-kettle and get supper jest as quick as I could.

His smile was like sunshine to my heart, as he told me he would be in by the time I got it ready, and I'd better hurry up.

As I walked towards the house I was feelin' beautiful, and very affectionate towards my pardner. For love, no matter how full and ardent it may be, will, like other great deeps, have its ebbs and flows, its high tides and its more dwindlin' ones.

At that moment my love and my confidence in my

Josiah swept up in my heart to the highest tide-level.
And I thought, as I walked along, that I would shet
up that eye of my spectacles—that I never would agin
let distrust and a Widder Bump cause me a moment's
disquiet and unhappiness.

And though I could not deny to myself that Josiah
Allen's conduct, in the spring of the year, and on a
Friday night, had been mysterious, I felt that I would
look back upon it as I look on scriptural passages that
I can't make out the meanin' of. I always feel in them
cases that it is the fault of the translator. No matter
how mysterious the meanin' may seem, I know that
the Scriptures are right, anyway. And I felt that I
would look back in that way upon my companion's
strange words and demeaners. I felt that I would
trust my Josiah.

And so, bein' full of love and confidence in Josiah
Allen and the world at large, I walked with a even
step up to the door-step, and as I did so I see the
kitchen-door was open. I thought that looked sort o'
strange, as I knew that my Josiah had been to the
barn to work all the time I was gone. But I went in,
and as I did so I see a man a standin' by the stove.
He was a short, stocky man, dressed middlin' well, but
he had a strange look.

He was considerable older than Josiah, I should
think. His face was red and bloated, and his hair
bein' white as snow, and his white whiskers runnin'
all round his chin, and up the sides of his face, it give

it considerable the look of a red pin-cushion with a white ruffle round it. Only the ruffle (still usin' the poetical simely) wuzn't white under his chin. No, he nsed too much tobacco for that. I s'pose he used it

MEETING THE ELDER.

for the good looks of it; I s'pose that is what folks use tobacco for. But good land! I can't see a single pretty look to it, nor never could, from the time a man takes in a half a plug or so, and wads it up in one side of his mouth, showin' his yeller, nasty-lookin' teeth, and lettin' the black, filthy-lookin' juice run down his mouth and whiskers, to the time he spits it all out agin onto carpets, stair-ways, church pews, concert halls, car floors, wimmen's dresses, and et cetery.

I can't see a mite of pretty looks about it. But I am reasonable and always was. And there probable may be some beauty in it that I hain't never seen, or there wouldn't so many foller it up.

For it must be for the looks of it that they use it. I have studied on it a sight, and there hain't no other reason that I can see. And if there had been any the keen eye of my spectacles would have ketched sight on it. They go awful deep into subjects, them spectacles do.

It can't be for the taste of it that they use it, for it don't taste good. That I *know*, for I got some into my mouth once by mistake, over to Miss Bobbet's, and so what I know, I know; I can take my oath on the taste of it. No, they don't use it for that.

It can't be for the profit of it, for it hain't profitable; quite the reverse. Why, there is about 30 million dollars' worth raised in the United States a year, and somebody has got to pay for it.

Why, I s'pose some poor men chew enough of this stuff,—chew it jest to spit it out agin,—and smoke it, —draw the smoke into their mouth jest to blow it out agin,—why, I s'pose this proceedin' costs 'em enough in ten or fifteen years to buy 'em a good little home. And there they are willin' to live and die homeless, themselves and them they love, jest for looks, jest to try to look pretty.

For it must be for that. It can't be for health, for doctors say it hurts the health awfully, makes folks weak and nervous, and sometimes leads to blindness and fits.

It hain't for morals, for folks say, and stick to it, that it makes 'em totter. Weakens a man's moral nature, his social and religious faculties, gives him a taste for the stronger stimulent of intoxicatin' drinks, and so leads him down to ruin gradual.

No, it hain't for the morals. I have most probable hit on the right reason. But good land! where the beauty is in it I can't see. But I am a episodin' fearfully.

As I was a sayin', this man, instead of beautifyin' himself with it, had jest spilte the looks of his whiskers, in my eye. They looked yeller and nasty. And the sides of his mouth was all streaked with it. In some places it was sort o' dried on. He looked to me as if it would do him good to put him asoak in weak lye, and let him lay in it 2 or 3 days till he got sweetened and cleansed.

His eyes was light-colored, and the lids was swelled and inflamed like. His mouth was drawed down into a dretful sanctimonious pucker; he had a awful big chew of tobacco in his mouth, and so it wasn't all hypocracy that drawed it down; it was probable about half and half—half hypocracy and half tobacco. And under all the other expressions of his face was a dissipated, bad look. I didn't like his looks a mite. But there he stood a kinder hangin' onto the table (I found out afterwards that he had been drinkin' all the hard cider he could to old Bobbet'ses).

He asked me, in a kind of a thick voice, for Josiah. And I, thinkin' it was some one on business, asked him in a polite tone, though cool, "if he wouldn't take a chair and set down."

"I would," says he, in that thick, husky voice, "I would set down, mum, but I am afraid if I should I couldn't get up agin."

And he looked at me in a curious, strange way; dretful wise, and yet foolish like.

Says I, gazin' sternly at him: "I am afraid you have been a drinkin', sir."

"No! No! I hain't! cider's good; good for the blood. Will take a glass, if you please."

"Not here you won't," says I firmly.

"I'll take a glass if you *please*, I said," says he, speakin' up kinder loud. "Cider's good; good for the blood."

Says I: "It will be good for your blood if you get out of this house as quick as you can. And I would love to know," says I, lookin' at him keenly over my specks, "what you are here for, anyway."

"I am here in the cause of—cider's good for the blood. Will take a drink."

Says I: "You start out of this house, or I'll call Josiah."

"I come, and I'm workin' for the cause of religion, if you please—and I'll take a glass of it, if you please."

He'd make a sort of a drunken bow, every word or two, and smiled sort o' foolish, and winked long, solemn winks.

Says I sternly: "You act as if you was a workin' for the cause of religion."

"Apple-cider's good. Hain't apples religious, easy entreated? Hain't apples peacible, long sufferin'? Will take a drink, if you please."

Says I, with a awful dignity: "I'd love to see myself givin' you anything to drink. You are drunk as a fool now; that is what ails you."

"Cider hain't tox-tox-toxicatin'; Bobbet said 'twuzn't. He said his cider-mill was harmless, easy 'ntreated, as peacible a one as he ever see. Will take a glass, if you please. I wouldn't drink a tox-tox-toxin' bevrig, not for dollar. Guess Bobbet knows what's pious drink and what hain't. Cider's pious bevrig—called so—peacible, pious drink."

"Pious drink!" says I, sternly. "I have seen more than one man made a fool and a wild man by it, pious or not. Oh!" says I, eppisodin' out loud and eloquent, entirely unbeknown to me, "how Satan must laugh in his sleeves (if he wears sleeves) to see how good men are deceived and blindered in this matter. Nothin' tickles Satan more than to get a good man, a church member, to work for him for nothin'. When he gets good, conscientious, christian folks to tackle his work of ruinin' souls, unbeknown to them, and let him rest off a spell,—why it tickles him most to death.

"And when anyone plants the first seeds of drunkenness in a person, no matter how good-naturedly it is done, no matter how good the ones are who do it, they are workin' for Satan and boardin' themselves, entirely unbeknown to them. That is, the good ones are; some know and realize what they are a doin', but keep at it through selfishness and love of gain."

"Likker's bad, wrong; but cider's in'cent, in'cent as a babe, a prattlin' little babe; it's called so."

"Good land!" says I, "do you s'pose I care a cent what a thing is called?" Says I: "I have seen cider that three glasses of it would fix a man out so he couldn't tell how many childern he had, or fathers and mothers, no more than he could count the stars in the zodiact. And couldn't walk straight and upright, no more than he could bump his old head aginst the moon. When a man is dead what difference does it make to him whether he died from a shotgun or billerous colic. or was skairt to death? And what difference does it make when a man is made a fool of, whether it is done by one spunefull or a dozen, or a quart? The important thing to him is, he is a fool."

"Yes, 'n I'll take a glass of cider, if you please."

I started right straight for the back stoop and hollered to Josiah.

That skairt him. He started kinder sideways for the door, got holt of the latch, and says he:

"I come to labor with you, n' I don't want to leave you goin' the broad road to destruction; but I will,"

says he, with a simple sort of a smile, and as foolish
a wink as I ever see wunk, "I will if you'll give me a
drink of cider, if you please."

Says I, firmly, "You will take a broader road than

A THREATNIN' ATTITUDE.

you have calculated on, if you don't clear out of this
house, instantly and to once." And as I still held my
umberell in my hand, I held it up in a threatnin' way
in my left hand, some like a spear. And he started
off and went staggerin' down the road.

I was a wonderin' awfully who he was, and what he
come for, when Miss Bobbet come in to bring home

a drawin' of tea, and she was so full of news that she most fell aginst the door, as wimmen will when they are freighted too heavy with gossip. And she said it was Elder Judas Wart, a Mormon Elder, who had come back to Jonesville again.

"And," says she, hurryin' to relieve herself, for her mind was truly loaded heavy with news beyond its strength, "what do you think now about the Widder Bump bein' a Mormon. I told you she was one, a year ago, and other wimmen told you so, but you would stick to it that she was a camel."

"Yes," says I, "in the name of principle I have upholded that woman and called her a camel."

"Wall," says she, "camel or not, she was sealed to Elder Judas Wart last week. You know she went home to her mother's in the spring. And he has been out there all summer holdin' his meetin's, and married her.

"He told us all about it to-day. He said he hadn't hardly a wife by him but what was disabled in some way from workin'. He said he was fairly discouraged. Eleven of 'em was took down with the tyfus, violent. A few of 'em, he didn't hardly know jest how many, but quite a number of 'em, had the chills. Two or three of 'em was bed-rid. Four of 'em had young babes; and he said he felt it was not good for man to be alone, and he needed a wife—so he married the Widder Bump and sent her on to Utah by express to take charge of things till he come. He had meetin's to Jonesville last spring, and Bobbet went to 'em."

MISS BOBBET TELLS ABOUT JOSIAH.

"Bobbet went to 'em," says I, mechanically. For oh! what strange and curious feelin's was a tacklin' of me. Memeries of that terrible crysis in my life when I heard the mutterin's of a earthquake, a rumblin' and a roarin' unbeknown to me. When everything in life seemed uncertain and wobblin' to a Samantha, and a Josiah talked in his slumbers of a Widder Bump.

"Yes," says she, "Bobbet owned it all up to me, jest now. He wouldn't, if the Elder hadn't come in and acted so glad to see him. But, if you'll believe it, Bobbet looked as if he would sink when he said he had married the Widder Bump. And he says he hain't goin' to have no new overcoat made this winter. And he has been sot on havin' one."

"Bobbet owned it all up to you," says I, speakin' agin mechanically, for I felt fairly stunted by the emotions that was rushin' onto me.

"Yes, I remember he used to go evenin's to Jonesville a sight, last spring, when I had the quinzy and was laid up. But I s'posed he went to the Methodist Conference meetin's. But he didn't, he went to hear Elder Judas Wart. And Bobbet says Josiah Allen went to 'em, too."

At them fearful words I groaned aloud. I wouldn't say a word aginst my pardner. But to save my life I couldn't keep that groan back. It fairly groaned itself (as it were), my feelin's was such.

It was a fearful groan, deep and melancholy in the extreme. I was determined to not say one word about

13

my feelin's concernin' my pardner, and I didn't, only
jest that groan. She is quite a case to make mischief
in families, but she hain't got a thing to carry from
me, only jest that groan. And there can't be much
done, even in a court of law, with one plain groan, and
nothin' else; there can't be much proved by it.

She is a pryin' woman, and I see she mistrusted
sunthin'. Says she:

"What is the matter, Josiah Allen's wife? What
are you groanin' for, so heavy?"

I wouldn't come right out and tell the awful emotions that was performin' through my mind—and at
the same time I wouldn't lie. So I broke out sort o'
eloquent, and says I:

"When I think what female wimmen have suffered,
and are sufferin', from this terrible sin of polygamy, it
is enough to make anybody groan." Says I, "I feel
guilty, awful guilty, to think I hain't done sunthin'
before now to stop it. Here I have," says I, growin'
fearfully excited, "here I have jest sot down here, with
my hands folded (as it were), and let them doin's go
on without doin' a single thing to break it up. And it
makes me feel fairly wicked when I think of that
address the sufferin' female wimmen of Utah sent out
to Miss Hays and me."

"To Miss Hays and you?" says Miss Bobbet, in a
sort of a jealous way. "I don't know as it was sent
to you special. It said Miss Hays, and the other wimmen of the United States."

"Wall," says I, "hain't I a woman, and hain't Jonesville right in the very center of the United States?"

"Why yes," says she. Miss Bobbet will always give up when she is convinced. I'll say that for her.

"Wall," says I, "that address that they sent out to us was one of the most powerful and touchin' appeals for help ever sent out by sufferin' humanity. And here I hain't done a thing about it, and I don't believe Emily has."

"Emily who?" says she.

"Why, Emily Hays," says I. "Rutherford Hays'es wife. She that was Emily Webb. As likely a woman as ever entered that White House. A woman of gentle dignity, sweet, womanly ways, earnest christian character, and firm principles. No better or better-loved woman has ever sot up in that high chair since Lady Washington got down out of it. A good-lookin' woman, too," says I proudly. "She has got a fair face and a fair soul. Her christian example is as pure and clear as the water she makes them old congressmen drink to her dinner-table, and is as refreshin', and as much of a rarity to 'em. I can tell you," says I, "it makes me and America proud, it tickles both of us most to death, to think our representative lady is one so admirable in every way. And foreigners can gaze at her all they are a mind to. We hain't afraid to let 'em peruse her through the biggest telescopes they can get; they won't find nothin' in her face nor her nature but what we are proud of, both of us.

"But in this matter I'll bet a cent Emily hain't made a move, no more than I have. We have been slack in it, both on us. But as for me," says I firmly, "I am determined to be up and a doin'."

And oh! how I sithed (to myself) as I thought it

"A RARITY TO 'EM."

over. Emily hadn't had the fearful lesson that I had had. Her pardner's morals never had wobbled round and tottered under the pressure of this pernicious doctrine, and a Widder Bump. My sithes was fearful, as I thought it over, but they was inward and silent ones. For my devotion to my pardner is such that I would not give even the testimony of a sithe against my Josiah.

When necessary, and occasion demands it, I scold Josiah myself, powerful; I have to. But I will protect him from all other blame and peril, as long as I have a breath left in my lung, or a strength left in my armpit.

But oh! what feelin's I felt, what deep, though silent, sithes I sithed, as I thought it over to myself. How the posy will not give out its perfume; will hang right onto it with its little, dainty, invisible hands till it is trod on; then it gives it up—has to. And gold won't drop a mite of its dross; obstinate, haughty, holdin' right onto it till it is throwed into the fire, and heat put to it.

And to foller up the simelys, Josiah Allen's wife's heart had to be tried in the fiery furnace of pain and mortifacture before it would give up and do its duty.

Oh! how my conscience smoted me as I thought it over. Thought how the hand of personal sufferin' had to fairly whip me into the right. There had hundreds and thousands of my own sect been for year after year a sufferin' and a agonizin'. Bearin' the heaviest of crosses with bleedin' hands, and eyes so blinded with tears they could hardly ketch a glimpse of the sweet heavens of promise above 'em. And how at last, bein' fairly drove to it in their despair, they writ to Emily and me for help: help to escape out of the deeps of personal and moral degradation; help to rescue them and the whole land from barberism and ruin. And there we hadn't paid no more attention to that letter than if it hadn't been wrote to us.

Oh! how guilty I felt. I felt as if I was more to

blame than Emily was, for her house was bigger than mine, and she had more to do. And she hadn't had the warnin' I had. I was the guilty one. In the spring of the year, and on a Friday night, right up on the ceilin' of our kitchen had those fearful words been writ, jest as they was in Bellshazzer'ses time:

"*Mean! mean!* tea-kettle!" and et cetery. Which bein' interpreted in various ways, held awful meanin's in every one of 'em. "*Mean! mean!*" showin' there was mean doin's a goin' on; "tea-kettle!" showin' there was bilin' water a heatin' to scald and torture me. And takin' it all together this awful meanin' could be read: "Josiah Allen is weighed in the ballances, and is found wantin'."

I hadn't heeded those fiery words of warnin'. I had covered my eyes, and turned away from interpretations (as it were). Forebodin's had foreboded, and I hadn't minded their 'bodin's. Forerunners had run right in front of me, and I wouldn't look at these forerunners, or see 'em run.

Blind trust and affection for a Josiah had blinded the eyes of a Samantha; but now, when the truth was brought to light by a Miss Bobbet, when I could see the awful danger that had hung over me on a Friday night and in the spring of the year, when I could almost hear the whizzin' of the fatal arrow aimed at my heart, my very life—now I could realize how them hearts felt where the arrows struck, where they was a quiverin' and a smartin' and a ranklin'.

Now, it felt a feelin', my heart did, that it was willin', while a throb of life remained in it, to give that throb to them fellow-sufferers (fellow-female-sufferers). And when Miss Bobbet said, jest as she started for home, that Elder Judas Wart wanted to have a talk with me on religion and mormonism, I said, in a loud, eloquent voice:

"Fetch him on! Bring him to me instantly! and let me argue with him, and convert him."

I s'pose my tone and my mean skairt her, she not knowin' what powerful performances had been a performin' in my mind. And I heard that she went right from our house and reported that I was after the Elder. So little is worldly judgment to be relied upon. But nobody believed it, and if they had, I shouldn't have cared, no more than I should have cared for the murmurin' of the summer breeze. When the conscience is easy, the mind is at rest. I knew there was three that knew the truth on't: the Lord, Elder Judas Wart, and myself. I count Josiah and me as one, which is lawful, though Josiah says that I am the one the biggest heft of the time. He said "he made calculations when he married me, when we was jined together as one, that he would be that one."

And I told him, "Man's calculations was blindin', and oft deceivin'."

I said it in a jokin' way. I let him be the "one" a good deal of the time, and he knows it.

But, as I was a sayin', them three that knew it was

all that was necessary to my comfort and peace of mind.

Josiah looked sad and depressted, and I knew, for I see old Bobbet leanin' over the barnyard fence while he

BOBBET AND JOSIAH TALKIN'.

was a milkin', and I knew they had been talkin' over the news. And when he come in with his second pail-full of milk, lookin' so extra depressted, my mean was some colder, probable about like ice cream, only not sweet; no, not at all sweet—quite the reverse.

After Miss Bobbet's departure, the night that ensued and followed on was fearful and agonizin'. What to do with Josiah Allen I knew not. But I made my mind up not to tackle him on the subject then, but wait till I was more calm and composed down. I also thought I would do better to take the daylight to it. So I treated him considerable the same as my common run of treatment towards him was, only a little more cool—not cold as ice, but coolish.

But oh! what emotions goared me that night, as I lay on my goose-feather pillow, with Josiah by my side a groanin' in his sleep frequent and mournful. He couldn't keep awake, that man couldn't, not if all the plagues of Egypt was a plaguin' him, as I often remarked to him.

But while such emotions was a performin' in my mind, there wuzn't no sleep for me. Some of the time I was mad at Josiah Allen, and then agin I was mad at the Government. Some of the time I would feel indignant at Josiah, clear Josiah; and then agin, as he would sithe out loud and heart-breakin' sithes, my affection for him would rise up powerful, and I would say to myself—oritorin' eloquent right there in the dead of the night—"Why should I lay all the blame of a pernicious system onto my sufferin' pardner? Human nater is weak and prone to evil, especially man human nater, which is proner. And when Government keeps such abysses for men to walk off of, and break their necks (morally), who should be scolded the most—them men after their necks are broke, or the ones who dug the abysses, or let 'em be dug?

13*

"Let this band of banditty flourish on shore—furnished land for 'em to flourish on—and furnished ships to go out over the ocian and hunt round for foreign souls to ruin. Who calmly looked on and beheld its ships bear to our shores hundreds and thousands of the ignorant peasantry of the old world—fair-faced Swedish and Danish maidens, blue-eyed German girls, and bright English and Irish lassies—lookin' with innocent, wonderin' eyes toward a new life—innocent youth, deceived by specious falsehoods, pourin' onto our shores like pure rills of water, to fall into that muddy gulf of corruption and become putrid also—and our Government lookin' calmly on, happy as a king, and pretendin' to be religious."

I declare! as I thought it all over, I was as mad with the Government as I was with my pardner, and I don't know but madder.

Scolded, Josiah Allen had got to be—that I knew. But I hankered, I hankered awfully, right there in the dead of the night, to tackle the Government, too, and scold it fearfully. I felt that I must be up and a doin'. I yearned to tackle Elder Judas Wart, and argue with him with a giant strength. But little did I think that in a few days I should be a doin' of it.

A SERENADING EPISODE, &c.

THESE verses of Betsey's come out in the last week's *Gimlet*, and I call it foolish stuff. Though (on measurin' 'em in a careless way with a yard-stick) I found the lines was pretty nigh of a equal length, and so I s'pose it would be called poetry.

A WIFE'S STORY.

Oh Gimlet ! back again I float,
　　With broken wings, a weary bard;
I cannot write as once I wrote,
　　I have to work so very hard;
So hard my lot, so tossed about,
My muse is fairly tuckered out.

My muse aforesaid once hath flown,
　　But now her back is broke, and breast;
And yet she fain would crumple down;
　　On Gimlet pages she would rest,
And sing plain words as there she's sot—
Haply they'll rhyme, and haply not.

(355)

I spake plain words in former days,
　No guile I showed, clear was my plan;
My gole it matrimony was;
　My earthly aim it was a man.
I gained my man, I won my gole;
Alas! I feel not as I fole.

Yes, ringing through my maiden thought
　This clear voice rose: "Oh come up higher."
To speak plain truth, with candor fraught,
　To married be was my desire.
Now, sweeter still this lot shall seem,
To be a widder is my theme.

For toil hath claimed me for her own,
　In wedlock I have found no ease;
I've cleaned and washed for neighbors round,
　And took my pay in beans and pease;
In boiling sap no rest I took,
Or husking corn, in barn, and shock.

Or picking wool from house to house,
　White-washing, painting, papering;
In stretching carpets, boiling souse;
　E'en picking hops, it hath a sting,
For spiders there assembled be,
Mosquitoes, bugs, and e t c.

I have to work, oh! very hard;
　Old Toil, I know your breadth and length;
I'm tired to death, and, in one word,
　I have to work beyond my strength.
And mortal men are very tough
To get along with,—hasty, rough.

OLD TOIL'S BRIDE.

Yes, tribulation's doomed to her
  Who weds a man, without no doubt.
In peace a man is singuler;
  His ways they are past findin' out.
And oh! the wrath of mortal males—
To point their ire, earth's language fails.

And thirteen children in our home
  Their buttons rend, their clothes they burst,
Much bread and such do they consume;
  Of children they do seem the worst.
And Simon and I do disagree;
He's prone to sin continuallee.

He horrors has, he oft doth kick,
  He prances, yells,—he will not work.
Sometimes I think he is too sick;
  Sometimes I think he tries to shirk.
But 'tis hard for her, in either case,
  Who B. Bobbet was in happier days.

Happier? Away! such thoughts I spurn.
  I count it true, from spring to fall,
'Tis better to be wed, and groan,
  Than never to be wed at all.
I'd work my hands down to the bone
Rather than rest a maiden lone.

This truth I will not, cannot shirk,
  I feel it when I sorrow most:
I'd rather break my back with work,
  And haggard look as any ghost,—
Rather than lonely vigils keep,
I'd wed and sigh, and groan and weep.

Yes, I can say, though tears fall quick,
  Can say, while briny tear-drops start,
I'd rather wed a crooked stick
  Than never wed no stick at all.
Sooner than laughed at be, as of yore,
  I'd rather laugh myself no more.

I'd rather go half-clad and starved,
  And mops and dish-cloths madly wave,
Than have the words "B. Bobbet" carved
  On headstun rising o'er my grave.
Proud thought! now, when that stun is risen,
'Twill bear two names—my name and hisen.

Methinks 'twould colder make the stun
  If but one name, the name of she,
Should linger there alone—alone.
  How different when the name of he
Does also deck the funeral urn;
Two wedded names,—his name and hurn.

And sweeter yet, oh blessed lot!
  Oh state most dignified and blest!
To be a widder, calmly sot,
  And have both dignity and rest.
Oh, Simon! strangely sweet 'twould be
To be a widder unto thee.

The warfare past, the horrors done,
  With maiden's ease and pride of wife,
The dignity of wedded one,
  The calm and peace of single life,—
Oh, strangely sweet this lot doth seem;
A female widder is my theme.

I would not hurt a hair of he,
Yet, did he from earth's toils escape,
I could most reconciléd be,
Could sweetly mourn, e'en without crape;
Could say, without a pang of pain,
That Simon's loss was Betsey's gain.

I've told the plain tale of my woes,
With no deceit, or language vain,
Have told whereon my hopes are rose,
Have sung my mournful song of pain.
And now I e'en will end my, tale,
I've sung my song, and wailed my wail.

I have made a practice of callin' that Poetry, bein'
one that despises envy and jealousy amongst female
authoresses. No, you never ketch me at it, bein' one
that would sooner help 'em up the ladder than upset
'em, and it is ever my practice so to do. But truth
must be spoke if subjects are brung up. Uronious
views must be condemned by Warriors of the Right,
whether ladders be upset or stand firm on their legs—
poetesses also.

I felt that this poetry attacted a tender subject, a
subject dearer to me than all the world besides—the
subject of Josiah. Josiah is a man.

And I say it, and I say it plain, that men hain't no
such creeters as she tries to make out they be. Men
are first-rate creeters in lots of things, and are as good
as wimmen be any day of the week.

Of course I agree with Betsey, that husbands are
tryin' in lots of things ; they need a firm hand to the
hellum to guide 'em along through the tempestuous

waves of married life, and get along with 'em. They are lots of trouble, but then I think they pay after all. Why, I wouldn't swap my Josiah for the best house and lot in Jonesville, or the crown of the Widder Albert. I love Josiah Allen. And I don't know but the very trouble he has caused me makes me cling closer to him. You know the harder a horse's head beats aginst burdock burs the tighter the burdocks will cling to its mane. Josiah makes me sights of trouble, but I cling to him closely.

I admit that men are curious creeters, and very vain, and they hain't willin' to let well enough alone. They over-do, and go beyond all sense and reason. A instance of these two strong traits of their's has jest occurred and took place, which, as a true historian relatin' solemn facts, I will relate in this epistol.

Yes, men are tejus creeters a good deal of the time. But then agin, so be wimmen, jest as tejus, and I don't know but tejuser. I believe my soul, if I had got to be born agin, I had jest as lieves be born a man as a woman, and I don't know but I drather.

No, I don't think one sect ort to boast over the other one. They are both about equally foolish and disagreeable, and both have their goodnesses and nobilities, and both ort to have their rights.

Now I hain't one to set up and say men hadn't ort to vote, that they don't know enough, and hain't good enough, and so forth and so on. No, you don't ketch me at it. I am one that stands up for justice and reason.

Now, the other day a wild-eyed woman, with short hair, who goes round a lecturin' on wimmen's rights, come to see me, a tryin' to inviggle me into a plot to keep men from votin'. Says she, "The time is a drawin' near when wimmen are a goin' to vote, without no doubt."

THE WILD-EYED WOMAN.

"Amen!" says I. "I can say amen to that with my hull heart and soul."

"And then," says she, "when the staff is in our own hands, less we wimmen all put in together and try to keep men from votin'."

"Never!" says I, "never will you get me into such a scrape as that," says I. "Men have jest exactly as good a right to vote as wimmen have. They are condemned, and protected, and controlled by the same laws that wimmen are, and so of course are equally interested in makin' 'em. And I won't hear another word of such talk. You needn't try to inviggle me into no plot to keep men from votin', for justice is ever my theme, and also Josiah."

Says she, bitterly, "I'd love to make these miserable sneaks try it once, and see how they would like it, to have to spend their property, and be hauled around, and hung by laws they hadn't no hand in makin'."

But I still says, with marble firmness, "Men have jest as good a right to vote as wimmen have. And you needn't try to inviggle me into no such plans, for I won't be inviggled."

And so she stopped invigglin', and went off.

And then again in Betsey's poetry (though as a neighbor and a female author I never would speak a word aginst it, and what I say I say as a warrior, and would wish to be so took) I would say in kindness, and strictly as a warrior, that besides the deep undercurrent of foolishness that is runnin' through it, there is another thought that I deeply condemn. Betsey sot out in married life expectin' too much. Now, she didn't marry in the right way, and so she ort to have expected tougher times than the usual run of married females ort to expect; more than the ordinary tribulations of matrimony. But she didn't; she expected too much.

And it won't do to expect too much in this world, anyway. If you can only bring your mind down to it, it is a sight better to expect nothing, and then you won't be disappointed if you get it, as you most probable will. And if you get something it will be a joyful surprise to you. But there are few indeed who has ever sot down on this calm hite of filosify.

Folks expect too much. As many and many times as their hopes have proved to be uronious, they think, well now, if I only had that certain thing, or was in that certain place, I should be happy. But they hain't. They find when they reach that certain gole, and have clim up and sot down on it, they'll find that somebody has got onto the gole before 'em, and is there a settin' on it. No matter how spry anybody may be, they'll find that Sorrow can climb faster than they can, and can set down on goles quicker. Yes, they'll find her there.

It hain't no matter how easy a seat anybody sets down in in this world, they'll find that they'll have to hunch along, and let Disappointment set down with 'em, and Anxiety, and Weariness, and et cetery, et cetery.

Now, the scholar thinks if he can only stand up on that certain hite of scientific discovery, he will be happy, for he will know all that he cares about or wants to. But when he gets up there, he'll see plain; for the higher he is riz above the mists of ignorance that floats around the lower lands, the clearer his vision; and he will see another peak right ahead of him, steeper and loftier and icier than the last, and so on ad infinitum, ad infinity.

Jest as it was with old Miss Peedick, our present Miss Peedick's mother-in-law. She said (she told me with her own lips) that she knew she should be happy when she got a glass butter-dish. But she said she wasn't; she told me with her own lips that jest as quick as she got that she wanted a sugar-bowl.

The lover thinks when he can once claim his sweetheart, call her his own, he will be blessed and content; but he hain't. No matter how well he loves her, no matter how fond she is of him, and how blest they are in each other's love, they must think, anyway, that the blessedness lacks one thing—permanence.

And though he calls her his own, yet he must feel, if he knows anything, that she is not his own; he must know that he has to dispute for the possession of her daily with one stronger than he is. And if he is tender-hearted and sensitive, the haunting fear must almost rack his soul; the horrible dread of seeing her slip away from him altogether; of sometime reaching out his arms, and finding that nowhere, nowhere can he find her; that in place of her warm, beating heart, whose every throb was full of love for him, is only the vacant spaces, the mysterious wave-beats of emptyness and void; in place of the tender sweetness of her voice, the everlasting silences of eternity.

And though he seek her forever and forever, he can never meet her; never, never, through all this earthly life, find her again. She, the nearest and the dearest, so lately a part of his own life, his own soul, gone from him so swiftly and so utterly, over such a trackless road, as to leave no trace of her footsteps that he may follow her. And though he throw himself upon the turf that covers her, and weary the calm heavens with his wild prayers and questionings, no answer comes;

NO ANSWER.

his words fall back again upon his heart, like dust upon dust.

And then, those who love him tell him that the loving hands were unclasped from his that he might forever reach upward, yearning, longing to clasp them again, that he might make his own hands purer, fitter to clasp an angel's fingers.

That the bright tresses were hidden away under the coffin-lid, that their immortal sheen might gleam through every sunset and every dawning; heaven's golden seal on the sunset of his joy, the morning of his hope, his faith. That the sweet eyes were darkened here that they might become to his sad heart the glowing light of the future. They say this to him, and he listens to them—maybe.

But if this does not happen to him, if his sweetheart lives on beside him, he finds that this mighty presence steals away—not love, for that is a bit of the infinite dropped down into our souls unbeknown to us, and so is immortal; but he steals the golden sheen of the hair, the eye's bright luster, the young form's strength and rounded beauty. Every day, every hour, he is losing something of what he proudly called his own.

You see we don't own much of anything in this world : it's curious, but so it is. And what we call our own don't belong to us, not at all. That is one of the things that makes this such an extremely curious world to live in. Yes, we are situated extremely curious, as much so as the robins and swallows who build their nests on the waving tree-boughs.

We smile at the robin, with our wise, amused pity, who builds her tiny nest with such laborious care high up, out on the waving tree-top, swinging back and forth, back and forth, in every idle wind. Gathering her straws and bits of wood with such patient and tireless care to weave about the frail homes that are to be blown away by the chilly autumn winds, and they also to be driven southward before the snows.

But are not our homes, the sweet homes of our tenderest love, built upon just as insecure foundations, hanging over more mysterious depths, rocking to and fro, and swept to their ruin by a breath from the Unknown? Our dreams, our hopes, our ambitions: what are ye all but the sticks and straws that we weave about our frail nests? Throwing our whole hearts and souls into them, toiling over them, building them for an evanescent summer, to be swept away by the autumn winds. And we also, poor voyagers, blown away through a pathless waste.

But shall we not go unfearing, believing that He who made a balmy south to fulfill the little summer bird's intuition, her blind hope and trust, has also prepared a place to fulfill our deathless longin's, our soul's strongest desires? And over the lonely way, the untried, desolate fields of the future, He will gently guide us thither.

But I am eppisodin'. I said I would relate in this epistol a instance of the devourin' and insatiable vanity of man, and their invincible unwillingness to let well enough alone. And so, although it is gaulin' to me, gaulin' in the extreme, to speak of my companion's weaknesses, yet, if medicine was not spread before patients, how could colic be cured, and cramps, and etcetery?

Yes, in the name of Duty, as a warnin' to the sect,

dear to me (in a meetin'-house way) for his sake of
whom I write, I will proceed, and give a plain and
unvarnished history of Josiah's serenade.

Eliab Gansey, or E. Wellington Gansey, as he has

E. WELLINGTON GANSEY.

rote his name for years, has been here to Jonesville on
a visit. He lives to the Ohio. He is jest about
Josiah's age, and used to be a neighbor of his'n. He
was born here, and lived round here till he got to be a
young man. But he went to the Ohio to live when

he was quite a young chap, and made money fast, and got high in station. Why, some say he got as high as clerk to town meetin'; I don't know about that, but we do know that he got to be a real big man anyway, and come home here on a visit, forehanded and weighin' over 300. He was slim as a lucifer match when he went away, or a darnin'-needle.

Wall, his comin' back as he did made a real commotion and stir in the neighberhood. The neighbers all wanted to do sunthin' to honor him, and make him happy, and we all sort o' clubbed together and got up a party for him, got as good a dinner as ever Jonesville afforded, and held it in old Squire Gansey's dinin'-room. He was cousin to Liab on his father's side, and had a big house and lived alone, and urged us to have the party there.

Wall, I approved of that dinner, and did all I could to help it along. Talked encouragin' about it to all the neighberin' wimmen, and baked two chicken-pies, and roasted a duck, and other vittles accordin'.

And the dinner was a great success. Liab seemed to enjoy himself dretfully, and eat more than was for his good, and so did Josiah; I told Josiah so afterwards.

Wall, we had that dinner for him, all together (as it were). And then we all of us invited him to our own homes seperate, to dinner or supper, as the case might be. We used him first-rate, and he appreciated it, that man did, and he would **have** gone home feelin'

14

perfectly delighted with our treatment of him, and leavin' us feelin' first-rate, if it hadn't been for Josiah Allen, if he had been willin' to take my advice and let well enough alone. And what a happyfyin' thing that is, if folks would only realize it, happyfyin' to the folks that let well enough alone, and happyfyin' to them that are let.

But some are bound to over-do and go beyond all sense and reason. And Josiah wasn't contented with what he had done for Liab, but wanted to do more—he was bound to serenade him. I argued and argued with him, and tried to get the idee out of his head, but the more I argued aginst the idee, the more firm he was sot onto it.

He said it stood Jonesville in hand to treat that man to all the honors they could heap onto him. And then he told me sunthin' that I hadn't heard on before; that Liab talked some of comin' back here to live: he was so pleased with his old neighbors, they had all used him so well, and seemed to think so much of him.

"And," says Josiah, "it will be the makin' of Jonesville if he comes back; and of me, too, for he talks of buyin' my west lot for a house-lot, and he has offered me 4 times what it is worth, of his own accord,—that is, if he makes up his mind to come back."

"Wall," says I, "you wouldn't take advantage of him, and take 4 times what it is worth, would you?" Says I sternly: "If you do you won't never prosper in your undertakin's."

"He offered it himself," says Josiah. "I didn't set no price; he sot it himself. And it wouldn't be no cheatin', nor nothin' out of the way, to take it, and I would take it with a easy conscience and a willin' mind. But the stick is," says he dreamily, "the stick is to get him to come back. He likes us now, and if we can only endear ourselves to him a little mite more he will come. And I am goin' to work for it; I am bound to serenade him."

Says I coldly: "If you want to endear yourself to him you are goin' to work in the wrong way." And says I, still more frigidly: "Was you a layin' out to sing yourself, Josiah Allen?"

"Yes," says he, in a animated way. "The way I thought of workin' it was to have about 8 of us old men, who used to be boys with him, get together and sing some affectin' piece under his winder; make up a piece a purpose for him. And I don't know but we might let some wimmen take a hand in it. Mebby you would want to, Samantha."

"No sir!" says I very coldly. "You needn't make no calculations on me. I shall have no hand in it at all. And," says I firmly, "if you know what is best for yourself, Josiah Allen, you will give up the idee. You will see trouble if you don't."

"Wall, I s'pose it will be some trouble to us; but I am willin' to take trouble to please Liab, as I know it will. Why, if I can carry it out, as I think we can, it will tickle that man most to death. Why, I'll bet after hearin' us sing, as we shall sing, you couldn't dog him from Jonesville. And it will be the makin' of the place if we can only keep him here, and will put more money into my pocket than I have seen for one spell. And I know we can sing perfectly beautiful, if we only set out to. I can speak for myself, anyway; I am a crackin' good singer, one of the best there is, if I only set out to do my best."

Oh! what a deep streak of vanity runs through the naters of human men. As many times as it had been proved right out to his face that he couldn't sing no more than a ginny-hen, or a fannin'-mill, that man still kep' up a calm and perennial idee that he was a sweet singer.

Yes, it is a deep scientific fact, as I have often remarked to Josiah Allen, that the spring of vanity that gushes up in men's naters can't be clogged up and choked. It is a gushin' fountain that forever bubbles over the brink with perennial and joyful freshness. No matter how many impediments you may put in its way, no matter how many hard stuns of disappointment and revilin' and agony you may throw into that fountain, it won't do no more than to check the foamin' current for a moment. But presently, or sometimes even before that, the irrepressible fountain will soar up as foamin'ly as ever.

As many times, and times agin, as Josiah's vanity had been trampled on and beat down and stunned, yet how constant and clear it was a bubblin' up and mean-derin' right before my sight. And before I had got through allegorin' in my own mind about the curious and scientific subject, he gave me another proof of it.

Says he: "I don't want you to think, Samantha, because I said I didn't know but we would let wimmen have a hand in it, I don't want you to think that we want any help in the singin'. We don't want any help in the singin', and don't need any; but I didn't know but you would want to help compose some poetry on Liab. Not but what we could do it first-rate, but its a kind o' busy time of year, and a little help might come good on that account."

Says I, in a very dry tone,—very: "What a lucky thing it is for Tennyson and Longfellow that you and old Bobbet are so cramped for time. There wouldn't probable be no call for their books at all, if you two old men only had time to write poetry; it is dretful lucky for them."

But I didn't keep up that dry, sarcastical tone long. No, I felt too solemn to. I felt that I must get his mind off of the idee if I possibly could. I knew it would be putting the wrong foot forward to come right out plain and tell him the truth, that he couldn't sing no more than a steam-whistle or a gong. No, I knew that would be the wrong way to manage. But I says, in a warnin' and a awful sort of a tone, and a look jest solemn and impressive enough to go with it:

"Remember, Josiah Allen, how many times your pardner has told you to let well enough alone. **You**

had better not try to go into any such doin's, Josiah
Allen.   You'll sup sorrow if you do."

But it was no use. In spite of all my entreaties and
arguments they got it up amongst 'em; composed
some poetry (or what they *called* poetry), and went
and sung it over (or what they *called* singin') night
after night to the school-house; practicin' it secret so
Liab shouldn't hear of it, for they was a lottin' on
givin' him such a joyful surprise.

Wall, they practised it over night after night, for
over a week. And Josiah would praise it up so to me,
and boast over it so, that I fairly hated the word serenade.

"Why," says he, "it is perfectly beautiful, the hull
thirteen pieces we have learnt, but specially the piece
we have made up about him; that is awful affectin'."
And says he: "I shouldn't wonder a mite if Liab
should shed tears when he hears it."

And I'd tell him I persumed it was enough to
bring tears from anybody.

And that would mad him agin.   He would get mad
as a hen at me.   But I didn't care.   I knew I was a
talkin' on principle, and I wasn't goin' to give in an
inch, and I didn't.

Wall, at last the night come that they had sot to
serenade him.   I felt like cryin' all the time he was a
fixin' to go.   For next to bein' a fool yourself, it is
gaulin' to have a pardner make a fool of himself.

But never, never, did I see Josiah Allen so highlarious in his most highlarious times. He acted almost perfectly happy. Why, you would have thought he was a young man to see him act. It was fairly sickish, and I told him so.

"Wall," says he, as he started out, "you can make light of me all you are a mind to, Samantha, but as long as Josiah Allen has the chance to make another fellow-mortal perfectly happy, and put money in his own pocket at the same time, he hain't the feller to let the chance slip."

"Wall," says I coldly, "shet the gate after you."

I knew there wuzn't no use in arguin' any more with him about it. And I think it is a great thing to know when to stop arguin' or preachin' or anythin'. It is a great thing to know enough to stop talkin' when you have got through sayin' anythin'. But this is a deep subject; one I might allegore hours and hours on, and still leave ample room for allegory.

And to resoom and continue on, he started off; and I wound up the clock, and undressed and went to bed, leavin' the back-kitchen door onlocked.

Wall, that was in the neighborhood of 10 o'clock. And I declare for't, and I hain't afraid to own it, that I felt afraid. There I was all alone in the house, sunthin' that hardly ever happened to me, for Josiah Allen was always one that you couldn't get away from home nights if he could possibly help it; and if he did go I almost always went with him. Yes, Josiah Allen is almost always near me; and though he hain't probable so much protection as he would be if he weighed more by the steelyards, yet such is my love for him that I feel safe when he is by my side.

I had read only a day or two before about a number of houses bein' broken open and plundered, besides several cases of rapine; and though I hain't, I persume, so afraid of burglers as I would be if I had ever been burgled, and though I tried to put my best foot forward, and be calm, still, the solemn thought would come to me, and I couldn't drive it away: Who knows but what this is the time that I shall be rapined and burgled?

Oh! what a fearful time I did have in my mind. as I lay there in my usually peaceful feather-bed.

Wall, I got wider and wider awake every minute, and thinkses I, I will get up and light the lamp, and read a little, and mebby that will quiet me down. So I got up and sot down by the buro, and took up the last *World*; and the very first piece I read was a account of a house bein' broke into, between ten o'clock and midnight, and four wimmen massacreed in their beds.

I laid down the *World*, and groaned loud. And then I sithed hard several times. And right there, while I was a sithin', sunthin' come kerslop aginst the window, right by my side. And though I hain't no doubt it was a June bug or a bat, still if it had been a burgler all saddled and bridled that had rode up aginst my winder, it couldn't have skairt me no worse, and I couldn't have jumped no higher, I was that wrought up and excited.

Wall, thinkses I, it is the light that has drawed that bat or June bug aginst the winder, and mebby it will

BURGLERS.

draw sunthin' worse, and I believe I will blow out the light and get into bed agin; I believe I will feel safer.

So I blowed the light out, and got into bed. Wall, I had lain there mebby ten minutes, a tremblin' and a quakin', growin' skairter and skairter every minute,

14*

when all of a sudden I heard a rappin' aginst my winder, and a hoarse sort of a whisper sayin':

"Josiah Allen! Josiah Allen! Miss Allen!"

It didn't sound like no voice that I had ever heard,

and I jest cov-
ered my head up
and lay there,
with my heart a
beatin' so you
c o u l d h a v e
heard it under
the bed. I *knew*
it was a burgler.
I knew my time
had come to be
burgled.

W a l l, t h e
whisperin' and
the rappin' kep'
up for quite a
spell, and then
it kinder died
off; and I got
up and peeked

THE GHOST.

through the winder, and then I see a long white figger
a movin' off round the corner of the house toward the
back-kitchen. And then I was skairter still, for I
knew it was a ghost that was a appearin' to me. And
I had always said, and say still, that I had ruther be
burgled than appeared to.

And there I lay, a tremblin' and a listenin', and pretty soon I heard steps a comin' into the back-kitchen, and so along through the house up to my bed-room door. And then there come a rap right onto my door. And though cold shivers was a runnin' down my back, and goose-pimples was present with me, I knew sunthin' had got to be done.

There I was alone in the house with a ghost. And thinkses I, I must try to use it well, so's to get rid of it; for I thought like as not if I madded it, it would stick right by me. And so I says, in as near the words I could remember, as I had hearn tell they talked to spirits:

"Are you a good spirit?" says I. "If you are a good spirit, raise up and rap three times."

I s'pose my voice sounded low and tremblin' down under the bed-clothes, and my teeth chattered so loud that they probable drounded the words some. But the rappin' kep' up.

And says I agin: "If you are a likely spirit, raise up and rap three times, and then leave." And then says I, for I happened to think what I had heard they done to get 'em away, for I had been that flustrated and horrer-struck that I couldn't think of nothin' hardly, says I:

"I will you away. I will you off out of this house, if you please," I added, for I was so afraid of maddin' it. Thinkses I to myself, I would ruther mad a bur-gler or a rapiner ten times over than to get a apperi-

tion out with me. I s'pose I had spoke up louder this
time, for the ghost (or what I thought was such) answered back to me, and says:

"I am Miss Moony."

Says I: "Not she that was Tamer Sansey?"

"Yes, I be."

Says I, in stern tones, for truth and rectitude is my
theme, even in talkin' with a apperition, and I felt,
skairt as I was, that it would be better to improve a
ghost than to not be a doin' anything in the cause of
right. And so says I firmly:

"Do you stop tellin' such stuff to me." Says I:
"You are a lyin' spirit. Tamer Moony is alive and
enjoyin' middlin' good health, if she wuzn't so nervous.
Eliab Gansey is a visitin' of her now. She never was
a ghost, nor nothin' like it, and apperition or not, you
shan't stand there and lie to me."

Says the voice "Let me in, Miss Allen; I am Miss
Moony, and I am most dead; I am skairt most to
death. And," says she, "I want Josiah Allen to go
over to our house right off. Oh! I am most dead,"
says she.

I begun to grow calmer. I see it wuzn't no ghost,
and says I: "Wait one minute, Miss Moony."

And I ketched up the first weepon I could get holt
of to defend myself, if she should prove to be a imposter. It was Fox'es Book of Martyrs, and I calculated
in case of need to jest throw them old martyrs at her
in a way she would remember. But it didn't prove to

be no imposter. When I opened the door there stood Tamer Moony a tremblin' in her night-gown, with not a sign of a shoe nor a stockin' on her feet, nor a bonnet on, nor nothin'.

"Why, for the land's sake, Tamer Moony,' says I,

TAMER MOONY.

"what is the matter? What are you here at this time of night for, and in this condition?" says I.

"Why," says she, a tremblin' like a popple-leaf, "there is the awfulest goin's on up to our house that you ever see. There is murderin' a goin' on! Liab has been murdered in cold blood!" says she, a wringin' her hands, and groanin' and sithin' like a wild woman.

"What makes you think so?" says I. "What have you seen? Have you been hurt? Where is Mandna?" says I.

"Oh, Mandy has gone over to Dagget's to roust them up. Oh! Oh! them awful sounds! They are a ringin' through my ears yet!" says she, a wringin' her hands and a groanin' wilder than ever.

THE SERENADING PARTY.

Says I firmly, but kindly: "Tamer Moony, try to be calm, and compose yourself down. Tell me jest what you have seen and heerd, and how it begun."

"Wall, in the first place, Mandana and I was rousted up out of sleep by hearin' a noise down in the the yard, and we got up and peeked through the winder, and we see 7 or 8 men,—wild, savage-lookin' men, —a prowlin' along through the yard; some of 'em walked with canes. I persume they had swords in 'em. Mandy thought she see the swords—bloody swords. And as we stood there a peekin' through the blinds, we see 'em prowl their way along round the house towards Liab's winder. And then, a minute or two after, we heerd the awfulest sounds we ever heerd, the most fearful and agonizin'. I s'pose it was Liab a groanin' and screechin' when they killed him. And then they seemed to screech out and yell the most harrowin' and blood-curdlin' sounds I ever heerd. Mandy said she knew they was Injuns. No other race could have made such hideous and unearthly noises. She said she had heerd that Injuns gin jest such awful and melancholy yells when they was on the war-path.

" Wall, them awful sounds took every mite of our strength away. We stood there tremblin' like two leaves, till finally we made out to totter down the back stairs; and she run to Dagget'ses, and I started acrost the lots here, for we thought the hull neighborhood ort to be rousted up. I am most dead ! Oh ! poor Liab ! poor Liab ! And his wife and childern happy at home ! Who will carry the awful news to 'em ? He was probable killed before I got out of the house. I thought I suffered when I lost my husband and 4 childern within a year, but this goes ahead of anything I ever see. So harrowin' and awful ; to have Liab, my only brother, killed right under my ruff, and I couldn't help it. Oh ! what shall I do ? What shall I do ?"

I see she was jest a tumblin' over into a historical fit, and I laid her down on my bed, and broke it to her gradual, what the trouble was. And then she had the historicks worse than ever. She broke out into a laugh so loud that you could hear her clear to the road, and then she broke out a cryin' so you could hear her et cetery and the same. And then she would claw right into me, and tear and rip round.

But good land! she didn't know what she was a doin', she was so full of the historicks. She was jest a pullin' and a tearin' at the bottom sheet when Josiah Allen came a meachin' in. A meachiner-lookin' creeter I never beheld. And from what I learned afterwards, well he might meach. And as bad as he looked, he looked worse when I says to him, says I:

"I told you, Josiah Allen, to let well enough alone, but you wouldn't; and you can see now what you have done with your serenadin' and foolery. You have killed Miss Moony, for what I know, and," says I, in still sterner axents, "a hull piece of factery cloth won't make our loss good."

Then Josiah groaned awful, and says I:

"What worse effects have follered on after your serenadin', I don't know."

Josiah kep' on a groanin' pitifuller and pitifuller, and I see then that his head was all bruised up. It looked as if he had been pelted with sunthin' hard, and there was a bunch riz up over his left eye as big as a banty's egg, and it was a swellin' all the time stiddy and constant. And from that night, right along, I kep' bread and milk poultices on it, changin' from lobelia to catnip, as I see the swellin' growed or diminished.

His sufferin's was awful, and so was mine, for all the first 3 days and nights I thought it would mortify, do the best I could, it looked that black and angry. His agony with it was intense, and also with his mind

THE BRUISED JOSIAH.

—his mind bein' near the swellin', made it worse, mebby—his mortification and disapointment was that overwhelmin' and terrible.   It was the water-pitcher, as I hearn afterwards, that Liab had pelted him with.

I s'pose from what I heerd afterwards, that they had the awfulest time that was ever heard of in Jonesville, or the world.   Liab jest throwed everything at 'em he could lay his hands on.   Why, them old men was jest about killed. He pretended to think they was burglers and tramps, but I never believed it for a minute. I believe it madded him to be waked up out of a sound sleep, and see them 8 old creeters makin' perfect fools of themselves.

Some think that he had been kinder sot up by some jealous-minded person, and made to think the Jonesvillians wanted to make money out of him, and cheat him; and he was always dretful quick-tempered, that everybody knows.

And some think that he thought it was a lot of young fellers dressed up in disguise, a tryin' to make fun of him, callin' him "Eliab." He always hated the name Eliab, and had felt above it for years, and wrote his name E. Wellington Gansey. But as he left on the first train in the morning, I don't s'pose we shall ever know the hull truth of the matter.

But anyway, whatever was the cause, he bruised up them old men fearful. Eliab was strong and perseverin', and a good calculator, or he never could have laid up the property he had. Every blow hit jest where it would hurt the worst. He pelted them old men perfectly fearful. They had composed a lot of verses —over 20 they say there was of 'em—that they was a layin' out to sing to him. They didn't sing but 3, I believe, when the first boot hit 'em, but they say they kep' on singin' the next verse, bein' determined to mollify him down, till they got so bruised and battered

THE SERENADE.

up that they had to flee for their very lives. The
verses run like this:

> Who did from the Ohio come
> To visit round in his old home,
> And make the neighbers happy, some?
> > Eliab.

> With melody we him will cheer,
> And keep Eliab Gansey here.
> Who is this man we love so dear?
> > Eliab.

> If music sweet as can be had
> Can sooth thee, make thee blest and glad,
> Then never more shalt thou be sad,
> > Eliab.

I s'pose it was jest at this very minute that the
washbowl flew and struck old Bobbet in the small of
the back, and crumpled him right down; he was sort
o' bent over the accordeon. They didn't play the
accordeon all the time they was singin', as I have been
told, but between the verses; jest after they would sing
"Eliab," they would play a few notes sort o' lively.

It was Josiah's idea, as I heard afterwards, their
takin' the accordeon. They couldn't one of 'em play
a tune, or anything that sounded like a tune, but he
insisted it would look more stylish to have some instru-
ment, and so they took that old accordeon that used to
belong to Shakespeare Bobbet.

They had planned it all out, and had boasted that

they had got up something in their own heads that hadn't never been heerd of in Jonesville. And well they might say so, well they might.

Wall, there wasn't one of them 8 old fellers that was good for anything for the next 4 weeks. Eliab's folks try to make the best of it. They say now that Eliab always did, when he was first rousted up out of a sound sleep, act kinder lost and crazy. They tell that now to kind o' smooth it over, but I think, and I always shall think, that he knew jest who he was a hittin', and what he was a hittin' 'em with. It was the glass soap-dish that struck old Dagget's nose. And I wish you could have seen that nose for the next 3 weeks. It used to be a Roman, but after that night it didn't look much like a Roman.

Eliab's boots was the very best of leather, and they had a new-fashioned kind of heels, some sort o' metal or other, and Cornelius Cook says they hit as powerful as any cannon balls would; he goes lame yet. You know the shin-bone is one of the tenderest bones in the hull body to be hit aginst.

It was the bootjack that hit the Editor of the Augur'ses head. His wife was skairt most to death about him, and she says to me—she had come over to see if she could get some wormwood—and she says:

" He never will get over that bootjack in the world, I don't believe. His head is swelled up as big as two heads ought to be."

And says I: "It always happens so, don't it, that the weakest spot is the one that always gets hit?"

I was sorry for her as I could be. And I gin her the wormwood, and recommended her to use about half and half smartweed. Says I: "Smartweed is good for the outside of his head, and if it strikes in it won't hurt him none."

I felt to sympathize with her. Old Sansey hain't got over the slop-jar yet. It brought on other complaints that he was subject to, and the Dr. says he may get over it, and he may not.

But as bad as it was for all the rest, it was the worst for Josiah Allen—as bad agin.

It wuzn't so much the hurt he got that night, though I thought for quite a spell that it would have to be operated on, and I didn't know but it would prove to be his death-blow. And it wuzn't so much our sufferin's with Miss Moony, though them was fearful, bein' up with her all that night, and workin' over her to keep the breath of life in her, and she a clawin' at us, and a ketchin' holt of us, and a laughin', and a cryin'. We had to send for the neighbors, we was that skairt about her, and Josiah had to go for the doctor right in the dead of night, with his head a achin' as if it would split open.

And it wuzn't so much the thought of losin' Eliab and money, though Josiah was dretfully attached to both, and he felt the loss of both on 'em more deeply than tongue can ever tell. But that wuzn't where the deepest piece of iron entered his soul. It was to think his singin' had got called so all to nort. He thought he was such a sweet, dulcet harmonist; he had gloated and boasted so over his lovely, melodious voice, and thought he was goin' to be admired so for it; and then to think his singin' had skairt two wimmen most to death, had skairt one into fits, anyway—for if ever a woman had a historical fit Tamer Moony had one that night. And instead of his serenade winnin' Liab's love and money, it had disgusted him so that he had pelted him most to death.

Oh! it was a fearfully humiliatin' blow to his vanity. The blow on his forward wasn't to be compared to the soreness of the blow onto his vanity, though the swellin' on his forward was bigger than a butnut, and as sore as any bile I ever see.

Yes, I have seen Josiah Allen in tryin' places, time and agin, and in places calculated to make a man meach, but never, never did I see him in a place of such deep meachin'ness and gloom as he was that night after he had come home with Doctor Bamber. There he was, at the very time, the very night, when he had lotted on bein' covered with admiration and glory like a mantilly, there he wuz lookin', oh, so pitiful and meek, bowed down by pain, contumily, and water-pitchers. And he happened to pass by the bed where Miss Moony lay, and she, bein' blind with historicks, laid holt of him, and called him "Mandana." She clutched right into his vest, and held him tight, and says she:

"Oh Mandana! Oh! them awful voices! Oh! them horrible, screechin' yells! I can't forget 'em," says she. "They are ringin' through my ears yet."

And then Dr. Bamber and the neighbors knew all about what it wuz that had skairt her so; there they stood a laughin' in their sleeves (as it were). And

MANDANA! MANDANA!

Josiah standin' there, lookin' as if he must sink. And there Samantha wuz, who had vainly argued with him, and entreated him to let well enough alone.

Yes, Josiah Allen was in a hard place, a very hard place. But he couldn't get away from her, so he had to grin and bear it. For he couldn't onclench her hands; she had a sort of a spazzum right there, a holdin' him tight. And every time she would come to a little, she would call him "Mandana," and yell about them "awful, blood-curdlin' screeches." It was a curious time—very.

Wall, she got better after a while. Dr. Bamber give her powerful doses of morpheen, and that quelled her down.

But morpheen couldn't quiet down Josiah Allen's feelin's, nor ease the sore spot in his vanity. No! all the poppies that ever grew in earthly gardens couldn't do it. He never will start out a seranadin' agin, I don't believe—never.

I hain't one to be a twittin' about things. But sun-thin' happened to bring the subject up the other mornin' jest after breakfast, and I says this, I merely observed this to him:

"Wall, you wanted to make a excitement, Josiah Allen, and you did make one."

"Wall, wall! who said I didn't?"

Says I: "You have most probable done your last seranadin'."

I said this in a mild and almost amiable axent, but you ort to heard how that man yelled up at me.

Says he: "If I was a woman, and couldn't keep from talkin' so dumb aggravatin', I'd tie my tongue to my teeth. And if you are a goin' to skim the milk for that calf, why don't you *skim* it?"

"Wall," says I mildly, "I hain't deef."

A STITCH IN THE BACK.

JUDAS WART AND SUFFERIN' WIMMIN.

ONE mornin', not long after Miss Bobbet's visit, I was a doin' up my mornin's work. I had been a little belated, for my companion Josiah, while fodderin', had been took in his back sudden and violent with a stitch.

He is subject to such stitches, but they are very painful and inconvenient. All the way he could walk round the house was by leanin' upon a broom-stick. He found the broom-handle in the barn, and come in leanin' heavy on it, and groanin' powerful and frequent. It skairt me awfully.

I never hinted to him that I thought more'n as likely as not that stitch was sent as a judgment; no, I held firm, and kep' my tongue still with almost giant force. That day, when the sun had rose up clear and lofty in the heavens, was the time I had calculated to tackle him. But I was too honorable to tackle a pardner who was down with a stitch.

No, I treated him well, bathed his back in linament,

and he was a lyin' behind the stove on the lounge, as comfortable as anybody could be in his situation of back and conscience.

As I said, I was a washin' up my dishes in the but-

ELDER JUDAS WART.

tery, when all of a sudden in walked Elder Judas Wart. The door was open, it bein' a pleasant mornin', and he jest rapped at the side of the door, and walked in.

I guess he didn't see Josiah, the lounge bein' kinder behind the door; but he seemed dretful tickled to see me—tickleder fur than I was. Though, havin' my mission in view, I used him well, and sot him a chair. But little did I think what was before me; little did I think what the awfulness of his first words to me would be. He hadn't been in that house five minutes, for I know I had only jest hung up my dish-cloth (for knowin' what a tussle of principle was ahead of me, and feelin' as if I should need all my strength in the conflict, I left the heaviest of my dishes to wash at noon, for the first time in over fourteen months).

Wall, if you can believe it, jest as I got that dish-

cloth hung up, that man, with no phraseoligies **or ex-**
cuses or anything, that man up and says:

"I have heard, and I see for myself, that you are **a**
very smart woman, and you could do wonders in the
true church if you was married to some leadin' man,

RESCUING THE ELDER.

—to me, for instance," says he, bold as brass, " or was
sealed to me," says he, spittin' hard onto the floor.
But that man hadn't hardly got that seal and that
tobacco-juice out of his mouth, when Josiah Allen
sprung up and leveled that broom-stick at him with a
deadly aim. I sprung forward and threw the end of
the broom-stick up jest in time to save the Elder's life.

I forced him to desist, I and the stitch; for truly the effort was too much for him. The stitch griped him awful, and he sunk back with a agonizin' groan.

I wanted Josiah to stay his hand and the broomstick for two reasons. One was, I didn't want the Elder killed quite so quick—not till after I had had a chance to convert him. And another reason was, I thought of my deep agony and a Widder Bump, and thinkses I to myself, though the medicine is fearful to administer, as gaulin' and bitter as wormwood and sicuta biled down in tar and vinegar, still I felt it was what my companion needed to show him the nefariousness and heniousness of Mormonism, in its true light.

I wouldn't in his present weakness of mind and back, throw the Widder Bump in his face, as I might have done. Some pardners would have jest turned round on him, as he lay there on that lounge, and throwed that woman full and square in his face. But I didn't. I see he was a sufferin' enough without that. He was takin' the matter to himself like a blister, as anybody has got to, in order to feel the smart. A blister don't draw half so powerful, nor feel half so bad, when it is on somebody else'es back, as it does when it is on our'n. He was a meditatin' how it would seem to his heart to lose the companion of his youth and middle age. He was a eatin' of that sass which ganders think is quite good for geese to eat. He was seein' now how it would relish to a gander. I pitied him from the bottom of my heart, his looks was such.

But Elder Judas Wart had no such feelin's of pity and sympathy, and bein' excited by Josiah's ragin' wrath, and maddened by the broom-stick, he spoke out, in a angry, sarcastical tone:

"Your husband felt different on this subject last spring. He seemed almost inclined at one time to take to himself another helpmate. There was a certain widder, there"—

"You lie, sir!" says Josiah, springin' up to his feet. "There wuzn't no widder there, and I never was there."

"Never was where?" says I, in a awful voice; for curiosity and various other emotions was a hunchin' me, as hard as ever a woman was hunched by 'em.

"I never was anywhere! I never was to their meetin's, nor to nowhere else."

"Where wuz you, then?" says I, in that same strange voice.

"I told you I wuzn't *nowhere*, didn't I?" he yelled out in fearful axents.

But Elder Judas Wart went right on a talkin' to me, stiddy as fate, and as hard to be turned round as she.

"He seemed then to look at the Widder"—

"I never looked at a widder! I never see none! I never see a widder in my life!"

Says I: "Josiah Allen, be calm!"

"I tell you I won't be calm! And I tell you there hain't no widders there—nor hain't never been any— nor nowhere else—nor I never heard of any."

He was delerious, and I see that he was. But Elder Judas Wart kep' right on, with a haughty, proud axent:

"He seemed then to look favorably upon the widder I have lately espoused. The Widder Bump; don't you remember her?"

"No! I don't remember no such widder, and I don't believe there was any by that name."

"Why," says I, "Josiah Allen, she made that coat you have got on. Don't you remember it?"

"No! I don't! She didn't make it! It wuzn't made! I never had none."

"Why, Josiah Allen," says I, "what will become of you if you tell such stories?"

"There won't nothin' become of me, nor never will; there never has nothin' become of me."

But jest as he said this, the stitch ketched him agin powerful and strong, and he sunk down on the lounge, a groanin' violent.

I see he was delerious with pain of body, and fur deeper, more agonizin' pain of mind, contrition, shame, remorse, and various other emotions.

And then, oh, the strength and power of woman's love! As that man lay there, with all his past weakness and wickedness brought out before me, stricken with agony, remorse, and stitches, I loved him, and I pitied him. I felt that devoted, yearnin', tender feelin' for him to that extent that I felt in my heart that if it were possible I could take that stitch upon me, and bear it onward myself, and relieve my pardner. Women's love is a beautiful thing, a holy thing, but curious, very.

I reviled my pardner not, but covered him tenderly up with my old woolen shawl, sot the broomstick up against the lounge, and he lay there and never said another word, only at intervals—when a pain of uncommon size would ketch him in his back or conscience, he would groan loud and agonizin'. But I see it was no use to argue with him then about the Widder Bump.

But if you'll believe it, I can't make him to this day say nothin' diffcrent. I have had a great many talks with him on the subject, but, he says, " She is a woman he never see."

And the nearest I ever made him own up to it was once when I had talked real good to him, talked to him about his past wickedness and tottlin' morals, and told him how I knew his morals was straightened and propped up now, good and sound, and his affections stabled and firm sot where they should be sot. I talked awful good to him, and he seemed to be sort o' melted down. And he owned up " that it did seem to him as if he had heard, when he was a child, of a woman by that name, that lived somewhere near here. It was either that name, or Bumper—he couldn't for his life tell which."

And I gin up then. Truly there are strange pages

in a man's nater, filled with curious language, curiouser than conundrums: who can read 'em?

As I said, havin' the aim in my mind that I did have, havin' a desire to let Josiah Allen get a full taste of that sass that he, as well as other ganders, find is fur different to eat themselves, and to stand haughtily on one leg (to foller out the gander simely) and see their mates eat it. Havin' a desire to let him get a full glimpse of the awful depth and blackness and horrer of the abyss he had suspended himself over, I did not rebuke Elder Judas Wart as I should, had it not been for that. I merely told him, when he said sunthin' agin about my bein' sealed to him—I merely said to him, with dignity and firmness:

Says I, "If you say that word seal to me agin, I'll seal you in a way you won't never want to be sealed!" Says I, in still more awful tones, glancin' at the bilin' teakettle, "If you say that word to me agin in my house, I'll scald you, if it is the last work I ever do in my life, and I am hung for it the next minute."

My face was red; I was fearfully excited with my almost giant efforts to control myself. To think that he should dare to approach me! me! Josiah Allen's wife! with his infamous offer. He see that my looks was gettin' terrible and scareful, and he hastened to say:

" I meant it in a religious way."

And I was that excited and mad, that I spoke right up and says, " Wall! I'll scald you in a religious way;"

and I added, in a firm, low tone, "But I'll bet a cent you won't never want to be scalded agin as long as you live."

Says he, in a sort of a apologizin', meachin' way, "It is my religion to marry various wives."

"Wall," says I, still clingin' to my simely, as great

HOT WATER.

oriters always do, "It is my religion to scald you, if you don't stop your insultin' talk instantly and to once! You can't talk no such stuff in the house of her who was once Smith," says I, glancin' agin at the teakettle, and steppin' up a little nearer to it.

"Be composed, mum," says he, a hitchin' up his

15*

chair a little nearer the door; " Be composed ! I was
speakin' in a strictly religious sense."

Says I, " You can't never make me think a crime
can be committed religiously." And agin I looked
longin'ly at that teakettle.

" Compose yourself down, mum, and let us argue for
a brief spell," says he.

His tone was sort o' implorin' and beseechin'. And
he took a plug of tobacco out of his coat-pocket, and
bit a great chew off'en it, and put it into his mouth,
I s'pose to try to show off and make himself attractive. But good land ! how foolish it was in him. He
didn't look half so well to me as he did before, and
that hain't sayin' but a very little, a very little indeed.

He wadded the tobacco all up on one side of his
mouth, till his cheek stood out some like a wen, and
the tobacco-juice started and run down on each side of
his chin. And so, havin' fixed himself, I s'pose, so his
looks suited him, he says agin :

" Less argue the subject."

I see that here was the chance I had wanted to convince him of his iniquity. I see that Duty was leadin'
a war-horse up in front of me all saddled and bridled,
ready for me to mount and career onward nobly on
the path of Right.

I see that Duty was holdin' in this charger by the
martingills with one hand, and with the other she was
holdin' out a pair of spurs to me. And though never,
never, did a war-horse look so prancin' and dangerous

"LESS ARGUE."

to me, and never did spurs look so heavy and sharp
and tejus to my achin' heels, yet Josiah Allen's wife
is not one to turn her back to Duty's call—no, my
desire to battle with the wrong, my martyrous spirit
curbed me in and let me hear him talk.

And he went on to tell me that in the first place he
wanted to lay before me the rise, progress, and glory
of the Mormon Church.   Says he, "In the first place,
you know, mum, that God made a distinct revelation
to us.   Our bible was found written on plates of gold.
Them plates "—

I am naturally very well-bread.   And thinkin' mebby
it would influence him towards the right, I didn't lay
out to interrupt him, or disturb his arguments, till he
had got through presentin' of 'em.   But the idee of
such imposture—imposture in the name of God—so
worked on me, that I spoke right out, in a firm, dignified tone, but very solemn:

"Elder Judas Wart, you jest pass them plates."

Says he: "Why should I pass 'em? The revelation
of God is written on 'em."

"Revelation!" says I.   "I should jest as soon go
into my buttery, and read my meat plates and platters,
as to read 'em.   I should find jest as much of a revelation on 'em."   And agin I says, with dignity: "You
pass them plates."

Says he: "I wont pass 'em."   And he begun agin,
in a sort of a boastin' way: "September 22, 1827, the

angel Moroni placed in Joseph Smith's hand our Mormon bible, or that is, the plates, that"—

Says I: "Hain't I told you to pass them plates? Your bible is a romance writ by Solomon Spaulding jest for fun, jest to see how near he could write like the bible. And it is a powerful lesson to me, and should be to everybody, of the terrible harvest that may spring up from one careless, thoughtless deed. The awful consequences, the sin, and the woe that followed that one irreverent, thoughtless act might well make us all more thoughtful, more mindful of the terrible responsibility that follows all our acts, the smallest as well as the greatest. We can't shake off that personal responsibility. It follers us tight as our shadders even into our hours of recreation, showin' us that we should not only work nobly, but recreate nobly and innocently and reverently."

"But," says he "them plates"—

But I was so rousted up with my emotions, that I waved out my right hand with awful dignity, and says I:

"You *shall* pass them plates."

And I held firm, and made him pass 'em. And he went to bringin' up the miracles that had been done by the early church—curing the lame and deaf, healing the sick, and et cetery, and so forth. Says he: "I have heard that you are a woman that loves reason and fair play," and says he, "you can't get over those miracles, can you?"

Says I candidly: "I don't want to get over no miracles, and hain't tried to. But I can say with the poet, that so far as believin' of 'em is concerned, miracles is sunthin' I had ruther see done myself than to hear of 'em. Howsumever, I hain't a goin' to say that you hain't done 'em. As to healin' the sick, the wonderful power and magnetism one strong mind can exert over a weaker one, when the weaker one has perfect faith in it, has a great many times performed deeds that looked miracilas, out of the Mormon church, and most probable in it. But even if you have raised the dead, which I don't think you claim you have done, it would make me no more a believer in mormonism; for we read of a woman not religious, who did that. And I never hankered after keepin' company with Miss Endor, or wanted to neighbor with her, or appear like her."

"You are unreasonable, mum," says he.

"I don't mean to be," says I. "I have allowed all you want me to, and more too. What more can you want?"

"You deride our holy church. Our church foundered on the Commandments of God."

"Which one?" says I enquirin'ly.

"Which one?" says he haughtily. "Every one of 'em; every one of 'em."

"Wall," says I calmly and reasonably, but with quite a lot of dignity, "we'll see." And I was risin' up to go and get the Bible offen the stand, for I was determined he should see 'em in black and white, when he spoke out haughtily and proudly:

"Keep your seat, mum; keep your seat. I have the Bible here in my breast pocket. Our church bein' foundered on the Commandments, leanin' up aginst 'em as we do for all our strength and safety, I don't depend on Bibles layin' round loose on stands, and so forth. I carry a copy all the time right over my heart, or pretty near over it—on the left side of my vest, anyway."

Says I: "There is different ways of carryin' things in the heart. But that is a deep subject, and I will not begin to episode upon it, for if I should begin, no knowin' how fur I should episode to, but will merely say that there is other ways of carryin' things in your heart besides carryin' 'em in your vest pocket. But howsumever, read off the first one." And he read it:

"Thou shalt have no other Gods before me."

He read it off jest like a text. And the minute he stopped I begun to talk on it a good deal like preachin', only shorter; but with jest about the same dignity and mean that preachers have.

Says I, in that firm, preachin' tone: "You have made Brigham Young a God. Your preacher, whom you call a 'model saint,' openly avowed that he was God. You have pretended to believe, and have taught to the people his blasphemus doctrine that he had power to save souls in the heavenly kingdom, or to shut 'em out of it." Says I: "I could spread out this awful idee, and cover hours with it, and then not make it very thin, either; there is so much that could be said on the awfulness of it. But 1 have got nine more jobs jest like it ahead on me to tackle, so enough, and suffice it to say, fetch on your next one.

He was goin' to branch out and say sunthin', but I held to my first idee, and wouldn't let him. I told him if I argued with him at all, he had got to read those Commandments off jest like texts, and let me preach on 'em. 1 told him after I had got through with 'em, then he could rise up and explain his mind, and talk; but jest at present it was the commands of God I wanted to hear—not the words of Elder Judas Wart. And I held firm, and made him. And when he would begin to argue I would call for another one, and kep' him at it.

"Thou shalt not make unto thee any graven image * * * * thou shalt not bow down to them, nor serve them"—

Says I: "You have done that and worse. You have worshipped and revered an image of clay—rather weak clay, too, though held up by a mighty will and ambition. Why, most anybody would say that a graven image would be sounder than he was—more sort o' solid and substantial. Anyway, it wouldn't wobble round as he wobbled, preachin' one thing to-day, and denyin' it to-morrow, jest as his own interests dictated. And the graven image wouldn't have been so selfish and graspin' and unscrupulus. It would have been fur honester, and wouldn't have wanted more'n a hundred wives. But that image of clay, such as it was, **you sot up and worshipped, and you needn't deny it.**"

He didn't try to.   He knew it wouldn't be no use to,
and says he :

"Thou shalt not take the name of the Lord thy God
in vain."

Says I, in a firm, awful axent, "You have taken it
in vain, the weakest kind of vanity, and you have
taken it wickedly, the wickedest kind of wickedness,
in darin' to commit this sin in the name of God."

Says he, "Remember the Sabbath day to keep it
holy."

Says I, "You have kept it holy, by teachin' this
unholy sin.   By assemblin' at the tabernacle to listen
to words so low, and vulgar, and weak that they would
be contemptible, if they were not so wicked and blas-
phemous."

Says he, "Honor thy father and thy mother."   He
spoke up awful quick and some haughty.   He felt
what I had said, I knew it by his mean, and he seemed
to read this with a air as if this was sunthin' he could
lean aginst hard, and nobody could hender its bein' a
support to him.   He looked sort o' independent and
overbearin' at me as he finished readin' it, and he spit
on the floor in a sort of a proud way.

But I went right on, in a deep and impressive axent,
and says I, "You have made that commandment impossible for your children to follow.   You have wickedly deprived your children of one of the holiest and
most sacred things in life.   A child's right to honor
the parents they love, and feel it their duty to rever-

ence.   But how can anybody, unless he is a fool or a
luny, honor what hain't honorable?   How can a child
honor a parent whose hands are stained with innocent
blood, who is enriched by theft and rapine, who is

MOUNTAIN MEADOWS.

living in open
shame — in open
defiance to the
commonest rules
of morality—who
breaks all the

commandments of God, and calls it religion?"

Says he, "Thou shalt not kill."

Says I, " The teachers of your religion say, Thou
shalt kill, if it is for the safety and enrichment of the
Mormon church.   And, following their commands
instead of God's, you killed one hundred and 20 inno-

cent men, wimmen, and children in one day. And how many other murders have been committed by orders of your church, in those lonely deserts and mountain roads and canyons, will never be known till the searchin' light of the great day of doom reveals all secret things. Why," says I, "Brigham Young taught that Mormons should shed each other's blood for the remission of sins."

He looked meachin', very. He didn't try to argue on this—he couldn't, for he knew I could prove what I had said. And he looked meachiner yet, as he read the next one :

" Thou shalt not commit adultery."

Says I, "The hull Mormon church is built up on the ruins of this broken commandment, and you know it. And you teach this doctrine, that the more pieces you break this commandment into, the higher it is goin' to boost you up into heaven. The meaner and lower you be on earth, the higher place you will have in the heavenly kingdom— "

Says he, interruptin' of me with a look of fearful meach restin' on his eyebrow, and speakin' up dretful quick :

" Thou shalt not steal."

Says I, " Your church teaches, 'thou *shalt* steal.' And you have to do it too, and you know it."

Says he, " Thou shalt not bear false witness against thy neighber."

Says I, " Ask the unhappy Gentiles who have incurred the displeasure or aroused the cupidity of the Mormon church, whether the Mormon commandment, 'Thou *shalt* bear false witness against thy neighber,' has not been followed, and followed, too, to the death."

"Thou shalt not covet"—and he said over the hull on 'em—wife, property, and maidservant.

Says I, "Your church teaches thou shalt covet 'em, every one of 'em, and get 'em, too, the hull on 'em— wife, property, and maidservant, 'specially the maid-servant."

He quailed. And right there, while he was a quail-in', I spoke, and says coldly :

"Now, Elder Judas Wart, you have read off the commandments of God, one by one, and I have preached on 'em ; now tell me, and tell me plain, which one do you lean on the hardest ?"

Says he, "As it were—that is, you know— "

"No!" says I, with dignity, "I don't know, nor you don't, nuther."

Says he, "I—that is—you—you are unreasonable, mum." And he looked curious, and spit fiercely onto the stone hearth and the floor.

"I don't mean to be," says I. "I sot out in this talk with principles as hefty as I ever hefted in my life, and if I hain't a good judge of the common heft of principles, nobody ever was. Why," says I, "the rights and wrongs of my sect has for years been held nearer to my heart than any earthly object, exceptin' my Josiah. And I can tell you, and tell you plain,

that I have laid awake nights a thinkin' over what my
sect has endured a settin' under that Mormon church.
And daytimes I have sot a knittin' and thought of the
agonies of them female wimmen till there wuzn't a
dry eye in my head, and I couldn't tell for my life
whether I was a seamin' or a knittin' plain, or what
I was a doin'. For of all the sufferin's my sect has
suffered from the hands of man, this doctrine of
polygamy is the very crown, the crown of thorns.
Other wrongs and woes have spilte earth for her time
and agin, but this destroys her hope of heaven. When
other sorrows and wrongs broke her heart, killed her,
she could still look to the time when she could take the
hand of Death, the Healer, and he would lead her into
Repose, give her the peace earth had denied her. She
could think that all her burdens of sorrows and wrongs
would drop from her into the grave; and in that land
where all tears are wiped away—that land of eternal
beauty—of sweet consolation for the weary—she could
find rest. But this last hope of the broken-hearted,
your accursed doctrine has destroyed. Your infamous
belief teaches that if a woman won't do wrong, won't
submit to man's tyrannical will on earth, commit sin
for his sake, he won't let her go to heaven! Good
land!" says I, "it makes me sweat to think on't."
And I wiped my forward on my apron.

Says he: "As it were, you know."

"No, I don't know it," says I warmly. "Nor I
never shall know it."

Says he: "And so forth, and so on."

He acted embarassed and skairt, and well he might. Why, the abomination of their doctrine is so abominable, that when it is presented to 'em in a eloquent, high-toned way by a woman who talks but little, but that little earnest and deep; when she places it before 'em in the axent she always handles when talkin' on principle, and with the soarin', deep look of her spectacles she always uses on them occasions—why, it is enough to skair anybody to death.

But in a moment or so he sort o' rousted up, and says he:

"If you think so much of female wimmen as you say you do, I should think you would think about what the position of these plural wives would be if polygimy were abolished. What would they be thought of? What would they be?"

Says I, in awful tones: "What be they now?"

"Wall," says he, "if they should be divorced they wouldn't be looked upon as they are now."

"No," says I, "that is very true; they wouldn't, not at all, not by me."

Says he: "They would be looked down upon more."

Says I, with dignity: "Stoppin' sinnin' hadn't ort to make anybody thought less on," says I. That hain't accordin' to my creed or my skripter."

Says he: "If they was divorced their situation would be very painful and humiliatin'."

Says I, very dryly: "It is now, in my estimation."

Says he : " Look at the position of the childern of these unions, that would be left fatherless. What a sad scene it would be; helpless infancy made a mark for contumely and sneers ; babyhood blamed, scorned."

Says I: " They wouldn't be scorned, not by anybody whose scorn would be worth havin'. Nobody but a fool or a luny is in the habit of blamin' folks for doin' what they can't help doin', and bein' what they can't help bein'. Blame the childern! Why, good land!" says I, " I should jest as soon set out and scold a mornin'-glory or a white violet for the looks of the ground they sprung from. God's own purity is writ in the clear eyes of babyhood, and in the blue heart of them mornin'-glories. Blossoms of light, mornin'-glories, springin', God knows how or why, out of the black mould, out of darkness and decay. Who could look scoffin'ly or irreverently on 'em, or on them other blossoms of innocence, springin' as mysteriously from as dark a soil, and touched by the hand of God with as pure and divine a beauty."

" Unpractical, unpractical female, led away as females ever are by sympathies and views of right and wrong. Oh! thank Heaven! thank Heaven! such dangerous qualities are not incorporated into politics. I should tremble for the nation if it were so."

And agin he looked fiercely at the stove-hearth.

"Unpractical female, what would become of the childern left, as it were, fatherless ?"

Says I: "If the parents of the childern are rich

enough, let 'em support 'em; and the poor ones—I
know a man who will adopt the hull lot, and be glad
of the chance," says I proudly. "It is a uncle of mine,
a uncle I am proud to own. Samuel is his name, and
nobility and generosity is his nater." Says I: "Let
these childern and the wimmen, if necessary, be took
care of by the government, and let the evil end with
this generation."

"But what would the position of these wimmen be
in society; what would they be?"

"What be they *now?*" says I agin. And I snapped
out that "now" considerable snappish, for I was gettin'
a good deal wore out with him. Says I: "You seem
to think it would be the death-blow to their reputation
to stop sinnin', stop livin' in wickedness; but there is
where you and I differ. I should think as much agin
of 'em."

And says I: "If a evil is a goin' to stop, it has got
to begin to stop sometime, or else it won't never get
stopped. More of these unholy unions have taken
place durin' the past year than ever before in the same
length of time. Powerful efforts are bein' made to
strengthen and extend the power of the system. And
it must either be stopped, or else go on widening and
spreading, and destroying this beautiful new world as it
destroyed so many other strong, proud nations that were
glorious in the past." Says I: "Can I set still and
see it go on, and can Josiah set still, and other female

pardners, and other Josiahs, and not long to lift a hand
to turn back this flood of woe and desolation?"

Here Josiah groaned aloud. He had his thoughts
there on that lounge, though he lay middlin' still. His
thoughts goared him worse than that stitch did, ten
times over. And I felt sorry for him, my feelin's for
him are such; and I brought his name in in a friendly
way, just because my love for him was so strong, and
I forgive him so.

Says I: "Elder Judas Wart, I won't take you back
to the old Jewish nations, round by Italy, Spain, and
other roundabout ways, as I might do, and as some
wimmen who are more talkative than I be probable
would, and show you all the way the ruins or the
nations ruined by this crime of polygimy. But I am
a woman who says but little, but that little I mean, and
I will merely hold up Turkey before you. And while
I am holdin' up that Turkey, I will merely mention the
fact to you, that you and everybody else knows, and
that Turkey knows it well, and if it should speak up
and own the truth it would say that it was the effects
of this system that made it so weak and impotent.
Weaker as a nation than our old turkey-gobbler; fur
weaker than a hen-turkey. (I make use of the gobbler
as a poetical metafor, and would wish to be so understood.)

"Will not America and Josiahs heed these warnin's?" says I, lookin' right up at the ceilin', in a
rapped way. "Will they not listen to the voice of

doom that rises from the ruins of other nations, glorious and proud and strong in the past, that has crumbled into ashes from the effects of this sin? Will they not," I went on in a still more rapped, eloquent way, " will they not bend down their ears and hear the wail of warnin' that seems to float along over the dust of the desert from old Babylon herself, warnin' to this new, fresh, western world to escape this enervatin', destroyin' sin, and escape her doom? Will not America and Josiahs take warnin by the fate of these nations? or will they go on in careless merriment and feastin', unheedin' those terrible words ' *mean! mean!* ' writ up in the blue vault above, till it is too late; till the land is given to the enimy; till weakness, ruin, and decay take the septer from Columbia's tremblin', shakin' grasp, and rain over this once strong, lovely land."

I sithed, I almost wept—I was so fearfully agitated —and says I : " If this threat'nin' doom that threatens our beloved land is to be averted, if this evil is to be stopped, when is there a better time than the present to stop it in, now," says I, wipin' my eyes on my apron, "now, while America has got me to help her ? " And agin I sithed, and agin I almost shed tears, and wept.

He see my agitation, and took advantage of it. Says he : " You seem to be tender-hearted, Josiah Allen's wife, and to have a great affection for the female sect, and yet you don't seem to think of the hearts that

16

would be wrung by the agony of seperation. Why," says he, "if they should part with their companions, they would be unhappy."

Says I, lookin' out of the open window, fur away over the tree-tops, over the blue lake beyond—and beyond—

My spectacles seemed to look very fur off. They had a very deep and sort o' soarin' look to 'em, somewhat happy, and somewhat sorrowful and solemn. And says I:

" I don't know as there has any law ever been made, in Heaven or on earth, that we had got to be happy. There is a law made that we should do right, should not do evil, but not that we must be happy. Why, some paths we have to foller lead right away from happiness. And says I, still lookin' fur off, in that same sort of a solemn, deep way:

"That path always leads to something better, more beautiful, more divine."

" What can be better than happiness?" says he, in a enquirin' way.

"Blessedness!" says I. "The two hain't to be compared no more than a flower growin' out of earthly soil is to be compared to one springin' up in the valleys of God. One is lit with earth's sun, and the other is shinin' with Heaven's own light. One is mortal, the other immortal."

Says he, still follerin' up his old theme, still **tryin'** **to** head me off in some way:

"Wouldn't you be sorry for these females, Josiah Allen's wife?"

Says I firmly: "If they suffered from the wrenchin' away of old ties, I should be sorry for 'em to that extent that there wouldn't be a sithe left in my breast, nor a dry eye in my head. At the same time, if they made the sacrifice willin'ly, from a sense of duty, for the ransom of their people, for the deliverance of the land from peril, my very soul would kneel in reverence to them, and they should be honored by all as those who come out of great tribulations.

"But," says I, in a slower, more thoughtful way, "there is different kinds of tribulations. And you can look at subjects with the sentimental eye of your specks, and then agin you can turn the other eye onto 'em. And in lookin' through that other eye at 'em, you might possibly see that the married life of these plural wives is wretched—full of jealousies, divisions, and sizms.

"Woman's love, when it has room to grow, is a tremendous thing to spread itself. But (still lookin' through that common sense eye of our specks) we would say that the divine plant of love *can't* grow so thrifty in one-twentieth part of a man's heart as it could in a more expanded and roomy place. We would say (still lookin' through that eye) that it was too cramped a spot—some like growin' a oak in a bottle. You can make it sprout; but there can't be so deep roots nor so strong a strength to it, and it wouldn't take nigh so much of a pull to wrench it up by the roots.

"And so, to foller up the simely, as simelys ort to be follered, we would think that the first wife is the one who would suffer most; she who thought she was marryin' a hull man, who dwelt for awhile in a hull heart, and whose affections, therefore, had naturally took deep root, and spread themselves. We would say (still lookin' through that eye of the speck, and still follerin' up simelys) that she is the one who would be most wrung with agony."

"Wall," says Elder Judas Wart, seemin'ly ketchin' holt of the first argument that presented itself in front of his mind, for truly he didn't seem to care how crooked his argument was, nor how wobblin'. Says he:

"Sufferin' is a divine agent to draw souls heavenward."

"Yes, heaven-sent sufferin'," says I, "will draw our hearts up nearer to the heavenly home it come from. But when sufferin' comes up from below, from another place, scented with brimstone, and loaded with iniquity, it will do its best to draw us down to it where it come from."

"Pain sometimes teaches divine lessons," says Elder Judas Wart. And I never see a mouth puckered and twisted down into a more hypocritical pucker than hisen was.

Says I: "Don't you s'pose I know that?" **And**

then I went on awful eloquent, and grew eloquenter and eloquenter all the time for as much as five minutes or more, entirely unbeknown to me, not thinkin' who was there, or who I was a talkin' to, or where, or when:

"Don't I know," says I, "that no soul has reached its full might, no soul has ever really lived, till it has learned to bless God for the divine ministry of sorrow? Don't I certainly know that of all God's angels the one who brings us divinest gifts is the blessed angel of Pain?"

And I went on again, in that fearfully eloquent way of mine, when I get entirely rousted up in eloquence, and know not where I am, or who is hearin' of me, or why, or which:

"If we bar this angel from our door, resist her gentle voice pleadin' at our heart, woe be to us; for she can come as a avenger, a destroyer. But if we greet her as indeed a heavenly visitant, believe that God sent her, hold her in our weak arms close to our hearts, she gives us divinest strength.

"Though we turn away, and fear her greeting, we find that the touch of her lips on our burning brow leaves calm. She lays on our throbbing, aching hearts soft hands of peace. Her eyes have a sorry look for us, that make our tears flow, and then we see that those sad, sweet eyes are looking up from earth to where our own, tear-blinded, are fain to follow—up beyond the vail, into that beautiful city where our treasures and our hopes are.

To no other angel has God given the power to so
reveal to us the glory and the mystery of life and
of death.   No other
hand but hers has
such power to unlock
the very doors of hea-
ven and send down
into our hearts hea-
ven's peace and glory.

AN ANGEL OF PEACE.

Don't I know this? don't I know that in the hour of
our bitterest sorrow, our deepest affliction, when the

one that made our world lies silent before us, deaf for the first time to our tears and our sorrow; when all the world looks black and desolate, and hatred and envy and malice seem to surround us, and our human strength is gone, and human help is vain; don't I know that this divine angel of Pain opens the very doors of Heaven, and lets down a perfect flood of glory into our soul—not happiness, but blessedness.

"Yes, the crosses this angel brings us from a lovin' Father we will bear in God's name. But," says I, firmly, "other folks must do as they are a mind to; but I never will, not if I know it, bend my back, and let old Belzebub lay one of his crosses acrost my shoulder-blades. No, I will throw off that cross, and stamp onto it. And this cross of Mormonism is one of hisen, if he ever had one. It is made out of Belzebub's own timber, nailed together by man's selfishness and brutality and cruelty, the very worst part of his nature. It is one of the very heaviest crosses ever tackled by wimmen, and bore along by 'em, wet with their blood and sweat and tears. And Samantha will do her best to stamp onto 'em, every one of 'em, and break 'em up into kindlin'-wood, and build fires with 'em to burn up this putryfyin' crime of polygimy, root and branch; make a cleansin' blaze of it to try to purify God's sweet air it has defiled."

"Oh!" says Elder Judas Wart, with a low deep groan, "oh! how unpractical females always are. Females are carried away by their sympathies and religious feelings and sense of right and duty, making them a most dangerous element in politics, a very striking and unwholesome contrast to the present admirable system of government, if they were ever incorporated into the body politic ; in short, if they ever vote. Let us look on the subject in a practical light."

And I was so beat out by my eloquent emotions (such emotions are beautiful to have by you, but fatiguin' to handle, as I handle 'em, and I can't deny it); and bein' also almost completely out of wind, I sot still, and let him go on.

And he talked, I should judge, well on to a quarter of a hour about Communism, Socialism, its principles, its rise, and progress ; and I let him go on, and didn't hardly say a word, only I would merely throw in little observations occasionally, such as, when he argued that everybody should own the same amount of property, and there should be no rich and no poor.

I merely threw in this question to him : Whether he thought shiftlessness and laziness should have the same reward as industry and frugality ?

And when he was a goin' on about everybody bein' educated the same so one could not be intellectually superior to the other, I simply asked him whether he thought Nature was a Socialist.

Says he : " Why ? "

" Oh ! " says I, " I was a thinkin' if she was one, she didn't live up to her belief. She didn't equalize brains and thrift and economy."

" Wall, as I was a sayin' " says he, " as it were, you know "—

" No," says I, coldly, " I don't know it, nor I never did. I know," says I, lookin' keen at him, " that some are born almost fools, and keep on so; and some," says I, with a sort of modest, becomin' look, " some are very smart."

He kep' perfectly still for a minute, or mebby a minute and a ½. And he seemed to collect his strength agin, and broke out, in a loud, haughty tone :

" The fault of our old civilization is that property is controlled by the few. How can a man have the same love for his home, for his hearth-stone, if he works the land of some great landed proprietor? In case of war, now, foreign invasion, if each man owned property of his own, if each man was a Mormon, in fact, he would be fighting for his own interest; not for the interest of some great landed lord. He would be fightin' for his own hearth-stone; the sacred and holy hearth-stone."

Says I, in reasonable axents: " I hain't a word to aginst the sacredness of the hearth-stun. I hain't a word to say aginst the stun. But wouldn't it be apt to take off a little of the sacredness of the stun to have thirty or forty wimmen a settin' on it; each claimin' it as her own stun? Wouldn't it have to be a pretty large stun, and a pretty firm one, to stand the gusts and whirl-winds of temper that would be raised round it? And to tell the plain truth, Elder Judas Wart, don't you believe that every man that owned such a stun, and 30

16*

or 40 wimmen a settin' on it, and childern accordin'ly, don't you believe that such a man instead of discouragin' war would do all in his power to welcome and encourage it, so he could go forth into the battle-field, and find a little peace and repose; that is, if he was a gentle, amiable man, who loved quiet?"

He never said one word in answer to this deep argument, he see it was too deep and sound for him to grapple with; but he kep' right on, and says, thinkin' mebby it would skair me, says he:

"Our order was founded by Thalos of Chalcedon."

"Wall," says I, "Mr. Thalos is a man that I hain't no acquaintance with,—I, nor Josiah; so I can't form any opinion what sort of a character he has got, or what for a man he would be to neighbor with."

Says he, in a still prouder and haughtier way: "Plato believed in it."

"How do you know?" says I. "He never told me that he did. If he had, I should have argued sound with him." And says I, lookin' keen and searchin' at him:

"Did he tell you that he believed in it?" says I. "You can hear most anything."

"Why, no," says he, "he didn't tell me. He died twenty-two hundred years ago."

"Wall," says I, coolly, "I thought you got it by hearsay. I didn't believe you got it from the old gentleman himself, or from any of his relations. I remember Mr. Plato myself, now. I have heard

Thomas J. read about him frequent. A sort of a schoolmaster, I believe—a man that travelled a good deal—and had considerable of a noble mean. If I remember right, I have seen him myself on a bust. But as I was a sayin', s'posen Mr. Plato did believe in it. Don't you s'pose that old gentleman had his faults? He was a nice old man, and very smart. His writings are truly beautiful and inspirin'.

" Why some of his dialogues are almost as keen and sensible and flowery as them that have taken place between a certain woman that I won't mention the name of, and her pardner Josiah. Why, jest the fact that he got sold once for talkin' so plain in the cause of Right, endeared him to me. And the fact that he didn't fetch only twenty minnys (and we all know what small fish they be) didn't make him seem any the less valuable to me. No, not at all so; it wouldn't, if he hadn't fetched more than one little chub.

" Them views of his'en, them witherin' idees aginst tyrany that he was preachin' to a tyrent, whales couldn't lug, nor sharks. They was too big and hefty to be bought or sold. But because Mr. Plato was all right in some things, we mustn't think he was in all. We are apt to think so, and we are apt to think that that because a gulf of a thousand or two years lay between us and a certain person, that it seperates them from all our mortal errors and simplicities.

" But it hain't so. That old man had other human weaknesses besides writin' poetry. I persume Miss

Plato had to deal real severe with him lots of times, jest as I do with Josiah. I dare persume to say she had hard work to get along with him more'n half the time. And if he believed in Mormonism, he believed in sunthin' wicked and abominable, and if I

MR. AND MRS. PLATO.

had been on intimate terms with him and her, I should have talked to him like a sister, right before her, so she would feel all right about it, and not get oneasy and jealous. I should have talked powerful to him, and if he is the man I take him to be, I could have convinced him in ten minutes, I know I could."

"Wall," says he, "bringin' the history of our church down to Christ's day: He was a believer in it."

I riz right up in a awful dignity and power, and I says, in a tone that was fearful to hear, it was so burnin' indignant:

"You say that agin in my house, if you dare."

He dassent, my tone was such. He never said a word, but sot kinder scroochin' and meachin' on his chair, and I went on, resumin' my seat agin, knowin' as I did that my principles was so hefty I had better save myself all the extra weariness that I could. Says I:

"You dare to say that He, the Deliverer of His people from sin and evil—He, the Teacher of all purity, morality, honesty, and all Christian virtues, who came bringin' peace on earth, good will to men —He, who taught that a man should have one wife, and be tender and constant to her, even as He loved the Church and gave Himself for it—He, whose life was so pure and self-denyin' and holy that it brought the divine down to the comprehension of the human— the love and purity of God manifest in the flesh—how dare you tell me that He was a Mormon?"

He dassent say it agin. He dast as well die as to say it. I s'pose, in fact I know, from my feelin's which I was a feelin', that my mean was awfuler and more majesticker than it had been for years and years.

Says he, "As it were—" and then he stopped short off, seemin'ly to collect his thoughts together, and then he kinder coughed, and begun agin—"And so forth, and so on," says he. He acted fairly afraid. And I don't wonder at it a mite. My looks must have been awful, and witherin' in the extreme.

But finally he says, " We read of this sect in the Bible, anyway. The Essenes was Mormons, or sort o' Mormony," says he, glancin' at me and then at the teakettle, in a sort of a fearful way.

But says I, coldly, " We read in the Bible of droves of swine that was full of evil spirits ; and we read in it of lunaticks, and barren fig-trees, and Judas, and the—the David—callin' him David, as a Methodist and member of the meetin'-house, who does not want to say Satan if she can possibly help it.

"Now," says I, " you have brought up every commandment of God, and I have preached on 'em, and you find every one of 'em is aginst you—the old law, and the divine new law made manifest in Christ. Now," says I, coolly, leanin' back in my chair, full of martyrdom and eloquence and victory and everything, "bring on your next argument, bring it right here, and let me lay holt of it, and vanquish it, and overthrow it."

" Wall," says he, "I hold that the perfect faith that thousands have in our religion and its founder, is one of the very strongest proofs of its divine origin."

"I don't think so," says I. " Faith is the substance of things hoped for, but things don't always turn out to be what you hoped they was. Now, there is hash,

for instance: and in order to enjoy hash, you have got
to have perfect confidence in it and its maker.   But
still you may have that perfect confidence in it, and
eat it in faith, believin' it is good beef and pork, while
at the same time there may be ingredients in it that
you know not of, such as Skotch snuff, lily white, hair-
pins, and etcetery.   Hash is a great mystery, and often
deceivin' to the partaker, no matter how strong his
faith in it may be.

"And I might foller up this strikin' simely of hash
into other eloquent metafors, such as pills, preachin',
wimmen's complexion, and etcetery.   Some is good
and true, and some hain't good and true, but they all
find somebody to believe in 'em.

"This is a very deep subject, and solemn, if handled
solemnly.   I have handled it only in a light parable
way, showin' that them that do honestly believe in this
Mormon doctrine, if there are any, are partakin' (unbeknown to them) of a hash that is full of abomination and uncleanness, full of humiliation, sorrow, and
degradation.   Oh!" says I, fallin' back on the side of
the subject nearest to my heart, " when I think of the
woes of my sect there in Utah, I feel feelin's that never
can be told or sung.   No, there never could be a tune
made mournful and solemn enough to sing 'em in."

Says he, bold as brass, and not thinkin' how he was
a wobblin' round in his argument, " They enjoy it."

Says I, firm as Bunker Hill, and as lofty, " They
don't enjoy it."

Says he, " They do."

Says I, " Elder Judas Wart, you tell me that agin, and I'll know the reason why."

" Why," says he, " they have petitioned Congress to not meddle with the laws."

Says I, " Can you tell me, Elder Judas Wart, can you tell me honestly that there wasn't man's influence lookin' right out of that petition ? "

" No, mum, there wuzn't. They done it of their own wills and acords."

Says I, firmly, " I don't believe it. And if I did, it would only show to me the blightin', corruptin', influence of your belief."

" Why," says he, " some of our wimmen are the most active in our church—full of religious zeal."

Says I, coolly, " All kinds of zeal hain't religious zeal." Says I, " The kind that makes a mother throw her child into the Ganges, and burn herself with the dead body of her husband—you can call it religious zeal, if you want to, but I call it fanatical frenzy."

Says he, " They are perfectly happy in their belief."

Says I, " You needn't never say that agin to me, thinkin' I will believe it, for before Mormonism was ever made, human nature was made, wimmen's hearts was made. And when you show me a man who would enjoy havin' his right hand cut off, or his eyes plucked out of his head, then I will show you a woman, a womanly woman, who enjoys sharin' the love of the man she worships—enjoys seein' it passin' away from her, given to another. Why, it is aginst nater, as much as it is for the sun to shine at midnight.

Blackness and despair and gloom is what rains when the sun of love is gone down—it's nater, and can't be helped, no more than the sun can, or the moon, or anything. No woman ever enjoyed this wretched doctrine—that is, no

THE HINDOO MOTHER.

good woman, no pure, tender-hearted, affectionate woman.''

" Why," says he, " I s'posed you thought all wimmen was perfect.''

" No, I don't, sir, no sir. A woman can lose all that is sweet and lovely in her nature—all the traits that make her so attractive, her tenderness, her affection, her constancy, her modesty, her purity. She can get very low down in the scale of being, lower, I think, than a man can get. You know the further up any one is, the worse it hurts 'em to fall.

" Now the angels that fell down from heaven, I s'pose it changed 'em, and disfigured 'em, and spilte 'em as bad agin as it would to fall down suller. Josiah fell a week ago last Wednesday night, with a hammer in one hand, and a box of nails in the other. He was fixin' up a cupboard for me in the sullerway. He fell flat down and lay his hull length on the suller bottom. Skairt me awfully. Skairt him, too, and sort o' madded him, as it always will a man when they fall. I was gettin' the supper onto the table, and I started on the run for the suller door, and says I, in agitated axents, and weak as a cat with my emotions:

" Did it hurt you, Josiah?''

Says he, sort o' surly, " It didn't do me any good.''

But he got up, and was all right the next day. I have used this poetical simely, of its hurtin' anybody worse to fall down from such a lofty height than to fall down the sullerway, to show my meanin' that a pure woman's nature is naturally very pure and lofty, and if she loses it she falls very low indeed.

"Lose it she can— all that makes her sweet and lovely and lovable; but while she keeps her woman's heart and nature, her life, in your religion, must be a constant martyrdom, and must be in its nature demoralizin' and debasin', dealin' the morals fearful and totterin' blows.

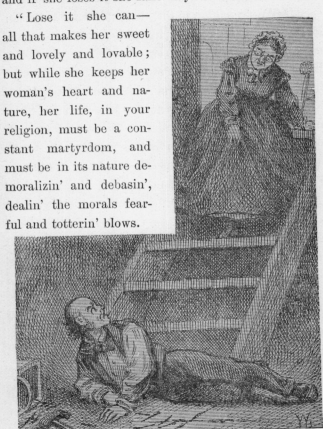

A FALLEN ANGEL.

"Why, don't you s'pose I can take it to myself? Now, Home is the most heavenly word we know. We hain't learnt the heavenly alphabet yet, none of us, and so can't spell out the word Heaven as it ort to be spelt. We are children that hain't learnt God's language yet. But Home in its true meanin' is sunthin' as near heaven as we can translate and spell out below. Home, when it is built as any home must be in order to stand, on a true love, and in the fear of God, such a home is almost a heaven below. I know it, for a certain home was built on these very foundations upwards of 20 years ago, and not a j'int has moved, not a sleeper decayed. Such a home means delight, rest, comfort. I know it, and my Josiah knows it.

" But let Josiah Allen bring home one more wife, let alone a dozen or fifteen of 'em—let him bring home one small wife besides Samantha, and I should find that home meant sunthin' very different from peace and rest and happiness. And Josiah Allen would find out that it did, too. He would, if I know my own heart, and am not deceived in myself. And when I think of it, think of what my own sect are a sufferin' right here in our own land, it makes my blood bile up in my vains, and the tears jest start to every eye in my head, and if I had two dozen eyes I could cry and weep with every one of 'em, a thinkin' how I should feel under them circumstances—a thinkin' of the desecration of all that is holiest, and purest, and most blessed. Thinkin' of the agony of remembrance, and regret, and despair that would sweep over me—remembrance of the old, happy days when I was blest with the love that had gone from me—regret for all the happy days, happy words of love and tenderness, happy hours of confidence and affection—mine once, gone forever. Despair, utter, black despair that all was past.

"And besides this sufferin', think of the ravages it would make in my morals, as well as his'en. I know jest how much my morals can stand, I know to a inch jest how much strain I can put onto 'em. And I know, jest as well as I know my name was once Smith, that another wife would make 'em totter. And, to be perfectly plain and truthful, I know that wife would make 'em fall perfectly flat down, and break 'em all into pieces, and ruin 'em. I shouldn't have a single moral left sound and hull, and I know it. I should be ugly."

Says I, with a added eloquence and bitterness of tone, as my mind roved back onto a certain widder:

"To have another woman come a snoopin' into my house and my pardner's heart—why, language hain't made mean enough to tell what my meanness would be under the circumstances. And her morals, too— why, don't you s'pose her morals would be flat as a pancake? Yea, verily. And where would my Josiah's morals be? He wouldn't have none, not a moral, nor a vestige of any. And there would be three likely persons spilte, entirely, and eternally spilte. And do you s'pose we three persons are so different from any other three persons? No, human nature (man human nature, and woman human nature) is considerable the same all over the world."

And agin as that fearful scene presented itself to my imagination, of another woman enterin' into my Josiah's heart, I sithed powerful, and went on with renewed eloquence. I was fearfully eloquent, and smart as I could be ; deep.

Says I, " One man's heart hain't of much account, viewed in a permiscus way, but to the woman that loves him it's a good deal, it is all. Wimmen are foolish about some things, and this is one of 'em. Her love is to her the very breath she breathes—it is the best part of her. Men don't feel this way as a general thing (my Josiah duz, but he is a shinin' exception). But as a general thing love is to them a sort of a sideshow, a tolerable good entertainment, but it hain't the hull circus.

" No, a man's heart hain't none too large for one woman to dwell in, especially if she is hefty, not at all too large, quite the reverse. And I can tell you, Elder Judas Wart, and tell it firm and ' solemn, that when it comes to dividin' up that heart that was a tight fit in the first place, and lettin' one woman after another come a troopin' in, a pushin' the lawful owner out of the way, jammin' her round, bruisin' of her, and in the end crowdin' her completely out in the cold, I say, may God pity such a woman, for human pity can't be made pitiful enough to reach her."

Says Elder Judas Wart, " Men that hain't Mormons sometimes has more than one woman inside of their hearts."

" I know it," says I. " But the law gets right onto such a man and stamps onto him. And public sentiment sets down on him hard. And I can tell you that when the hull community and law and religion and everything are all a settin' on a man, and settin' heavy, that man finds it is a pretty tuckerin' business; he gets sick of it, and is glad to do better and be let up. But you make the iniquity lawful. You make law and religion and public sentiment all get under such a man, and boost him up—make out that the more crimes a man commits, the more wives he has, the higher place he will have in heaven. Why," says I, " when I think it over, it hain't no wonder to me that the Mormon leaders, before they let loose this shameful doctrine and putrifyin' sin of polygamy, they settled down by a salt lake. I should have thought they would have needed salt. But salt never was made salt enough to save 'em, and they'll find out so."

He quailed a very little, or, that is, it looked like quail, though it might have been meachin'ness strong and severe. Powerful meach looks some like quail, at a first look. But he recovered himself in half a moment, and went on, in the haughtiest, impudentest tone he had used as yet:

" Wall, whether salt has helped us, or whatever did, we have flourished—nobody can deny that. We have made the desert blossom like a rose. We are industrious, stiddy, prudent, equinomical, hard-working.

You can't deny the good we have done in that way.
We are full of good qualities, brim full of 'em."

Says I, coldly, almost frigidly, "No amount of white-
wash can cover up a whited sepulker so that my specks
can't see through it, and see the sepulker. Good store
clothes can't cover up a bad soul worth a cent. A blue
satin vest, or even a pink velvet one, buttoned up over
a bad heart, can't make that heart none the purer.
The vest might look well, and probable would. But
when you know the bad heart beats under it, vile and
wicked beats, why, that vest don't seem no better to
you, nor seem to set the man off no more, than if it
was calico, with leather buttons. Material good can
never make up for moral degradation.

"And your good qualities only make your sinful
practices more dangerous, more successful in luring
souls to destruction. It is like wreathin' a sword with
flowers, for folks to grip holt of and get their hands
cut off (morally). It is like coverin' a bottomless
gulf with blossoming boughs, for folks to walk off on,
and break their necks (as it were)."

"Wall," says he proudly, "we have flourished, and
are flourishin' and are goin' to still more. We are
goin' to extend our doctrine of polygamy further and
further. We are goin' to carry it into Arizona and all
the other new territories— "

I riz right up, I was so agitated, and says I: "You
shan't carry it, not one step."

Says he, firmly: "We will!"

Says I: "I tell you agin that you shan't; and if you do I'll know the reason why. I tell you that you shall drop it right there, by that salt lake, and let it lay there. It needs brine if anything ever did. You shan't make no move to carry it a step further. You shall not carry this godless crime, a disgrace to religion and civilization, into new territories. The green turf of them lands is too fresh and bright to be blood-stained by the feet of weepin' wimmen, bearin' this heaviest of crosses that was ever tackled by 'em. You shall not darken the sunny skies and pollute the sweet air of new lands with this moral pestilence."

Says he: "We will!"

Says I, firmly and sternly: "You won't; and when I say you won't, I mean it."

"Wall," says he, with a proud mean, "how are you goin' to help yourself?"

Says I, in loud, excited axents: "If I can't stop you myself, I know who can, and I will go to Uncle Sam myself. I'll have a plain talk with that good old man. I'll jest put it into his head what you are a tryin' to do, and I'll hunch him up, and make him stop you."

Says he: "Don't you s'pose sin and sorrow will ever be carried into the territories only as they are carried in by Mormons?"

"Yes, I do," says I. "I s'pose that whenever humanity is sot down under the light of the Eternal, it will forevermore, as it has forever in the past, be followed by two shadows, the joyful and the sorrowful.

17

Human nature can't help itself; the Eternal Soul above will shine on, and the human nature below will throw its shadows—the dark one and the light one, first one and then the other, unbeknown to us, followin' us all the time, and will follow us till the darkness of the human is all lost in the light of the divine. There hain't no territories been discovered distant enough for the human soul to escape from itself—from the shadow of sorrow. I hain't said there wuz. Neither have I said it could escape from sin. I s'pose the old man in human nature won't never be wholly drove out of it this side of Eternity; and I s'pose wherever that old man is there will

THE OLD MAN.

be caperin' and cuttin' up and actin'. But, as I have said more'n forty times, you ort to whip that old man, make him behave himself as well as you possibly can, be awful severe with him, and keep him under. But you don't try to. You jest pet that old man, and humor him, and encourage him in his caperin's. You try to make sin and cuttin' up and actin' respectable; protect it by the law.

"Why, sin is what all good men and wimmen must fight aginst; educate public sentiment aginst it; make it obnoxious; or what will become of everybody and the world if they don't? Why, they will be ondone, they and the hull world, if they don't. I will," says I firmly, "I will see Uncle Sam about it at once."

"Oh," says he, in a impudent, pert tone, "Uncle Sam won't do nothin' to hinder us. He has always protected us. He has done well by us. He has let us do about as we was a mind to."

"I know it," says I, "but I'll tell you," says I, on-tyin' my apron-strings in a absent-minded sort of a mechanicle way, and then tyin' 'em up agin in the same way (or about the same), "I'll tell you what," says I, for I was fairly determined to find some excuse for Samuel, if I possibly could, "the fact is, that old man hain't been well for quite a number of years. He has seemed to be sort o' runnin' down; his constitu tion hain't seemed right to me. And he has had mis-erable doctors; or that is, he has got help in some directions, good help, and in others he has had the poorest kind of physic. But," says I, firmly, " that old man means well; there hain't a well-meanin'er, conscientiouser old creeter on the face of the earth than that old man is."

"Yes," says he, " he has done well by us. We hain't no fault to find with him."

Oh! how that madded me. But I was determined to find all the excuses for Samuel that I could (though I was at my wit's end, or pretty nigh there, to find 'em, and I can't deny it). Says I,

" That old man has been more than half crazy for a number of years back. What with fightin' and blood-shed right in his own family, amongst his own chil-dern—and the injins screechin' and warhoopin' round his frontiers, and the Chinamen a cuttin' up behind his back, and his neighbors a fightin' amongst them-selves, and jabbin' at him every chance they got ; and congressmen and everybody a stealin' everything they could, right under his nose, and cuttin' up and actin' It is a wonder to me that the old man hain't gin up long ago, and died off. I guess lots of folks thought, a number of years ago, that he wouldn't live a year. And it wasn't nothin' but his goodness and solid principles that kep' him up, and everybody knows it. He's had enough to bear to kill a ox."

" We ort to speak well of him," says he agin. " He has done first-rate by us. He has seemed to like us."

" Shet up!" says I. "I won't hear another word from you aginst that old man. Your doin's has wor-

ried Samuel almost to
death — I know it has. I
wouldn't be afraid to bet
(if I believed in bettin')
that it has wore on him
more than all the work
he has done for years.

"He wants to do right,
that old Uncle does.
He would be jest as glad
to get rid of all of you,—

Mormons, Oneida Communities, Free Lovers, and the hull caboodle of you,—as our old mare would be glad to get rid of flies in fly-time. But the thing of it is, with Samuel and the mare, how to go to work to do it. He can't see to everything without help. I know what he needs. He needs a good, strong friend to help him. He wants to have somebody tell him the plain truth, to get his dander completely up; and then he wants to have that same female stand right by him, with a cast-iron determination, and hand him bullets and cartridges, while he aims his old revolutionary musket, and shoots down iniquities on every side of him.

"Why, where would Josiah Allen be, if it wuzn't for me? He would come to nothin', morals and all, if it wuzn't for me to hunch him up. And Samuel has as much agin to worry him as Josiah has.

"Why, there is no tellin' how many things that old man has to plague him and torment the very life out of him. Little things, too, some of 'em, but how uncommon little things will worry anybody, 'specially in the night. Curious things, too, some of 'em, that has worried me most to death way off here in Jonesville, and what feelin's I should have felt to have had it a goin' on right under my nose, as Samuel did.

"Now, when they made that new silver dollar, right there in his house I s'pose they done it, or in his wood-shed or barn—anyway, it was right where he could see it a goin' on, and worry over it—you know they put onto it, 'In God we trust.' And it has fairly hanted me

THE CALL TO DUTY.

to find out what the government really meant by it—
whether they meant that God wouldn't let 'em get
found out in their cheatin' seven cents on every dollar,
or trusted He would let 'em cheat fourteen cents on the
next ones they made.

" Why, it has worried me awfully, and how Samuel
must have felt about it. And that is only one little
thing.

" There is the trade dollars we made on purpose to

HELPS FOR THE HEATHEN.

cheat China with, and sent over in the same ship we
sent missionaries to convert 'em. I presume to say
that old man has laid awake nights a worryin' over
what the heathens would think about it—about our
sendin' religion and robbery over to 'em in the same
ship—about our sendin' religious tracts, exhortin' 'em
to be honest, or they would certainly go to that bad place
which I do not, as a Methodist, wish to speak of, and
send these dollars to cheat 'em with in the same box—

sendin' eloquent and heartrendin' tracts provin' out to
'em that no drunkard can possibly go to Heaven,
packed side by side with barrels of whiskey to teach
'em how to get drunk, so they will be sure not to go
there.   I know it has wore on him, so afraid that the
heathens would be perfectly disgusted with a religion
taught by professed followers of Him who come down
to earth bearing peace, good-will to men, and then,
after 1800 years of professed loyalty to Him, and His
pure and exalted teachings, bore to their shores such
fruit as cheating, falsehood, and drunkenness.

"It has hanted Samuel, I know it has.   Hantin' me
as it has, it must have hanted him fur worse.   He has
had severe trials, that old gentleman has, and he has
needed somebody to hunch him up, and lock arms with
him, and draw him along on the path of Right.   And
I tell you when I talk with him I shan't spare no pains
with him.   I shall use my eloquent tone freely.   I
shan't be savin' of gestures or wind.   I shall use sharp
reason, and, if necessary, irony and sarcasm.   And I
shall ask him (usin' a ironicle tone, if necessary) how
he thinks it looks in the eyes of the other nations to
see him, who ort to be a model for 'em all to foller,
allow such iniquity as Mormonism to flourish in his
borders.   To let a regular organized band of banditty
murder and plunder and commit all sorts of abomina-
tions right under his honest old nose.   And how it
must look to them foreign nations to see such a good,
moral old gentleman as he is lift his venerable old eye-

winker and wink at such crime and sin. How insignificant and humiliatin' it must look to 'em to see him allow a man in Congress to make laws that will imprison a man for havin' two wives when the same man has got four of 'em, and is lookin' round hungry for more.

"And I shall hunch him up sharp about sellin' licenses to do wrong for money—licenses to make drunkards, and unfit men for earth or heaven—licenses to commit other crimes that are worse—sellin' indulgences to sin as truly as ever Mr. Pope did.

"I don't s'pose, in fact, I know, that Sam hain't never thought it over, and took a solemn, realizin' sense of how bad he was a cuttin' up (entirely unbeknown to him). And, if necessary, to convince him and make him see his situation, I shall poke fun at him (in a jokin' way, so's not to get him mad). And I shall ask him if he thinks it is any nobler for him to set up in his high chair at Washington and sell indulgences to sin, than it was in Mr. Pope to set up in his high chair in Vatican village and sell 'em.

"And I shall skare him mebby, that is, if I have to, and ask him in a impressive, skareful tone that if he can't be broke in any other way, if he don't think he ort to be brought down to a diet of Worms.

"It will go aginst my feelin's to skare the excellent old gentleman. But I shall feel it to be my duty to not spare no pains. But at the same time I shall be very clever to him. I shall resk it. I don't believe

17*

he will get mad at me. He knows my feelin's for him too well. He knows there hain't a old man on the face of the earth I love so devotedly, now father Smith is dead, and father Allen, and all the other old male relatives on my side, and on his'en. I'll bet a cent I can convince him where he is in the wrong on't."

Here I paused for a moment for wind, for truly I was almost completely exhausted. But I was so full and runnin' over with emotions that I couldn't stop, wind or no wind. And I went on:

"He hain't realized, and he won't, till I go right there and hunch him up about it, how it looks for him to talk eloquent about the sanctity of home. How the household, the Christian home, is the safeguard, the anchor of church and state, and then make his words seem emptier and hollower than a drum, or a hogsit, by allowin' this sin of Mormonism to undermind and beat down the walls of home."

And then (this theme always did make me talk beautiful), as I thought of home and Josiah, and the fearful dangers that had threatened 'em both, why, as I thought of this, I begun to feel eloquenter far than I had felt durin' the hull interview, and I don't know as the feelin's I felt then had been gone ahead of by me in five years. Why, I branched out perfectly beautiful, and very deep, and says I:

"Home! The Christian home! The mightiest power on earth for good. Each home seperate and perfect in itself, like the little crystal drops of water, each one on 'em round and complete and all floatin' on together, unbeknown to them, makin' a mighty ocian floatin' right into that serene bay into which all our hopes and life dreams empty. That soundless sea that floats human souls right up to the eternal city.

"The love of parents, wives, and childern, like golden rings, bindin' the hearts to the happy hearthstone, and then widenin' out in other golden rings, bindin' them hearth-stones to loyalty and patriotism, love of country, love of law and order, and love of Heaven, why, them gold rings within rings, they all make a chain that can't be broke down; they twist all together into a rope that binds this crazy old world to the throne of God.

"And," says I, lookin' at Elder Judas Wart, with a arrow in each eye (as it were): "This most wholesome restraint, this strongest of ropes that is stretched firm and solid between safety and old Error, you are tryin' to break down. But you'll find you can't do it. No sir! You may all get onto it,—the whole caboodle of you, Mormons, Oneida Communities, Free Lovers, the hull set on you,—and you'll find it is a rope you can't break! You'll find that the most you can do is to teter and swing on it, and stretch it out a little ways, mebby. You can't break it! No sir! Uncle Samuel (after I have hunched him up) will hold one end of it firm and strong, and Principle and Public Sentiment the other end of it; and if necessary, if danger is at hand, she that was Samantha Smith will lay holt of it, too ; and I'd love to see any shacks, or set of shacks, a gettin' it out of our hands then."

Oh, how eloquent I had been. But he wuzn't convinced. I don't s'pose anybody would hardly believe that a man could listen to such talk, and not be proselyted and converted. But he wuzn't. After all my outlay and expenditure of eloquence and wind and everything, he wuzn't convinced a mite. And after he had got his hat all on to go, he jest stood there in front of me, with his hands in his pockets, and says he, bold as brass, and as impudent as brass ever was:

"I am a goin', mum, and I don't never expect to see you agin. I never shall see you in the kingdom."

"I am afraid you won't," says I, givin' him a awful keen look, but pityin'. "I am afraid if you don't turn right square round, and stop actin', you won't be there."

"I shall be there," says he, "but you won't."

Says I, "How do you know I won't?"

Says he, "Because I do know it."

Says I, with dignity, "You don't know it."

"Why," says he, comin' out plain with his biggest and heftiest argument, the main pillow in the Mormon church, "a woman can't be saved unless some man saves 'em, some Mormon. That is one reason," says he, "why I would have bore my cross, and married you; obtained an entrance for you in the heavenly kingdom. But now it is too late. I won't save you."

"You won't save me?" says I, lookin' keen at him,

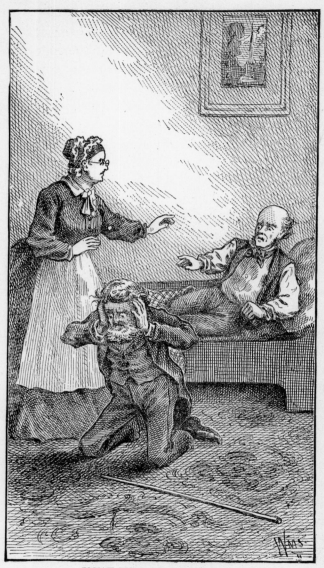

JOSIAH ENDS THE ARGUMENT.

as he stood there before me, with his red bloated face, a face that had that low, disipated, animal expression lookin' out so plain under the sanctimonious, hypocritical look he had tried to cover it with. "You won't save me! Won't take me into the heavenly kingdom! Wall, I rather think you won't."

I was so engaged and bound up in my indignant emotions and principles and everything that I didn't see what was goin' on behind me. But there was a fearful scene ensuin' and goin' on there. A awful scene of vengeance and just retribution. For my faithful pardner, maddened by the terrible insult to his Samantha, jest lifted himself up on one elbo, his righteous anger liftin' him up for the moment above stitches and all other earthly infirmities, and he threw that broom-handle at Elder Judas Wart with terrific force, and aimed it so perfect that it hit him right on the nap of the neck. It was a fearful blow. I s'pose it come jest as near breakin' his neck as anything ever did and miss.

And it skairt him fearfully, too; for Josiah had been so still for a spell that he thought he was asleep. And it had come onto him as swift and severe as a judgment right out of the heavens. (Not that I would wish to be understood that broom-handles are judgments, and should be handled as such; not as a general thing. I am speakin' in a poetical way, and would wish to be took poetically.)

But oh! how fearful Elder Judas Wart looked. **It**

squshed him right down for a minute where he ort to
be squshed—right onto his knees. He couldn't get
up for a number of minutes, bein' stunted and wild
with the blow and the fearful horrow of his skare.
And oh! how Josiah Allen did converse with him, as
he knelt there helpless before him; hollered! it wasn't
conversation, it was hollerin'; loud, wild holler! almost
a beller!

He ordered him out of the house, and threatened
him with instant and immediate execution on the galluses. Though he knew we hadn't no gallus built,
and no timber suitable to build one; and he disabled
with a stitch, and nobody but me to do anything. But
he vowed, in that loud, skareful axent, that he would
hang him in five minutes' time; and chop his head off
with a broad-axe; and gulotine him; and saw his neck
off with our old cross-cut saw; and shoot him down
like a dog; and burn him to the stake; and scalp him.

Why, Josiah ort to have known that one of these
punishments was enough for any man to bear, and
more than any man could stand up under. And he
knew we hadn't the conveniences by us for half of
these punishments. But he didn't think of that. He
didn't think of nothin', nor nobody, only jest anger
and vengeance. He was more delerious and wild in
his conversation and mean than I had ever known him
to be during our entire aquaintenship. It was a fearful scene. It was harrowin' to me to see it go on.
And Elder Judas Wart, as quick as he could get **up,**

—started off on a quick run, almost a canter. I s'pose, I have heerd sense, and then I could see from his looks and actions, that a skairter man never lived. And well he might be. I don't blame him for it a mite.

DEPARTURE OF THE ELDER.

I blame him for lots of things, but not for that; for the words and mean of Josiah was enough to apaul a iron man, or a mule.

But as I told Josiah afterwards, after the crazy delerium begun to disperse off of his mean, says I,

"Why is it any more of a insult to me than it is to them other poor wimmen who have to endure it?" Says I, "You feel awfully to have that doctrine jest throwed at your pardner, as you may say. And look at the thousands of wimmen that have to submit to the humiliation and degredation of this belief, live in it, and die in it."

"Wall," says he, chucklin', "I jest choked old Wart off of it pretty sudden. I brought him down onto his knees pretty suple. He won't talk about savin' wimmen's souls agin right away. He won't till his neck gets well, anyway." And he chuckled agin.

I don't believe in fightin', and am the last woman to encourage it; but I could not help sayin', in fervid axents:

"Oh! if Uncle Samuel, that dear, blunderin', noble old man, would only hit old Polygamy jest another such a blow, jest as sudden and unexpected, and bring him down on his polluted old knees in front of the nation. Oh! what a day that would be for America and Samantha. What feelin's we should feel, both on us."

"Yes," says Josiah, "I wish it could be did." In the case of Josiah Allen my powerful talk (aided by previous and more late occurrences) had fell on good ground, I knew. The seed was springin' up strong. I knew it was by the way he threw that broom-handle, and I knew also by his looks and axents.

He was perfectly and entirely convinced of the

awfulness and vile horrors of Mormonism. I knew
he was. He looked so good and sort o' noble at me.
And his tone was so sweet and kind of affectin', somehow, as he added, in gentle and plaintive axents:

"I believe, Samantha, I could relish a little briled
steak and some mashed-up potatoes."

Says I, "So could I, and I will get dinner to once."
And I did.

A CRISIS WITH KELLUP.

THE very next day after I gin the Elder such a talkin to, Cassandra and Nathan Spooner come to our house a visitin, or that is, Nathan brought Cassandra up as far as there for a drive, in the mornin', and I made 'em come in and stay to dinner, Cassandra not bein' very strong. They have got a young babe, a boy, five weeks old that very day. Wall, while they was there, while I was a gettin' dinner, I had a letter from Kitty. Kitty had gone home two weeks before, unexpected. A letter bein' had by her from her mother, to that effect.

I never shall forget the day Kitty went. Never. Josiah had hitched up to take her to say good bye to the children, and they hadn't been gone more'n several moments, when Kellup Cobb come. He had heerd the news of her goin' home, and he looked anxious and careworn. And his hair and whiskers and eyebrows bein' a sort of a dark mournful color that day, made him look worse. He had been foolin' with logwood and alum, and a lot of such stuff.

(470)

He said, " he was fairly beat out a layin' awake the night before."

" What ails you?" says I. " What is the matter?"

" Wimmen is what ails me!" says he with a bitter look. " Wimmen is what is the matter! Why," says he, " wimmen make such fools of themselves about me, that it is a wonder that I get any sleep at all; I shouldn't," says he firmly, " I know I shouldn't, if I didn't get so sleepy and sort o' drowse off."

" Well," says I reasonably, " I don't s'pose we should any of us get much sleep, if it wasn't for that."

Says he, speakin' out firm and decided, " I want to do right. I want to do the fair thing by wimmen. But there it is. How can I? Now here is Kitty Smith goin off droopin' and low-sperited, I s'pose, jest on my account. And situated as I be, how be I goin' to help myself, or chirk her up before she goes?

" I think my eyes of that girl. And I jest about made up my mind, last night, in the dead of night (for I don't believe I slept a wink before ten o'clock), I jest about made up my mind that marry her I would, and let the rest of the wimmen live or die, jist as they was a mind to.

" Why, I think so much of that girl, that it jest about kills me to think of her goin off home, as them without hope. But what can I do? I dassent say right out that I will marry her, till I look round and see what would foller. I want to see the doctor! I want to see what he thinks, if he thinks the effects of such

a terrible blow onto the fair sect would be worse at
this time of the year. It is a sickly time. Mebby
they would stand it better some other time of the year.

" But," says he, " this I think I may safely promise
you; this, I think, will chirk her up a good deal: I
will write to her. I will kinder watch things, and
enquire 'round, and see what I can do—see how they
would seem likely to stand it, and if I see it haint
likely to kill ten or fifteen, I will try to get round and
marry her. You tell her so from me. And tell her I
will write to her, anyway. My very heart-strings
seemed wrapped round that girl," says he, sithin' hard,
" and how I am a goin' to stand it is more than I can
tell, to think of her bein' way off there alone, a sufferin' and droopin' round, on my account.

" But this letter will probable be the greatest comfort
she can have next to havin' me myself. You will be
apt to write to her ? " says he anxiously.

" Yes," says I, " most probable I shall."

" Wall," says he, " I will put in a letter with you
when you write. It haint the postage that is the stick
with me, it haint the 3 cents I mind. But if I can't,
after all my efforts, see my way clear to marry her, it
would seem more cruel and cold-blooded in me, to have
gin her the encouragement of sendin her a letter by
myself, all stamped and paid for by me, than it would
to send it in with somebody else." Says he, " Don't
you think so ? "

"Says I, in a sort of a blind way, "I think of a great many things that it wouldn't do to tell of."

"Yes," says he, "you probable pity me, and realize the situation I am placed in, more than you feel free to tell. You probable think that sympathy would break me down—make me feel worse "

"Yes," says I firmly, "I don't feel free to tell my opinion of you. It would be apt to make you feel worse."

"You are a woman of principle, Josiah Allen's wife, and a woman of strong sense. You realize my situation—you feel for the condition of my heart."

"Yes, and your head too," says I; "I realize jist what has ailed you, ever sense you was born. But," says I, wantin' to turn the subject, for I was sick of it, sick as a dog. Says I "you wuzn't to meetin' last night wuz you?" Says I, "We wimmen talked it over after the meetin', and we are goin to take up a collection to make Miss Bamber a present of a new black dress. We are goin' to ask each church-member to give jest one sixpence, and one sixpence apiece from the 250 members will get her a good bumbazeen dress, or a very nice alpacka. And so," says I, "I thought I would ask you for your sixpence."

Knowin' it is Kellup's duty to be tackled for the good of the meetin-house, I will, no matter whether he will give anything or not, I will insist on tacklin' him.

Says I, "You know Miss Bamber has lost her

mother-in-law and wants to mourn for her—wants to the worst kind, and can't."

" Why can't she mourn ?" says Kellup.

" Why," says I, " She can't mourn, because she haint got no dress suitable to mourn in, thats why Miss Bamber feels like death about it. She knows it is her duty to mourn, and she wants to, like a dog, but can't."

Says Kellup, lookin stingy, awful unwillin' to give anything, " She can mourn jest as bad in one dress as another, or without any."

" Wall," says I reasonably, " So I think. But everybody has their little different ways and excentricities, and it don't look well for us to meddle with 'em. Now that feller by the name of Procrustes, at Attica village. Now, I always thought he went too far. He had a iron bedstead, and he used to make everybody that traveled his way lay down on it, and if their legs was too short, he would stretch 'em out to fit that bedstead, and if they was too long, he would saw 'em off."

Now Mr. Procrustes wuzn't doin' exactly the fair thing. What earthly business was it of his, if other folks'es legs was too long to be convenient, or too short ? It wuzn't his place to trim 'em off, or stretch 'em.

And I always thought that if I had had business in his neighborhood, and been travelin' that way, and he had tried to fit me or Josiah to that bedstead, why, I always thought he would have seen trouble. I should have gin him a awful talkin' to, and kicked.

Mr. Procrustes is dead. Yes, I believe old Thesius, a neighber of his'en, killed him upon some mountain or other. I presume he got to stretchin' old Thesius'es legs out, or begun to saw 'em off, and got the old man mad, and he jest laid to and killed him.

Yes, I believe old Mr. Procrustes hain't livin' at the present time, but he left a large, a very large family. And every one of 'em inherits the old gentleman's traits and disposition. I have seen lots of 'em that, if

TAKIN' A REEF.

they dast, would have every leg in the world jest the length of their'n. If they dast, they would tackle you in a minute with a saw or a broad-axe.

" But I never felt that way. Now, as fur as my own feelin's are concerned, I think memories can haunt anybody, and hearts can ache jest as severe under a white dress as a black one, and visey versey. Hearts can beat gay and triumphant aginst bumbuzeen bodist waists and crape trimmin's. But Miss Bamber feels different. She feels that she can't mourn without certain conveniences. And feelin' in that way, and feelin' that it would be a duty and a privilege for her to mourn for her mother-in-law, I say that woman shall have the wherewith to do it with. I say she shall mourn if she wants to ; she shall be helped to a black dress. There hain't a member of the meetin'-house but what can give a six-pence without feelin' it. We want to keep it all still from Miss Bamber, and get it, and get it all made for her before she knows a thing about it. And," says I, "mebby you had better give me the six-pence to-day, as we have got it about all collected, and want to get the dress right away."

Says he, " Hain't there nobody else whose duty it is to get the dress ? Her relations ? I should think it was their duty to help."

Never did I ask a stingy human creeter for help for the poor, or help for the meetin'-house, but what this argument was dragged up by 'em. Tryin' to shirk off their own duty onto somebody else.

" No," says I, " her family is all dead. She hain't got but one relation in the world, and that is an aunt of her grandmother's; and she is supported by the town."

" Wall," says he, cheerfully, " mebby the town would feel like gettin' this dress."

I jest give him a look, and never said another word, —only jest that look. But I s'pose that look spoke louder and awfuler than words, for he hastened to say, in a apologizin' way :

" I didn't know but the town would want to—would feel it a privilege to—"

I still didn't say nothin', only jest that awful look. And agin he says, in a apologizin' way :

" I would advance the six-pence to you, I would try to raise it some way for you, but the hard times we have had, and are havin', have depressed all sorts of business so, we have suffered terribly financially as well as the other public. We have got a great deal of money to make out this fall—over 10 dollars. Father hain't a bit well ; my health hain't what it once was ; our expenses are enormious—taxes, household expenses, clothin' ; and takin' all these things into consideration, together with the public debt, the withdrawal of funds by foreign capitalists, the almost total stagnation of public enterprize, the total lack of public confidence, the total—"

Says I, " Put in total selfishness and total meanness, and keep your six-pence."

I don't beheve I have been more wore out in over seven months,—and mad.

" Wall," says he, lookin' relieved, " if you will excuse me, I won't make no move towards raisin' the money for you. It would probable cramp me considerable to raise the sum jest at this present time."

And then he begun about Kitty agin. Says he, knittin' up his eyebrow hard, and lookin' gloomy:

"I never calculated to fall in love with a poor girl. It never used to pass my mind that I ever should select such a one out of the hundreds that stand round me, hankerin' to marry me. But I have done it. Why, sometimes I think I couldn't love that girl any more if she was worth two hundred and 50 dollars. I think so much of her that it is as hard for me as loosin' a limb, almost like loosin' my pocket-book, to think of her bein' way off there a pinin' for me, and bein' on a perfect rack, not knowin' whether she will get me or not.

" When I think of that side of the question, Josiah Allen's wife, I feel jest like leavin' word here with you for her, that I will marry her, whether or no. But then, jest like a blow aginst the side of my head, comes the thought of them other wimmen, that had hopes before she come to Jonesville that they would get me. I believe, anyway, it will be safe to leave word here for her to keep up good courage, and try not to get too cast down and melancholy; to hope for the best; and I'll do everything I can. I'll enquire round about the wimmen, see the doctor, and try to arrange things for her good and happiness; try to get round and marry her. At the same time," says he, with a cautious look, " I would feel it my duty to warn her to not get so bound up in me that the disappointment would kill her, if she should lose me."

" Wall," says I, bein' wore almost completely out, " I must go and skim the milk for the calves."

And he took the hint and started off, and glad enough was I to see him go. But jest as he went down the steps, and I turned to go into the buttery, I see a paper of indigo that Marier Burpey had left here that very day. She had forgot it, and I knew she was in a hurry a colorin'; so I jest carried it to the door, and asked Kellup if he would carry it to her, knowin' he had to go right by her door.

" No," says he, firmly, " I dassent do it." And he looked anxious and skairt as he said it. " I'd be glad to, but I dassent," says he. " I have to make my demeanor perfectly stunny towards that girl, in order to keep her affection anywhere within bounds. She don't show it any by her looks or actions—she has got almost marble self-control; but I see right through it. I see that she almost worships me. I see that I am makin' her perfectly unhappy; and when I think of Sofier's fate, I tremble for Marier. I am careful; I am a careful feller; I am on my guard. And at the present time, situated as I be in regard to Kitty, I feel that I ort to be doubly careful. But at any and every time a young man like me can't be too careful when they are round amongst wimmen."

"Nobody wouldn't mistrust you was makin' such havock," says I, mechanically, for I really didn't know what to say.

MARIER BURPEY.

"Yes, if a young man like me is unprincipled enough to go headlong into wimmen's company without lookin' where he is goin', without actin' offish and cold to 'em, why, before that man knows it, he is a wadin' through **goar**. Bleedin' hearts lay round him on **every side a** bleedin'. Why don't other young men think of these things? Why hain't they more careful, more offish?"

Says I, with feelin', "That's so, why hain't they? The offisher some men be, the more I think on 'em." And I looked longin'ly at the path down to the gate, and the road to Jonesville.

"Yes, you know what actin' on principle means. That is why I respect you, confide in you."

"Then you don't think you can carry the indigo?" says I, turnin' to go in.

"No," says he, firm as marble, and as sot as that stun. "I'd love to accommodate you, but I dassent. When I think of the fate of Sofier, when I think of the deadly blows my conscience dealt to me every minute, as I drove her hearse to the buryin'-ground—then I feel as if I had almost ruther lose ten cents than go through it agin with Marier. I feel that I must not be resky, and do anything to ensnare her affections."

"Good land!" says I, "indigo won't be likely to ensnare 'em, will it?"

"Other men might handle it safe, men with less attractions than I have got, but I can't, I dassent."

And I wouldn't demean myself by urgin' him another word. And I went into the house, and he started off.

Wall, as I was a sayin', Kitty had been gone two weeks, the day Nathan and Cassandra visited me, and this letter from her, brought in to me while I was a gettin' the dinner onto the table, brought news that was startlin' and agitatin' in the extreme. I was jest a stirrin' some sweet cream and butter together over the stove, havin' a fresh salmon trout for dinner, and Josiah bein' fond of that kind of gravy to eat with it, and Nathan bein' such a clever creeter, offered to stir it for me, while I read the letter. And I was so anxious to git the news, that I let him do it, though, the stove bein' so hot, take it with that and his burnin' blushes, it made a pretty hot time for him.

But the news was this: Kitty was married. But the curiousest and most agitatin' part of the news was, the old gentleman, Mark's father, had got after Kitty's mother. He went to give her a scoldin', and fell in love with her on the spot. Like Hamen, he got hung on his own gallowses—went to smite her, and got smit himself, awful. So he courted her up violent and powerful, and they all got married the same day.

It was very pleasant and agreeable news to me, and to Josiah. And Cassandra and Nathan acted well about it. They said they was glad it all turned out so well, but their minds didn't seem to be on the news so much as they was on their babe. And it is a very good-lookin' child, and appears middlin' well for a child of its age. Takes after its father some—sort o' sandy, with red hair. It don't look much, as little Samantha Jo did, nor it don't have that noble, beautiful appearance she had at that age. But then you can't expect that any other child is ever goin' to look and **act like** her. I do despise people bein' so **bound up in**

their own childern and grandchildern that they can't
see no good qualities in any other childern.   Thank
fortune that hain't my way, nor never was.   And I
say, and I always shall say, that Cassandra's babe
hain't a babe to be ashamed of, and feel above, not by
any means.

Bein' so awful bashful, Nathan don't probable associate with it so much, and act on such intimate terms
with it as he would if it wuzn't for that.   But in a
mild, sheepish way, he seems to think the world of it,
and seems to want to do everything he can to make it
feel to home with 'em, and happy.   But he don't come
out openly and express his admiration and affection, as
he would if it wuzn't for that drawback.

Now, he dassent hold it much, or that is, he don't
seem to dast.   But Cassandra bein' proud-spirited, and
wantin' Nathan to show off some, would once in a
while put the babe in his lap.

He never would make any move to stop her.   He
never would refuse to take it.   He would set and hold
it jest as long as she felt disposed to leave it there.
But he would look down on it in a skairt, wonderin',
breathless way, as if the child got there in his lap
through some mysterious and inscrutable decree of
Providence, and it wuzn't for him to resist.   But he
suffered intensely at such times, I could see.

And every little while Cassandra (bein' determined
to make Nathan show off) would tell him to say sunthin' to the babe, talk baby-talk to it.   And he would

always try to. He would always do jest as Cassandra
told him to (a cleverer critter never walked). His

"DO YOU WANT A PAIR OF BOOTS?"

face would be as red as a red handkerchief, but he
would ask the babe, up in a little, high, fine voice:

"Do you want a pair of boots?"

He never made any other remark to the child that
I heard, only jest that. I heard him say that to it

THRILLING NEWS.

more'n 20 times, I dare persume to say. For Cassandra, bein' so anxious to have him show off, kep' tellin' him to talk to it. And it seemed as if that remark was all he could think of that would be agreeable to the child. But Josiah said, as we was talkin' it over afterwards, that he heard him say two or three times to it:

"Yes, it shall have a pair of boots."

But it must have been when I was out a gettin' dinner. For if I was under oath I would say that I didn't hear him say a single thing to it, only jest this:

"Do you want a pair of boots?"

They started for home jest after dinner, Nathan havin' left some work that must be done. And Josiah hitched up and went to Jonesville to mill. And I s'pose he told the news about Kitty there. But it wuzn't till the next afternoon that I heard what the effects of that news wuz in a certain place and to a certain feller.

And though it hain't always best to mention names, and come right out plain and talk, yet it probable won't do no hurt to mention that you might expect Kellup Cobb, under any circumstances, would act like a fool.

I was down to the creek lot, pickin' a few berries for supper, when Josiah told me on't. It had got a little later than I thought for, and Josiah had come down after me, bein' worried about me. It was only a little ways from the house. I had put the tea-kettle

on, and sot the table, before I had come out, and the
tea-kettle was a bilin', so Josiah said, after he told me
the news.   The news was thrillin' and agitatin' in the
extreme. He said Kellup Cobb had disappeared the
night before, after the news of Kitty's marriage had
got abroad in Jonesville. They said that he felt so
that he disappeared, he and the hearse and Elder
Judas Wart—the hull three on 'em. Kellup had been
on intimate terms with Judas Wart for some time ; and
some think that Kellup bein' so cut down by Kitty's
marriage, and the Elder bein' so cut down by my witherin' eloquence and Josiah's broom-handle, that they
both got into the hearse, and drove off in it to Utah to
jine the Mormons. And some think that they sold the
hearse, and took the money, and went to Salt Lake by
rail. Which last way, I told my Josiah, when he mentioned it, was the proper way to go there, if it wuz the
right kind of a rail. But anyway, they had gone, the
hull three on 'em, and there hain't been a word heard
from 'em sense in Jonesville.

Josiah said old Cobb felt awfully.

Says I, "To lose Kellup ? "

" No," says he, "to lose the hearse."

But I jest repeated this line of poetry to my pardner.
Says I :

" Poetry, Josiah, will somehow express the feelin's
of the soul better than you can express them yourself."
And says I, "Josiah, as for Elder Judas Wart and

Kellup, I say with the poet, good riddance to bad rub-
bidge."

"Wall," says Josiah, with a sort of a dreamy look,
—that man loves poetry, though he seldom quotes it—
"don't you s'pose, Samantha, that you have got about
enough berries for supper, for I am gettin' hungry as
a bear."

"Yes," says I, "because I have got stewed peaches
and cold chicken and everything else good for supper
besides them. But," says I, lookin' sort o' longin'ly
at some berries that was a hangin' over the water,
"there is a few extra big and ripe ones that do look
too good to leave."

"Wall," says he, sweetly (for his mean sense I told
him what we was goin' to have for supper had looked
perfectly beautiful), "you set down and rest, Samantha,
and I will pick 'em for you."

And so he took my little tin pail, and with a happy
frame bent down to pick 'em. And I, bein' tired, sot
down, and looked into the water. And I see that
everything was reflected in it. The trees, the nodding
red sumac feathers, my Josiah and me, gay golden-rod
and wild blue china-oysters, the berry bushes, the
thorny stalks and the ripe fruit, fresh posys, and withered leaves ; all imaged there in the water ; and the
water was a runnin' swift.

And out on the end of a slender bush that hung over
the water, a bird swayed and swung to and fro, and
sung out a dretful sort of a sweet song, yet sad like.
18*

Some as if it was practicin' over a farewell song to its home, its happy nest, before it sailed away south in search of a balmier climate.

So the bird sailed back and forth on that slender twig, over the deep waters, a singin' about a happier country, sweet and sad, sweet and low. And my pardner picked the ripe berries, and I sot there peaceful and serene (though some sweaty), a thinkin' how, over all that was pictured on the changing face of the waters, the changeless blue heavens was reflected, shining down over all, the old and the new, the mournful and the sorrowful; over all, and beneath all. That thought was perfectly beautiful to me, and dretful comfortin'. And I sot there a thinkin' of that, and a thinkin' how swift the water was a runnin' towards the sea.

THE END.